1980   250

THE BOYS
IN THE MAIL ROOM

THE BOYS IN THE MAIL ROOM

A *novel by*
Iris Rainer

WILLIAM MORROW AND COMPANY, INC.
New York

acknowledgments

Special thank-yous to
George Eckstein
Bernie Weintraub
Elaine Markson
Pat Golbitz
Sharleen Cooper Cohen
Richard Grossman
David Knopf
Jay Cooper
Mary Blann
P. W. Davidson
Sandy Ferguson
Maria Padilla
Colleen Collins
and
Katzie

THE BOYS . . .

one

When David Kane was seventeen and his mother was thirty-five, at first glance people who saw them together thought they were a young attractive couple. Marlene Kane had fiery red hair and freckles and green eyes, and she wore jeans and T-shirts on her slim body, long before dressing that way was chic. Her son, also a redhead, was six foot one, and the extensive sports program offered at his posh Beverly Hills private school helped him to develop an exquisite athlete's body.

David could never remember Marlene treating him like a child. When his father walked out David was seven. He heard the shouting in the middle of the night but he was used to that, so he managed to get back to sleep. When he woke up again it was light outside, and Marlene was sitting silently at the bottom of his bed. She was holding the G.I. Joe doll he had been playing with and left on the bed the night before.

"Daddy's gone, Davey," she said.

David searched his mother's face for even a trace of sadness. There was none. He also tried to cry. He emitted a few sounds that sounded more like coughing than anything else, and then he stopped. Marlene and David were both feeling relieved. David was even more relieved when Marlene assured him his father would "never be back again." Filled with the Oedipal leanings of the average seven-year-old boy, David's future looked bright to him. He was glad Marlene didn't fall apart this time, the way she had in the past when she fought with his father. Instead she got up and said she'd make breakfast. David climbed out of bed and padded after her into the kitchen. It wasn't until later, when David was putting his toys away that he realized that somehow, since last night, G.I. Joe's head had been broken off his body.

Marlene didn't start going on dates for a very long time. Men would call her, David knew that, because many times he answered the phone when they did. She was polite, but she always told them, "No, thank you. I'm very busy with my son." Then the man would say something, and Marlene would reply, "Sorry, I can't do that, but thank you," and David imagined the man was saying, "Why not bring your son along, too?" And he would wonder how it would be to sit in a restaurant in a big round booth with his mother and a man, instead of at the little tables for two to which he and Marlene were inevitably ushered when they went to restaurants alone. But, though David wanted a dad, he wanted having Marlene to himself more, so he never asked her what the men on the phone said to her.

By the time Marlene started having any noticeable social life, David was in his early teens and too busy to care. She was working in Saks in Beverly Hills in the cosmetics department, and he knew sometimes she met men there who worked in the store, or customers who stopped to buy gifts there, and they would call her.

One of the men was an actor. When Marlene came home from her dates with him she looked disheveled but happy. After a while the actor finished making the movie, which was why he was in town to begin with, and went back to New York, and Marlene started going out with another man. This one worked in the men's department at Saks. He was nice. On David's birthday the man brought him a blue Oxford cloth button-down-collar shirt. It wasn't until David was fourteen that Marlene met Charles Wolfson. Wolfson was tall and elegant and graying at the temples, and he always had a tan, and he wore nicer suits than David saw in the men's department at Saks the time he stopped in to say hi to the guy who gave him the shirt.

To David, Wolfson was kind of dull, even though he seemed to want to be friendly. He called David "Davey" the way Marlene did, and he always wanted to discuss the ball scores on nights when Marlene was finishing dressing and he and David would end up face to face in the living room of the tiny apartment. Marlene, however, didn't think Wolfson was dull at all. David could see that by the way she looked at him. He could also see that she was starting to use a lot of the stuff she sold in the cosmetics department. Mascara and other dark eye makeup that David didn't like on her. It reminded him of the kind of stuff the drippy girls at school wore.

After she'd been seeing Wolfson for about six months or so, Marlene started turning down dates with everyone else. It seemed funny to David though because Wolfson only saw her a few days a week, and she would end up being home alone a lot. But she didn't seem to mind. David didn't spend too much time thinking about Marlene because his own life was beginning to take shape now. He lost his virginity with the help of a girl in the senior class who called him every night from her personal Princess phone to say good night, and frequently mentioned to him that she was sleeping naked and thinking of him. And he had an after-school job he liked at the offices of the Beverly Hills *Messenger*. The *Messenger* was a throwaway local newspaper. The job was mostly doing errands for the editor, but all the people at the paper were very nice to him, and they laughed a lot, and he felt as though he fit in.

David never even read the *Messenger*. It wasn't really a newspaper. It was kind of a community service filled with stories about who did this charitable thing, or what citizen was being presented with which award. So that day when he happened to be waiting in the gas station for the attendant to take a look under his hood, it was just out of boredom that he looked at the copy of the paper that was sitting next to him.

When he saw the photograph of a familiar face he looked closer. It was Charlie. Charlie Wolfson. How about that. He looked at the printing. Charles Wolfson, Beverly Hills banker, presenting check to organization's president Meyer D. Coleman. On his right, Mrs. Charles Wolfson. David looked back at the picture. The dark-haired woman who was smiling at Charlie in the picture was Mrs. Charles Wolfson. David looked at the picture for a long time trying to work it out in his mind. The woman was very pretty. She was older than Marlene. Probably the same age as Charlie Wolfson. But she was—oh, shit—she was his wife. Charlie Wolfson was married. David felt queasy. He ached from his throat all the way to his stomach. Wait until Marlene found out. God damn it. She'd really be pissed.

David carried the secret around with him for several days. No wonder Charlie only saw Marlene during the week. God damn that son of a bitch. Married. On the weekends he had to be at home with the smiling Mrs. Charles Wolfson.

On Sunday night, Marlene was in her room watching Ed Sullivan. David summoned up all his courage and went in to talk to her. The only light in the room was the light from the television show, where a bunch of little dogs wearing coats were running around the feet of some couple. The dogs were yapping, and the audience was laughing and applauding.

"Mah."

"Hi, honey. What are you doing here? I thought you were going to a movie."

"I changed my mind. Mah, I have to tell you something."

Marlene's eyes opened wide. She looked afraid. She got up and turned off the television. David's heart was pounding.

"Are you in some kind of trouble?" she asked.

"Mah, Carlie Wolfson's married." There. He'd said it. Oh, Jesus, that was hard, but he was glad he did it because now it would be okay. Marlene would call Wolfson or send him a nasty letter. David would help her write it, and she'd really lay into that lying bastard. Thank God he'd seen the picture of that schmuck or they never would have—

"I know, Davey," she said calmly. "I've always known that."

"What?"

"It doesn't matter," she said. "I love him. And that's all that counts."

David couldn't believe it. This was crazy. She was acting like one of those dramatic women characters in some soapy movie. A woman someone had to grab by the shoulders and shake. A woman who was told by everyone, "Come to your senses!" Not *his* mother.

"Davey, he wants to leave her and marry me. Honest. And he will. It's just that he doesn't know how to tell his children yet—so we're waiting. Just a little longer. He's a very devoted father. Otherwise he'd marry me tomorrow."

David took a long look at her. She hadn't put on any of the makeup today and she looked like a very young girl. He felt as though she were his child. That *he* was the parent and not her.

"Mah . . ."

"He's crazy about you, Davey," she interrupted. "He wanted me to tell you right away that he was married. I said no, but he thought you should know. He hoped you'd understand. He respects you, Davey." She paused for a moment. Then her eyes filled. "He doesn't love Diane, you know. That's been over for years. He loves me."

Diane. That must be Mrs. Charles Wolfson. David stood up. He felt very tired. Very helpless. It occurred to him that when Marlene had stopped dating the others, he figured she would marry Charles Wolfson and he'd been glad. He wanted his mother to stop working and to live in a big beautiful house, and go to the beauty parlor and shop for expensive clothes the way the mothers of his friends did. Now he didn't know what would happen. Maybe Marlene was right. Maybe Wolfson would leave Diane for her.

The relationship between Marlene and Wolfson went on for a long time after that, and David tried to block it out. He couldn't bear to look at Marlene's face when it was a holiday, and he sat with her at a dinner she had cooked, and she couldn't enjoy it until the phone rang, and she heard Wolfson's voice from Acapulco or Honolulu, telling her he loved her.

Every time Wolfson was coming over, David found someplace else to be. It wasn't difficult to avoid the situation. Wolfson and Marlene never spent much time in the apartment. Just as long as it took for Wolfson to pick her up and go. Where? David wondered about it constantly. Certainly nowhere in public. David had done some more investigating about Wolfson. One night he stayed late at the office and found himself poring over the *Messenger*'s files, when he discovered that C. W. Wolfson didn't simply work at the First Beverly Hills Bank. He and his three brothers owned it. Charles and Diane lived at the corner of Lexington and Crescent in an enormous Tudor mansion and had another home in the South of France. There were more pictures of Diane. She collected antiques and furnished the house with them. It made David nauseous. And it didn't look as if Wolfson didn't love his wife. There were pictures of him gazing at her lovingly. More lovingly than David had ever seen him gaze at Marlene. And time was passing. David would be graduating from high school in June. So it was nearly three years Marlene and Wolfson had been together. Three years of Wolfson coming to their apartment to get Marlene, David's mother, his beautiful mother, and take her somewhere—just to fuck her. Oh, Christ. And her walking around with this bullshit dream about Wolfson marrying her. That's what it was, David thought. Bullshit! And he was going to go home right now and tell her so. She was still young and she was very beautiful, and Wolfson was wasting her time.

David parked the green Volkswagen that the editor of the *Messenger* had loaned him for errands in front of the apartment building on South Almont Drive. No one would miss him at the *Messenger*. They'd think he was out picking something up. It was Monday. Marlene's day off from Saks. She'd be bustling around cleaning the apartment. Saks. Cleaning the apartment. Diane Wolfson probably never lifted a finger. And David was sure she spent more at Saks every week than his mother made there.

He took the steps up, three at a time. The door was unlocked.

"Mah?"

The television was on in Marlene's bedroom. Maybe she was in there.

"Mah?"

Maybe she went downstairs to the laundry room, David thought, and he started to turn when he saw the blood. He took a deep breath and walked slowly toward the door.

"Mah?"

Marlene was lying on the bathroom floor. The tile and the chenille rug under her were covered with blood. Other things were covered with blood, too. A lot of towels that sat on the lid of the toilet, and a robe that was thrown across the sink. Marlene's eyes were closed but she was, oh, God, she was still breathing. David kept repeating the words be calm to himself. Be calm. Oh, God. He ran into the bedroom and grabbed a pillow from the bed. He brought it back and put it under Marlene's head. Her eyes opened slowly and she looked at him.

"Mah," he softly. "Mah, I'm gonna call an ambulance."

"No," she said. "No ambulance. You take me. Take me to U.C.L.A. I don't want anybody to know, Davey."

The doctor at U.C.L.A. told David Marlene was pregnant and had tried unsuccessfully to abort herself. She had lost a lot of blood and would have to stay in intensive care. David was nauseous at first, then very angry. He went to the phone and called information. He asked for Charles Wolfson's home phone number. He didn't care if the son of a bitch's wife knew. His mother had lost a lot of blood. Maybe she would—unlisted. The bank. First Bank of Beverly . . . fuck. It was five o'clock. His boss at the *Messenger*. Maybe *he* had Wolfson's number.

I don't want anybody to know, Davey.

He could see Marlene's ashen face as she said that.

"Mah!" he cried out aloud, still holding the receiver of the pay phone. David Kane stood in the hospital corridor sobbing. A nurse came through the swinging doors of the intensive-care unit and walked toward the nurses' station where she leaned forward and said something to the nurse who was sitting next to the phone. David turned cold. He sensed what it was the first nurse had said, but he couldn't move. The nurse who was next to the phone picked the phone up and dialed a few numbers. A moment passed and David heard the page: "Dr. Seligson. Dr. Howard Seligson." The doctor who had admitted Marlene.

Marlene was dead. David saw it on Seligson's face as he got off the elevator and walked down the hall. Seligson didn't notice him standing there, and David didn't make himself known. He watched Seligson enter the I.C.U., and continued to stand paralyzed by the pay phone. Maybe it wasn't Marlene. Oh, please, God. Maybe it was someone else. Someone old. Someone who had lived a full life. Someone—Seligson emerged from the swinging doors and spotted David immediately. He began to walk toward him.

"Mr. Kane."

No, David thought. Maybe if I run. But he didn't.

"Mr. Kane. I'm sorry," the doctor told him. "Your mother is dead."

Charles Wolfson had a regular doubles match very early every Tuesday morning. The other three men arrived at Wolfson's at seven. By that time he had already been up for two hours, having his morning coffee and making calls to the East Coast from the elaborate poolhouse-office, which was adjacent to the tennis court. Wolfson was looking forward to the game. He'd had two lessons over the weekend, and his serve was a killer ace. He wished he'd gone to bed a little earlier last night but that dinner party he and Diane threw was worth losing sleep for. The cook had outdone herself. Wolfson patted his middle. Never mind. He'd work the dinner off this morning. Maybe ask one of the men to stay later for a set of singles.

The figure in the doorway startled him. It was back-lit, and he jumped when he saw it. Martine always brought him the coffee and took away the silver service after the men were out on the court. Wolfson squinted.

"Yes?"

"Charlie?" a young man's voice said.

Wolfson was nervous. Slowly the figure moved into the room. Good God. Wolfson's heart sank. It was Davey. David Kane. Marlene's boy. Was he crazy? What could he be thinking? Why would he come here? How could he even dream of coming here? Wolfson would send the little bastard on his way.

"Look, Davey," he said, getting up. That's when he noticed David was carrying a gun.

Wolfson stopped in his tracks. David was holding the gun with two hands and it was pointed right at Wolfson's chest.

"David," he said gently. "You found out I'm married and you've come here to vindicate your mother. Is that it?"

"No," David said.

He looked bad. His face was bright red and tear-stained, his eyes were bloodshot. Maybe he smoked marijuana. A lot of these kids were doing that now.

"I've known for over two years you were married," he said.

Wolfson was getting very nervous. Given some time, he knew he could calm the kid down, cool him off. But that gun. He'd seen the statistics. Handgun deaths were common fare. Many times the guns just went off by accident. He read about it at least once a week. And saw it on the news. Innocent people were—he tried to see the clock on the bar. Maybe the others would drive up and frighten the kid off. Oh, Jesus. Maybe their arrival would scare the kid into pulling the trigger. Wolfson was trembling visibly.

"Upset, Mr. Wolfson?" David asked thickly.

"David," Wolfson said, "I love your mother. I swear to God I do. I love her goodness, and her sweetness and all of the things *you* love about her. And I want to marry her. She knows that. I tell her that every time we're together. You ask her. It's true. But my littlest daughter. Kate? She's only seven. And, well, I couldn't leave her now." Wolfson was talking very fast.

"I mean, it's such a formative time. You know? Marlene understands that, Davey, and she's willing to wait. But I swear I'm going to . . ."

David's arms dropped to his side and he let the gun fall to the floor. He closed his eyes in exhaustion and sank into a chair, sobbing.

"She's dead," he managed to say through the tears. "Dead. Abortion. Didn't want anyone to know," he coughed.

Wolfson stood silently for a long time. The only sound was the boy's terrible agonized sobbing.

"Davey," he said. "Go home and get some rest. Stay by the phone. I'll call you later today. I'll take care of everything. Including you."

David didn't say another word. He was too numb. He got up, left the gun on the floor and walked out to the car. He drove back to the apartment and cleaned up his mother's blood from her bathroom. When he finished, he fell asleep on her bed. At three o'clock Wolfson called. He had made arrangements for a small funeral at a nearby mortuary. He had also found David a job he could start right after graduation. It didn't pay much, but it didn't require a college degree, and it was a steppingstone to bigger things. The job was in the mail room at Hemisphere Studios.

two

Mickey Ashman's brother, Harvey, was a genius. When Mickey was seven and Harvey was ten, Harvey was attending special classes at the University of Chicago. Mickey and Harvey looked alike. Sometimes relatives would grab Mickey and pinch his cute little face and say, "Your parents are so proud of you, Harvey. You are the greatest joy they could ever ask for." And Mickey would say, "I'm not Harvey. I'm *Mickey*." Then the relatives would look closer at him and realize that what he had just said was true. He was Mickey. Not Harvey. And they would be disappointed and say, "Oh. Right. Well, Mickey, you're a nice boy, too."

Actually, Mickey was a very special boy. In any other family he would have been the star. But in a family that also had Harvey, he could never be more than second best. Every time company came to visit the Ashmans. Harvey was trotted out, and the people would ask him questions and marvel at his knowledge. Mickey always stayed in the bedroom during those sessions and watched television.

At least once a year there would be a feature article in one of the newspapers about Harvey; in fact, one night while Harvey was in the living room performing for the company and Mickey was watching television, there was a special news feature report on, which had been shot earlier that year, and there was Harvey on television at the same time.

Little by little it occurred to Mickey that in order for him to get any attention at all from his parents (who always referred to Harvey as "our Harvey" and to Mickey as "Michael," which was his real name) he would have to be special in his own way.

Maybe because Harvey had a very busy schedule and Mr. and Mrs. Ashman always seemed to be taking him to this seminar or to that interview, Mickey spent a lot of time alone. He and Harvey had a television in the room they shared, which Harvey had won as a prize in some contest, and Mickey liked watching television. Even more than that, what Mickey liked doing when he was alone was looking in the mirror. Not just looking in the mirror to look. But to make faces, and try out reactions, and make himself look like other people, and then to talk in voices that seemed to go with the various faces. He could even do imitations of some of the people on television.

When Mickey was eleven and Harvey was fourteen and a chess master, there were tryouts for the sixth-grade play entitled *What Is Health?* Mickey auditioned for the part of Mr. Pneumonia and won the role over several other candidates. Mr. Pneumonia had lots of good lines, and everyone agreed that Mickey was very funny and the best one in the play. His parents and Harvey came to see him in it. The teacher who directed the play told Mr. and Mrs. Ashman that Mickey was "a natural comedian." When the family went out for ice cream afterward and they bumped into a woman Mrs. Ashman knew from the P.T.A., and Mrs. Ashman asked the woman, "Have you met my Harvey and my Mickey?" Mickey knew he was on the right track.

When Mickey was fifteen he played the part of Fancourt Babberley in the Senn High School production of *Charley's Aunt.* Every time he took his curtain call during the entire run, he got a standing ovation. On closing night he was in his dressing room and a girl who was a senior and seventeen came backstage and told him he was so funny in the show that she was in love with him. Mickey was still wearing a hoop skirt at the time, because of the scene where Fancourt pretends to be Charley's aunt, but he managed to lift the skirt sufficiently so the girl could get under it, because she also told him that she wanted to suck his cock. Even though his appearances in *What Is Health?* and *Charley's Aunt* were several years apart, somewhere along the line Mickey was able to formulate an equation from his experiences with these two productions, which was that being in show business meant getting a lot of approval.

In Chicago the advertising agencies frequently used local talent in commercials. So after he finished high school, Mickey got a part-time evening job cleaning up the floors and counters at the Sara Lee Kitchens, had some black-and-white pictures taken and printed of himself, and, still living at home, paid visits to the various advertising agencies, to try out for jobs in commercials during the day. His parents liked his decision. Harvey was in graduate school at Yale. It was costing them a fortune to keep him there, and Mickey's lack of interest in college lightened some of their financial pressure.

It didn't take long for Mickey to start getting jobs in commercials. He was chubby and sweet-faced and the clients knew the viewers would relate to him. The account executives told one another, as they each took the credit for finding him, that he looked "ordinary." Mickey played the kid who begs Dad for the car keys in a car commercial, he played the guy whose potato chip falls apart in the dip in a potato chip commercial, he played a guy who cringes because his grandfather has bad breath in a mouthwash commercial. After that he quit the job at the Sara Lee Kitchens.

Things were great. He was starting to know the executives at the advertising agencies by their first names, and they loved him.

One year when Harvey came home for Easter vacation Mickey took him on location to a shoot. It was a local bank commercial. Mickey played a newly married groom. The bride was a pretty blond girl, and Mickey had to kiss her. Later, on their way home, Harvey told Mickey he'd heard of many strange things in his life, but never anything as strange as a creep like Mickey getting paid a lot of money to kiss a gorgeous girl like that. Mickey was the happiest he'd ever been in his life. People would see him on the street or in a store and recognize him and not know why.

"Did you go to Roosevelt High School?" they'd ask, trying to figure out why he looked so familiar. Or, "Did you ever live in Evanston?"

Sometimes Mickey would just smile mysteriously and walk away without telling them why they recognized his face. Other times he'd tell the people which commercial they'd seen him appear in that particular month, and they would really get excited. He loved it.

And the girls. They all saw the commercials on TV, too, and they called his house and invited him to parties, and wanted to be with him. And the more forward ones touched him and undressed him and caressed him, and one of them asked if she could please leave the light on when he made love to her so she could watch a mouth that had been on television sucking on her nipples.

After he did the peanut butter commercial Mickey bought his first car. It was used. A '58 Ford convertible. Black with a white top and a gold metal streak across the body. He loved driving it with the top down, and when he'd stop at a light, sometimes the person in the adjacent lane would look at him, look away, and then look back in recognition.

"You're Mr. Chunky!" they'd say.

Mickey would give a little wave as if he were running for office. He was getting used to it.

He had just decided to take his own apartment. After all, he had what seemed to be wealth beyond his wildest dreams.

He was shaving that morning when the phone rang. In fact, he left the shaving cream on his face because he was at the end of the can and didn't want to waste it by wiping it off just to come to the phone.

It was Howie Krakow, one of the advertising agency guys he'd worked for.

"Mick? I have some incredible news. I mean you're not gonna believe this."

"Don't tell me. You're rerunning Chunky for an added thirteen weeks."

"No."

"You're casting me in a spot opposite Gina Lollobrigida?"

"No. Sit down, you lucky putz. Did you ever hear of Lowell Spears?"

"No."

"He's a producer in Hollywood. He saw you in the Chunky spot, tracked us down and wants you to come to California to do a television series."

Mickey knew Krakow was kidding. Not that he hadn't thought about the possibility of someday trying to work in Hollywood but . . .

"Bullshit, Krakow," Mickey said.

This was really a dumb joke. The other guys at the agency were probably on extensions right now listening to his reaction. Jerking him off. Big joke. Mickey was getting pissed.

"I can't talk now. I have an interview in a half an hour and I gotta get dressed."

He was waiting for Howie to laugh and then admit it was bullshit. But he didn't.

"Mickey, I'm serious."

Mickey closed his eyes. It was true. Of course he'd heard of Lowell Spears. Now, in context, he remembered. A Lowell Spears Production. It was all over television. On comedy shows, dramatic shows. Everywhere.

"What do I do?" he asked nervously.

"Call Spears' office collect." Krakow gave him the number, excitedly. "They're waiting for you now. Good luck, killer. And don't forget, when you're big, who cast you as Mr. Chunky!"

Mickey hung up the phone. A television series. He took a deep breath. Jesus Christ. He hadn't written the number down, but he remembered it. He dialed the operator.

"I'd like to call Hollywood, please," he said. "Person-to-person to Mr. Lowell Spears, and make it—" That was when he decided it was better not to have the call be collect. "Uh, make it fast, Operator," he said instead.

* * *

Mickey was picked up at the Los Angeles Airport by a long black Cadillac limousine. The driver called him "Mr. Ashman" and drove him to the Sportsmen's Lodge in North Hollywood. The bellhop told Mickey there was a stream outside his room with trout in it, and patrons could fish there for their own dinners. Mickey laughed and gave the bellhop five dollars. His meeting with Lowell Spears wasn't until the next day. It would be at Hemisphere Studios where the series was being produced. Actually it wasn't a series at all, but what they called a pilot for a potential series. The lead character was described in the script they'd sent over to Mickey as zany, ambitious, energetic and audacious. Kind of like Mr. Chunky in the peanut butter commercial.

Mickey was confused. Spears obviously liked him well enough to bring him all the way to Los Angeles and get him a car and a driver and a room near the trout, but then why did he still have the feeling he was going to be auditioning tomorrow instead of signing a contract?

BOBBY *(sweetly)*
Can I carry your briefcase, Mr. Holloway? Looks awfully heavy to me.

Was that line supposed to be a joke? Was Bobby trying to butter Mr. Holloway up, or was it just meant to be straight? Mickey read the script over and over. He never left the room. He ordered room service for dinner, and at eleven that night wheeled the untouched meal into the hallway outside the room. He wasn't hungry. He wasn't sleepy. Looks awfully hollow to me, Mr. Heavyway. No. Shit. Was he supposed to memorize the lines or read them? Did he have the part or didn't he? Maybe he'd look outside the door and see if his room service tray was still there. At least he could eat the piece of cake he'd left there. The tray was gone. He paced. The telephone. Sure. Hemisphere was picking up the tab. He'd call Harvey. Harvey would still be up because of the time change.

Mickey got the operator to dial the number at Harvey's apartment in New Haven. The phone rang for a long time.

"H'lo!"

"Hey, Harv. It's me, your brother, calling from Hollywood. Can you beat that?"

"Hmm!"

"Harv? It's Mick."

"Jesus, Mickey. It's—what the hell time is it?—three o'clock in the morning?"

Mickey was embarrassed. He knew the time difference was three hours. But he thought it was in the other direction.

"Ahh, shit, Harv. I'm really sorry."

"No. It's okay. How are you doing?"

"Great. Oh, it's great. I've got a room in this hotel right near Hemisphere Studios, and my own driver and stuff."

"Whaddya mean?"

"Well, I mean he's not exactly my own guy. But he drove me here and he's picking me up in the morning and he calls me mister—"

"Hey, Mick. Could you do me a favor?"

"Sure, Harv. Are you kidding? Anything. Sure. I'll do you a favor."

"Call me another time, okay? I got a final tomorrow."

"Yeah, but, Harv, see I—"

Harvey hung up. Mickey put the phone down and looked around the room. In the room next door he heard a toilet flush. He lay down on the bed and looked at the script again.

BOBBY
Can I carry your briefcase, Mr. Holloway? Can I carry your brief-case, Mr. Holloway? Can I . . .

When the bellman dropped a copy of the morning *Los Angeles Times* outside Mickey's room, Mickey had slept for a total of fifteen minutes. He was feeling rotten. He wanted to get dressed and go to the dining room for breakfast—but what if Spears called? He opened the door and took in the morning paper. Finally the phone rang. Thank God. Mickey let it ring three times, even though his hand was on the receiver the minute it started ringing.

"Mr. Ashman?" It was a woman. "This is Lowell Spears' secretary. Mr. Spears would like to see you in his office at ten this morning. Is that all right with you?"

"Uh . . . ten?" Mickey said. "Let's see, well, uh, yes. Ten. Ten is good. Ten at his office."

"We'll send a car for you," the woman said and hung up.

Hemisphere Studios, my God. Mickey had to take a deep breath to stop himself from screaming out "There it is!" to the driver as they rounded the corner and the big gold building came into view. Of course the driver knew where it was. And what it was. But Mickey, who had only seen the photograph on picture postcards, or the logo at the end of television shows, or movies, was dazzled. It was better than he had ever imagined. And now he would be part of it.

The guard at the gate waved them by, and the driver maneuvered the car with ease through a Western street filled with façades of saloons and bathhouses, past a metal truck where a lot of men dressed in cowboy clothes stood drinking coffee, eating donuts and laughing. Probably about some funny show business story. Mickey couldn't see enough. He wanted the driver to slow down so he could wallow in it, memorize it, remember every second to tell Harvey, to tell his parents. The car stopped and Mickey looked anxiously around. Obviously they were there. Where? Wherever it was he was supposed to meet Spears.

The driver got out of the car and came around and opened Mickey's door for him.

Mickey could now see that the car was parked in front of a pink stucco house with a tile roof that was one of several of those houses. There was a wooden sign nailed to the door that said "Casita de Lowell Spears." Mickey was clutching his now dog-eared script in his hand, and he looked at the driver. It was the first time he really had. The man was about fifty years old and very trim and handsome. This guy had probably driven major big-time people to premieres and parties. Why hadn't Mickey thought to ask him? Well, he would later. He stood for a moment, hoping the driver would wish him good luck or give him some advice about how to behave with Hollywood producers or something. But the guy just tipped his hat, got back in the car, picked up a newspaper and started to read.

Mickey opened the door to Spears' office. As the blast of air conditioning blew at him, he realized how hot it was outside the casita. Spears' secretary was an old, very tiny woman. She got up immediately and walked to the door to greet Mickey.

"Why, you're Mr. Ashman," she smiled, putting her hand out to take his. Mickey was clutching his rolled-up script in both hands. "I'm Vera, Mr. Spears' secretary. How 'bout some coffee?"

"No, thanks," Mickey said. Mickey looked at the door to the inner office. It was closed and he could make out the murmur of various voices inside.

"He's finishing a production meeting," Vera said, seeing Mickey's face. "It won't be long."

Vera returned to her desk. Mickey paced and looked around. On the wall was a Perma-Plaqued picture of President Eisenhower standing with a man who must be Lowell Spears. Actually Spears sort of resembled Eisenhower. Mickey looked out the window and saw his driver still sitting in the limousine reading the paper. He looked through the now curly pages of his script.

BOBBY
Can I carry your briefcase, Mr. Holloway?

No. No more of that. He'd go crazy.

Vera took some phone calls. Mickey looked through a copy of *Variety*. HOLLYWOOD IATSE LOCALS SEETHE OVER CURBS IN PACT TALK WITH PRODUCERS. Whatever that meant. NAME NETWORK ADVICE FOR SEASON'S PROBLEMS. Jesus, this waiting was the worst.

The voices got a little louder. Maybe they were finishing up. The buzzer on Vera's phone sounded twice.

"You can go in now, Mr. Ashman," she said. Mickey tried to keep the nervous smile from his face as he entered Lowell Spears' office.

Three men were standing facing the door as he entered. Two wore suits. Lowell Spears wore a pale-blue bouclé golf sweater. For the first time it occurred to Mickey that he'd never even thought about how he himself was supposed to dress for this occasion. Maybe the T-shirt and jeans weren't right. It was too late. Shake hands. Arthur someone from the network, Tom something else from casting or something, and Spears himself. His mentor. Smiling. Does look like Eisenhower.

"Well, we've all seen your work, son," Spears said. "And we know you're good."

"Thank you." Mickey was okay. He was monitoring himself. Still trying to record every beat. And he was doing okay.

"How'd you like the script?" Spears asked.

"A whole lot," Mickey said, smiling. His voice sounded a little hollow. Maybe he should work to get ride of the Chicago accent. Maybe the studio would get a coach for him.

"Good. Tom will read with you on page four."

Read. Thank God. He didn't have to know it by heart.

"The thing we saw in you that made us bring you here was the aggressiveness of that Mr. Nutty character you played. That's what we liked."

"Chunky," Mickey said.

"What?" Spears asked.

"Mr. Chunky!"

"Right. Page four!"

Mickey froze. He'd left his curled-up script on the chair in the outer office. The guy from casting handed him a new one. Shit. His own had some words underlined—some inflections marked. But he couldn't ask to go get it now. He turned to page four. Before he could even take a breath, the guy named Tom started to read from the script in a flat voice.

> HOLLOWAY (*hurriedly*)
> Good morning, Emerson. Nice day today.

> BOBBY (*sweetly*)
> Can I carry your briefcase, Mr. Holloway? Looks awfully heavy to me.

Perfect.

> HOLLOWAY
> No, thank you, dear boy. I must say it's nice to see at least one of my employees gets to the office early.

> BOBBY
> That's because I remembered what you always say, Mr. Holloway.

Mickey paused here. He remembered marking a pause in his own script. Then he said the next part very slowly.

> BOBBY (*continuing*)
> The early bird always catches the worm.

Out of the corner of his eye Mickey saw Spears look at Arthur from the network. The man from casting went on.

> HOLLOWAY
> So . . . you memorized that, did you, Emerson?

> BOBBY
> Oh, of course, sir. I even put it on tape.

Here comes the joke, God.

BOBBY (*continuing*)
In fact you might even say now it's kind of a . . . taped worm.

Two-three-four.

They laughed. All three of them. Mickey flushed. Fighting off the nervous smile. The man from casting stood.

"Okay?" he asked Spears.

"Thanks, Tom." Spears shook Tom's hand.

"Thanks, Lowell," Arthur from the network said. "Nice job," he said to Mickey and left.

Mickey couldn't believe it was over so fast. He kept waiting for Spears to ask him to read more, but Spears called out a list of names of people for Vera to get him on the phone, thanked Mickey a lot, shook his hand, ushered him to the door of the casita and went back into his office and closed the door.

When the chauffeur saw Mickey, he got out of the car and opened the door for him. Tom, from casting, stood at the car with Mickey.

"You're good," Tom said to Mickey. Tom Rich. That was it. Tom Rich. He was probably thirty, but he had thinning blond hair and was paunchy and craggy-faced so he could have been older.

"If I were you I'd start looking for a place to live. Someplace in the Valley. And leave your number with my office so I'll know exactly where you'll be. Okay?"

Mickey was buoyant. He gave the driver a playful punch and rolled into the back seat.

The minute he got to the hotel, he opened the paper and started looking. Apts. Furn. S.F. Valley. He'd forgotten to make arrangements with the driver for the rest of the day, but fuck the driver. He'd rent a car. A new Chevy Bel-Aire.

By three o'clock that afternoon he'd rented a one-bedroom house! Not just an apartment. It was on the corner of Moorpark and Beck, and it even had a yard. It was two twenty-five a month. And he paid first and last month's rent with his traveler's checks. But so what! By next week he'd be rehearsing. By next month he'd be written up in *Variety*. And by next year—my God!—maybe he'd even be buying a house.

He'd call Harvey. As soon as he had the phone installed tomorrow he'd call Harvey. And Howie Krakow—and that girl Janet who he'd met on the Pillsbury interview last month, and Jesus. Tom Rich! The casting guy. Tomorrow he'd call him. With the new number. No more hotels. He lived here now. In Hollywood. Well, North Hollywood. But still. The furniture in the house was only fair, but the landlady said she'd put in some new carpeting and eventually it would look great. And maybe his parents would come out, and Harvey, too. There would be a party for the night the show was on. Or maybe he'd go to Chicago just for that night and there would be a party for him there. He drove the Chevy Bel-Aire back to the Sportsmen's Lodge, ordered a huge room service dinner, and fell happily asleep almost immediately after finishing the last bite.

The next morning Mickey opened a checking account in a bank in Studio City. He deposited the five hundred dollars he had left and took his temporary checks with him.

When he got to the house the landlady was there and a carpet man was there, and the telephone man was there, and the old man who lived next door was there to help the landlady move some furniture out of the garage. The minute the phone was hooked up, Mickey dialed the number at Hemisphere.

"Hemisphere Studios."

"Tom Rich's office, please," Mickey said. His first call on his new phone.

"Tom Rich's office."

"Hi. Is Tom there?"

"Who's calling?"

"Mickey Ashman."

"Mr. Rich is on another line right now."

"It's okay," Mickey said, "tell him it's me." Mickey saw the carpet man going out to his truck. There were brightly colored rolls of shag rug. Mickey wanted to have white.

"Uh, will he know what this is regarding?"

"Yeah. My new phone number. I'm the guy from Chicago who read for—"

"Why don't you just give the number to me, Mr. Ashman. I'll see that he gets it."

As Mickey continued watching the carpet man through the window, he didn't know why, but the phone felt heavy in his hand and there was a vague discomfort creeping over him. It started in his back and moved up to his shoulders.

"Look," he said into the phone, "I'll wait till Tom gets off the other line. Okay? I mean, I don't mind."

"He's talking to New York," the secretary said emphatically, with the implication that those particular words meant the phone call could be extended indefinitely. "Why don't I have him call you?" she offered.

Mickey gave her his new number.

When three days had passed and he hadn't heard, he called again.

"He's in a meeting."

He called Spears.

"Oh, yes, Mr. Ashman," Vera said brightly. "He's out of town. I'll have him get back to you."

Seven days. Ten.

"He's been so busy," Rich's secretary said. "Anything I can help you with?"

"Had to rush off to New York, honey," Spears' secretary said. "Back on Thursday."

Mickey had nothing to do. He bought the trades. There was no point in going to MALES—CASTING CHORUS BYE-BYE BIRDIE. MUST SING. SANTA BARBARA PLAYHOUSE. He was going to start shooting the pilot any minute. Any day. The Chevy Bel-Aire was getting expensive. He'd have to get rid of it and buy himself an inexpensive car. Back home his mother was driving the Ford. Maybe he could hire someone to drive it to Los Angeles for him. Oh, well. As soon as the series started he'd probably buy a sports car.

Mickey was getting very lonely. A friend of his mother's mailed him the telephone number of a niece of hers who went to U.C.L.A. The niece's name was Zyra, and Mickey called and asked her out to dinner. She told him that she was too busy. That she had a boy friend. That she hated her aunt for giving out her phone number, and that she thought actors were jerks.

Mickey had been in town for four weeks and he hadn't met anyone besides his landlady and the old man who lived next door. He also hadn't heard one word from Lowell Spears or Tom Rich. In fact, that night when the phone in his house rang for the first time, he was so surprised he literally jumped.

"Mick?" It was Harvey. And Mickey's parents. God damn, it was great to hear their voices. Harvey was in Chicago for a few days so they decided to call.

"Hey, star," Harvey said, "too big to call us up, huh?" Sometimes for a genius Harvey sounded like an idiot.

Mickey's mother wanted to know if Mickey had seen any movie stars. Mickey's father wanted to know if Mickey had signed his contracts yet. Harvey wanted to know what all those Hollywood starlets were like. Mickey's mother said all of her friends wanted to know what the name of the show was. Mickey's father asked if there were any big-time actors in the supporting cast to help Mickey along. Harvey said he was checking around to see if there were any special low-fare flights to Los Angeles from New Haven so he could come out to visit.

Mickey didn't know what to say to them. He hemmed and hawed and shuffled around, but thankfully they didn't seem to notice. It was as if they'd already made up the answers to the questions they were asking and weren't listening anyway. The call went on for quite a while. The Ashmans only had two extensions on their number, and there were three people who wanted to talk to Mickey, so there was a lot of changing phones and repetition of questions, and it was all very shrill, and finally when everyone said goodbye and Mickey put the phone down, he realized that he was sweating and his heart was pounding.

He was embarrassed. And upset. And he had a right to be. Jesus Christ! He had a fucking right to be. Why didn't he have any answers for his family? What was going on? These people out here brought him to Hollywood. He didn't ask to be brought here.

These people. Spears, Hemisphere Studios, Tom Rich. And now, not only were they not telling him anything, but it felt like they were avoiding him. Couldn't someone just call and say, "Hey, Mick, listen. The network is slowing us down a little but stop by for lunch?" Or, "Sorry, kid, there's been a delay, how's your new place?" No one said shit.

He tried to calm down. He *would* calm down. It would be okay. This was probably always the way it was in real show business. Not like the small-time bullshit world of commercials he'd been involved in in Chicago.

Things in network television took time. Decisions were crucial and slow in the making. He had to learn how to accept that. He would be able to explain that to his family the next time they called. By then he would be in rehearsal.

Carry your briefcase, Mr. Holloway?

Mickey stayed awake that entire night, because even after he'd told himself all of those things, and tried so hard to calm himself, his heart wouldn't stop pounding. He did everything he could to try not to think the thoughts that kept creeping into his head. He read, he counted backwards from a thousand, he watched television. At 1 A.M., without knowing what he would say, he even called Zyra. When she answered, he hung up.

At eight thirty the next morning he sat in his living room, nervous and unshaven and still wearing the same clothes from the day before. He had to do something. He didn't know what, but he had to do something about the way he was feeling.

Slowly he got up, went into the bathroom and showered and shaved. Then he picked out his favorite Oxford cloth shirt from the closet, and some newly cleaned blue jeans, and filled with the heady tension of the sleepless night, he got into his car and headed for Hemisphere Studios.

All the way to the studio Mickey tried to think of what he would say to get past the gate, but when he drove up there was a man in a suit inside the security booth having a heated discussion with the guard, so Mickey was able to drive right through and onto the lot.

There was no question that he remembered the route perfectly. Past the Western town, make a left, and the casitas should be straight ahead. They were. He was sweating. All the parking spaces had cars in them or names on them. Reserved for Al Dietrich, reserved for Mike Nichols, reserved for John Gavin, reserved for . . . Who gives a shit? He'd pull into the next space and not even look at whose name was on it. Mickey got out of the car and walked toward Lowell Spears' casita.

Spears would be surprised to see him. But glad. Maybe glad. It would be a break in his day and they'd go to lunch, and— Mickey opened the door. Vera wasn't there. No one was in the outer office and the door to Spears' office was closed. This was wrong. He should have called first and he'd better leave. But maybe not. God, he was tired. Why hadn't he slept? Because of the phone call is why. Because of no answer is why. He was getting a headache. He could feel it. That fucking tension headache that started in his back. He tapped on the door to Spears' office.

"Yeah?"

Mickey opened the door. Lowell Spears was sitting at his desk. Boy, he really did look like Eisenhower.

"Hi," Mickey said.

Spears looks at him blankly.

"Mr. Spears." Shit. He should have called him Lowell. "Mickey Ashman," Mickey said. Jesus. Why did he have to announce his name? Spears was the one who discovered him. But the blank look on Spears' face was still there.

"Bobby Emerson," Mickey said, kind of jumping into the room the way the character he was going to play in the pilot would.

Spears looked confused.

There was a very long moment of silence. Mickey could hear himself breathing. Maybe Spears was a drunk or something like that. He'd heard stories about people who couldn't remember because they . . . the dawn broke. Mickey saw the recognition.

"Mr. Nutty."

"Chunky."

"How are you, kid? On the lot to read for something?"

Mickey started to laugh, then stopped when he looked at Spears' face.

"No. Not to read. Just came to see—" The headache was pounding.

"Mister Spears. Listen. I really came by to ask you, uh, when are we starting to shoot our pilot? *Big Business?* The one you brought me here for?"

Spears' eyes narrowed. "What do you mean?" he said.

"I mean I've been trying to reach you for four weeks," Mickey said. "And you haven't called me back, and I didn't know what to do about the rest of my life because I knew that we'd be starting to shoot any day, so I—" Mickey could feel himself sounding a little choked up, and he had a quick flash of one time, a million years before, when he'd gone to his father to tell him that it wasn't fair that Harvey got to stay up until eleven and *he* had to go to bed at nine, and his father had looked at him that night and was so preoccupied he didn't seem to see him standing there, just the way Spears was looking at him right this minute. ". . . So I came to tell you all of that in person because I . . ." Mickey remembered later that he heard himself go on with that speech for a very long time, and while he did, Spears said nothing at all. In fact, he never even got up from his desk. He also remembered later that somewhere in the middle of it all he realized that he was afraid to stop talking. Afraid, because all of a sudden he knew that when he finished telling Spears his story, Spears would say just what he did say.

"Get out of my office, Ashman. You asshole. Are you crazy coming over here at nine o'clock in the morning and walking into my office unannounced, with that bullshit about *our* pilot? How the fuck did you ever get on the lot, you no-talent pushy bastard? Get your stupid face out of my sight or I'll call security and have them drag you out of here by the balls."

The phone rang. Spears picked it up.

"Yes?" he said brusquely into the phone.

Mickey couldn't move. This was a joke. It had to be a joke. Spears was going to put down the phone now and smile at him and laugh, and admit it was nothing but a joke.

"I'll be right there," Spears said into the phone. Then he slammed the phone down and stood.

Mickey still hadn't moved. His mouth was dry and his eyes were starting to water.

Spears walked around the desk, past Mickey to the door.

"Please," Mickey heard himself say, "just tell me what happened."

"Kid," Spears said, turning back, "don't make something out of this. Because there's nothing to make. And that's it. You came in here like a million other kids did to read for Bobby, and you stunk. So you come on a plane from Chicago, instead of in a Volkswagen from Laurel Canyon. What do you think that makes you? I'll tell you. It makes you an actor from Chicago who stinks. Go take acting lessons."

Spears turned away and had his hand on the doorknob when Mickey grabbed him. It was more like a hug from behind, but Spears stiffened.

"Wait," Mickey said. "You can't say things like that. They're not true."

Spears shook Mickey off and turned to face him. He was glaring. His face was ugly.

"Keep your hands off me, you little piece of shit. I paid for your ticket here and gave you a chance. Then you walked in here after I got network brass to sit in, and you read like some two-bit amateur and made me look like a schmuck. Then you had the nerve to start calling here and bugging my secretary, and calling casting and bugging them like you were somebody in the business. Well, you're not. You're a lowlife. All actors are lowlifes. Even the big ones. So that makes you the lowest of the low. And you can tell your agent never to submit you for any jobs on this lot. Because I'll make sure you don't get them."

Spears left the office and the casita.

Mickey stood frozen to the spot for a few minutes, then walked out and got into the Chevy. His head throbbed and the rest of him was numb.

He closed his eyes and put his head on the steering wheel and cried. He was weak and tired and Spears was right about him. He was an asshole. A naïve asshole. Oh, shit. He stunk. Stunk? What a crappy fucking word to use. The network guy thought so. Thought he stunk. Smelled. Couldn't act. But what about . . . what about Chicago? And the agencies? What did they know? Spears was right. Why hadn't he taken acting lessons? Mickey banged his fist on the dashboard. He had to pull himself together. And get back to the house. And pack. Yes. He'd go back to Chicago.

Probably he wouldn't act anymore. Maybe now that Harvey was finally approaching the end of all his schooling and . . . He wanted to get out of here. His face was covered with tears and his breath was still coming in gasps. He rolled down the window and looked straight into the face of Tom Rich.

"I *thought* that was you, Ashman," Rich said. Warmly? It sounded that way—but then they were *all* full of shit—and he knew that Rich knew what the network guy knew. That Mickey Ashman had no talent. Stunk.

"I submitted you for a two-line part in an episode," Rich said, still smiling. "Last week. They used the director's brother. Say, I was real sorry to hear about the way Spears decided to go in *Big Business*," Rich went on. "They wanted a name actor. You know?"

Mickey still hadn't said one word.

"You were good, though. Hey . . ." Rich moved closer to the car. "Are you all right?"

Mickey was trembling.

"Jeez, Ashman, what the hell happened?"

Mickey was afraid if he spoke he would burst into tears. Tom Rich looked genuinely concerned, and he walked around to the passenger side of the Bel-Aire and got in.

"Back out and make a left over there," he said to Mickey, pointing out the turn. Mickey started the car and followed Tom Rich's directions. "Now a right. Pull up there."

Mickey saw another group of casitas. The one he was in front of bore a sign that said CASTING.

"Come into my office," Rich said gently. "I'll buy you a drink."

Mickey nodded weakly and followed Rich past a few desks of chattering secretaries into a small office containing a metal desk, a Naugahyde chair and a small Naugahyde sofa. Rich locked the door and took a bottle of scotch and two paper cups from his desk drawer. Without asking Mickey, he poured a cup for each of them and gestured for Mickey to sit down.

Mickey took a sip of the scotch. It occurred to him as the thick taste filled his mouth and his ears, and his eyes began to water, that it was only nine fifteen in the morning. Rich had already drained his cup. They were both silent while he poured himself another. Then he looked at Mickey.

"Visiting Spears?" he asked.

Mickey nodded. Rich nodded, too. A knowing nod that said he could probably guess the whole story.

"Son of a bitch is worth fifty million dollars," Rich said. He took another taste of the scotch. So did Mickey. Mickey's face felt hot and Rich's office was beginning to feel confining to him. Maybe if he got up and walked around. There wasn't even a window. Rich looked a little glazed as Mickey stood.

"Sit down, Ashman," Rich said, "and I'll tell you something. Something which if you're smart you'll listen to carefully, and live by forever, because I swear to you it comes from knowledge and wisdom, and years of observing the system, and being in on the secrets of many of the most important people in this town."

Mickey sat. If he had been his usual self he would have laughed at a statement like that because it sounded so full of shit. But he was exhausted, and he knew Rich meant well, and the scotch was going to his head.

Rich's com-line buzzer buzzed and he picked up the phone. He listened, nodded, promised to be somewhere by ten and hung up. For a minute he sat quietly as if he weren't sure where he'd left off, then he looked at Mickey with what Mickey remembered later looked very much like tears in his eyes.

"Ashman," he said, "don't be an actor. Find another life, my friend. But don't be an actor."

"That's what Spears said," Mickey told him.

"But it's different," Rich said, and poured himself some more scotch. "More?"

Mickey nodded. What the fuck. His career was over. Now it was Rich who was going to tell him he stunk. Maybe it would be a good idea to start every day with a glass of scotch.

"It's different," Tom Rich began, "because Lowell Spears hates actors."

"He told me."

Rich shook his head sadly. "That bastard. And he treats them like shit, and goes home to tell his friends about it. Makes young girls suck his cock for parts they'll never get, and young boys kiss his ass for the same. And he hates you all."

"But I didn't—"

"No. He treated you okay. At first. Because he thought you would do him some good. And he needed you. As soon as he decided he didn't need you anymore, you were nothing. Like the others."

"You mean after I read so badly?"

"Huh?"

"He told me what the network guy said."

"What do you mean?"

"That I stunk."

"Arthur? He never said that. He couldn't have. You were great. I was there." Rich's brow was furrowed.

Mickey was sweating. He'd had a cup and a half of the scotch and he was hot and heady.

"Are you sure he didn't say it sometime later?"

"Of course I'm sure. It had nothing to do with Arthur Brand. Or Lowell Spears. At all. It was because the sponsor wanted a name actor to play Bobby, and that's why you were out. Ashman, you gave a great reading. Oh, fuck," Rich said. "Oh, fuck." And as he shook his head sadly he really did look as if he would cry.

"Which only brings us back to my original point, Ashman. Don't be an actor. Because actors, in this town, never ever get treated a hell of a lot better than that."

"I don't believe that," Mickey said. "How can it be? What about the stars of—"

"Stars, yes. Actors, no," Rich said. "And there's a difference. You don't have to be an actor to be a star. Look behind you."

Mickey did, and for the first time, he noticed that the bulletin board above the sofa where he sat contained a dozen black-and-white eight-by-ten glossy photographs of young Hemisphere Studios contract players. He recognized them all.

"The contractees," Rich said to him. "I sat with the heads of this studio and auditioned seven hundred and fifty people to get those twelve. I heard Hamlet's soliloquy delivered, and I use the term loosely, seventy-four times. Emily's 'goodbye Grover's Corners' speech from *Our Town* twenty-six times. I saw eight versions of the George-and-Martha scene from *Who's Afraid of Virginia Woolf?*— one of them where the parts of George and Martha were both played by men. I saw a grown man who was about to do a monologue throw up from sheer terror in front of an entire staff of studio executives, and learned that later that week that same man killed himself, and I ended up offering contracts to those twelve people you see there. Why? The blonde on the far left has a thirty-six D bust and gives allegedly great head on a regular basis to Al Dietrich, who is the next in line to Harold Greenfield, who is the president and chief executive of Hemisphere Studios. The dark-eyed lady to her right, though not nearly so enormously endowed or reputationed, is the daughter of one of Hemisphere's in-house lawyers."

"Jesus," Mickey said softly.

"And the boy with the blond curls, Ashman," he said, "who I'm sure you can recognize as the star of a currently running cowboy series, is a master of S&M, of which a certain elderly film director cannot get enough."

"Stop," Mickey said.

"Are you getting the point?" Rich said to him. Now his teeth were clenched angrily.

"I'm trying to tell you that actors don't matter," he spat at Mickey. "I love them. They're vulnerable, beautiful, emotional, needy people. But not to these guys, Ashman. I swear to you that there were some really good auditions done during that hyped-up talent search. That's what those assholes had the nerve to name it. And not one of the good ones got so much as a phone call, or a thank-you, or even a two-line bit on this lot."

Mickey was slumped down in the Naugahyde couch. He wanted to die. Maybe kill himself. Like the guy who threw up.

"I need a job," he said finally. "I'm running out of money." He couldn't even look at Rich's face when he said it. What did it matter to Rich? He must know thousands of actors. He was in casting. Knowing actors was what he did for a living.

"I need a job," Mickey repeated. "If I want to stay here, and not go back to Chicago and face the"—he was crying—"and face, well, it isn't even my parents so much as the whole—" He couldn't go on. He just sat there on the sofa without covering his eyes, letting the tears drip in his lap.

Rich took a few Kleenexes from a plastic box on top of his desk, then walked over to Mickey and handed them to him.

Mickey felt like such a schmuck. Such a schmuck.

He wiped his eyes.

Rich helped him to his feet. He probably had to leave for his ten-o'clock meeting.

"I'll work on it, Ashman," Rich said. "I promise I will."

"But Spears said—"

"Spears is a bad-ass motherfucker and I don't give a shit what he said," Rich told him, opening the door. Mickey handed Rich the paper cup he was still holding, and Rich downed the remaining scotch. Mickey guessed Rich didn't care if anyone knew about his morning drinking habits, because the door to his office was open now, and lots of people were bustling past.

Rich gave Mickey a warm slap on the arm and Mickey walked outside to his car. Later he didn't even remember the drive home. When he got there it was ten thirty in the morning. He fell asleep on the couch in his living room and slept until noon the next day. When he woke up, he ate a Swanson's TV dinner and sat in a hot tub. He had dragged the phone with its extra long cord into the bathroom just in case. He was about to add more hot water when the phone rang at last.

It was Tom Rich's secretary. "Mr. Ashman?" she said. "Tom's in a meeting but he asked me to call and tell you that you've got a job!"

Mickey heaved a sigh. He was on his way. Fuck Lowell Spears and all the bullshit. Somehow Tom Rich had managed to come through with a job for him.

"On what?" he asked the girl on the phone.

"I beg your pardon?"

"On what show? Is the job?"

"Oh, no, Mr. Ashman," she said, "it's nothing like that."

She told Mickey that the message Tom Rich had given her said Mickey could start work on Monday if he wanted to. Tom would call him personally later to tell him about the pay and the insurance benefits. The job was in the mail room at Hemisphere Studios.

three

Barry Golden was the smallest boy in his class at P.S. 19 in Brooklyn. That's why he was glad that when the class lined up to go anywhere they did it alphabetically and not by height. Even when they went to toilet recess, as Miss Hausman called it, they went in alphabetical order. Barry always felt sorry for Arnold Zalmonowitz, who had to pee last, and felt glad that he himself only had to be third after Eddie Berkowitz and Marshall Feldman. But then Barry felt sorry for a lot of people. Not just Arnold Zalmonowitz. That's why he was referred to as "a sensitive child" by his aunt, "a little jewel" by his mother and "moldy-goldy" by a bunch of boys on his street who didn't like him.

Barry's uncle, Mashe, who was married to Barry's mother's sister, was very rich. At least he seemed rich to Barry's family because he was in the business of manufacturing ladies' clothing. The company was named Eldor Dresses, after Mashe's wife, Barry's aunt Eleanor, and Mashe's mother, Dora (not really related to Barry), and its label was carried in some stores that Barry's mother referred to as "fancy."

Barry couldn't quite remember exactly when his father got laid off from the job he had in the cleaning plant, but he did remember hearing his father tell his mother the news. Barry was supposed to be asleep but he crept into the kitchen and stood in the doorway and watched them both cry. His mother and his father, sobbing with their heads in their arms leaning on the kitchen table. Barry started to cry too, and crept back into his bed.

The next day, while Barry sat out on the front steps, a taxi pulled up and Mashe stepped out of it. Mashe always looked elegant, combed, rich. He didn't even acknowledge Barry as he walked past him and up the three flights to the Goldens' apartment.

Barry wasn't sure exactly what happened between Mashe and his mother and father that day. He knew it had something to do with a call Barry's mother had made to her sister, Aunt Eleanor, the night before with crying and what Barry's father called "shrying gevalt." It also had something to do with what Uncle Mashe called "seconds," and soon racks of dresses were being delivered to the Goldens' apartment by some men in trucks and then the Eldor label was being torn out, and lots of ladies in the neighborhood were coming over to the

Goldens' apartment to look through the racks, which now lined the living room so you could hardly even see the furniture.

Most of the time Barry was at school when the ladies came to try on the dresses, but sometimes they would still be there when he got home and his mother would caution him, "No, no. Someone's trying on in the bathroom. Just a second, Barelah." And Barry would have to wait if he wanted to pee, the way Arnold Zalmonowitz always had to wait at school.

After a while, there seemed to be more and more dresses and more and more ladies, and sometimes they would come early before Barry left for school, and if there were a lot of them they would change in his room. He would pretend to be reading or getting his books together, and the ladies mostly acted as if he weren't even there, so he would get to see their breasts and their tushes and sometimes even the curly hair between their legs.

Most of them were ugly. Mrs. Pivar had breasts that were big and wrinkled, and even after she put on one of the dresses, the part that was her cleavage, as Barry heard his mother call it, was still crinkly and ugly. But she bought lots of dresses and gave Mrs. Golden cash for them, and there was no more crying at the kitchen table, and Mashe kept sending over more racks.

Barry's parents were much happier now. His mother smiled and sometimes served coffee to the "yentas" (as his father called them) who came by, and there was even talk that maybe the two of them would take Barry and go on a trip someplace soon. A real vacation.

Then Eugene died. Eugene was Mashe and Eleanor's son. He had meningitis. Meningitis. For the rest of his life, when Barry Golden heard that word, the horror surrounding the death of Eugene came rushing back. Barry was eleven, Eugene was thirteen. In fact, he had just had his bar mitzvah. It was vague what and where and how Eugene got the meningitis, but one minute he was in the hospital, and there were screaming phone calls, and Barry was left in the apartment with a neighbor while his parents rushed away and told him not to go anywhere. Where could he go? He was stuck staying at home with old Mrs. Farkus. Very old Mrs. Farkus, who sat all day and read the *Forward,* which another neighbor brought her. She also cooked a big soup pot of soggy vegetables and boiled chicken on the stove, from which she took a small portion every few hours.

Despite Mrs. Farkus's urging, Barry didn't eat the soup. Meningitis could be in it. Meningitis could be everywhere. When Mrs. Farkus answered the phone, Barry knew Eugene was dead. She only nodded, then handed the phone to him. By the time he took it, his mother or father had hung up. They must have told Mrs. Farkus to tell him.

"A zachen vay," Mrs. Farkus said, putting her hands on Barry's head and holding it tightly. "Nicht far dere gedacht, mein kind," she said, and then spit gently on his face three times, saying, "pooh pooh pooh" with each spit, and even though Barry knew it was supposed to be some nice thing she was doing to ward off evil, he ran into the bathroom and threw up. In fact, he stayed in the bathroom for four hours after that. Until his parents came home. For a while they didn't look for him.

They sat at the kitchen table and said things like, "See. No matter how much money you have it doesn't mean anything at a time like this." Then they each had some of Mrs. Farkus's soup, for which they thanked her profusely.

Eugene's funeral was the first funeral Barry ever attended. He wore a suit from last year, and his mother combed his hair down with water, which is what she usually only did once a year, before they went to high holiday services. He was very nervous. There were some familiar faces at the funeral home. In a big outer room were relatives Barry had seen at family parties. Eugene's bar mitzvah party, in fact. One was a pretty young cousin who had recently been married. Barry flushed when he saw her now. She had tried on some Eldor seconds in his room and he had seen her naked. The memory was getting him very excited. At Eugene's funeral. Oh, shit. Maybe God would give Barry meningitis for thinking of the cousin's naked body.

He felt a nudge from behind him. His mother was moving him from the big room. They were heading into a smaller room where Eugene's immediate family was seated. Maybe Barry could forget the cousin's big breasts and her furry— Oh, my God. It was the first time he'd seen the casket. He reeled for a moment and leaned back against his mother. Maybe because everyone else had been grown-ups and Barry was so short he hadn't noticed it before—but there in the middle of an archway, in what looked kind of like a puppet theater, was this big box. And the top half of it was open and Barry could see the face of Eugene. Dead Eugene. Wearing a yarmulke. Barry closed his eyes. Maybe if he looked at Eugene he would get meningitis. His mother was moving more quickly now into the back room. In the small room was Dora, Mashe's mother. She was in her eighties. She sat like a queen, all in black, holding her cane like a scepter. Relatives surrounded her. The relatives cried. Dora only nodded her head. Barry panicked. He remembered now he'd forgotten to ask his mother what you were supposed to say to someone when this happened. Now he was right in front of Dora. Dora only stared. Barry's mother leaned over and hugged her.

"We're sorry," she said. "We're very very sorry." That was good, Barry thought. Now he looked at his father, who merely touched Dora's hand with his own and moved his head in a gesture that was somewhere in between a nod and a shake. Barry's mother nudged him on ahead.

Mashe and Eleanor were surrounded by a whole group. The Goldens would have to wait. Barry wondered why his mother hadn't been sitting in this room, since she was, after all, Aunt Eleanor's sister. Maybe it was because they weren't so close. In fact, before Barry's father lost his job and the Goldens started selling Eldor, his mother and Aunt Eleanor talked to each other very little. Occasionally Barry had overheard conversations about "they think they're too good for us" from his father, and his mother would always make excuses and blame it on Mashe.

The crowd ahead of them was moving forward. Barry rehearsed in his mind. "We're sorry. We're very sorry." But before he could say a word Aunt Eleanor grabbed him.

"Barry," she said. "Oh, my God, Barelah," and she began to wail and sob. Barry looked at his mother, whose mouth was set stoically but whose eyes were filled with tears. He was stunned. He didn't even know Aunt Eleanor that well. This must all be because he was a boy and Eugene was a boy and Aunt Eleanor thought of Eugene when she looked at Barry. Or something. But she wouldn't let him go. And worse yet, she was moving him toward Mashe, who was also sobbing. And Mashe grabbed him now and they both held him and hugged him, and other relatives were coming in and "tsking" and nodding their heads knowingly, and Barry thought maybe he should say something, but all he could do was stand there watching them cry all over him.

Some very soft music started to play, and the rabbi, whom Barry recognized as the same one from Eugene's bar mitzvah, came into the little room. Thank God. Mashe and Eleanor let go of Barry and stood. Someone helped Dora to her feet and she followed the rabbi back toward the main room, where the family would sit in the front row. Eleanor walked behind Dora and then Mashe. Barry looked at his mother. She nodded and gave him a shove. He was next. In line. In importance. To Mashe. At Eugene's funeral. Barry was surprised to see that everyone else was already seated. As they filed into the front row he caught a glimpse of the pretty cousin. She smiled gently at him. Please, God, not now. He turned and sat down. They had closed the casket.

Barry felt very small sitting there with Mashe on one side and his mother on the other. Mashe had stopped crying now. But while he listened to the rabbi speaking, he did take out a handkerchief and blow his nose loudly for what seemed like five minutes. Barry didn't hear much of what the rabbi said. Not just because Mashe was blowing his nose—but because he was deep in thought. Especially after Mashe put the used handkerchief away—and took his big manicured right hand and placed it over Barry's little one. Why? What does this mean all of a sudden? Barry thought. Barry remembered a fairy tale he'd read once about a rich king whose wife was barren—that was the word the fairy-tale book used—so the king went into the town and gave gold to a very poor family of peasants and they gave him their baby daughter. Maybe Uncle Mashe was going to try and buy him from his parents now that Eugene was dead. Barry couldn't remember whether the baby daughter had grown up happy to be the daughter of the king or not. But he did remember how spectacular Eugene's bar mitzvah had been. Maybe after Mashe bought him there would be a bar mitzvah like that for him, too.

It was over, and everyone was going to the cemetery. Barry's mother was not. She was going back to Mashe and Eleanor's. Barry went with her in a taxi. The apartment was at Ninety-second and Park Avenue. Eleven rooms. Not counting bathrooms. A colored maid answered the door looking sad, and Barry's mother hugged her. Barry had never seen his mother hug a colored person before. Especially not Eva Jones, who came to clean their apartment once in a while. Barry figured this colored maid must be someone important. Barry's mother didn't really need him to do much. He was free to wander around. He had been to the apartment before, but of course this time he looked at it differently. After all. Who knew what could happen now? The door to Eugene's room was closed. Did he dare? His mother and the maid were in the kitchen removing waxed paper from trays of corned beef. They'd never notice.

He opened the door slowly. If he went in and closed the door behind him, they probably wouldn't even look for him.

It was better than he remembered. The football pennants and sports equipment and a giant desk with a real typewriter, and bookshelves with two sets of encyclopedias, and a fur rug on the floor, and a double bed with a huge comforter monogrammed with a giant "E." That would have to go. Barry closed his eyes. My God. In his mind he was already moved in. He sat down at the desk chair to think.

How could he be planning this? To become the replacement child of Uncle Mashe and Aunt Eleanor. What about his mother, who loved him so much she called him her little jewel? And what about his nice father, who—who what? He was trying very hard to think of something special about his father when he heard the voices. Oh, no. The people. The people were there. Already. Probably back from the cemetery. Maybe some didn't go to the cemetery. It sounded like there were a lot of them. They would be out there eating the corned beef and they would see him coming out of Eugene's room. And they would know his plans. He walked to the door and opened it. No one was looking. Slowly he walked out of Eugene's room, closed the door behind him and went into the dining room to make himself a corned-beef sandwich.

For the first few months after Eugene died, everything went back to being the way it had been before, and Barry was beginning to feel really foolish about the idea he'd had that Mashe and Eleanor were going to buy him. Eleanor and Barry's mother were talking on the phone to one another more often now than before Eugene died, so Barry would get to hear bits of information. Like the fact that Eleanor and Mashe had given all of Eugene's clothes away to some charity, and that Eugene's two sets of encyclopedias, both bar mitz-vah presents, had been donated to the Sunday-school library at the temple, where they were putting his name on a plaque in his memory. Barry could tell that Aunt Eleanor was crying during these conver-sations even though he could only hear his mother's side, because his mother would say into the phone: "Please, Elly. Don't, honey girl. Please."

Barry always felt a rush of love for his mother when he saw how sweet she was to her sister on the phone, and how much she cared for a woman who didn't seem to start being nice to her until she needed her.

Then one night it began. Almost the way Barry had imagined it might. Just when he had stopped thinking about it.

Barry was in his room doing his homework. He hated his god-damned homework, and he hated junior high school, and worse yet he was going to Hebrew school and being tutored by the rabbi. And the rabbi had bad breath, and there was almost nothing about

Barry's life that was exciting or different or important, and Mashe called.

Barry's father answered the phone and Barry knew already that it wasn't just one of his mother's friends or one of the yentas asking when she could come over to try on dresses, because his father put on this voice that Barry recognized as his talking-to-someone-important voice.

"Why, isn't that a lovely thought!" Barry heard his father say into the phone. Not once in his life had he ever heard his father speak the word "lovely."

"Oh, Barelah," his father called out to him in a phony singsong, which really seemed silly, since Barry was standing next to him at the time. "Your Uncle Mashe would like to talk to you on the telephone," went the rest of the song.

Barry took the phone nervously. He hadn't seen Mashe since the day of the funeral. What could this be? The buying? Was it actually going to happen?

"Barelah?" Mashe said.

"Hello, Uncle Mashe," Barry said, thinking that his own voice sounded very babyish. He was talking to Mashe on the phone. He felt important.

"You know, your Aunt Eleanor and I belong to an organization that has theater parties on Broadway. Do you know what that means, Barry?"

"No." He sort of knew. Why hadn't he said yes?

"It means we buy theater tickets in a group," Mashe said patiently. "So . . . since we ordered several months ago, we had three."

Silence. The implication was clear. The ticket had been ordered for Eugene. More silence. Who was supposed to say something now?

"You want to maybe go with us to *Gypsy?*"

Gypsy. Barry had seen the signs in the subway station. On the buses. Everywhere. Best damned musical I've seen in years. Mashe, Eleanor. Eugene's ticket. Meningitis. The E on the comforter would have to go.

"Uh, yeah, Uncle Mashe," Barry said, looking around and realizing his father had been standing right there next to him the whole time smiling. It was the smile that went along with the phony singsong voice.

"Next Thursday," Mashe said and hung up.

Mashe and Eleanor's seats for *Gypsy* were fantastic. They were in the third row on the right-hand side, directly opposite the drummer. Barry got the chills when he heard Ethel Merman's voice say "Sing out, Louise" from the back of the theater. The whole audience turned to see her make her entrance down the aisle, and they all burst into applause. It was exciting. The most exciting thing Barry had ever seen. Mashe and Eleanor were excited, too. They laughed at the cow and Mr. Goldstone, and when the sister, June, went away with Tulsa, the tap dancer, Barry sneaked a look at Eleanor and she had her face screwed up as if she might cry.

During intermission in the lobby Mashe bought Barry an orange drink and a giant Hershey bar. Then Eleanor introduced him as her favorite nephew to a lot of her lady friends in mink coats, who in turn introduced him to their various daughters and sons, and there were so many of them that afterward Barry couldn't remember any of their names. He did wonder if some of them hadn't maybe read the same fairy tale he had, and figured out the truth, which was that he was really only the child of the poor people. But no one said anything. And two weeks later, when Mashe and Eleanor picked him up and took him along on Eugene's preordered ticket to see *West Side Story,* all the same kids were there, and some of them greeted him by name.

On the night they took him to see *Gypsy,* Aunt Eleanor had a headache so they took Barry back to Brooklyn and went straight home. But after *West Side Story,* it was Sardi's. For supper. The three of them. And Mashe asked Barry what he thought of the show, and Aunt Eleanor asked Barry to tell her what his sizes were, and she wrote them down. And even though it was Tuesday night, a school night, Barry didn't get home to Brooklyn until midnight, and when he got into bed he couldn't sleep because he was thinking about the theater and being rich. And knowing he wanted somehow to have a part of each of those things. And wondering if Mashe and Eleanor would ever ask him to live in the room with the pennants, because it seemed like a better place to start what Barry was all of a sudden certain would be some kind of fabulous future, that far outshined the drabness of his Brooklyn life.

Barry's bar mitzvah was nice. It couldn't even be compared to Eugene's, but Aunt Eleanor helped his mother decorate the social hall at the shul with crepe paper, and even though no one said anything to him about it, the catering for the reception was so elaborate and the band was such a good one that Barry was sure that Mashe had probably contributed a few dollars to help pay for it.

Barry's whole class from junior high school was invited and his whole class from Sunday school, too, and many of them came to shul that morning to hear him read his haftara, which Mashe told him he did magnificently, which his mother told him made her "kvell," which his father said was "Very good, Barelah," and which made Aunt Eleanor cry.

The party went on until 1 A.M. and afterward when everyone left, Barry and his mother and father and Mashe and Eleanor drove back to the Goldens' apartment in Uncle Mashe's Cadillac. Barry was surprised when his mother asked Mashe and Eleanor to stop in for a late-night cup of tea and they said yes. He knew that even though his mother and Eleanor could yak for hours, Mashe was bored to tears by Barry's father. Barry was exhausted, and while the four of them sat at the kitchen table laughing and talking about the other relatives, Barry went to put on his pajamas. When he came in to say good night, Uncle Mashe put an arm around him.

"Nu, bar mitzvah bocher," he said. "Maybe you didn't notice, but your uncle Mashe didn't give you your present yet."

Barry had noticed. He had already totaled and retotaled the cash, checks and bonds he'd received from the other relatives combined, and they added up to a thousand dollars. He knew Mashe would give him some large amount, even if it was just so Barry's parents could tell the other relatives what a generous man Mashe was, and not just because he was eyeing Barry as potential son material. Barry's mind raced. How much would it be? Two hundred? Five hundred?

"Instead of money," Mashe said—Barry's heart sank—"which anybody can give," Mashe went on. That cheap bastard. "Your Aunt Eleanor and I thought maybe you would like to go on a little trip with us. So, as your bar mitzvah present, we want to take you to Hawaii."

Barry's mother gasped. "Oh, my goodness!" she said. "How lucky for you, Barelah!"

Shit! Barry thought.

"In December," Aunt Eleanor said.

It was September and still warm in New York, but Barry knew in December when the cold weather came, his aunt and uncle always went off to vacation in a warm climate. Yes. Now he remembered the way Eugene used to always be suntanned around Christmas vacation. First Barry got Eugene's theater tickets, now he was going to get his suntan.

"So, what do you say?"

Barry smiled. "Oh, thank you, Uncle Mashe," he answered. He wondered if Mashe could tell that behind the smile he was worried about whether or not suntans caused meningitis.

Barry's parents came to the airport to see Mashe, Eleanor and Barry off. It was Barry's first flight and they kept telling him, "Don't be nervous. There's no reason to be nervous." He wasn't nervous at all. He was exhilarated. When he discovered that every single person getting on the plane knew Uncle Mashe because the flight was a charter of several companies in the garment industry for a "shmatah" (Mashe's word) convention, Barry was surprised.

So were his parents. He heard his father say softly to his mother, "Big deal, a convention." But Barry liked the idea. There were lots of other kids of all ages going along. He kissed his parents goodbye and looked back at them briefly before he walked outside to board. They looked jealous.

It was a wonderful feeling to get on a plane in New York where it was nine degrees the day they left, arrive that night in Los Angeles where it was seventy-eight degrees, and be in Hawaii the next morning where it was eighty-four degrees. And so beautiful.

The Royal Hawaiian Hotel in Honolulu was pink. As far as Barry knew there weren't any pink buildings in New York and it was the first time he'd ever seen one.

Mashe and Eleanor had what was called a one-bedroom suite, and there was a cot in the living room for Barry. The living room faced the Pacific Ocean, and the beach was better than anything Barry ever imagined. If he stood outside on the little balcony he could look to his left and see the huge crater called Diamond Head. Mashe pointed it out to him. Mashe had been in Honolulu before, so he was able to tell Barry a lot of things about it on the plane ride over. The most important thing he told him had to do with the beach.

"Use a lot of lotion."

Mashe and Eleanor put their lotion on in the room. That precluded the risk of sandy hands, they told Barry, so he put lotion on, too. By the time they got outside, a lot of the other people from the charter already had their blankets spread on the sand. Some of the older couples waved at Mashe.

Barry noticed on one blanket very near the water were three boys not far from his age. He remembered seeing them on the plane. Separately. With their parents. He was amazed that they had all become friendly so fast. Those things usually took him a while. Maybe they'd known each other before. Must have. The boys had a portable radio which was playing pretty loud. Eleanor saw Barry looking at them.

"Why don't you go over there, Barry?" she said. "Those boys look nice." It sounded like something his mother would say.

Why didn't grown-ups understand that you didn't just go over to a group of people expecting them to immediately make you a part of their group? That wasn't how it was at all. People who walked up to other people like that were jerks. The guys had to decide to include you and then ask you. Maybe. Maybe not. Maybe Aunt Eleanor was telling him to go over because Eugene would have gone over with no trouble at all.

The three boys had been sitting, but now they all got up and ran into the water. All three of them swam out a distance and stopped. They were far enough out in the water so it looked as though it would be very deep—but they were standing, and the water was only as high as their chests. They were laughing and roughhousing.

Eleanor was spreading the blanket. Barry looked at Mashe, who was taking off the flower-printed shirt that matched his bathing suit. Mashe was very white and pale and paunchy and had no hair on his chest at all. Barry looked back at the boys.

"Swim out there, Barelah," Mashe said. "The boys are on a sandbar."

"I can't swim."

"No! You're joking. Your mother never sent you to the Y?"

Barry shook his head. He felt very badly. Maybe he should go back to the room. He couldn't swim. Even if those guys did want to include him, they would laugh at him when it was time to go in the water and he had to admit he couldn't. Maybe they would say he was a queer, which is what one of the guys in his gym class called him last week when the volleyball hit Barry's hand so hard that it bent back and hurt his wrist and he dropped out of the game.

Barry sat down on the blanket. He was depressed. He knew that he shouldn't be because here he was on the first real vacation in his life, in Hawaii, with so many things to do. The tour of Pearl Harbor, and the tour of the pineapple factory, and the parties that were part of the convention. It was more important than anything he'd ever done.

The boys were coming out of the water. They ran to their blankets and shook themselves off. They were all laughing and one of them turned the volume up on the radio. Barry wished he had a portable radio. Maybe he would buy himself one when he got home, with his bar mitzvah money. One of the boys stood up again and started walking toward the hotel pool area. He was obviously looking for someone as he passed their blanket and saw Mashe.

"Hey, Mashe," the kid said. Barry was surprised. He was used to kids calling grown-ups Mr. or Mrs., not by their first name.

Mashe shaded his eyes with his manicured hand and looked up at the boy.

"Hello, Howard," Mashe said smiling. "You know, it took me a second to recognize you. You're so grown-up." The boy Howard grinned. He had great teeth. He had great hair.

"Look, Elly," Mashe said to Aunt Eleanor, who was dozing. "Here's Howard. Did you ever meet my nephew Barry Golden?" Mashe asked Howard.

Howard extended his hand to shake. Barry felt shy. He put his hand out. They shook.

"Howard was Eugene's best friend," Eleanor said, smiling.

Howard looked uncomfortable.

"I'm looking for my dad," Howard said. "He was supposed to take some of the kids to lunch. Wanna come along?"

The last three words, directed at Barry, were so much a part of the first sentence that it took Barry a few seconds to realize Howard meant him.

"Huh?"

"Lunch. Hungry?" Howard asked.

"Uh . . ."

"Go ahead, Barelah," Mashe said. Barelah. Shit. Why did Mashe have to call him that in front of Howard?

"Your aunt and I will eat later. Go ahead."

Barry got up slowly. It was what he wished would happen, but those boys were all older and what would he talk about with them?

Lunch was in the outdoor dining room. It was beautiful. Birds flew right in and landed on the floor, under the tables, eating the dropped crumbs. Howard's father wasn't hungry, so he didn't join them after all, but Howard's sister, Joan, who was eleven, did. She brought her friend named Mattie, who was also about eleven and who wore braces on her teeth.

Howard was nice but the other two boys were saying dirty things about the waitresses in front of the girls, and punching each other on the arm and doing corny stuff like blowing the straw papers in each other's faces. Barry ordered a cheeseburger and it was delicious. They served it with a piece of pineapple beside it, and it was the first time he'd ever tasted pineapple that wasn't "chunk style" from a can. It was great. Restaurant food was so much better than his mother's cooking. When they'd finished eating, the waitress brought checks and pencils. Barry didn't know what the pencils were for. The others were all writing something on their checks. Barry looked at Howard.

"Oh," Howard said, "I forgot." And he took Barry's check from Barry. "My dad said I should sign for you, too." Then Barry saw that Howard was writing his parents' name and room number on the check and the words "add tip" and adding up the numbers. Howard was treating him to lunch. Barry's mother's face flashed through his mind.

"Tell your father 'Thank you,' Howard," he said.

Howard smiled that great teeth smile.

One of the other boys belched really loud, and the one who didn't belch laughed hysterically. Barry held his breath for a second. They might be doing that as a criticism of him. But neither of them was even looking at him. They were both already on their feet and running out the door, back to the beach, poking and shoving one another.

The two girls said they were going to get dressed and go to the hotel shops.

"Want to come to my room?" Howard asked.

Oh, yeah, Barry thought to himself. This guy with the good teeth and the good hair wants to be my friend, in beautiful fabulous Hawaii. Oh, thank you, God and Uncle Mashe and poor dead Eugene since now it's your best friend I'm stealing. Thank you, he thought happily.

What he said was "Sure."

Barry must have gotten more sun than he thought in the short time he was on the beach, because he could feel the elastic around the waist of his bathing suit rubbing against his body, and it hurt as he walked down the air-conditioned hallway behind Howard toward Howard's room. Howard was dark-skinned and already looked as though he had a tan. He stopped at a room and took a key out of a pocket in his suit. Howard was fifteen. He got to have his own room. Not a cot in the living room. Of course, he was in Hawaii with his parents, not his aunt and uncle. It wasn't just a room. It was a suite. Howard had his own suite. Much fancier than Mashe and Eleanor's. Barry tried not to look impressed. But he was.

"Well, c'mon in," Howard said. Barry was still standing in the doorway.

Barry noticed that the television was on, and there was the remains of a room-service breakfast still on the table in the living room.

"Those jerks haven't cleaned up yet," Howard said.

The other thing Barry noticed was the newspaper. It was spread all over the sofa. Howard had obviously been reading it. Barry didn't know anyone but grown-ups who read the newspaper.

"You look a little like Gene," Howard said to him.

"Who?" Barry asked.

"Gene. Your cousin."

Barry didn't know who Howard meant. Then it hit him.

"You mean Eugene?"

Howard laughed. "His parents were the only ones who called him Eugene. He hated it."

Barry smiled. "The way they call me Barelah."

"Right," Howard said. He was sitting at the table now, shaping and reshaping a little pile of sugar he'd spilled there from the room service leftovers. He had stopped smiling.

"I loved him," he said to Barry, not looking up. "I loved Gene."

"Yeah," Barry heard himself mutter. "He was a nice guy." Why was Howard saying that about Eugene? Because when someone was dead you could say things like that about them and no one thought you were soppy or—or what? Queer? Is that what Howard meant when he said he loved Gene, who was fast becoming in Barry's mind a different person than the Eugene of the bar mitzvah and the encyclopedias.

"Want a cigarette?" Howard asked him.

Barry shook his head. A lot of the kids at school smoked cigarettes. He'd never tried it.

Howard got up and walked toward the bedroom. "I've got some L&M's somewhere," he said.

As Howard walked into the bedroom Barry thought about leaving. But he didn't. He told himself he was staying because Howard paid for lunch, and leaving would be rude. Howard was talking to him from the other room.

"You can't blame Mashe and Elly," he was saying. "Parents don't ever know their kids. I guess if you think about your own parents, you'll know what I mean."

What was he talking about?

"Come in here," Howard said.

Later when he thought back about that afternoon he remembered there was something about the way Howard said "Come in here" that made Barry know exactly what would happen next, and that made him get slowly to his feet as if under a spell and walk into the bedroom. The blackout curtains were closed so it took a moment for Barry's eyes to adjust. When they did he saw Howard was naked. With a hard on. Barry's breathing was heavy and he had a hard on too.

Howard smiled. Barry wanted to look away from Howard's body and especially from his penis. But he was riveted to the spot.

"You can touch it," Howard said.

Barry felt a rush of blood all through him.

"No?" Howard said, tauntingly. "Then how 'bout taste it?"

This was it. He would run now. Run out of this room and down to the beach to the safety of Mashe and Eleanor and he could find a book to read. A good book to read all day, every day, and not once look up to see Howard and the other boys. If he could get out of this one, he would read three books. Yes, God, I promise. Three books over Christmas vacation was a major achievement. His English teacher had said so just last week.

He walked slowly toward the bed.

"Take your suit off, Barry," Howard said.

He did. It excited him even more as he watched the suit fall to his feet and then felt Howard's strong hand take his arm and pull him into the bed.

Howard was touching him, caressing him, tasting his body. Barry was filled with heat. He kept his eyes closed tightly. Howard's mouth was on his balls, then around his penis. Barry opened his eyes now and looked down at Howard's beautiful hair. He was amazed at what was going on. Oh, God. It felt so good. A queer. Oh, God. The frenzy built inside him to such a pitch he didn't even hear the key turn in the door.

Howard heard it. He jumped to his feet, pulled on a nearby robe and ran to the living room.

Barry's heart was pounding. He heard the voices.

"Maid service."

"Not now."

"I'm the last shift, sir."

"I don't care. Not now."

"I have orders to take the tray back to the kitchen."

"Fuck your orders."

"Hey, listen, mister—"

"Take the goddamned tray."

Barry was on his feet. He didn't want to be here. He was really afraid. He was a queer. He'd suspected it for a long time. But now. Letting another boy do that to him. He didn't feel very well. He remembered that party he'd gone to in Brooklyn, where Gloria Heller had suggested they all play Five Minutes in Paradise, and he found himself in somebody's parents' bedroom. He was on top of a big pile of coats that were on top of a bed, and Judy Krassner was on top of him. Crawling all over him, and he could smell perfume from the dresser of somebody's mother, he forgot whose house it was, and it made him queasy. At least he thought it was the perfume.

He picked his bathing suit up from the floor and slid it on. He heard the maid say the word "Mahalo" to Howard and the door to the corridor closed. A second later Howard stood in the door to the bedroom.

"Scared?"

"Yeah."

Howard moved into the room and sat on the bed.

"If you wanna leave you can," he said, and he took another cigarette from a pack of L&M's on the night table. "And I don't even care if you tell Mashe and Eleanor." His voice was very even. Not angry at all.

"I never would," Barry told him.

Was he crazy? Tell Mashe and Eleanor that he'd been in bed with Howard?

"Gene was always afraid of them," Howard said, inhaling deeply on the L&M, and blowing out a large cloud of smoke, then a smoke ring.

He's beautiful, Barry thought.

"The first night we were together he got so nervous he made himself sick," Howard said. "He was afraid if he went home they could look at his face and know. So he called them and told them he was staying overnight with me."

Eugene and Howard. That was what he meant. Howard looked at Barry. "You look like him. Like a shorter version of him." Howard smiled. Barry smiled. Howard liked him a lot. He felt that. Howard was so beautiful it made him weak. Eugene had been with Howard when they were both his age. Maybe queerness ran in his family. Maybe it caused meningitis.

"Don't be scared," Howard said.

"I'm not," Barry lied.

Howard put the cigarette out, untied his robe, and dropped it to the floor.

During the seven-day Hawaii stay Barry and Howard were together a lot but there wasn't any more sex or even any talk about it. Even though the experience was never out of Barry's mind and he was anxious to try to be with Howard again, he was relieved.

When they arrived at the New York airport, Howard got into a taxi behind his parents, closed the door and then looked out the window and waved at Barry, who was standing on the curb. That was the last time Barry ever saw him.

During the four years of high school that followed, Barry had two girl friends. Sarah Levy, an intellectual with giant breasts who asked him to squeeze her nipples hard while he kissed her but thought other sexual activity was whorey. And Margo Barnes, a shiksah, who would only kiss and no tongue please or I'll take a cab home. There were no more homosexual affairs and Barry was relieved that he hadn't met anyone who brought those feelings out in him since Howard.

When he was seventeen and a senior and working as a delivery boy for Eldor, Barry met Andy May, one of Mashe's designers.

Andy was twenty-five, very good looking and slim and funny. He made Barry laugh. A few times after work some of the other people at the office would get together and go to the movies, or to get dinner and Barry would join them and end up sitting near Andy. Andy would tell jokes about the models he worked with and after the group got to know Barry and to trust him, there were lots of jokes about Mashe from all of them.

Andy did a brilliant imitation of Mashe that killed Barry.

He did Mashe's bow-legged walk and supercilious raised eyebrow to perfection. Everyone loved it.

Barry knew Andy would ask him to come home with him eventually. Not just because when Mashe talked about Andy he ended the conversation by saying, "That faygelah," which always made Barry cringe, but because there was some very warm feeling between them.

When he finally did go to Andy's tasteful apartment in the Village that first night, the release was enormous for him. And he was sure he was in love. After the sex, which they both wanted so badly that it began the moment they closed the door behind them, Barry told

Andy about Howard and about Sarah Levy and Margo Barnes and Andy laughed a lot at the stories and made Barry laugh at them, too. And it was only because Mrs. Golden still peeked into his room every morning that Barry crept out of Andy's bedroom at 4 A.M. and took the long subway ride home.

The next few months were wonderful. High school really seemed like more bullshit than ever. Barry couldn't wait to get to Eldor to work. Even though he and Andy had to act as though nothing was going on, the restraint was sweet and the longing delicious. Barry's only problem now was college. One night early that year Mashe had called the Goldens to say he was coming over. He wanted to talk about something important. Barry's mother put on makeup. Barry's father "took a shave," as he called it. Barry was told to stay home. It might concern him. It did.

It seems that with Eugene dead, Mashe was worried about not having anyone to whom he could pass on his business if, in case, God forbid he should drop dead himself someday. Therefore, because Barelah had become so dear to him, he would like to pay his way to go and study business at the Wharton School of Finance at the University of Pennsylvania next year. Provided, of course, that during the summer and after he graduated he would come to work at Eldor in a capacity which would have increasing importance as the years went on.

Barry's father sighed. Why not? He wouldn't have to pay the kid's tuition himself. Barry's mother threw her arms around Mashe and told him there was surely a place in heaven waiting for him.

Barry was confused. He didn't know what he wanted to do. Granted he was impressed with Mashe's wheeling and dealing, and the way he manipulated not only his employees but everyone he did business with, but he wasn't so sure shmatahs was what he wanted. He still had some feeling about show business, and was curious about how people got into that. But somehow it got away from him. Somehow everyone was hugging and saying how blessed they all were to have their health, and by the time Mashe left that day it felt as if the deal was closed. Barry sent a letter off the next day to the University of Pennsylvania asking for an application, but he continued to feel uneasy about it.

By the time he met Andy he'd already been accepted to Wharton and the families had celebrated the acceptance at Mamma Leone's. Barry's mother told him she had never been so happy about anything in her life.

"Philadelphia? In business school?" Andy liked to tease him about it.

When Andy said it it sounded funny, even though the thought of it when he was alone made Barry ache.

The day of Barry's high school graduation his mother had a small party. Andy came and brought a few of the people from Eldor. Mashe and Eleanor were there, of course. It was weird for Barry to see Andy in his parents' living room. So out of context. One of the people who came to the party was Rita, a secretary from the front office at Eldor, who sometimes went out to dinner in the group with them. She was brazenly flirting with Mashe in front of Eleanor, and Barry kept wishing the party would be over. Finally it was, and Barry said a small prayer as Andy shook Mr. Golden's hand and said "Nice meeting you, sir." And kissed Mrs. Golden's hand and left with the girl Rita and some others.

Barry slept late the next day. It was the first day of summer vacation and Mashe said he could come in at noon. The group was going to dinner after work, so he'd wear something special. Barry turned over lazily and was surprised to see his mother in his room. She was leaning against the door, as if she'd been there for a while. Her face was pale and her mouth was contorted in a sneer of rage. Barry, now wide awake, sat up.

"Mah?"

"Pack your bags," she said quietly.

Barry knew something was deeply wrong. But what?

"Why?" he asked tentatively. "What do you mean?"

"Pack up. And get out of this apartment. We tried. God knows, your father and I tried to raise you and make you a decent man, and you did this to us, you ungrateful little louse! You will be out of here by noon, and we'll say kaddish for you because as far as we're concerned you're dead."

Barry's mother turned and ran out of the room.

Oh, my God. She knew. But how? And how much?

Barry jumped out of bed and ran after her. She was already in her room. She'd thrown herself across her unmade bed, sobbing.

"Mother. Talk to me."

Terrible agonizing sobs.

"Mother."

She raised her head and looked at him. That face. So filled with pain. She was gasping for air and then she coughed.

"Where's Daddy?" Barry asked.

"Not here. Couldn't stand the shame," she managed to get out. "Of you. You're a freak. You're a fairy. My own son. Tell me it's a lie. Tell me."

"Mah. It's not like that."

"Not like what? I'm talking about you and that Andy." She was screaming. "That goyishe sissy. Don't you get in bed together and touch each other? Don't you? Don't you do things with him you're supposed to do with a girl? Maybe you are a girl, my Barry? Maybe?"

Barry could see himself in the mirror of his mother's dresser. He was only wearing his pajama bottoms and his body was lean and hairless. If not a girl, he looked like a very young boy. He felt like that, too. Young and helpless and afraid. What could he say to her?

Now she was staring at him.

"How did you find out?" he asked quietly.

"From Mashe," she said. "I called there this morning and Eleanor, my sister Eleanor who's been so good to you, sounded very strange. We talked a few minutes and she said to me, 'Listen, Mashe would like to tell you something.' So Mashe got on and told me that about you. He heard it from one of the secretaries."

"Rita," Barry said, realizing out loud.

"He told me he can't fire that boy. He needs him. So you can't work there anymore. And no college either. He's too ashamed and sick to even know you. And so am I."

"That bitch Rita," Barry said. "I'm going over there." He ran to his room to get dressed.

"Don't you go to Eldor," Barry's mother shrieked at him. "Don't you embarrass my brother-in-law who is a saint. You get out of town and go be in a freak show somewhere."

Barry rushed past her on his way to the door. She would calm down and he'd deal with her later.

Barry bolted up the steps from the subway, moving around the people who were walking, and then headed down the street briskly. He didn't know what he'd say to Mashe, but he had to make this right. The elevator doors opened on the Eldor floor and Barry looked directly into the face of Rita. She flushed. She was shocked to see him there.

"You cunt," he yelled at her. There were a few people in the outer lobby.

"You filthy big-mouthed cunt," he screamed.

"Drop dead, you little fairy," she said. "So you finally got caught. Big deal."

Barry was amazed at how tough she was.

She picked up her phone and dialed.

"He's here," she said into the phone. She was warning Mashe.

Barry stormed through the reception door and down the corridor to Mashe's office. His jaw was clenched and his nose was running when he threw the door open. Mashe sat on the sofa across from his desk. Over his head was a portrait of Eugene in his tallis and yarmulke.

"Barelah," Mashe said, "what is there to say?"

"Uncle Mashe," Barry began. But Mashe was right. There was nothing.

"If you came here to look for your boy friend, don't bother. I sent him away for a few days. He won't see you when he gets back either, because if he does and I find out, I'll fire him. And he needs the job more than he needs to put your cock in his mouth, or his in your ass, or vice versa."

Mashe winced at the thought.

"Oh, God, and to think my wife and I took you into our lives like you were our son. And my own son, who was an angel and a perfect human being, is dead. Oh, God."

Mashe was crying. Barry looked at the portrait of Eugene. By the time Eugene was bar mitzvahed he'd already been in bed with Howard many times. If Mashe only knew that. Well, he would. Barry would tell him. Now.

"You know what, Uncle Mashe, you poor bastard," Barry said.

"What?" Mashe looked up at him.

Mashe, the saint, the millionaire, the president of Eldor Dresses, and the buyer, or at least the renter, of Barry Golden for the last six years, was reduced, falling apart, ashamed, and humiliated because his wife's nephew was having a sexual relationship with a member of his own sex. Barry knew he couldn't say what he planned.

"I'm leaving for California," he said instead.

For a moment he thought someone else had said those words instead of him, because he didn't remember even thinking about doing that before. But once he realized he'd said it, he also realized it was right. Mashe only nodded.

Barry had no trouble leaving town. When he got home that day his parents had sequestered themselves in their room. He packed in twenty minutes, only taking a few pairs of jeans and some shirts, then went to the bank and took out the five hundred dollars he'd saved from working at Eldor and his bar mitzvah money plus interest which he'd never touched, got into a taxi, and headed for the airport. As the taxi got close to the New York airport the driver asked, "Which airline?" and Barry didn't know.

"American," he guessed.

In Los Angeles he told the cab driver to take him to the Hollywood Roosevelt Hotel because he'd heard the name once on television. He checked into a room there, and cried and slept for three days. At the end of the three days he placed a long distance call to Andy's apartment. For a moment when Andy answered, Barry froze. "Andy?" he finally managed to get out.

"Who is this?" Andy asked.

"Barry."

There was a long silence.

"Where are you?"

"Hollywood."

Andy began to laugh. "Hollywood!" he kept saying as he laughed. "Hollywood!" And Barry thought probably someone was with Andy and that was why he kept repeating Hollywood, and he felt bad to think maybe Andy had already found someone else to be with.

Andy laughed so much he began to cough.

"Listen, kiddo," he said after he stopped coughing, "I hate to sound like *Foreign Intrigue* and all, but if anyone knew we were talking, my cute little ass would be, how you say, grass, so I better jump off."

Barry was silent. Why didn't Andy mention anything about Mashe and Rita and what had happened in New York?

"Bar? You there?" Andy asked.

"Yeah," Barry said softly.

Andy's tone changed now. "Listen, Barry," he said. "Your uncle's an asshole, but I need the job. He said you were a minor, and he'd get me for contributing to your delinquency, and rape and all sorts of bullshit if I didn't end it with you. I had no choice. Barry?"

"Yeah?"

"I have a friend in Hollywood. It's Michael Allred, the designer. I'll call him tomorrow. No, I'll call him now and you call him tomorrow and remind him. Maybe he can help you get a job."

That night Barry went downstairs to the Cine-Grill and had a cheeseburger and a Coke. He bought *Life* magazine from the newsstand on the corner and fell asleep in his room reading it. The next morning he called Michael Allred. Allred was effusive. Andy had been a student of his years ago. He called Andy "a beautiful boy." He told Barry how Andy raved about him over the phone last night when he called Allred. He asked Barry to come over to the studio for lunch.

Barry was impressed. Michael Allred had won Oscar after Oscar for costume design.

When Barry got to the lot that day to meet Allred he wasn't surprised that the man was a supercilious old queen, but he was surprised that Allred had already found him a job. The job was in the mail room at Hemisphere Studios.

four

On January 3, 1943, when Stanley Rose was born, his mother, Lena, received fifteen bouquets of flowers. The nurses were very impressed. Lena also received a pink-satin quilted bed jacket, a Teddy bear that was dressed in a blue crocheted suit, and a book called *Watching Our Baby Grow*. The book contained blanks which Lena could fill in, regarding the child's development.

Lena Rose told the nurses she would only keep the bouquet sent to her by her husband, but that the other fourteen could be distributed among some of the less fortunate people in the hospital. Then she donned the pink-satin quilted bed jacket, tucked the Teddy bear under the sheet next to her, opened the book called *Watching Our Baby Grow* and began to fill in the blanks.

> BABY'S NAME: *Stanley Rose.* BABY'S WEIGHT: *Seven pounds, fifteen ounces.* BABY'S HEIGHT: *Twenty and one-half inches.* BABY'S MOTHER: *Lena Rose.* BABY'S FATHER: *Albert Rose, D.D.S.* LOCATION OF BLESSED EVENT: *Jackson Memorial Hospital, Miami, Florida.*

Lena wrote in the book faithfully for a long time. She wrote about every gurgle and every coo Stanley uttered. She wrote about every hair and every tooth he sprouted. And as he got older and verbal, she wrote about the things he said.

"Stanley already displays a keen mind and a great wit," was the entry Lena made when Stanley was three. "Today was his third birthday and Albert and I gave a party. All of Stanley's cousins were there and his aunt Sally and his aunt Belle were both there too. Belle was devouring the cake (as usual) and Stanley said, 'Aunt Belle, I think the reason I love you so much is because it's like loving two people!' Belle put her fork down and swore to go on a diet tomorrow."

When Stanley was seven years old he made up a riddle which he wrote out in newly learned cursive script. The riddle was about a dentist, and Stanley's father, Albert, was a dentist so his parents loved it. The riddle was "Why is a cat like a dentist's drill?" And the answer was "Because they both make me ow!" Lena saved the blue-lined paper sheet where the riddle was written, in a pocket in the back of the book for "Mementos."

By the time he was nine, Stanley thought the book was stupid, mainly because it was called *Watching Our Baby Grow* and he wasn't a baby anymore. He teased Lena about the envelope she kept in the book that contained curls she'd retrieved from his first visit to the barber, by calling the book "a hairy tale." But by the time he was ten, Stanley was glad Lena had kept the book, because in it she had written over and over how much she loved him. And though she'd kept a book just like that one for his younger sister, Bonny, she didn't write nearly the wonderful things in Bonny's book about Bonny that she wrote in Stanley's book about Stanley. He checked one day to be sure. The other reason he was glad Lena had kept the book was that by the time he was ten she had died of cancer.

Stanley watched Albert do everything he could to try and save Lena. Taking her to doctor after doctor, to hospitals and clinics, but nothing worked. Stanley remembered never really thinking about romantic love before he stood with Bonny and watched his father lying on the bed next to poor sickly Lena promising her, assuring her, that she would be fine, and all of them knowing it wasn't true, except for Bonny, who was too young to really understand what was going on. Stanley's father loved Stanley's mother more than anything. He didn't even go to the office most of the time while she was sick. Just stayed with her, near her, caring for her until the end.

When Stanley saw the look on Albert's face the day Lena died, for a minute he hated his father. Albert looked almost glad. Then Stanley realized that he himself was glad. There was a reason to be glad. There would be no more nurses in the house, no more having to be quiet all the time. No more visits from his big fat aunts, Sally and Belle, his mother's sisters, who would go to see Lena in her room wearing big phony smiles on their faces, and then come out when she fell asleep to sit in the living room and smoke cigarettes and cry to Albert, who would comfort them. Comfort them? Poor tired Albert. And the two aunts so fresh from shopping they had their bags from Burdine's with them in the back seat of Aunt Belle's car. Stanley saw them.

Stanley couldn't understand how his beautiful mother had two sisters who looked like that. Maybe they weren't really her sisters. Like in "Cinderella." That's what it was. Sally and Belle were the ugly sisters. As he watched them coming up the walk to the house, Stanley would shout, "Hey, Dad, here come the sisty uglers," and sometimes Lena would hear him from her bed and laugh, and Albert would try to stifle a giggle as he opened the door to let the aunts in. For years after that, Stanley and Bonny referred to Sally and Belle as the S.U.

The S.U. were certain that Albert would never be able to handle the job of raising two young children, as well as return to his dental office, which was only still functioning thanks to his associate, Dr. Charles, because Albert had spent so much time trying to take care of Lena. But Albert surprised them. He hired a daily cleaning lady named Vivian, then made car pool deals which allowed him to drive in the morning and another parent to pick up while he was at work in the afternoon. He marketed at night, packed lunches early in the morning, left tooth fairy money and made the best Halloween costumes the kids ever had. Stanley and Bonny adored him, even though Stanley prayed every night that Albert would get married again someday soon so the children could have a father and a mother, instead of a father and a cleaning lady, and Bonny, who was very young, prayed that Lena would come back to life.

Stanley was watching television in the living room that afternoon when his throat started hurting. It was a Friday and Albert had promised to take Stanley and Bonny out for Chinese food and then bowling when he got home. It was their favorite evening out together. Stanley wouldn't mention the sore throat. Anyway, the hot won ton soup would fix him right up.

Vivian was carrying the last load of ironing upstairs and muttering to herself when she stopped and looked at him.

"You got somethin' wrong?" she asked.

"Huh?"

"You sure lookin' sick to me, my friend." Vivian dumped the pile of ironing on the sofa. "What's achin' you?"

Shit. She would tell his father.

"My throat."

"You go get in bed now till your daddy gets home, hear?"

Stanley wanted to go bowling tonight. Albert promised him if he started doing well he'd get him his own bowling ball. If he was in bed when Albert got home, Albert would never take him out tonight. But Vivian had picked up the pile of ironing again and wouldn't walk up the steps until Stanley went ahead of her, so he did.

Bonny was in her room holding a doll that was wearing leggings. She was trying to get teeny little red rubber galoshes on the doll's feet.

Stanley went right to bed and fell asleep. When he woke up a few hours later he was sweating. Covered with sweat. And his throat still hurt. Worse now. Much worse. And his foot. His foot was aching. Maybe he'd tripped or something. But his foot was really hurting. What could this be? Suddenly, as he lay in the darkened bedroom, Stanley was filled with terror.

He knew what it was. No one had to tell him. Polio. It was going around. Public pools had been closed down. Children were told not to drink from public fountains. Polio. Oh, God. He would be in a wheelchair. Maybe an iron lung. And Albert would look at him with sad eyes the way he'd looked at Lena when she was sick and helpless, like Stanley was going to be now. Oh, please. His crying was loud and the door opened. Albert. He was home.

"Baby?"

Albert called Stanley baby. He also called Bonny baby. It was his favorite endearment.

"Anything wrong?" he asked.

"No," came the tearful, through a clogged nose answer.

"What is it?" Albert asked, turning on the light.

"I—I—" Stanley couldn't say it.

"Are you ready for bowling?" Albert asked.

"Daddy," Stanley managed to say. "I'm afraid. I think I have polio," he blurted out and began to cry.

"What?" Albert said, still standing in the doorway. "That's silly. Don't you think that. You must have been having a bad dream. Now your sister's all ready. So you wash your face and comb your hair and we'll go."

"I can't."

Albert Rose walked over to the bed and took the boy in his arms.

"Well, you do have a fever, baby," he said. "You're hot as hell."

"And my throat hurts . . ."

"Just some flu bug or other." Albert rocked him now. He was so strong and sure.

"But my foot," Stanley said. He was afraid to say the rest. "My foot hurts real bad, Daddy."

Albert no longer looked so sure.

"I'll call Dr. Grogen," he said.

A few minutes later, after making a phone call and asking Vivian to stay with Bonny, Albert bustled his son into the car and drove him to Harry Grogen's office. After the examination, the white-haired pediatrician told Stanley to dress and took Albert into his office. He put his hands on Albert's arms as if to hold him up.

"I think the boy has polio, Al," he said. "I want to do a spinal."

"You're crazy," Albert said. But there was fear in his voice.

"He's got all the signs," Grogen said.

The door to Grogen's office opened. The eleven-year-old boy stood in the door dressed and pale and shivering. He looked at Grogen's long face looking back at him. And then at Albert's face. He recognized Albert's expression of helplessness. He'd seen it before. Stanley broke the silence.

"I guess this sort of rules out bowling," he said softly.

Albert closed his eyes for a moment to stop the tears.

"Let's go home, baby," he said then, and he lifted the boy into his arms and carried him out to the car.

Bulbar polio. Crippling. That was the diagnosis. Grogen wanted Stanley to move into the hospital immediately. Albert said no.

"He could need oxygen fast, Al," Grogen told him. "You can't care for him the way we can."

"The hell I can't," Albert Rose said. "I don't want my boy in any goddamned hospital."

"You plannin' to give up your life again?" Grogen snapped. "The way you did with Lena for so long? Staying around that house doin' twenty-four-hour-a-day service, giving up your own life? What about Bonny? That poor baby probably only knows you as a nurse, Al."

Albert was stone-faced.

"You bring that boy into the hospital tomorrow, Albert Rose, or you're making a mistake. I'll fill out the forms right now."

"Shove the goddamned forms, Grogen," Albert said.

Stanley was afraid. He was glad his father wouldn't let him go to the hospital. On the day he had to go there to have his tests, he saw children in wheelchairs. Children on crutches. It was awful. The hospital must have done that to them. But then there was the other side. What if Albert was wrong and Stanley was supposed to be in the hospital? Couldn't get better without the hospital? Then what would happen?

Albert began treating him the next day.

"What's that?" Stanley asked.

He was lying in his bed upstairs and Albert was carrying a big tray that had something on it that looked like giant versions of the steaming dumplings they served in the Chinese restaurant.

"Hot packs, baby," Albert said. "We're gonna do these every two hours till we make you well."

The packs were boiling. Blankets. Boiled. Packed on Stanley's legs. The first few times Stanley cried and begged Albert to stop, but Albert said, "Now, now, Daddy loves you. Daddy wouldn't hurt you. This is what we have to do." And sometimes Bonny would stand wide-eyed in the doorway of Stanley's room to watch.

"Get out of here," he screamed at her one day. "I wish you had polio and not me."

Stanley would be crippled for life. He knew it. His father didn't tell him that, but he knew it. Just like he knew other things his father didn't tell him. That he never went to work anymore, and that he was giving up his practice totally to Dr. Charles so he would have nothing to do every day but be home with Stanley. And he was very worried, Stanley could see it in his eyes. Just the way he knew Albert's helpless expression, he knew the worried one too.

When he wasn't hovering over Stanley, Albert was taking care of Bonny. Shopping with her, making sure she had a portion of his time every day.

Albert moved the television set into Stanley's room, to distract the boy from what was becoming an agonizing process.

The television set. Stanley always had it on. Every waking minute. Even some sleeping minutes. Amazing. Sometimes he would wake up at night and the postprogram flurry of dots would be on and he would stare at them, seeing colors and shapes. It wasn't long before he knew everything about every show. News, Westerns, detective shows, *Beat the Clock, Kukla, Fran and Ollie*. He played a game with himself, where he tried to remember who each of the writers was, and who the producers and the directors were, and where the shows were made. He loved *Boston Blackie*. It was on on Friday nights at nine thirty. Albert and Bonny joined him to wait for it. First they would watch *I Remember Mama* at eight because Bonny liked the little girl named Dagmar. Then at eight thirty they'd watch *Life of Riley*. Then Bonny would go to sleep and Albert and Stanley would watch *The Big Story* and Albert would fall asleep in his chair. By the time *Boston Blackie* came on, Stanley would have to try to hear it over Albert's snoring.

Blackie was played by Kent Taylor. He was handsome and tough and smart. And sometimes he got into his convertible without even opening the door. He just vaulted over the side into the front seat and drove away. Stanley wanted to do that. To move and be like that. Watching *Boston Blackie* helped him decide he couldn't and wouldn't be crippled. He would endure the hot packs his father told him were called the Sister Kenny treatment. Even though in his mind he was sure Sister Kenny must be some monster who hated children.

Dr. Grogen came by once a week to examine Stanley. For the first few months, every time he came, he took Albert aside and chastised him for doing this to Stanley, to himself and to Bonny. Albert never said a word in response. After a while Grogen stopped commenting. To begin with, the boy didn't look so bad. But mainly, Grogen knew Albert never even heard him anymore.

Once, in a sort of joke, Grogen made a remark to Albert about his being like Florence Nightingale. It made Albert laugh and became Grogen's nickname for him.

"You're tough, Flo," Grogen would say, and the two of them would laugh heartily. Grogen was right. Albert was tough, but he was getting tired, too. He was only thirty-four years old, but he felt as though he were ancient. The stairway leading to the bedrooms seemed more and more difficult to climb when he carried up Stanley's meals. And then, every day, so many times, boiling those blankets, over and over, twisting them, wringing them out. Carrying them upstairs, too. And watching his baby. His wonderful boy, trying bravely not to cry out from the pain of the heat. Stanley only joked and called him the Bully with the Blankets.

Sometimes Albert thought maybe Stanley would be better off . . . No. He had to be there for him. If the boy was in a hospital, Albert couldn't be on top of everything. In control. He had to stay with it. He would.

"God damn you, Flo, you devil," Grogen said to him. It had been nearly a year. "You did it. He's perfect."

Stanley had licked the polio. Albert had licked it. The boy and his father both grinned, then squeezed one another's hands conspiratorially. Albert bought himself a bottle of wine. Stanley wrote a poem called "God Bless Sister Kenny," and after he'd printed a neat copy of it and showed it to Albert, they mailed it to the Sister Kenny Institute in Minnesota.

After Stanley recovered from polio, Albert was a different person. Happier. Less serious. It was almost as though curing Stanley relieved him of the guilt he had for being unable to cure Lena. The young dentist was anxious to have the well-loved Albert come back to the office, so they made arrangements for his return to the practice.

Stanley was a different person, too. The year he'd spent at home in bed had changed him. Made him quiet. Introspective. And reentering the world of other kids was hard for him. He had spent so much time watching television that he'd never once opened the math book or the spelling book the school sent to him, accompanied by a get-well-soon card a year ago. So he was behind academically. But there was something else wrong, too. Something about the way the kids were acting now. And even the way they looked. Especially the girls.

A couple of them had real bad pimples, and all of them were giggly and secretive and would sometimes just start crying for no reason at all. Yuch! The only thing he liked about school was coming home every day after it was over. He would turn on the television and watch anything and everything. He even watched WEBU, the educational channel. And when he realized the station was located in downtown Miami, without asking Albert's permission he took a bus there one day after school.

There it was. All of it. Cameras and lights and microphones. And the sets. He recognized the sets from a show called *Wendy's World.* It was a puppet show and Wendy was a pudgy blond woman who was a very bad ventriloquist. Each day, in a fifteen-minute segment, Wendy and the puppets would deal with some moral issue, then resolve it, and end the segment with a song. Wendy was on her set today and Stanley stood wide-eyed on the sidelines, and watched as she slipped Winnie on her left hand and Wally on her right.

"Okay, let's take the song from the top," Wendy yelled to someone who was controlling the tape-recorded music. Her voice sounded a lot different from the way it did on the show when she would say, "Welcome to Wendy's wide and wonderful world," or when she was talking to the puppets. But then the music started and she was using the Wendy voice that Stanley remembered. And the Winnie voice. And the Wally voice. They all sounded pretty much alike.

> *"We're Wendy, we're Winnie and we're Wally*
> *And we want to welcome you to Wendy's World*
> *Where whimsy and wisdom and wishes all abound*
> *Where weakness and worries and woes just can't be found."*

It was really neat to hear it in person. Stanley decided to come back the next day, too. For a few months he visited WEBU every day, and the people there were beginning to think he belonged there, so they started giving him jobs to do. Little jobs, like going to the coffee machine in the hallway to bring back coffee, or running out-side to close someone's car window when it started raining unex-pectedly. But it wasn't until Stanley got up the nerve to ask Arnold West, the station manager, if they would pay him a small wage, and West agreed, that Stanley even mentioned to Albert where he had been going every day after school.

Albert was concerned. Stanley's report cards were pretty disap-pointing. But after Stanley swore he'd bring his grades up, Albert agreed to let him take a real job at WEBU. It became the most im-portant thing in his life.

After two years of sweeping the studio and emptying the trash cans and ashtrays, and making sure he always had quarters in his pocket for the coffee machine, Stanley got his first big break.

The station was short-handed that week and they needed someone to turn the TelePrompTer for a professor who was speaking on "Comedy and Tragedy in Literature." Stanley was chosen, and Ar-nold West told him he did a great job. "A great job means I didn't fall asleep from boredom," Stanley said. As a result, the next week they asked him to pull the photographs, one at a time and in order, while an expert in ornithology gave a lecture on endangered birds. Stanley asked Bonny to watch that day. "This could be stardom," he told her. "Maybe part of my hand will be seen on camera and then, who knows? My own show." Bonny told him later that his hand was never visible.

Finally, when he was a senior in high school, they let Stanley oper-ate a camera during a geography lecture. He was thrilled. "This is creativity. Great art. And I'm grateful for the opportunity," he said to West, who laughed. Stanley's camera was focused, throughout the entire lecture, on a map of South America.

Stanley didn't want to go to college, but Albert insisted. So he ap-plied to and was accepted by the University of Miami. The school was in his neighborhood, and if he didn't take a full load of credits he would be able to continue at WEBU. By now he was telling his ideas for new programming to Arnold West and West liked them. West liked Stanley. Stanley's best idea wasn't really original. He stole it from the television series *You Are There*. He wrote a series of short plays telling stories from history in a simple way. He would combine the use of drawings with scenes performed by members of the school's drama department. And the actors answered questions from the narrator, played by Stanley.

The first show was about Christopher Columbus discovering

America. A boy named Michael Tucker played Columbus. He was a very good actor. Queen Isabella was played by Carol Sue Schwartz. Carol Sue was from Memphis, so her portrayal of Queen Isabella included a Southern accent. But that didn't bother Stanley. He was willing to give her other parts too. He told her that one night in the doorway of her Coral Gables apartment.

"Would you like to play the part of Betsy Ross in my next production and go to bed with me?"

"Huh?"

"It's a yes-or-no question."

"Now wait—"

"Would you?"

"It's a good thing ah lahk you, Stanley Rose, or ah'd slap you."

"Sounds like a no to me."

"There were two parts to that question," she said.

"Not really."

"You mean you'd use your power at that station to get a girl to bed?"

"Not really."

"Oh, I'm glad you wouldn't."

"No. No. 'Not really' was me repeating the answer to the question before."

"Then you would."

"In your case. Maybe."

"I don't know whether to laugh or—"

"Laugh."

She did. They went to bed together that night. They also went steady for his whole senior year.

Stanley was starting to think of himself as the creative force behind WEBU. He was, after all, a writer, a director and a producer. So when graduation time came, he informed Albert he was heading "out West" to get an agent. He kissed Carol Sue Schwartz goodbye. "I'll send for you," he said, and they both laughed, knowing it was B.S., as Carol Sue called it. Then he told Arnold West he would be using him as a reference, took the money he'd saved from his job at WEBU and flew to Los Angeles.

For weeks Stanley made phone calls but he couldn't reach anyone at the William Morris Agency or at GAC who wanted to represent his directing career. He made the rounds of the local television stations, but only got as far as the receptionists, who told him, "Leave a résumé." He did. But no one called. He was beginning to understand that being a great director at WEBU didn't, as he later put it, "mean shit, or anything else of equal or lesser importance."

After Stanley had been in Los Angeles for eight months and still didn't have a job, his father, Albert, decided to take the matter into his own hands.

Albert called Larry Portner, a guy he'd known in dental school. Lawrence Portner, D.D.S., had his practice at 9255 Sunset Boulevard, which was between Hollywood and Beverly Hills. Portner and his wife, Sylvia, always called Albert and took him out to dinner when they came through Miami to see Sylvia's mother, Sadie, who lived in Miami Beach. Lawrence Portner showed Albert his clippings once. They were from columns where they referred to him as "Larry Portner . . . the dentist to the stars."

"My son is a director and a writer and a producer," Albert told Portner on the phone. "Twenty-two years old."

Portner wanted to know what Stanley's credits were.

"Local television," Albert said. "But he's brilliant."

"I'll see what I can do."

After a few days Portner called Albert Rose back.

"My contact is a guy named Joe Rabinowitz, a patient of mine," he said. "He has bad gums, but a good heart. He's some kind of executive in the television business, and he says, on my say-so, he'll recommend your Stanley for a job at the studio."

Albert thanked Portner, said someday he'd return the favor and he would have Stanley call Joe Rabinowitz right away.

When Albert told Stanley, Stanley said, "I can't believe I spent the last eight years of my life learning about television, and I'm getting a job in show business through the root-canal underground."

Stanley called Joe Rabinowitz's secretary. Rabinowitz was in the hospital. Portner was wrong. Rabinowitz's heart was as bad as his gums. Worse, maybe. He'd had a heart attack that morning and, as the secretary told Stanley, it didn't look good. Rabinowitz had, however, already written a letter to personnel regarding Stanley Rose, only yesterday. And she would send it off today. She wished Stanley luck, and when her other phone rang she said, "Just a sec," and put him on hold.

"Rabinowitz is dead," she said to Stanley when she came back on the line.

A few days later Stan got a call from the personnel office. If it wasn't too soon after his friend Joe Rabinowitz's death, they said, they'd like him to come in and start working right away. The job was in the mail room at Hemisphere Studios.

IN THE
MAIL ROOM . . .

five

The first stop on any tour of Hollywood was always Hemisphere Studios.

In the middle of the arid San Fernando Valley, the Hemisphere executive building rose majestically from the bustling lot like a shrine to the film, television and music industries. The architect had worked closely with Harold Greenfield, the president and chief executive officer of Hemisphere, Inc., on the design.

Greenfield wanted the building to be twenty stories high with hundreds of windows that had an orange, yellow and brown cast, so that when they caught the California sun it would look as though the building were made of gold. Like a piece of fine jewelry. Maybe that was the reason the Hemisphere tower was sometimes referred to by people as "Greenfield's mezuzah." Or maybe because, as one well-known comedy writer quipped, "Inside there is a religious experience."

The personnel office was in the basement of the gold building. Stan Rose sat in a chair across from the receptionist reading *Variety* while he waited.

FILMWAYS FOUNDED IN 1953 WITH $200, SPENDING $25 MILLION ON PRODUCTION THIS YEAR. UNITED ARTISTS QUARTERLY NET RECORD $3,042,000, UP 46% OVER 1964. PREXY PREDICTS $12,000,000 PROFIT THIS YEAR.

The numbers fascinated him. The amounts were always so enormous. He wondered how much of it was true.

"Sorry you have to wait so long," the receptionist said. "They promised somebody would be right over to get you, but they're always real slow."

"I'll change all that," he said. She smiled.

She was great-looking. Probably wants to be an actress, Stan thought. He was playing a game with himself trying to decide what her name might be when he heard the door open and a very loud voice shout, "Judy baby!"

Stan turned to see who made the loud entrance. The young man was chubby and sweet-faced.

"Hi, Mickey," the receptionist, Judy, said, grinning, and before she could protest, the guy named Mickey had lifted her from her chair and was dancing her around the room singing like one of the Supremes. "Baby love, my baby love. I need you, oh how I need your love." Judy was screaming with laughter. Mickey pulled her against him. "Let's dance close, baby," he said, and whirled her around again.

"Mickey," she screamed through her laughter. "Get out of here." Mickey let Judy go, then he made an entire show of fanning himself, unzipping his pants, adjusting himself, and extending the hand he'd used to Stan Rose.

"No, thanks," Stan said, laughing.

"I'm Mickey Ashman."

"I'm Stan Rose."

"Welcome to Hemisphere Studios," Ashman said to Stan. "You'll love the mail room. It's the asshole of show business. Contrary to what some people believe, which is that *I* am. C'mon, I'll take you over there."

Stan nodded to Judy, who was sitting at her desk, combing her hair, trying to put herself back together.

"I love you, Judy," Mickey said, "and remember that any time you want to touch my penis it's okay with me because, after all, what are friends for?"

Judy shrieked at the outrage then giggled, and Mickey led the way for Stan out the door and onto the Hemisphere lot.

As they walked toward the gold cart that had the words Mail Room stenciled on it, Stan couldn't believe his eyes. Right in front of him was Lorne Greene. It look Stan a minute to realize who it was, and when he did his heart started to pound. It was one thing to see a star's footprints or parking place somewhere, and another to see the actual person. So real. Just walking by talking to someone, as if he were just a regular guy. Mickey saw the look on Stan's face and laughed. "Yeah," he said, "that's really him. You'll get used to it. There's Natalie Wood."

Stan turned quickly to look where Mickey was pointing. It was true. Natalie Wood and a man in a dark suit were entering the gold building. This job was going to be better than he imagined. It reminded Stan of the joke about the shy little man who was a janitor in a burlesque house. He came there every night to clean and watched the beautiful girls go by. One day, after the man had been there a few weeks, the boss asked him why he hadn't come by to pick up his pay check, and the janitor asked, "You mean I get paid for this, too?"

"Actually, the M.R. is right near the personnel office where you came in," Mickey told Stan as the cart started off with a lurch, "but I have to show you around the lot so you'll know where the routes are.

"The costume department is in that four-story building over there. The first floor is made up of sewing rooms and offices. And the second, third and fourth floors are lined with racks, covered with every kind of costume you can imagine. There's one huge room that's just shoes. Another one is only hats. Thousands of goddamned hats."

Stan shook his head in amazement.

"Last Halloween, someone on the lot had a party and all the guys went over to costume and some of the designers helped us out."

"Sounds great."

"It was. I went as a pizza."

Stan laughed.

"I looked adorable," Mickey said, grinning.

"Have you been in the mail room a long time?" Stan asked. When Mickey's face tensed, Stan realized that was the wrong question. The mail room was a means to an end. The end was getting out and into a good studio job.

"Yeah," was the answer. Stan didn't pursue it.

They rode for a long distance and Stan was amazed at how large the Hemisphere lot was.

"Makeup," Mickey said, pointing to a smaller building in front of which were parked half a dozen long black limousines. The drivers stood next to their cars talking to one another. A few of them waved at Mickey.

"All of the stars have to stop there first. Those guys are their drivers. When the actors come out, the drivers take them to the sound stages."

Mickey turned the cart and they drove through the Western town. It was empty and looked very flat and Stan recognized it with a grin.

"Is this where they did *Desperado?*" he asked.

"That's right," Mickey laughed. "God," he said, "I love to take the new guys on the lot for the first time. I guess I forget how used to all of this I am till I see someone else seeing Lorne Greene."

He made a left turn and passed several pink one-story Spanish buildings.

"The casitas," Mickey told him. "Up until this year when the gold building went up, the hotshot execs were out here. Now they stick writers and the young executives in the little buildings and anybody important is in the big building. Even casting moved upstairs."

Stan spotted an ambulance with its red lights flashing up ahead and craned his neck to see.

"Don't panic," Mickey said. "It's not a real one; we're about to pass transportation. The shop there services all the vehicles used on the lot. That's the ambulance from *Med School*. It's a new show this year." As they passed the big garage, Stan saw several black-and-white police cars and a fire truck inside.

"And these are the places where it all happens," Mickey said, making a sweeping gesture as they passed several buildings that looked like airplane hangars. "Stages one through thirty-five, which have been converted at one time or another to look like the inside of an airplane, the bottom of the sea, the top of a mountain in a snowstorm, the surface of the moon, the giants' living room in *Here Come the Little Folk,* and more. You probably won't have to take any mail to those stages, unless something special comes up, but we're allowed to watch anything that's shooting on our off time, unless the director says it's a closed set."

"Really?" Stan had never found himself at a loss for words before, but the idea of being able to walk into any set on the lot made him too excited to speak.

Mickey nodded. "By the time you've been here as long as I have," he said, "you'll get tired of it." Mickey turned the cart back toward the gold building. "That's pretty much all you need to know today," he said to Stan, turning the cart again. "There's the tour department over there," he said, pointing to a long trailer in the distance. "They're just starting out. They'll be building the thing within the year. Universal's tour is so successful I guess Greenfield figured Hemisphere should have one, too."

They were almost at the gold building. "Now I'll show you the mail room and introduce you to the guys."

He drove the cart under the building into a large parking area and stopped in a space that was right next to a bicycle rack containing half a dozen rickety-looking bicycles with bright metal baskets on the handlebars. Before Stan could ask, Mickey answered.

"That's right," he said, "this cart's only for emergencies. One of those bikes is for you. That's how we all get around. So if you don't get a better job out of all this, at least you'll get great legs."

As the two walked into the building, Mickey was slightly ahead, and when they reached the door marked Mail Room, he stopped. There was a cardboard sign tacked to the door. BE KIND TO THE BOYS IN THE MAIL ROOM, it said in block letters. SOMEDAY YOU'LL BE WORKING FOR THEM.

"Like that?" Mickey asked. "I made that sign. It's what keeps me going."

He pushed the door open.

In the middle of the large room was a high table with a postage machine on it. A redheaded fellow was arguing with another guy who was sitting on a stool by the table.

"I have this building until next month," the redhead said.

"David, I wasn't trying to bird-dog your goddamned route," the other guy said. He was short and had thick black hair. Stan noticed that he couldn't stop shifting nervously. "So just fuck off. I was talking to Milt Fredericks' secretary yesterday about an article I read in *The New Yorker* and she asked if I'd save it for her. That's what was in the envelope you saw me giving to her."

The redhead's face was very flushed.

"This is Stan Rose," Mickey said. The two young men were so locked in their argument neither of them even looked over.

"That's David Kane and Barry Golden," Mickey said to Stan.

"Did you ask Fredericks for a job?" Kane demanded.

"No, I didn't," Golden answered. "Fredericks is in Europe."

"Oh."

Stan looked around at the large room. One wall was covered with pigeonholes for the mail. A name was printed under each box and the boxes were divided into sections. The wall on the other side of the room was covered with larger pigeonholes. "That's where the outgoing stuff goes, in the pouches."

"Pouches?"

"The airborne service picks those up and gets them almost anywhere in the world within twenty-four hours. The small pigeonholes are like individual mailboxes. Twice a day we go to the post office and pick up mail. We sort it, then run it."

Kane and Golden had finished their fight. Kane was leafing through today's *Variety* and Golden came over.

"Ned quit," he told Mickey. Not even acknowledging Stan. "There was a note from upstairs. So we don't have a boss."

Mickey explained it to Stan. Ned Carr had been the head of the mail room. He was a sniveling spoiled boy whose family owned one of the country's largest wholesale food companies. "This'll give you a picture of Ned Carr," Mickey said to Stan. "He once said to me, 'You've never had an onion ring in the West that didn't belong to my family.' So you know what I said back to him? I said, 'I never *touch* fried foods.'"

Everyone laughed.

"Ned's father didn't want him in the food business, so they tried getting him into show business through friends," Barry said. "Unfortunately for him, according to the system, in order for a mail room employee to get out of the mail room, an executive has to make him an assistant, and no one wanted Ned Carr as an assistant."

"Yeah," Kane said. "He was in the mail room for five years, watching everyone else come and go. This year it looked as if he was on the verge of having a nervous breakdown."

"Well, we better get busy," Mickey said. "Golden, why don't you and Kane get to the post office for pick up. Then Rose here and I can do a run at eleven so he can see how it's done. I'll call personnel and find out if there are any more candidates for these fabulous jobs, and I'll stamp the few things left on the table." Golden nodded and he started out with David Kane behind him. Mickey watched them go and then turned slowly to Stan.

"Uh-oh," he said. "I think something terrible just happened."

"What's that?" Stan asked.

"I think I just became the head of the mail room," Mickey said.

He tried to say that as though it made him angry, but Stan noticed there was a look of pride in Mickey Ashman's eyes.

six

It was Stan Rose who always insisted that the four mail room boys take their lunch break in the main dining room of the commissary.

"It's exposure, you guys," he'd say, hyping them with a twinkle in his eyes. "You know what I mean? You can bury yourself in here with a brown-bag lunch at the postage table, or you can have a tuna melt in the same room where the biggies are having their tuna melts, and pretty soon they think they have something in common with you, so they start talking to you."

Stan Rose had turned from an awkward boy into an attractive man during his college years and his days at WEBU. Maybe because of his childhood bout with polio he seldom participated in any athletic activities, so his body wasn't particularly toned. But he had a kind, toothy smile and beautiful eyes. His best quality, which was a razor-sharp mind and a wit to match, made everyone ask his advice. Not because they were necessarily planning to take it, but just to see what he'd say and how he'd say it.

He brought an attitude with him that made the place more like a fraternity house than a studio mail room. And it was that attitude that brought the guys closer together.

To begin with, there were the nicknames. Stan was kidding David Kane about his bright-red hair and he called him Archie, like Archie Andrews from the comic book—and the others laughed.

"Then you should be Jughead," Mickey said to Stan. "Remember that time when Archie asked Jughead doesn't he have any clothes besides that one long sweater and those dark pants and that little hat he always wore that looks like a crown?"

"It's nice to see you remember great moments from important literature, Ashman," Stan said. The four of them were stuffing the pigeonholes from the newly arrived bags of incoming mail one morning.

"So Jughead takes Archie to his closet," Mickey went on, "to show him he's got plenty more clothes."

"I can hardly wait to hear what happened next," Barry said. He was standing on a step stool to reach the top row of pigeonholes.

"And he opens the goddamned closet and," Mickey started to laugh, "and he does have a lot of clothes. Only they're all the same.

Ten of those long sweaters, and ten pairs of those dark pants and ten of those hats that look like crowns."

No one else was laughing.

"Yeah," Stan said. "So?"

"So you're like that, Rose, with your goddamned plaid shirts and khaki pants. That's all you ever wear. You should be Jughead."

"And Golden can be Big Moose," Stan said.

Barry smiled. Stan Rose was boring, but at least he was a nice guy, not like that cold bastard Kane.

"And Mickey?"

"I'll be Reggie," Mickey said.

"Because he's Archie's rival?" Barry asked.

"No, because if I don't pick *him,* all that's left is Betty or Veronica. And I'd have to go out and rent some tits."

It was expensive to have lunch in the commissary every day; the prices were not made for the mail room salary. But the others knew Stan was right about being seen there, so they each managed to work their budgets around to afford it. After a few weeks they'd established a regular table near the entrance and the favorite game was to figure out what was going on in town by who was having lunch together. The room was always bustling, and the passing faces were impressive.

"Don't look now, but Al Dietrich is meeting in the last booth with Sandy Koufax. Big-time movie offers to the Jewish baseball player," Stan said.

"Would I look like a jerk if I asked Koufax for an autograph?" Mickey said.

"You always look like a jerk, Ashman," Barry said.

"Listen, I was very cool last week when Lynda Bird Johnson and George Hamilton were in here," Mickey said. "I went over to their table and I was very charming and I said, 'I think your father is a great old boy. I used to think he was just a shit-kicker but now he's all right with me.'"

"Right," said Stan. "Unfortunately you said that to George Hamilton."

"Oh, yeah," Mickey said, furrowing his brow, pretending to be confused. Stan and Barry laughed.

Most of the time David stayed out of those exchanges. He liked Rose but he thought Ashman was a loudmouth and Golden a frantic little nobody.

"Hey, Archie," Mickey would say to David. "How come you're so quiet?"

"Leave him alone, Reg," Stan would tell Mickey.

David wouldn't even reply. Frequently he'd get up, leaving enough cash on the table to cover his part of the check, excuse himself and spend the last part of the lunch hour wandering around the lot.

"Don't go," Stan Rose said to him one day as David was reaching for his wallet. "Wait for dessert."

"I don't want dessert," David said.

"You'll want this one. Here it comes."

David looked up to see what Stan was talking about. Five of the commissary waitresses were walking toward their table. One was carrying a piece of cake with a lit candle on it. The waitresses were all smiling and they began to sing.

"Happy birthday to you," they sang.

"Happy birthday to you," Barry, Mickey and Stan chimed in.

"Happy birthday, dear David." People at the other tables in the commissary were looking over.

"Happy birthday to you."

How in the hell did they know?

Everyone in the entire commissary burst into applause. David flushed. Jesus Christ.

One of the waitresses kissed him on the cheek. His birthday last year was a few weeks after Marlene died and he'd sat in a chair in the living room of the apartment all day knowing that nobody he could think of knew it was his birthday or cared either.

"Make a wish," Mickey said.

A wish. What could he wish? That he could get out of the mail room. That someone would care about him? He couldn't decide what to wish but he knew everyone wouldn't stop staring at him unless he blew out the goddamned candle, so he closed his eyes as if he were wishing something important, then opened them and blew. There was another burst of applause.

"How did you know?" David asked Stan.

"Ashman knew," Stan replied. "He's seen all of our job applications."

David looked at Mickey Ashman.

"Don't get sentimental about me, Arch," Mickey said. "I only did it because I wanted everybody to look at our table instead of staring over there at Mia and Frank."

It was true. Mia Farrow and Frank Sinatra were having lunch with Harold Greenfield. In fact, they were just getting up to leave now.

"Happy birthday, David," a woman David didn't even know said to him as she walked by their table.

"Happy birthday!" a guy from accounting said, grinning at David.

Mia and Frank and Greenfield were in animated conversation as they walked toward the door of the commissary to leave. All eyes were on them. Mia stopped near their table.

"Happy birthday, David," Mia said smiling. "Have a nice day." The four of them discussed it for weeks afterwards, and the general consensus was that Sinatra smiled too.

"Yes, David, happy birthday," Harold Greenfield said. Mia and Frank kept walking, but Greenfield stopped and stood looking closely at the four of them.

"How's it going, boys, Making the deliveries through rain and sleet and dark of night?"

Greenfield was tall and thin. He had white hair and wore black horn-rimmed glasses. He also wore dark-blue suits. Only dark-blue suits, and so did all the other studio executives at Hemisphere. All four of them were thinking the same thing as he stood there. He didn't have any idea who they were besides delivery boys. He couldn't possibly. None of them had ever even seen him this close before.

"Your team got trounced last week, eh, Rose?" he said.

Stan was startled. The University of Miami team had indeed been trounced by Tulane.

"That why you didn't go to homecoming?"

"No, sir. Too expensive to fly back there for just a weekend."

"Good point," Greenfield said. "Well—it's nice that you're all looking so well."

"Golden," Greenfield nodded at Barry, then at Mickey. "Ashman, good to see you." Then he looked at David. "Happy birthday, Kane," he said. "Many happy returns."

"Thank you, sir," David said, and Harold Greenfield turned and walked out of the commissary to rejoin Mia and Frank.

The four looked at one another silently for a moment, then laughed.

"Can you beat that?" Mickey said. "He knows us. He really knows our names and everything."

"And what football team I root for," Stan said. They were incredulous. "But how?"

"It's part of what makes him who he is, I guess," Barry said.

"Amazing." They were about to do their usual dividing of the check.

"You don't pay today, Arch. It's your birthday," Stan said to David. "We'll divide the total by three." He hadn't consulted the others but they nodded in agreement.

"Thanks, Jug," David said. It was the first time he'd used one of the nicknames. It was also the first time he'd had any feelings for any of them.

seven

Days passed when they felt as if they were robots. Pick up the morning mail, sort the morning mail, run the morning mail, pick up the outgoing, sort the outgoing, eat lunch. Pick up the afternoon mail, sort the afternoon mail, run the afternoon mail, pick up the outgoing, sort the outgoing, go home. Sometimes they joked that the rickety bikes they drove on their routes could probably find the way to their deliveries alone.

Finally they found something to break the monotony.

To: Mr. Noel Gordon
      Director of Business Affairs
      Hemisphere Studios
      North Hollywood, Calif.

Dear Noel,

Please note that this letter has been hand-delivered to you personally because of its highly confidential nature. I trust you will respect the secrecy surrounding its contents exactly as instructed herein, in order to facilitate the security measures with which the following issue must be handled. I specifically chose not to meet with you personally regarding this issue, so as not to arouse the suspicions of our respective staffs.

As I am sure you are aware, the Russian film director Milton Pinsky has defected from the Soviet Union and is now trying to find a place for himself in the American film community. For obvious reasons, Pinsky is a frightened and secretive man and wishes to keep his new-found association with Hemisphere Studios unknown and above all, unpublished. It is for this reason I have gone to elaborate lengths to maintain his cover. Even so far as making it appear as though his remuneration for services comes from outside sources. Which is why, to date, none of his paperwork has passed through your offices.

Henceforth, however, to our great fortune, Pinsky has chosen to emerge from hiding, as it were, if only slightly, and will be making use of some of our facilities. Because of the complicated political ramifications of his alliance with Hemisphere, and here I use the word political in both the personal and territorial senses, it is imperative that my association with him appear nonexistent.

Therefore, I have an emissary who will be tending to

Pinsky's needs, as well as acting under my instruction as a liaison between Pinsky and your office. The man is called Stan Rose and he has unwittingly been chosen as my liaison, based on his low profile as a mail room employee. He knows nothing of his mission. Merely that he is doing a service for the studio.

Certain that you will carry this out with discretion and haste, and without further correspondence, I remain,

Sincerely yours,

HAROLD GREENFIELD

(P.S. Naturally you will destroy this letter.)

"I'm gonna piss in my pants," Mickey said.

Tears were streaming down David Kane's face. He couldn't stop laughing. None of them could.

"It's brilliant," Barry said.

"I love that part where you say you don't know anything about it."

"Yeah," Stan said, "that was kind of my favorite part, too. Okay, what do we want?"

"Four parking spaces on the lot," Barry said. The walk to the mail room from the lot the boys called "peon parking" was nearly half a mile away. On rainy days it was miserable, and by the time they were dry it was time to ride the bikes back out into the rain.

"Pinsky wouldn't ask for four spaces," Stan said. "What if we try for one space and we take turns using it?"

"Okay," they all agreed.

"Jesus," Barry said, looking at the letterhead. FROM THE DESK OF HAROLD GREENFIELD. "This stationery looks real."

"It *is* real," Stan said. "Greenfield ordered twelve new boxes. I delivered eleven and kept one for us."

"What else does Pinsky want?"

"An office. But make it around here. With a television, and a secretary," Mickey said.

"Great." David couldn't believe it.

"I'll interview the secretaries," Mickey said.

"Don't get crazy," Stan told him. Stan made notes while the others looked over his shoulder.

"Pinsky's Russian," Barry said. "He probably likes vodka. Maybe caviar."

"My guess is that Pinsky would like to see a print of *Tomorrow We Live* in a private studio screening room with just a few of his close friends," Stan said.

"*Tomorrow We Live* hasn't been released yet. No one can screen it. Those guys aren't gonna release their biggest picture for next year to be screened," David said.

"Hey, Arch," Stan said, "why tell me? Tell that to Pinsky."

The four of them laughed and Stan sealed the letter, then rose to his feet. He stood at attention, his face a mask of seriousness.

Mickey couldn't stand it. "I swear to God I'm gonna piss in my pants."

"Wish me luck, boys," Stan said.

The other three were holding on to one another, convulsed with laughter as Stan walked out of the mail room to take the letter to Noel Gordon.

By the end of the week Rose had delivered two other letters.

"Coffee, Mr. Rose?" Gordon's secretary said.

"Huh?" No one ever offered a mail room boy coffee.

Stan knew by the look on the woman's face that even though Gordon may not have told her why, he obviously had told her to be nice to Stan Rose. She was a bitchy old spinster who up until the past week had called him "kid." She always covered the work she was doing with a cupped hand when he came near her desk to get the mail, as though she were the class goody-goody and he were a potential copycat.

"That bleached-out bitch," Barry said gleefully when Stan told the others she'd offered him coffee. "She must hate it that you bring the letters straight to Gordon and she doesn't see them first."

"She does," Stan said, "and you should see Gordon," he went on, describing the reaction the Milquetoast head of business affairs was having to the Pinsky letters. "He thinks it's a James Bond movie. He lets me into the office, and then he closes the blinds."

"He's on the eighteenth floor," David said laughing. "Who's going to see you? A bird?"

"It's fabulous," Stan said.

Late that day when Mickey came back from a run, he saw the painter with the stencil in the parking lot. The message to Gordon was that, of course, Pinsky, fearing discovery, could not have his own name on his parking space. So, to avoid suspicion, they would paint an alias on his space. The name chosen was Sorrel Naft. Sorrel Naft was the name of a boy who had been in the third grade with David Kane.

"Oh, Jesus," Mickey said, bursting in on the others. "I swear to God. It says Sorrel Naft on a parking space."

"Gordon gave me an envelope this morning with a parking pass in it for Pinsky. Pinsky's supposed to put it inside his windshield when he drives on the lot."

One at a time they strolled out to the parking lot just to see the sign.

On Monday David and Stan were coming in from the post office. Moving men were carrying a desk off a truck.

"Oh, look," Stan said. "Someone's moving into an office down here."

By the time the boys finished their first run that morning, the office near the mail room was completely and quite elegantly furnished.

"Oh, my God," Stan said as the four of them passed the open door of the new office on their way to lunch. "I'll bet this is our office. Pinsky's office!"

"No!"

"I think so."

The four of them looked up and down the hall to make sure no one was around, then went into the new office.

There was a reception room, complete with coffee-making para- phernalia and phones, and an inner office with a carpet, a television and a bar. It was Barry who opened the bar. Inside was a case of Crown Russe.

"Oh, my God," Mickey said.

"I'm gonna—"

"Don't piss in your pants, Reg. Do it in here," Stan said, and he opened the door to Pinsky's bathroom. It was wallpapered in mylar, and it had a shower.

"I'll stop by Gordon's office today to get Pinsky the key," Stan told them.

"Let's hit the commissary. I'm starved," David said.

"Yeah. I love to watch Gordon trying not to look over at our table," Barry said.

"Or at Greenfield's," Mickey said.

The Pinsky Caper, as they later called it, went on for quite a while.

Dear Gordon,

For the past few months our correspondence has been solely in the form of lists written on my letterhead regarding items which Pinsky needed. Your quick action in obtaining them was splendid, and your use of the service of my innocent mail room boy convinced me that your future with Hemisphere will be long and profound. I am particularly impressed with the catering service you chose for Pinsky's private party (Pinsky told me about it; I did not attend) and the alacrity with which the studio limousine was able, via your instructions, with merely a call from your home late one night, to pick up Pinsky and his friends at a bar and drive them to the beach. (You see I am aware of it all.)

My next request is complicated. It may surprise you to discover that Pinsky is ready to step out in public. Appropriately, I think he wishes this emergence to occur at the Oscar telecast and he would like the studio to obtain V.I.P. seating as well as parking for him and his wife, Natasha. Unfortunately, because of circumstances, Pinsky can go nowhere alone. He must travel in a group so he may remain protected. Therefore, I am hoping through the Academy you will secure two additional tickets for Pinsky's bodyguards. With continuing faith in your confidence, I remain,

Sincerely,

Harold Greenfield

The four tickets arrived two hours after Stan dropped off the note.

"Oh, Reggie, what's Pinsky gonna wear to this?" Mickey asked Stan. "We know you're wearin' khaki and plaid 'cause that's all you've got."

"And what about us? The Pinsky-ettes?" Barry said.

"How 'bout your pal Allred?" David said to Barry. Barry flushed. "Maybe he'd spring for four tuxes. He's got access to a roomful of them."

"No, I don't—I—"

"It's okay," Stan said. "Pinsky can order the suits."

"I think we've gotta be a little cool with Pinsky," David said. "He's gonna get caught."

"Not until after Oscar night."

The next day Pinsky's friends sent their sizes to costumes. The suits arrived within three hours. They were perfect. The boys each used Pinsky's bathroom to dress. Raised Pinsky's glasses filled with

Pinsky's champagne, left over from Pinsky's party, in a toast to Pinsky, and took Pinsky's limo to Santa Monica Civic.

David had loved the whole Pinsky thing. It scared him a little but it made him laugh to think of pulling the wool over the eyes of those assholes in the gold building. But now, as the car drove up outside the auditorium, as he saw the bright searchlights and the paparazzi, he was afraid the four of them would be caught and punished and told to find jobs somewhere else.

And he couldn't do that. He was busting his nuts to make good relationships at the studio. This could fuck it all up. Someone would surely see them—recognize them. The others were climbing out of the car. David was tempted to stay inside the car and wait. Wait with the limousine driver. Probably the driver was a nice guy. A smart guy. A guy who was once headed for a vice-president's job until he fucked around with Harold Greenfield.

"C'mon, Arch," Barry said, looking into the car.

"Yeah, okay."

As the boys made their way through the crowd and down to their seats, they passed Jack Shear and his wife, Al Dietrich and a date, and Lonny Paxton, who nodded absently to them. David was sweating. Stan shook his head and grinned knowingly as they sat down.

"It's like being invisible," he said. "Those guys look at us in these tuxes and they don't have a clue who we are."

David was starting to relax. The Oscarcast was exciting for all of them, and Rose was right. At the party afterward, executives pushed past them, either ignoring them totally or grabbing their hands to shake, with an absent look in their eyes that proved Stan was right. They knew they'd seen those four young men. But they didn't know where.

The boys found the table near the back that had been reserved in Pinsky's name. It was a good vantage point and they made a game of pointing out the stars to one another.

"Milton Pinsky. Paging Mr. Milton Pinsky." Barry, who was the first to hear it, turned pale and dropped his fork.

"Jug?" he said. "Did you hear that?"

The music was very loud and so was the chatter.

"Listen."

David and Mickey were having a discussion about how bad the food was. "Milton Pinsky." The P.A. was full of static, but there was no mistaking it. David and Mickey turned to Stan. David looked panicky.

"Oh, shit," he said.

"Relax," Stan told him. "It's got to be Gordon. He's the only one who knows. He's probably checking to see if Pinsky's having a good time."

"No," David said. "Pinsky's supposed to be kept a secret, Rose. Gordon would never page him on the P.A. at a place like this." He stood, nervous and red-faced.

"Jesus, Kane," Barry said. "Sit down. Don't get crazy."

"Fuck you," David said hotly. "This could be our jobs. My job." The page was more clear this time.

"I'll go," Stan said.

As he walked into the lobby of the hotel, the sound level changed drastically, and he took a deep breath. It must be Gordon. He headed for the sign that said House Phones. Gordon probably was at home, and since the show wasn't telecast until later, he was making sure Pinsky was—

"Operator?"

"Yes," Rose said, placing two fingers under his collar to loosen it a little. "I'm taking the call for Mr. Pinsky."

"One moment."

It'll be Gordon, Stan thought, but his heart was pounding.

"Hello." It was a familiar voice. Not Gordon's.

"Hello," Stan said. Maybe he should try to use a Russian accent.

"Good evening, Rose. This is Harold Greenfield."

Stan's mouth was very dry. He pulled at the black satin tie until it opened.

"Uh, hi there, sir," he said.

"Having a good time, Rose?" Greenfield said. Stan looked around the lobby quickly. If this was a movie, Greenfield would be at the phone right next to his, and they would be standing back to back with phones to their ears. Greenfield was nowhere in sight.

"Yes, sir," Stan said. Oh, shit. Maybe he could get a job back in Florida.

"And the others?"

"Yes, sir."

"What about Pinsky, Rose?" Greenfield asked.

"What about him, sir?" Stan said, wincing.

"Is he having a good time? Shall I send him a glass of wine, or do you think I've done enough for him, Rose?"

Stan tried to figure out exactly what it was he was hearing in Greenfield's voice. For some reason it didn't sound like anger, but then he'd read books about these big movie moguls. The key to their enormous power was that they never lost control. They could ruin people's entire lives with smiles on their faces. Oh, what the hell. Florida was nice all year round, and Stan's father would be glad to have him back.

"How long have you known about this, sir?" Stan asked, looking around nervously. At the entrance to the ballroom, Mickey, Barry and David were waiting. Mickey smoked a cigar and paced. Barry and David looked like they were arguing.

"From the beginning," Greenfield answered. Stan closed his eyes. How could that be? "But I loved watching it, Rose. And you. You're quite remarkable and I like your style. Your group of boys has been happier than any group I've ever had in the mail room. It was worth every penny. Now, however, I think it's time for Pinsky to go the way of all legends."

Stan was grinning. He was holding back a relieved laugh. "You bet, Mr. Greenfield," he said.

The others must have seen Stan's face because they were heading in his direction. By the time he hung the phone up they were beside him.

"Well?"

"Boys," Stan said, "someone very close to us just passed on."

VARIETY PERSONALS

DEATHS

Milton Pinsky. Russian film director, from natural causes. Recently defected to U.S. in order to carry on his brilliant filmmaking career here in association with Hemisphere Studios. Pinsky leaves behind his four boys Stanley, Barry, David and Mickey. In lieu of flowers, the family requests donations sent to Actors Fund.

INTEROFFICE MEMO FROM THE DESK OF HAROLD GREENFIELD

Nice work. Send me the rest of my stationery.

Best, H.G.

By Tuesday morning Pinsky's office was empty, but the boys barely noticed. Stan Rose had an appointment for a job interview on the lot with a man named Walter Barton. Barry Golden was waiting for a return call from Henry Shmidt's office at World Records. Mickey was meeting after work with a new commercial agent, and David had decided to try to become the assistant to Harold Greenfield.

eight

David Kane pushed the up button on the elevator in the lobby of the gold building. He was carrying an armful of mail for the executive office upstairs, and that made him nervous. It never occurred to him to feel nervous on the days he was delivering and picking up the mail at costumes or makeup or transportation. That's because there was no one in those departments he wanted to impress. But in this building, the executive manpower overwhelmed him. And he needed those men to notice him. They had to notice him. It was the only way he'd ever get out of the fucking mail room. Jesus, he hated it there.

First that little prick Ned Carr, and now Ashman running the place, telling him what to do. And as the months went by, David kept thinking it would be over any day and someone would take him out of there and make him their assistant. But hustling around the gold building, visiting their offices, getting to know their secretaries, the standard mail room pattern, didn't seem to be doing him much good.

"So, how's it goin' there, Red?"

Willie the guard, whose domain was the lobby of the gold building, yelled across the hollow space to David.

David didn't answer. Just nodded. He wasn't going to get into a conversation with some guard.

The elevator doors opened and Al Dietrich got off.

"Morning, Mr. Dietrich," David said.

Dietrich nodded and headed for the glass doors leading to the parking lot.

"Sir?" David would ask him if he needed an assistant. This was a great time. He hadn't been able to get past that bitchy secretary of his. "Uh, Mr. Dietrich?"

Dietrich kept walking.

"He didn't even hear ya, Red," Willie the guard said.

The elevator doors had closed and David pushed the button again. When the doors opened, he got on and stood for a moment shaking his head. Shit!

David pushed the button marked nineteen. He was carrying mail for several of the producers whose offices were on that floor. He had already asked around if any of them needed an assistant, but if there was any response at all it was usually something on the order of "I'd love to give you a job, kid, but by next season I may not have one myself."

It was true. The television producers and many of the film producers came and went quickly. That's why David wanted to work upstairs. With the studio heads. For Harold Greenfield. But Greenfield was never available. He was in Europe, or in a meeting, or at lunch, or too busy, or not seeing anyone this month or something like that. But David was hanging in. Calling and leaving messages with Greenfield's secretary. He believed that if he could have a half hour of Greenfield's time just to talk, Greenfield would see how aggressive he could be and take him on as an assistant. David got off the elevator, sorting the mail as he walked. He would hurry through nineteen and get to twenty quickly.

"Hi, David."

Lonny Paxton's secretary. Big tits. What was her name? "Hi, honey," David said.

Harry Mann's secretary. Tough old broad. He liked her.

"Morning."

"Take that pile in the box for outgoing, will you?" she said. The telephone was at her ear, a cigarette hung from her mouth and she was typing rapidly. David grinned.

Part of the nineteenth floor was casting. Tom Rich's office. Three blond girls, each wearing too much makeup for that hour of the morning, sat in three chairs lined up just next to Rich's door. Each was holding a picture portfolio on her lap. Rich's fat secretary, Enid, was reading a novel.

"Got my trades, mail boy?" she asked. She had a thick New York accent.

David put a copy of *Variety* and one of the *Hollywood Reporter* addressed to Rich on her desk. She was a cunt, a fat ugly cunt, and he hated her and the way she called him "mail boy."

But Rich listened to every word she said about everything. "Here you go, Enid," David said, smiling at her.

The door from Rich's office opened and a fourth girl who looked like the three girls in the chairs emerged.

"Thank you very much, Mr. Rich," she said over her shoulder. "And thank you," she said to Enid who didn't even look up. Then she turned to the three girls in the three chairs. "Good luck," she said insincerely to them.

Tom Rich came out after her. He was red-faced and looked very haggard.

"Next," he said. "Llewellyn?"

"Me!" one of the three blond girls said and jumped up.

"Hiya, Tom," David said.

"Whaddya say, Dave?"

Tom Rich was a real warm guy. Honest and sincere. And everyone knew he'd never get anywhere. He'd been stuck as a casting director for ten years because he was a yes man. He had no opinion. And he drank too much. There were three different heads of casting since Tom Rich started working at Hemisphere, but Rich had never been considered for the job.

The girl named Llewellyn brushed seductively past Rich into his office. Rich didn't even notice. That was the other thing. Ten years in the job of casting beautiful women and there had never been even one rumor about him.

"So how 'bout it, Tom?" David said to Rich. "Looking for an assistant?"

"Huh?"

The secretary, Enid, looked up at David and narrowed her eyes. "Nevah mind, Kane," she said, "he's gonna hayah me if he needs someone to help him. Not one of you mail room creeps."

Rich shrugged at David and closed the door. David walked down the corridor dropping trade papers on desks, testing himself to see how many of the secretaries' names he could remember, and clenching his teeth trying not to think about that cunt Enid.

He looked to see what he had left to deliver. All the rest was on twenty. He'd stop in the men's room on the nineteenth floor and comb his hair before he went up.

The men's room was empty. David took a paper towel and wiped off one of the sinks so he could put the papers he was carrying down on it. Then he took a comb out of his pocket, and stood in front of the mirror that was over the next sink. He looked at his face. He was only nineteen, but his eyes looked like the eyes of an old man. Since Marlene died, he'd been living alone in the apartment in Beverly Hills, living carefully on Social Security checks and his small mail room paychecks, making the drive into the Valley every morning, occasionally having dinner or a beer with some of his high school friends in the evening, but most of the time staying late at the studio.

Mail room chores were usually finished by six every night. Mickey Ashman would run off to his acting workshop or some such bullshit and the others seemed in a hurry to get away each evening, too. Not David. He would wander around to see what was going on. There was frequently nighttime shooting of a picture on the back lot. David would find a spot behind the cameras and sit quietly watching. Occasionally there would be a pretty young actress or extra around who would flirt with him and he would join her on her dinner break, then take her home for some casual sex. But watching the movies being made got him more excited than any woman ever could.

David finished with the comb and looked at himself with satisfaction. His hair was his best feature. Besides being thick and healthy-looking, the bright carrot color that made people call him "Hey, Red" was outstanding. And he'd spent some of his Social Security check on this new seersucker blazer he was wearing, so he looked exceptional today. Maybe he would see Greenfield today. Maybe Jack Shear needed an assistant. He took the mail and headed for the elevator.

On the east side of the twentieth floor were the offices of World Records, a subsidiary of Hemisphere. The record company was headed by Henry Shmidt, a giant bear of a man who knew a lot about business and nothing about music except what some of his underlings and his teenaged daughter told him. There were three photographs on Shmidt's desk. David had seen them once when Shmidt was in New York, and Shmidt's secretary had been busy on the phone and waved to David to take the mail right in and put it on Shmidt's desk. One of the photographs was of Shmidt's wife, Jenna, currently a socialite, formerly a Las Vegas showgirl. The second picture was made as a joke. It was a shot of Shmidt in a World War II Nazi uniform complete with helmet. And the third was a photograph of Shmidt and his teenaged daughter, Anna.

The girl was very tall and blond and statuesque and she was laughing. And Shmidt was standing behind her with his arm around her and had his left hand cupping her left breast. His daughter. Jesus. David had heard Shmidt was strange. The three pictures convinced him. Today he only had *Billboard* and *Cash Box* for Shmidt's office. The secretary was away from her desk so David dropped the papers off and left quickly.

He headed for Jack Shear's office. Shear's secretary was—let's see. A girl with a guy's name. Jean? No. Allyn Grant. With a "y." She wasn't at her desk.

"Allyn?" David said.

"Hi," she shouted out. She was sitting in Shear's empty office, looking out the window.

"Got anything for outgoing?" he asked. He dropped Shear's mail on her desk.

"No," she replied, "he's in Europe."

"Oh."

"Did you want to see him about something?" Allyn emerged.

David hesitated. Maybe he shouldn't say. Maybe this girl wanted to move up from being Shear's secretary the way Tom Rich's fat secretary wanted to be Rich's assistant. No, he thought. This one's too pretty to want to be an executive. She's probably looking for a husband. He could trust his instincts about women.

"Yeah," he said. "Think he needs an assistant?"

"Don't know," she said. She was twisting the end of her thick straight black hair. "I'll be glad to ask him."

"You been here long?" he asked. Secretaries were so boring, but if they didn't like you they could make your life miserable.

"A year," she said.

"I thought you'd been here longer," he said. "Usually girls are in the typing pool first."

She shook her head and laughed.

"Typing pool. I'd never have made it through that."

"Shear find you through an agency?" Who cares? David thought to himself. He'd go and talk to Dietrich's secretary. Or Greenfield's. Shear was out of the country. This girl had nothing to offer him. He was halfway to the door, not even listening, when he heard her reply.

"No. Harold Greenfield is a friend of my family's. In fact, we're nearly related."

David stopped and tried to look nonchalant.

"Really?"

"It's kind of silly," she added smiling. "My grandmother and his mother are best friends. He adores his mother so he gave me a job here and he and his wife, Julia, have been like parents to me. It's a sordid admission, I guess," she continued, bubbling on. "I mean everyone wants to think they got their jobs because of their own merits, not their grandmother's contacts—but if I hadn't taken this job . . . My God. I could have ended up staying in Pittsburgh married to some doctor or something. So here I am. With Harold Greenfield as my mentor." She laughed. "Not bad, huh?"

The story was totally guileless. The girl had no affectations about her closeness to the most powerful man in Hollywood. It was very matter-of-fact.

"Is Greenfield a good person?" David asked, moving back toward Allyn's desk.

"The best," she said, smiling. "I have dinner at his home nearly once a week and he sits at the dinner table and talks about the industry. And it's fascinating because Harold knows every detail of every film and TV show that's being shot on this lot, including what time the coffee catering truck stops at which sound stage. And he cares. He really cares. I guess he and his wife probably always wanted to have a daughter. I mean, I know that's true, so they're very kind to me. I'm very lucky," she said.

David had never heard anyone, anyone at all, call Harold Greenfield Harold. At the studio he was known as Mr. G. or Mr. Greenfield or "he," as in "he" doesn't want to make war movies, or "he" won't approve that budget, etc. This girl must really know Greenfield well.

"I like your jacket," Allyn said. "That look reminds me of the East."

David's mind was racing. Harold's incredible. I have dinner at his home nearly once a week. He and his wife are like parents to me.

"Hey, listen," he said, "want to have dinner with me sometime?" he asked.

It looked to David as though she blushed. "Sure."

"I'll call you tonight."

"Great," she said. "I live in South Beverly Hills."

"So do I," he said. "Maybe I'll stop by . . ." She grinned. He made himself smile. She wrote down her phone number. He put it in the pocket of his seersucker blazer and headed for the elevator. He was elated.

nine

Allyn Grant walked back into the inner office, sat in the big swivel chair and looked out the window of Jack Shear's office. It was Jack Shear's swivel chair, the one behind his desk. Allyn liked sitting there when Shear was in Europe. It was just as easy for her to answer the phone from his desk as it was from the reception area. Besides, Shear had a window and she didn't.

Allyn loved looking out at the Hemisphere lot from the window. She had plenty of time to do it. In the year she'd worked for Shear, he had spent most of his time in Europe.

It was an easy job.

Allyn didn't want an easy job. She wanted a job that would keep her so busy day and night that she could stop thinking about Phil Gruber. How dumb. Phil Gruber. Here she was in the glamour capital of the world, in a cushy job at a movie studio, had been for a year, and she was still thinking about some ophthalmologist in Pittsburgh.

Of course. It made perfect sense. She was raised in Pittsburgh where ophthalmologists who were in love with you were a valuable commodity. Better than money in the bank. Or at least the same as money in the bank. Allyn Grant marrying Phil Gruber was a very logical step. According to her mother, her mother's friends, and her grandmother.

Except that Allyn was never sure she loved Phil Gruber. Really loved him. In fact, sometimes she didn't even like him. Until he said he couldn't see her anymore.

What a move. What a spectacular move on the part of boring Phil Gruber. There he was, deeply involved with tall, brunette, blue-eyed Allyn Grant. A bright English major at the University of Pittsburgh who had been the most popular girl in her high school, and very sought after in college—and he was dumping her. Kissing her off. Now she was sure she loved him. Had all along. Wanted him back. Wanted his babies. Hurt when she saw his car or a car that looked as if it might be his car, sobbed when she heard love songs on the radio and sat for hours in her room writing love poems, the first line of which was frequently "If you come back I swear I'll change." Rejection is a powerful force. Phil Gruber broke up with Allyn to go back with Janet Blumenthal, a girl he'd dated when he was at Penn State who had once rejected him.

Allyn slept through her own graduation ceremony. She wouldn't take phone calls from any of her friends for fear they'd tell her they'd seen Phil somewhere with Janet. She appeared at the family dinner table once with very bloodshot eyes and a red nose, and excused herself to go back to her room right after the salad, which she barely touched. Her nineteen-year-old brother raised his eyes heavenward, said "Oh, fuck," and was asked to please leave the table.

Allyn's mother, Sarah, was afraid to tell her own mother, Ethel, about the breakup because she knew Ethel was counting on walking down the aisle at a summer wedding. But when Allyn emerged from her room for the first time in something other than her old plaid bathrobe and announced that she was grateful to all of them for putting up with her childish ways, and that they'd soon be rid of her, because she was packing to go to New York where she would find a job in advertising, Sarah called Ethel. It was hard to be certain over the phone, but after she told her the news, Sarah thought the old woman might be hyperventilating.

"I'll call a cab and be right over," Ethel said.

When the old woman saw how bad her beautiful granddaughter looked, she clutched herself somewhere around the area of her chest.

"Grandma," Allyn told her. "It's for the best. If I married Phil I would have stayed in Pittsburgh and been a housewife all my life. In New York it's exciting and I'll have some kind of career."

Ethel uttered the word career, nodded, went to the phone and called Rosie Greenfield, née Dworkin, who had been her best friend for sixty years. Ethel and Rosie lived two blocks apart. Both were widows and both were active in the Temple Sisterhood.

"Call Harold," Ethel said to Rosie.

Everyone knew that Rosie Greenfield's son was someone important in Hollywood. His exact title didn't matter. What mattered was that he was a "big shot."

Before Allyn even decided what to pack for her move to New York, Rosie Greenfield, as directed, had secured a secretarial job for her at Hemisphere Studios in Hollywood.

Hollywood. That was crazy.

"Oh, yeah," Ethel said. "Not as crazy as you think. At least I know Rosie's boy will keep an eye on you." Allyn laughed at that. The man her grandmother called "Rosie's boy" was fifty-three years old.

The instructions were for Allyn to call Harold Greenfield the minute she arrived in Hollywood. She did and he invited her to come to his house for dinner. What a house.

It was in Beverly Hills, on a corner, and the taxi driver who drove Allyn there whistled as he drove up the long tree-lined driveway.

"Geez, lady," he said to the fare he'd picked up at the run-down motel in Hollywood where she was staying, "you sure got some classy friends."

The Greenfields told Allyn later they had been surprised when she walked into their living room that evening. From the story they heard about Allyn being jilted they were expecting to receive a pudgy unattractive little heartbroken girl.

"And only the heartbroken part was true," Allyn laughed.

The Greenfields considered themselves connoisseurs of people. And because of their position in the community they were exposed to some exceptional people. On any given evening their palatial home was filled with political figures, foreign dignitaries, business tycoons and, of course, movie stars. Despite Allyn's inability to qualify as noteworthy, both Harold and Julia immediately took a liking to the pretty but downcast girl. She would mix well at their parties. And certainly Julia could find her a husband as was requested on Ethel Cutler's behalf in a recent phone call from Harold's mother, Rosie. A far more interesting husband than some dull whatever-he-was in Pittsburgh.

Julia Greenfield was elegant and warm. She spoke with humor about the one time Harold had taken her along on his annual Pittsburgh visits. She even remembered meeting Allyn's grandmother, Ethel, once, and both she and Harold agreed that Rosie's friendship with Ethel was the most important thing either old woman had.

Allyn told Greenfield her only qualification for getting a job anywhere was good typing. She had taken a typing course one summer a few years back so she could type her English papers. Greenfield smiled.

"You don't have to be that good. You'll be an executive secretary. Just a few letters and memos here and there."

She would start on Monday of the following week. Julia helped her find a one-bedroom furnished apartment in South Beverly Hills, and after she'd been in California one week, Allyn Grant sat down and wrote:

Dear Grandma,
    Harold got me a job as a secretary for Jack Shear who is an executive at Hemisphere Studios (that is the place you and Mrs.

Greenfield call "Harold's Studio"). Please thank Mrs. Greenfield for
me even though I will write her a thank you note myself. I love it
here, Gran. It's very exciting and they tell me it's warm all year
round.

Who would have thought that a woman who came over from Rus-
sia at thirteen and spent the next sixty years of her life living in
Pittsburgh would have so much pull in Hollywood?

I love you,

Allyn

Ethel Cutler framed the letter.

The first year went by and quickly Allyn's relationship with the
Greenfields flourished. In fact it provided her with almost all the social activity she had that year. Harold taught her how to shoot pool
at the antique pool table in the Greenfields' playroom, and she was
getting very good at the game. Julia gave her some decorating tips for
the new apartment and shopped for fabrics with her.

Parties at the Greenfields were heady affairs, filled with faces
Allyn had seen before only in magazines. She was fascinated by the
interesting people. Still, there wasn't a man in the crowd she wanted
to date or, especially, to go to bed with. But now, that darling David
Kane said he was going to call. She could hardly wait.

ten

Barry Golden spent three weeks avoiding Michael Allred. At first, when he asked to not have the route that included the costume department, saying he'd take any other available run, he thought there might be questions. On the contrary. Everyone seemed to have similar peculiarities about where he did and didn't want to be, so no one questioned him. Once the group began eating their lunch in the commissary, there was no avoiding the situation. The mail room table was right near the entrance and a few times Allred raced over to their table, recognizing Stan, who delivered his mail, and Mickey, who sometimes did, too, and, of course, Barry.

"Why don't you ever stop by?" Allred asked Barry. Barry was embarrassed. He was certain the others knew the whole story, that he and Allred had a former lover in common. But instead the others were impressed.

"He's the best," Stan Rose said after Allred left. "One of the major biggies in this business."

After he got the job in the mail room, Barry took an apartment on Flores in West Hollywood. He never called home, and only called Andy's apartment one time after their last conversation. A man Barry didn't know answered and when the man asked who was calling, and Barry told him, there was a muffled sound as if the man was holding the phone against his chest, a few muffled voices, and then the man got back on the line.

"Andrew is in Europe," he said, "on business. So how about if I tell him you called, when he gets back?"

It was a lie. "Great," Barry said. "When will that be?"

Muffled phone voices. Laughter.

"Uh . . ." the man said. "Oh, sometime next year." Laughter in the background.

"Right," Barry said and hung up.

That was when he decided he ought to accept the fact that he was in California to stay. He also wrote several letters to his parents, but didn't mail any of them. He was lonely. His building had a swimming pool so he went to the Broadway on Hollywood Boulevard and Vine Street and bought himself a bathing suit. He was so slight and narrow and so much skinnier than he'd been in New York, when his mother was cooking dinner for him, and Mashe was paying for his lunches, that the only suit he could find to fit him was in the boys' department. Hang-Ten boxer trunks.

He sat at the pool every Saturday and Sunday reading Friday's *Variety*. He'd already read it on Friday, but he was hoping perhaps someone would see him reading it and know he was in "the business."

The only person at the pool on most days was Yona. Yona had brown frizzy hair, pimples and a roll around her midriff. The first time Barry saw her she was wearing only the bottom of her leopardskin suit, and her sagging bananalike breasts were tanned dark like the rest of her skin. Barry must have looked at her, looked back at the real estate section, then looked back again because he couldn't believe it when Yona shouted.

"I can sit here any goddamned way I want. I pay rent here, too, asshole."

Barry was so surprised all he could emit was a polite "Good morning."

There was a peal of laughter from a balcony overlooking the pool. "That's tellin' her, kid," the voice said. Barry squinted and looked up.

A pudgy dark-haired man stood in the balcony of his pool-view apartment wearing an orange terry-cloth robe and holding a beer.

"Fuck off, you fat suckhole," Yona yelled at the man.

"Oh, my God," he responded, "we finally found you, Princess Anastasia."

Yona sneered and turned over on her stomach, and the guy disappeared into his apartment.

Barry went back to *Variety* until a few minutes later when there was a giant splash, and he was covered with water. His copy of *Variety* was soaked. Before he even looked, he knew Yona got wet, too, because he heard her bloodcurdling scream.

"Mothafuckah!"

The diver was swimming laps underwater. It was the fat guy. He would come up occasionally and gasp noisily, then swim lengths underwater again. When he had done the length about ten times he pulled himself up at the edge of the pool, his suit sliding down to reveal the top of his large pink ass. Then he walked over to Yona and shook himself so hard the water went all over her. "Take that, you bitch," he said. Yona opened her eyes slowly and looked up. Barry was sure she was going to say something really horrible now.

"Hi, baby," she said, grinning.

The fat guy leaned over and kissed her, then caressed one of the banana tits and she laughed. The guy looked over at Barry.

"We're the Bakers. I'm Marty, she's Yona."

Barry laughed.

"I'm Barry Golden."

"In the business?"

Barry nodded.

"Us, too," Yona said. "We do clubs and stuff, but we're studio musicians mostly."

"I play the piano and vibes and Yona plays the harp," Marty said. "She was in the scoring sessions for *Sound of Music!*"

Yona scratched herself under her suit. "Yeah. That was good fucking bread. You know?"

Barry had to giggle to himself when he thought what it would be like if Julie Andrews ever met Yona.

After that day, Marty and Yona practically adopted Barry. They invited him to their apartment for dinner every night and he loved going there. They were wonderfully zany and had stories to tell about everyone in the music business. They knew the Beach Boys, they had each played on Andy Williams' albums, one time Yona had replaced someone at the last minute on the road with Johnny Mathis. They were becoming not just the only friends Barry had, but a family for him as well. By the second week after he met them, he found himself at work wondering if it was close to six so he could get home, and what Yona would be cooking.

Once Yona mentioned fixing him up with her sister who was a manicurist. She must have noticed the look that flickered across his face.

"Gay, huh?" she asked matter-of-factly.

Barry nodded.

"Then how 'bout my brother?"

There was a beat and then both of them laughed for a long time.

One night Yona and Marty were both playing on the same session and they invited Barry to come along. Sonny and Cher were there. Barry recognized them as the ones who sang "I Got You, Babe," and he remembered seeing them on *Hullabaloo* or one of those shows. They sat in the same control room as he did. The musicians, and there were a lot of them, were on the other side of the glass in a large studio. There was a lot of laughing and talking. Sonny and Cher were friends with the man who was in charge, Jim Garland. Garland was very tall and skinny and he had buckteeth. He was producing the session. He had a lot of energy and ran back and forth between the room where the recording equipment was and the room where the musicians were. Cher smoked a cigarette and didn't smile.

Barry realized he hadn't even asked Yona and Marty, now busy in the crowd of musicians who were tuning up and chattering and laughing on the other side of the glass, who was recording. Maybe it was Sonny and Cher. No. Yona would have told him.

The door from the outside hall opened and a boy's face peeked in tentatively.

"Hello?"

Garland and Sonny and Cher all jumped to their feet and ran to the door.

"Hey, Harley," they said, escorting the boy into the room. "How you doin', man?" they asked him.

Barry was sitting with about six or seven other people in a row of chairs that looked like they'd been removed from a movie house but faced directly into the studio. All the people looked over. Barry had never seen the boy before. He looked about eighteen, and he had shoulder-length straight brown hair, and he was carrying a guitar case, which Garland immediately took out of his hand and carried for him. Garland walked him into the studio. Most of the musicians didn't even look up.

At the front of the group of musicians was a stool with a microphone in front of it. Garland was hovering over Harley so much he practically lifted him right onto the stool.

Finally, after a big discussion about whether or not Harley should play his guitar while he sang, the decision was that he should, even though Garland didn't seem to like the idea. They started to rehearse. It was exciting. It reminded Barry of the live orchestras on Broadway. Marty was conducting, and the music gave Barry the chills. No one else was too excited, though. Sonny and Cher left after a while, and Garland was getting very nervous, and you couldn't hear Harley's guitar at all, and Harley's voice sounded very thin.

"Let's lay one down," Garland said. Harley looked scared but he nodded, and Marty who was conducting from the piano counted and the orchestra played and Harley started singing the song he'd been rehearsing, "The Rain Is Like My Tears." When they played it back it was awful.

"Great, Har!" Jim Garland said over the intercom into the studio. Harley didn't believe it. No one did.

"One more, baby!" Garland said.

Five takes later, Harley looked very sad.

It seemed as if Garland had already smoked two packs of cigarettes.

"Fuck," Garland said. Only the engineer and the seven people could hear him muttering angrily. His switch into the studio was off. "Suck. Rat piss. This eats it, and it's not the kid's fault."

"Doin' great, Harley," he said with a smile into the box. "Band, take ten, okay?"

The whole orchestra rose noisily to their feet and filed out into the corridor of the recording studio. Yona and Marty motioned for Barry to join them. There were machines that dispensed coffee, hot chocolate, milk, candy, crackers, even soup. Barry waited in line to get a Hershey bar, realizing now that there had been about thirty people in the orchestra. There was a lot of laughter. A couple of guys lit up joints. No one in the group even commented or looked over. It was just as though they'd lit cigarettes.

At one point Barry noticed Jim Garland come to the door of the studio and close it from the inside. When the ten minutes had passed, the group began to drift back toward the studio but the red light was on.

"Shhh," someone said. They all listened. Harley's sweet voice was singing, alone with his guitar. Garland was recording it. The red light went off. Garland opened the door and gestured for the others to come in. When everyone was inside, Garland silenced them.

"People," he shouted. "People! I want you to hear something."

The engineer rolled back the tape and they played what they'd recorded while the band was on their break. "The Rain Is Like My Tears." One voice. One guitar. It was perfect. Harley's voice was clear and true, and Barry realized now that the boy had written the song, too. When it finished, all the musicians applauded. Harley blushed.

"Call it a night," Garland said.

Harley hugged Yona and then Marty as they congratulated him.

"Wanna get a bite?" Marty asked him. Marty looked even more like a big bear with his arms around the delicate Harley.

"Sure."

Barry couldn't believe it. He'd get to meet Harley.

Ah Fong's was empty.

"Anybody home?"

An old Chinese man appeared. "Yes. We home," he said, grinning.

The four of them took a booth. Barry and Yona across from Marty and Harley.

"Harley was a studio guitarist," Marty told Barry.

"But he's so adorable he's becoming a star. Right, you little baby-faced fart?" Yona said.

Harley grinned. "Right."

"He's really fifty years old," Marty told Barry. "He just lives clean. Doesn't smoke any of this stuff, right?"

Marty was holding a joint in his hand.

Barry was surprised. He had suspected that Yona and Marty smoked pot. He knew a lot of musicians did. But they never talked about it. And now. In a restaurant. Marty was being so open about it.

The waiter came over to the table. Marty ordered for all of them, still moving the joint around in his pudgy hand the whole time. The waiter disappeared into the back and Marty lit the joint. He inhaled deeply but kept talking while he held the smoke in so his voice sounded weird. "I think Garland has taste in his tuchus," he said. "And he'll never get a full album cut a take at a time like that." He exhaled. Yona took the joint and inhaled in short sucking sounds. She held her pinky poised while she puffed, as if she were a fancy lady having tea. A few more puffs and she handed it to Harley. Barry watched him take it eagerly. The waiter was coming with the soup. Barry was afraid. Maybe the waiter would call the police. Harley puffed on the joint as the waiter put small soup bowls in front of each of them and the large soup tureen in the middle of the table, not looking at any of them. As the waiter turned to walk back to the kitchen, Harley handed the joint to Barry. Barry was embarrassed. He wasn't sure what to do. Marty understood.

"Inhale and hold it in your lungs for as long as you can," he said gently.

No one laughed. No one said, "First time, huh?"

Barry held the smoke in his lungs for a long time. Released it. Then again. Then again.

By the time the fortune cookies came, the four of them were still the only ones in the restaurant and they were all bleary. Barry knew he must be stoned because Yona looked beautiful to him.

"You will take an exciting trip," she read from the tiny piece of paper she'd pulled out of the cookie. "Oooh, baby. Maybe it means Disneyland," she said to Marty, pouting like a little girl.

"You did promise me that, you big turd," she said.

"Yeah. Yeah." Marty took a handful of the hard noodles and tossed them into his mouth as if they were popcorn.

"Let's go tomorrow," she urged. "We'll get stoned in the morning and drive out."

"Stoned in Disneyland? Far out," Harley said. "Too bad I've got a rehearsal."

"Bar, will you come? Fuck the mail room," Yona said.

Stoned in Disneyland. Barry loved the idea. He'd call in sick to work—but he wanted Harley to come with them, too. He wanted Harley to be everywhere with him. The warm feeling in his chest was about Harley and the way Barry wanted to touch him. Oh, Jesus. He was stoned. Harley would probably recoil from him if he knew what he was feeling.

"Are you going to go, Barry?" Harley asked.

As Barry looked at him, he thought about Howard and Eugene and Andy and Mashe, and his parents, and all of the things that had happened in the last five or six years. And it was clear and plain as things seem to be after smoking dope, things that are obvious in a flash but later feel obscured again, that he had always let himself be a victim. Allowing things to happen to him, but never making them happen. And that was the wrong way to live. Wrong if he wanted to have the things he knew he had to have out of life. He thought of David Kane, who approached everyone on the lot asking them for jobs, and when the others teased Kane about it or called him pushy, he said, "You have to ask for what you want," and Stan Rose, who always bragged about himself that he had "Chutzpah" with a capital "Chu," and even that jerk-off Ashman who was always grab-assing every woman, seemed to end up in bed with anyone he wanted. So. So what? The original thought was blurred. Yes, change that. Barry wanted to change that. He could change that.

"I'm going to go to Disneyland," he said to Harley, "skip your rehearsal and join us."

"Okay."

Some days in our lives are only historical in retrospect. The obvious ones, like wedding days, or funeral days, may seem to be pivotal, but later, when we look back, we find that the ones we didn't consider crucial may have been truly the most important. The day Barry spent in Disneyland with Yona, Marty and Harley changed his life.

At eight thirty in the morning, Yona, with a joint in her left hand and a spatula in her right, made them all scrambled eggs in her kitchen. By nine fifteen they were on the freeway. Barry had seen Disneyland on the news on television when it opened, and he vaguely remembered seeing a ride that looked like teacups, but he wasn't prepared for this. Yona wanted to go on everything. She dragged them all by the hand from ride to ride laughing and hugging them. It was a blur of joy and sweet sensations, and eating too much, and thinking everyone was funny, and Harley and Barry would look at each other and laugh till the tears came. And finally it was getting dark and they took the tram to Marty's car and drove home exhausted. Yona fell asleep in the front seat with her head against the window, snoring. Barry looked at Harley. How could he know what to say? It was Howard and then Andy who initiated the sexual contact he'd had with them. How did they know he would want it?

When Marty got off the freeway at Highland Avenue, he cleared his throat.

"Uh . . . Har. You want me to take you home?"

Barry clenched his teeth and looked straight ahead.

"No," Harley said. "Uh-uh."

The rest was understood. There wasn't much conversation when Harley and Barry got to Barry's apartment.

When Harley took his clothes off, he was smooth and hairless like Barry, and when Barry was touching him and sucking him he had a picture in his mind that they were two innocent cherubs. And when Harley came, moaning gently, Barry could hear "The Rain Is Like My Tears" in his mind, and it played over and over again when he came himself, and until he fell asleep.

When Barry woke up it was four o'clock in the morning. Harley was awake, too. They were both hungry, so they went into the kitchen and had salami sandwiches and beer.

Harley told Barry what it was like to grow up in California in a big family, and how going off somewhere to just play his guitar was his only escape from the other kids. And that he still lived at home with his family except when he was on the road with some band. And Barry told Harley about the reason he'd left Brooklyn, and then Harley told Barry about the time when he was a kid that his mom's brother gave him a blow job and then said he'd kill him if he told his mom. And Barry told Harley about the episode in Hawaii with Howard, which he'd left out of the story before. And a few hours later, when Barry was about to leave for the mail room, and Harley was lying in the bed half asleep, Barry said:

"Go over to your folks' house today and pack your stuff and move in here."

Harley looked up, thought for a long moment and then nodded. "Yeah. Okay," he said. "I will."

eleven

Inured. Allyn Grant was stoned. She'd tried pot for the first time at a party a few weeks ago. The girl who had the party, who was one of the other secretaries at the studio, served some chocolate chip cookies still in the box, and after Allyn took a few puffs of what was left of a joint that was so small one of the girls was holding it with a bobby pin, she ate ten cookies. They were the best cookies on earth. Better than Silverman's bakery in Pittsburgh. Inured. Later that week, she went out and bought the same cookies. They were dry. Tasteless. Yes. She must have been stoned at that party. So that's what it was like.

Allyn would never make a "buy" and get some pot of her own, but Norah, George Marvin's secretary, gave her three joints as a gift. And tonight she was using the first one. She'd only required a few puffs. Hits, they were called. Now she was lying on the sofa in the living room of her apartment. Inured. That's how it made her feel. It was funny to her that she was thinking that word, inured, to describe her feelings, because she had no recollection of ever having used the word before. It meant something like being so numb that you were getting used to pain, and she was. The pain of her loneliness and her isolation from her old friends. And the pain of having no relationship with a man. No one to hold her. No sex. It reminded her of the way she'd felt in high school.

High school. Somehow she had managed to stay a virgin through all of it. In the late fifties and early sixties that was what unmarried girls were supposed to be. That's what their parents told them, and that's what they told each other, and they turned their collective and cliquey backs on the girls who were rumored to "do it."

Most of the girls in Allyn's group of friends had done everything except "it," but that was allowed. Unspoken. Ken Mitchell made Allyn come with his fingers under her short shorts when she was fifteen. She'd been doing it herself for years and it was wonderful to have someone else do it to her. She didn't know very much about sex and she was sure that Ken Mitchell's fingers inside her couldn't be as good as his penis, but penises made you pregnant so she'd have to avoid them. She was hot all the time, and very afraid the other girls would suspect how lusty she was feeling. She would rush through her homework, promising herself the reward, when she finished the last algebra problem, of locking the bedroom door, turning off the light, closing the venetian blinds and crawling under the covers to masturbate until she'd had three or four orgasms before falling asleep.

She was afraid of Ken Mitchell even though his hands were magic inside her, because she knew eventually she'd have to return the favor in some way. In the back of his father's car her blouse was unbuttoned and her bra unfastened and Ken's mouth was sucking and drooling on her left nipple with his right hand manipulating her right nipple. She always kept her underpants on, but Ken's left hand was inside them rhythmically moving the inflamed button of her clitoris toward the explosion she had to have. And Ken was fully clothed, sweat shirt and jeans with that big bump in them that he rubbed on any part of her, or any part of the car he could get near.

Pregnant. Allyn knew girls who'd been sent away for a year to have babies they gave up because they got pregnant. From having penises inside them. And they were never popular again. Yes, there were rubbers, but rubbers broke. There was "the rhythm method." Allyn knew that had something to do with figuring out when you ovulated, but everyone told the joke that went "What do you call people who use the rhythm method?" and the answer was "Parents."

It became more and more difficult to avoid the issue. Especially when she got to college. Only a few of the girls in college were the disapproving and judgmental girls from high school, and there was much more freedom now, but there were still expressions like "the town pump" about girls, that made Allyn continue to say no during a session of heavy petting when a fraternity boy began to tug at her panties.

In the dorm it was harder to find time alone to masturbate because she had a roommate, but Allyn copied her roommate Leslie's schedule onto a piece of paper she kept in her wallet so she would know exactly when Leslie would be in class and it was safe.

One afternoon about two days before summer vacation, after she was freshly showered and sprinkled with Jean Naté, the sight of her own body in the full-length mirror made Allyn hot. She wanted it. To come hard and strong. Instead of getting into bed she leaned against a wall a few feet from the mirror so she could watch. Teasing herself, she began pulling at her own nipples with the thumb and forefinger of each hand. Squeezing them hard, then pulling them outward, all the time feeling her clitoris swell, getting hotter and wilder. But she wouldn't touch it yet, because the wait was so agonizingly good. Finally, with her left hand still on her nipple, she slid her right hand slowly down to her pubic hair, pulling the hair hard to tease herself even further before she touched her clitoris, exquisitely hot, watching in the mirror as her fingers now approached the inside of the folds and entered them. Oh, God. She wanted it. She was unable to look in the mirror at her own eyes, which she knew would be filled with guilt. She would close them. Her nipple was hard in her fingers. Her clit ached for more, just a little more, and some more, baby, oh, God. Was it Ken she was picturing? Ken with the bump in his jeans? Oh, God, more, it didn't matter, the frenzy was filling her, she was close, oh, baby, I want it. So close. And, oh, my God. Now. It filled her. Exploded. Again and again and oh, God. Her insides were deliciously achy. And she slowly opened her eyes.

"Hi."

Allyn flushed from head to toe. It was Bob Burdett, Leslie's steady boy friend. She'd forgotten to lock the door and he had just watched her make herself come. She'd been so hot she hadn't heard the door open. Allyn started to grab for a blanket to cover herself.

"Don't bother," Burdett said, locking the door behind him. "I came by to pick up a book, but God knows this is a hell of a lot better." He slid his arm around Allyn's naked waist, and with his body on top of hers dropped them both onto Leslie's bed. Burdett was a football player. Allyn weighed one hundred pounds.

"Bob," Allyn said. She was so humiliated she could hardly speak.

"I'm gonna fix it for you, baby," he said. "So you don't have to do that to yourself." Allyn felt his hard penis pushing against her leg. Everything about him was hard and she was afraid. He was all over her, his wet tongue on her face, in her ears, on her breasts, and trying to get his pants off at the same time. When he got them off, Allyn gasped. This was the first penis she'd ever seen. She was nineteen years old. It was leathery and shiny and Bob Burdett was holding it with his big pudgy hand and spreading her legs with the other. "Yes," was all Bob Burdett kept saying. "Yes. Yes. Uh-huh. Yes."

Allyn was speechless. She didn't want this. This wasn't how it should be.

"No," she said finally, finding her voice. "Bob. Bob. No. Please." Now she was talking fast. "Please, what about Leslie? She loves you so much. Bob?"

Burdett was poking at her with his penis as if to tease her. Allyn was getting frantic.

"Bob." He was heavy on top of her. She knew it was hopeless. What did it matter? Why had she saved it? For this? She began to cry. She was sobbing hard from all the embarrassment and anger and frustration.

And Bob was losing his hard on.

"Hey!" he said, looking at her. "What the hell is this?"

"Bob. I don't want you. Please. I don't want you," she said. She was afraid. Maybe he'd hit her.

His penis was shriveled now, and he put his feet on the floor and stood up pulling his boxer shorts up, then his jeans. Allyn was still spread-eagled and naked. She was afraid to move. He took a blanket that was folded at the bottom of her bed and threw it at her.

"Here you go, you little whore," he said. "You can cover up now. You probably left that door open for me so I could watch you doing yourself. Boy, you are scum."

Allyn was nauseated.

"Please get out," she said quietly, pulling the blanket over herself.

"When I'm ready." He walked over to Leslie's bookshelf and scanned it, found the book he wanted and walked to the door. Allyn hadn't moved. "You're lucky it was me," he said, shaking with anger. "Anyone else would have raped you," and he walked out.

After that Allyn was certain Bob Burdett was telling everyone at school the story, and she was afraid she would be labeled scum. That awful name he'd called her. And then she would never find a husband, which was, of course, the plan that had been set for her life since the day she was born. So one week later, when she met Phil Gruber, older, presentable, Phil Gruber, ophthalmologist, there was no question in her mind that he could rescue her from scumdom. Make her appear respectable. Even though she'd been caught— No, she couldn't even think about it. Slowly, she let Phil Gruber think he was seducing her and finally he took her virginity, technical though it was, and told her he was "honored" to do it. Allyn remembered trying not to laugh when he said that.

In the arms of Phil Gruber, she was able to release all of her sexual energy. Try everything. Experiment on his body. Act out all of her fantasies. After all. He said he was probably going to marry her. But he didn't. He broke up with her. And she hadn't been laid since. And the first man she wanted, had any sexual interest in since that day Phil Gruber told her goodbye, was David Kane. And he wasn't calling. So she was inured.

She had run home from the studio that night he told her he might stop by, and started the tub running before she even put her car keys down. Then she took all her clothes off, put a towel down on the hardwood floor and did fifty sit-ups. Bath oil? She had some Estee Super she'd been saving. The water was steaming. Allyn looked at her body. Was it good enough? She did everything. Makeup. Perfect. Hair. Thank God for electric rollers. And then she sat there. All evening. And the phone never rang. At ten o'clock she realized it had just been polite conversation. Maybe I'll stop by. And she went to sleep.

Allyn had hoped David would come by her office the next morning with some excuse. But he didn't. In fact, he didn't deliver on her route that day. Or the next either. Ah, that must be it! Something was wrong. She'd ask one of the other guys.

"Hiya, gorgeous, wanna fuck a rising star?"

"Hi, Mickey," Allyn said.

"Mail for Mr. Shear from the industry, and adoration for your gorgeous knockers from me."

"Thanks." She was afraid to ask him. He was leaving.

"Mickey?" she said. "How's David?"

"You mean Arch, the old redhead? That David?"

She nodded.

"You having a thing with him?"

"Mickey, is he—I mean, how come you're—"

"Running this route? 'Cause we switch off for variety. Arch doesn't like the other routes, 'cause he likes coming up here to kiss ass and look for jobs—but he's running another section for a while."

Allyn nodded. "Okay."

That's when the ache began. And it wasn't gone yet. And it was three weeks later. So she was inured. Maybe coming down from the inurement now. Realizing she'd spent every night rushing home, pulling the phone on its long cord into the kitchen while she was cooking herself a meal, pulling the phone into the bathroom while she took her bath, and lying awake in her bed with the phone sitting right next to her. And it never rang. And it wasn't ringing now. And she was so lonely.

The phone rang.

"Hello?"

"Allyn?"

"Uh-huh."

"David Kane."

Allyn was grateful she was so mellow on the grass or she might have shouted, "Thank God!" right into the phone.

It was eerie. He talked to her almost as if the three weeks that had gone by hadn't existed.

"So what about our dinner?"

"Dinner?"

"Can we make it tomorrow night?"

The double meaning wasn't lost on her. She was wishing she could pretend to be busy. Tomorrow was a Saturday. But she wanted, needed someone so badly.

"Yes."

"Where's your place?"

"It's one twenty-nine South Oakhurst."

"I'm on South Almont. That's really close by."

"Yes."

"How about Mario's in Westwood?"

"Sure."

"Seven thirty."

"Great."

"See you tomorrow."

"Okay."

He hung up.

"David . . ." Why didn't she suggest making the dinner herself? It would have been cozier, different. It was too late. She didn't move from the sofa. She was thinking about that day three weeks ago when they talked. He really seemed interested in her then. What did she wear? Maybe she'd remember and wear that again. Maybe it was something she said that got his attention. It didn't matter. What mattered was that tomorrow night David Kane was taking her to dinner—and she'd obviously done something right to make him choose her.

twelve

Stan opened the heavy door to stage 15 and walked into the cavernous silent studio. There was no one around yet. It was just six o'clock. In one hour the place would be filled with the crew, cast and audience of *Give 'em the Hook,* a television show which, as Stan described it, "made nice ordinary people look like assholes."

The show was a hit and it had been for years. Walter Barton, who produced *Give 'em the Hook* and hosted it, was a local Los Angeles personality. First he was a disc jockey who called himself Big Wally. On all of Big Wally's shows, Barton did the voice of a teenaged kid named Animal who pestered Big Wally. Animal was always getting into trouble and Big Wally would have to bail him out. The comedy relationship bridged the spaces between the top forty records in a funny way, and the teenagers loved it when Animal got the best of Big Wally, which was always, so Barton achieved a kind of local fame. He made a career of doing personal appearances and was so available for any event it caused another L.A. disc jockey to say, "I was leaving for work this morning, and Walter Barton was there for the opening of my garage door."

After a while, though, just being known on the local scene wasn't enough for Barton, and he came up with some ideas for television game shows and variety shows and took them to the networks. The best one was a show called *Give 'em the Hook*. Barton was such a colorful hustler and so charming in his sales pitch for the show that the network not only bought it but they bought Barton as well to produce and host it.

Give 'em the Hook was a kind of amateur talent show where a performer would audition and act for the studio audience. If the audience didn't like the performer's act they would scream out, "Give 'em the hook," and a big hook would appear from offstage and pull the rejected singer or dancer into the wings. If the performer was a pretty girl singer or a pretty girl dancer, as the hook pulled her off the stage, Barton would run on as if in protest and shout at the audience, "Ahh, why do you wanta hook 'er?"

And the word play made the audience scream with laughter. They loved the show's sexuality.

"Make 'em hot and they love your ass," Barton muttered aloud backstage one day.

"Sounds like a sampler in a porno shop," Stan Rose answered.

Barton smiled. Stan was around the stage so often Barton felt like he knew him.

"You're smart, kid. I like you."

Stan visited the set of *Give 'em the Hook* for weeks. He continued to be fascinated with the television business, and live game shows were much more exciting than the WEBU history plays. He watched the frenetic little man with the gravelly voice who could say to a sexy female contestant before she sang, "Do your thing, honey, and remember, if you're no good I'm gonna get my hook into you," and the audience loved it, because Barton's delivery was boyish, and cute, and nonthreatening. And if a contestant looked offended, Barton would look offended, too, and then embarrassed and say, "Ooh, how awful. I'm the worst. Call the producer and tell him to fire me. Call the producer. Oh, no! I *am* the producer. Now what?" And everyone would laugh and the female contestants would hug him, and he'd rest his face on their bosoms and giggle innocently. Stan wanted to be Barton's assistant producer, but most of the time when he dropped by the studio Barton was too busy to get into a real conversation with him, so finally Stan left a note for Barton in his dressing room, asking for a few minutes of his time. Barton's secretary called the mail room the next morning.

"Mr. Rose?" she said, "Mr. Barton will see you in his dressing room next Friday at six." Stan was pleased. He felt as if his career could go in any one of several directions, so there was no anxiety about the meeting. If it didn't work out with Barton there would be other choices. The dressing room door was open.

"Hiya, Stanley!" Barton got to his feet as Stan entered the room. No one ever called him Stanley anymore but his father Albert.

"Howsa bouta drinkie?" Barton asked.

"No, thanks, Walter," Stan said. "Don't get up." Walter reminded him of an animated cartoon character.

"So what's the haps?" Walter said. "Gettin' tired of runnin' the mail?"

Stan nodded.

"That's what I figured. So what can I do for ya?"

"Well," Stan said, "how about making me assistant to the producer on *Give 'em the Hook?*"

Barton pursed his lips, frowned and pursed his lips again. He stared into space thinking for a long time. Stan watched him.

"I got a better idea," Barton said. "A much better idea than that for the both of us. Are you ready?"

"Sure." Stan was certain he was about to get a brushoff.

"Did you go to the Beatles' concert last year?" Barton asked him.

"No." Stan remembered reading about the Beatles at the Hollywood Bowl in '64.

"Well, I did. And I'm gonna take you to the one this year," Barton said. "Because I want you to see something incredible. Bob Eubanks was the promoter and, boy, did he have a good idea. The rock 'n' roll business is the business to be in, not this television bullshit, Stanley."

Stan wasn't sure he knew what Barton meant.

"You mean producing rock concerts?"

"Yeah."

Stan was disappointed. Rock 'n' Roll. It was something he'd never even considered. He wanted to be in television. That's what he'd always wanted.

"Let me tell you something, Stanley. There were over eighteen thousand kids there last year. The show grossed fifty-eight thousand. And the tickets were sold out three months in advance. You know what that says to me? It says a lot of little girls get hot lookin' at the Beatles."

Stan laughed.

"I'm not joking," Barton said. "They screamed their asses off. One little honey down in front took her shirt off and shook her tits at the stage. Police threw her out. Too bad. Cute tits." Barton smiled.

"Here's what I'm proposing," he went on. "Eighty-six the mailroom, and you become my legman. You and I will become promoters together."

"Aren't the promoters the guys who put up cash?" Stan asked.

"I'll be the cash. You be the front. I got contacts. You quit the mail room, you got time. Sound fair?"

"Yeah . . . sure it does, but—"

"But you're not sure it's the kind of show business you had in mind? Right?"

Stan didn't answer. Barton picked up an envelope that was sitting on the dressing table. "See these?" he said, taking two tickets out of the envelope and handing them to Stan. "Bob Eubanks and KRLA present the Beatles at the Hollywood Bowl, August 30th, 1965." Stan read aloud from the ticket. It was a week away.

"You'll go with me, and I promise you the next day you'll start looking for an office for our new company. Barton and Rose Concerts."

Stan grinned at Barton's style.

"Why you smiling? Okay, you win. Rose and Barton Concerts."

Stan and Walter got to the Bowl early but the place was already crawling with kids. Mostly teenaged girls, or at least that's how it looked. Backstage, policemen were milling and everyone had to have a special pass. The feeling of excitement was already generating. Walter knew a lot of the people and he introduced Stan to them. A few of them had something to do with the Beatles, others were people in the music business who had enough influence to get their names on the backstage list.

"They're takin' 'em outta here afterwards in an armored car," one of the guys Walter knew said. " 'Cause if they don't, man, those little teenaged chicks'll kill 'em. You dig?"

Stan nodded.

"Jumped on by a horde of prepubescent girls," Walter said. "You can kill me like that anytime."

Stan smiled and looked at Walter, wondering if there wasn't some seriousness in what the little man just said. He'd met Barton's wife, Phyllis, a few times and never saw any display of affection between them. The first time Stan met her she was overweight and she was wearing a red fox coat which made her look even wider than she was. The coat was the same color as her red hair. The staff and crew of *Give 'em the Hook* were having a buffet dinner after the shooting of the show and Phyllis was piling her plate with food.

"Eat up, fatso," Barton shouted at her from across the studio. "Eat all that starchy shit. 'Cause you need it, honey. You're a growing girl."

Everyone became very quiet and Phyllis didn't even look up. She put the plate with a sandwich and potato salad and macaroni salad and cole slaw and French fries down where she was standing and walked toward the door. No one said a word while she crossed the length of the stage. As soon as she was out the door everyone resumed their chattering and kept taking food. They walked past the piled-up plate she'd left on the table as if it weren't there, and as if Phyllis had never been there.

The next time Stan saw Phyllis Barton, it was six months later, and he didn't recognize her. She couldn't be described as skinny, no, it was more like gaunt. Her cheeks were hollow, and her eyes looked corpsishly deep-set. She was wearing a tight sweater and her chest was very flat, and the bell-bottomed jeans she wore seemed small enough to fit a pre-teenaged girl. That's how she looked. Like a teenaged girl with an old face. It was awful.

The noise from the stadium was getting louder and Barton pulled Stan over to one of the wings to watch the people pour in. Stan and Walter had entered the Bowl through an interior back door, so this was Stan's first real look at the seats and the massive capacity of the house. Jesus Christ. It was exciting. The rows were filling in with poeple.

"Thousands and thousands of people," said Barton, giving voice to Stan's thoughts, "times seven bucks, kiddo. You dig?" he added, imitating the guy who'd told them the story about the armored car. Stan grinned and Walter took out their tickets.

"Let's find our seats."

Walter and Stan's seats were close to the front of the Bowl, and when Stan turned around and looked back, there were teenaged girls as far as he could see.

"What'd I tell you?" Barton said. The buzzing from the crowd was loud and frantic and a helicopter was circling over the Bowl with flashing lights. Onstage the huge red letters KRLA glittered. It was exciting all right. Stan hadn't imagined anything like this. Barton grinned. "So, Stanley. This is the concert business. What do you think?"

Stan was about to tell him when the screaming began. Eighteen thousand voices were shrill and piercing and it must have begun spontaneously because no one was on the stage, and no one had done anything. It was just getting close to the time and everyone knew it. And then the lights dimmed.

Someone was singing some KRLA song, then an announcer was trying to be heard over the screaming, and flashbulbs were popping like a fireworks display. It was so outrageous it made Stan laugh. Barton was laughing, too, and the orchestra began to play. Now the kids were screaming for each song in the overture.

Dick Biondi, an L.A. disc jockey, came out. More screaming.

Stan never even got the name of the opening act. Something like Headhunters. The kids didn't care. The roar was as loud as if there were no act out there. Another disc jockey, Casey Kasem. Another act, Brenda Holloway. Several times Stan wanted to say something to Barton but before he could another surge of screaming would go up. Another group. Stan looked at his watch. Barton saw him and grinned. The third group was a six-piece band, playing something very loud that sounded remarkably like the *William Tell Overture*. It must have been good publicity for these acts to open for the Beatles, Stan thought, because they sure weren't doing it to be heard. Nobody was listening.

The band finished. Dave Hull, the president of the Beatles' fan club, came out and introduced Bob Eubanks, the promoter, who introduced the Beatles. My God. There they were. Stan had seen them on television. Their music filled the last year of his life but this. This chaos, this madness, this had nothing to do with the music. Most of the time you couldn't even hear the music.

"Paullll. I'll kill myself. I love you."

"Ringo. Oh, God. Ringo!"

"I wanna hold your . . ."

"John. Oh, John. I can't stand it."

Stan shook his head in disbelief.

The Beatles. The rock business. It was overwhelming. Rose and Barton Concerts. Barton and Rose Concerts. What did it matter? It could be good. Sensational maybe. The worst it could be was a ticket out of the mail room. Hell. He was only twenty-three years old.

The Beatles played their last song and, from all the way in the back, the crowd began moving toward the stage.

Stan looked around again and saw the waves of people heading right toward where he and Walter were sitting. All of them screaming. He shook his head in disbelief.

Suddenly the fountains that separated the stage from the seats went on, and bursts of water sailed into the air. Clearly it was an effort on the part of the promoters to keep the kids back.

"I don't care," a girl yelled, and dove into the fountain.

Announcements came over the P.A. The screaming was now combined with crying.

"Stanley?" Barton said over the noise. "Are we in business or what?"

Stan heard him and smiled.

"We are," he said, and Stan Rose and Walter Barton shook hands on the formation of their partnership.

thirteen

Mickey was in three actors' workshops that he attended regularly after work. One of them was called the Underground, and since he'd joined they'd only done one production, García Lorca's *House of Bernarda Alba,* which had an all-female cast, so he was bored there. Another one was a small group that got together casually on Wednesdays to practice cold readings. They would bring scripts of plays, and take turns reading them in front of one another, and then creatively evaluate one another's work. But Mickey's favorite was his Monday-night group, the Jackie Levitz comedy workshop.

Jackie Levitz was a character actor who had appeared briefly on Broadway, unnoticed in a few television series, and with a line here or there in numerous commercials. He was always a second or third banana. Agents referred to him as an ethnic character type because he had dark hair and dark eyes and was short and pudgy. His timing was good and his style was broad in the manner of vaudeville comics, which he was too young to have been, a fate he bemoaned aloud frequently. Levitz's decision to teach a comedy workshop came at a time when he had been out of work for a whole year. Both Jackie and his wife, Ruth, a former Broadway dancer, knew if he spent one more day during which walking to the corner newsstand to buy the trade papers was his only activity, he would soon be telling jokes in the lockup ward at Camarillo.

Five years after Levitz's comedy workshop began, there was a waiting list to get in. It was well known among young actors. Mickey applied right after his incident with Lowell Spears and was invited to come as an observer. For months he sat in the back row of the small theater where Levitz's group worked out. He watched carefully as the regulars did improvisations, rehearsed sketches, played theater games and performed exercises that Levitz made up. Most of them tried too hard and weren't funny. There were only a few good ones. Even fewer very good ones. And according to Levitz, after Mickey had finally waited long enough for Levitz to allow him to try out, "There was only one great one, and that was Mickey Ashman."

"I can't teach you a thing, Ash!" Levitz said to him one night when the others had left the theater for a coffee break. "You are a pro, my friend. Better than nearly anyone I know."

Mickey's heart swelled. God, he needed to hear that. His career had been nothing if not shitty. Even now at the studio, where he was rubbing elbows with dozens of producers every day, he couldn't get a day of acting work. Acting work? He couldn't even get a goddamned agent. And he'd tried. Hard. He had the list to prove it. Thirty-two agents. He'd met and talked to thirty-two agents, some when they came to make calls on the Hemisphere lot, some after he left work and rushed to their office with his picture portfolio, and some during his lunch break. And not one of them wanted to sign him.

"How old are you?"

"Twenty-two," Mickey said, trying to sound spritely. Sometimes he felt like a hundred and five.

"Gee, you look a lot older," one agent said, looking at Mickey's most recent photographs. "You're a character type. I already got plenty of those."

Then there was that woman agent who loved him. At least that's what she said.

"I love you. Oh, God. I absolutely love you. I mean I love your type. I mean you're funny. You're silly. You're just a riot. I love you. But there's no work in the industry for someone like you."

"Thank you."

He had some photographs in his book of himself as Mr. Chunky which were taken on the set when he was shooting the commercial. One of the agents he saw looked at them while he was leafing through Mickey's book, squinted and said, "Oh, yeah. That was you. God, that was a million years ago."

Nevertheless, in Jackie Levitz's class Mickey was a star. He was fast on his feet in the improvisations, and creative, and every time he got up to do an exercise the rest of the group paid attention. They knew what they were about to see would be good.

But they were all working in the industry. And he wasn't.

Dal Mitchell was skinny and unshaven and did a great Western dialect and he always played the hero's sidekick in cowboy pictures. Beans and Mitzi Cass were a husband-and-wife comedy team and they had just done a series of coffee commercials that helped them make a down payment on a new home in Studio City. Barbara Rogers, a buxom blonde whose stock-in-trade was playing the part of a dumb blonde, and whose secret was she was as dumb as she acted, was the "game girl" on a daytime quiz show. She stood beside the prizes when they showed them to the audience. It wasn't exactly acting, but she was paid two hundred and fifty dollars a show. And they shot five shows a week.

Mickey couldn't stand it.

"It's a fluke," Jackie Levitz told him. "A guy with all that talent should have his own series." Mickey smiled and shrugged, but he wasn't sure when Jackie said that if he was talking about Mickey or himself. And Jackie would call agents on Mickey's behalf. But even though everyone knew who Jackie Levitz was, everyone also knew he hardly ever worked anymore, and they connected Mickey with him. So the answer to Jackie was always some variation of "Hey, Jackson baby, I'm up to my ass in comic types," or "Love to see the kid, Jackie, but it's almost hiatus, so gimme a call in June. Okay? Ciao."

One Monday night Mickey left the studio and drove home. He stopped to pick up his cleaning on Ventura Boulevard, then he stopped at a small market near his house and bought a package of sliced bologna and a loaf of bread and a bottle of orange juice, because for some reason that's what he felt like eating. Then he drove home and had a bologna sandwich and a glass of orange juice.

After he finished eating, he sat at the tiny kitchen table and looked at the clock. It was seven thirty. Levitz's workshop met at eight o'clock. Ordinarily Mickey couldn't wait to get there. He would be the first one to arrive. Even before Levitz. But tonight it was different. He couldn't go. Couldn't. He couldn't move from the table. He felt as if his body were tied to the chair. There was a pounding behind his eyes that made his whole face and head ache.

The mail room. Maybe he was stuck there. Forever. Running the mail. Incoming. Outgoing. Mailboy, leave those on my desk. Mailboy, send these out. Stan Rose and Walter Barton. David would be leaving the mail room soon. So would Golden. Mickey had been there before all of them, and there he was. Still. Everyone was moving ahead but Ashman. Mickey Ashman. Carry your briefcase, Mr. Holloway. God damn it, he was tired. Maybe he should skip Levitz's class tonight. Yes, skip it. That's what he would do. And sleep.

He walked into his bedroom and looked at the unmade bed. The pounding behind his eyes was getting harder. It would be good to lie down. Take the phone off the hook and sleep. The phone. Who would call? Stan Rose sometimes called and the two of them would go to a movie in the Valley. But Rose was pretty busy now with the concert business, and . . . yeah. Everyone was busy. Everyone was making money. Big money. Everyone in Levitz's class but him. Everyone in the mail room but him. Maybe he'd take a couple of aspirins.

The water in the bathroom sink was dripping. The sink was dirty and the soggy towel from his morning shower was on the floor where he'd left it. He hated the house when it looked like this. But lately he had no strength, no energy, to keep it clean. Aspirins. He opened the medicine cabinet. Contac Nasal Mist, Rise, Naturade one-a-day vitamins, Valium. Valium. This was an old bottle from Dr. Sobel in Chicago. Mickey never took them. The plastic container was full. The cotton was still in it. Valium. He had been having some lower back problems a few years ago and Dr. Sobel said these would ease the muscle spasms and relax him. But he'd never even opened the bottle. Maybe he should take one now. Maybe he would take more than one. All of them. Mickey picked up a plastic cup. The rim of the cup was caked with toothpaste from the sink. He rinsed the cup carefully, put some water in it and took it and the Valium bottle into the bedroom. It was dark in the bedroom now except for the light from the bathroom. Mickey sat on the bed and held the plastic Valium bottle in his hand. Who would miss him? Harvey? Maybe. His parents? Yeah. That was it. He had nobody. He was nobody.

He put the cup of water on the night table and pulled the plastic lid off the container and took the cotton out. Blue pills. Ten milligrams, it said on the label. Lots of them. Little blue pills. Fuck. Fuck. Fuck. Little blue pills and he would never have to pick up the trades and see who else was working. Little blue pills and he wouldn't have to hear any more agents say, "You can't work, Mickey. You're too character. You're too young. Maybe you'll grow into yourself." Can't work. Fuck. Fuck. Fuck. He threw the open bottle of Valium hard against the wall. The little blue pills flew everywhere. Fuck. Can't work. Can't even commit suicide.

Five or six of the pills were scattered on the floor next to the bed. Maybe that would be enough. He stooped down on the floor to pick them up, and as he did he could see his reflection in the mirror on the bathroom door.

Chubby, schmucky Mickey Ashman killed himself last night by swallowing a bunch of dusty Valiums that he picked up off the floor of his slovenly room. Tears welled in Mickey's eyes and he laughed. At himself. He was schmucky. That part was true. But he wouldn't kill himself. At least not tonight. He'd go to Levitz's class and let everyone tell him how wonderful he was.

fourteen

David Kane had it figured out. Finally. Maybe. The maybe was because he wasn't sure it would work. When you were dealing with something as elusive and uncertain as romance it was hard to be positive about what the results would be. Romance. It was romance that had brought his parents together. Marlene hadn't told him too many details, but every time she'd spoken to him about her relationship with his father she used the word "passionate," and even though David remembered very little about the two of them together, one of his memories had to do with tiptoeing into their room in the morning, and always finding them locked in one another's arms whether they were asleep or awake. Big deal. Then the son of a bitch left her. And never even came back, or called or sent a fucking cent.

And Wolfson? Wasn't he romantic? That rotten asshole. He knocked Marlene up and never had any intention of leaving his wife. Wolfson. God, how David hated him. Marlene's funeral had been very small. A few of David's high school friends saw the announcement in the paper and came. Two women from the cosmetics department at Saks came, and they cried until their very heavy black mascara ran, and Wolfson was late. David was sure he wouldn't be there at all and he was surprised when he looked back to see him in his three-piece pinstripe suit, leaning against the back wall of the tiny room where Marlene was laid out. David hated Wolfson when he looked at him, and wished he'd killed him that morning in the poolhouse. At the cemetery Wolfson called him Davey and gave him a piece of paper where he'd written the time and date David was supposed to report to Hemisphere. He never said how he got him the job; probably the Bank of Beverly Hills did business with the studio. What difference did it make?

"Good luck, boy," Wolfson said to him. Then he got into his Rolls-Royce and drove away.

The friends from school looked sadly at David and left. The women from Saks had apologized but they couldn't come to the cemetery because they had to get back to work. David went home alone to the apartment and sat in a chair in the living room for hours, alternately staring into space silently and then sobbing loudly. He had no one. Romance had seen to that. He would never get caught up in it. But he knew how to use it. And that's what he would do with Allyn Grant.

The mail room was the lowest. And he couldn't stay there anymore. It was demeaning and he wanted more money than that piddly-shit salary. And status, too. A car. A good car, not Marlene's old Ford Falcon. Allyn Grant was close with Harold Greenfield. Maybe she would get David to Greenfield. Take him there. Not maybe. She would. He was playing it cool with her. First he said he'd call her, and then he didn't call. That always drove women crazy. He could see it in her eyes after the three weeks on the other runs when he went back to the gold building. She was aching to say something to him but she was afraid. That was the system. Women waited. Men were the aggressors. The askers, the callers. He was running the show. She'd be there waiting when he called.

She tried to be cool but there was no mistaking what was in her voice that night. For a Saturday date. He'd known he was going to call her for days, but he wanted to wait, to see if she'd admit that her other choice was to stay at home. It was a game he'd learned in high school. But so what? It worked. And she was a great-looking bitch, too. Long straight black hair, almost to her waist, and those blue eyes and—why was he saving her tits for third on the list? They were nice tits. High and round and lots of times it looked like she wasn't wearing a bra under her shirt.

Dinner in Westwood was perfect. Mario's. David ordered wine and they didn't even ask him for I.D. He knew Allyn was a few years older and other guys she went out with were probably more sophisticated, but he could tell by the way she looked at him that she was interested, and he knew by her almost inaudible intake of breath when he touched her leg as she sat next to him in the booth that there were vibrations. Hot ones. That's why he didn't fuck her that night. Or on the next two dates. Just brief good-night kisses at her door and "See you, babe." He loved it. She would smile and say "Great" but the frustration on her face was clear.

She'd wait. Until he was good and ready. Tonight he'd tease her a little more just to get her really good and hot. Maybe touch those tits. He was getting hard thinking about it, but he couldn't get carried away. His phone rang.

"Hello."

"David? Allyn."

"Hi, gorgeous." Why in the hell was she calling him?

She laughed. "Hi. Say, listen, did you make dinner reservations for tonight yet?"

"Yeah. Why?"

"Oh, uh . . . nothing. I just thought maybe instead of going out, I would, uh . . . make dinner here. But if you already made them I—"

The kill. She was going to try to seduce him with a dinner.

"Yeah. I already made them." Play hard to get.

"Oh . . . okay. It's just that I'm a really good cook, and—"

"Hey, if you really want to cook, it's okay. I just thought you'd like going out," David said.

"Well. Dinner here would be more casual."

"Okay. I'll cancel." He hadn't made a reservation anywhere. "What time?"

"Eight."

Allyn Grant's apartment looked like a model apartment in a magazine. There were plants everywhere, and all the fabrics were brightly colored, and David noticed the table was already set with wineglasses, and lots of forks at both places, and a tablecloth. Allyn Grant. He watched her ass as she gave him a tour of the place. Tight. And she was tidy. Neat. Everything in place. Not like him in his apartment, with yesterday's socks still on the floor.

"What would you like to drink?" she asked. "I made some great hors d'oeuvres."

Drinks. Hors d'oeuvres. Casual. David smiled to himself. And that slinky dress. It looked like a goddamned nightgown.

She made bullshots for both of them and they sat on the sofa in the living room. The hors d'oeuvres were shrimp puffs. He hated shrimp.

"Nice place."

"Do you really like it? Julia helped me do everything. Actually she more than helped. She did it."

Julia Greenfield. They're very close.

"Excuse me for just a second," Allyn said.

He watched her walk to the kitchen. Very close. Soon the closeness would pay off for him.

"Dinner's ready." She was carrying a platter to the table. Then she was twitching around serving the salad and the roast, and she was leaning over the table to serve him until he could see everything but her nipples. Maybe he wouldn't wait. He didn't want to wait. He ate the meal slowly. Trying to decide. When they'd both finished, they sat quietly until Allyn moved for the kitchen.

"I'll get dessert."

"Allyn." He grabbed her arm, and pulled her to him. He was sitting in the chair in her tiny dining room. As he pulled her toward him those tits were right above his face. He nuzzled the right one, then the left one. He could see that her nipples were tough and hard under the silken dress. He lifted his hand and pulled the top of the dress down two inches and released her right nipple. It was brown and large, and he put his lips around it and flicked it with his tongue.

"Mmmm, David," she said softly.

He pulled the other side of the dress down and now both of her breasts were free.

Another tug and the dress was at her waist.

"Oh, David," she said. David's cock was hard. Still sitting in the chair, he slipped his arm around her ass. The hot cunt. She wasn't wearing panties. He tugged down on the dress. What a great-looking black bush.

"David," she said. Her head was thrown back and she was moaning. "Oh, God."

The dress was around her feet. He was sucking the tit of a naked broad in her dining room, and he had all his clothes on. He moved his left hand up and down between her thighs quickly—careful, just so he could momentarily touch her cunt every few strokes.

"Oh, God. David. Baby. Oh, God."

He squeezed the inside of her right thigh hard. Then the left. Then quickly he slipped his finger inside her wet cunt. She wanted it. He'd make her beg for it. She reached for him, to undress him, but he moved her arms away. He'd heard it somewhere. Women loved to be naked while the man is dressed. It was hot and demeaning.

"Oh, David."

He did want her. But he had to stay in control. He got up and pinned her against the dining room wall. Now he had his hands and mouth all over her—and she was frenzied—but still he knew he was in total control.

"I want you, baby," she said. "I want you."

"I know you do," he said, looking in her eyes. He knew she wanted to hear more. "But I can't." It was perfect. He was in total control. Her cunt was dripping wet and her legs were spread and he was leaving her cold.

"What?"

He moved away from her and sat down in his chair. She looked like a fool standing there naked. He smiled his best sweet smile.

"I can't make love to you, Allyn."

He watched her passion subside and the self-consciousness take over.

"I—don't understand." She stooped down to reach for the dress. David wished he could move it out of her way with his foot, but that would be going too far. She picked up the dress and held it in front of herself.

"Why not?" she asked, biting her lower lip.

"Because I care about you. I really do." Oh, Jesus. What shit.

"David. That's crazy."

"No, it isn't. It really makes sense. Come sit on the sofa with me."

"I'll get a robe."

He watched her naked back as she walked to her room still holding the dress in front of her. It was working.

God he was smooth. That's what the young actresses he'd met at the studio told him. It must have been from growing up in Beverly Hills where teenaged fucking was commonplace. Sometimes he'd spent the night with girls in their own bedrooms—while their parents were home. Usually the parents were too drunk or too drugged to care. Or the daughters knew so many incriminating things about the parents that the parents didn't dare object.

Allyn emerged from the bedroom. Even the robe was part of the act. Bright pink and cuddly like a stuffed animal. David was totally pulled together by the time she came out of the bedroom.

"Sit here," he said, patting the sofa.

Allyn was pulled together, too. She had added some blusher to her makeup, and she smelled as if she'd splashed on more cologne.

"Well," she said.

David was prepared. Rehearsed, in fact.

"Please don't think I'm a jerk," he said.

"David, my God, I'd never think that."

He blinked a few times as if grateful.

"Thank you. You really are a terrific lady. Honest to God. You know that?"

She smiled.

"Look, Allyn," he said, touching her hand. "I'm going to be as honest with you as I can."

"Great," she said.

"I already knew before you told me last month about how close you are with the Greenfields."

"You did?" How could he possibly have known that?

"It's common knowledge," he said.

She looked surprised. Maybe he'd gone too far.

"Well . . . not really common knowledge, but a number of people know. And . . . well . . . I'm incredibly attracted to you. You saw that a few minutes ago. But, I would never want you to think that I would—just because I'm looking for a job that I'd— I'm too embarrassed to say it." Thank God it was easy for a redhead to look as if he was blushing.

"David. Did you think I thought you were trying to get to know Harold through me?"

He wouldn't say anything. He looked down at his hand on hers.

"Is that it?" she asked.

He bit the side of his cheek as if talking about this any longer would be too painful.

"I do think you're a jerk," she said, moving closer to him. "That's adorable." She put her arms around his neck and kissed his cheek. "It's so silly of you. I mean, I never once thought that."

He smiled an apologetic smile.

"You're not, are you?" she asked, joking.

He looked away.

"I'm sorry, David. That was a joke."

He turned back slowly and looked into her eyes for a long time. "I want you," he said finally.

Allyn rose to her feet and took his hand.

"Then let's go."

Slowly they walked toward the bedroom.

"Julia? Allyn!"

"Darling, how in heaven's name are you? I was saying to Harold only this morning I hadn't spoken to you in days. Will you come for dinner tonight?"

It was Sunday morning and Allyn sat on her bed surrounded by the frilly eyelet pillow shams, dust ruffles and comforter, talking on the telephone.

"Julia," Allyn said, the delight filling her voice. "I got laid last night."

Julia laughed. "Thank God," she said. "I was about to offer you Harold for a quickie."

Both women laughed.

"Well?" Julia said. "Who was it? A prince? A count? A duke?

Don't tell me it was someone in the business. And, above all, don't you dare tell me you're in love."

"Well . . ." Allyn hesitated. "No, I'm not yet. And he's just a boy really. I mean he's younger than I am."

"Ooh, please—no one is younger than you are," Julia said.

Allyn had grown to admire Julia Greenfield. To her, Julia was the perfect example of the woman behind the man. A woman whose primary purpose in life was to make her husband's life better, and she did it with great flair. *Architectural Digest* printed an article with magnificent photographs of the Greenfields' palatial home, *Gourmet* magazine printed a feature article on Julia's sensational cooking and original recipes, *Women's Wear Daily* constantly reported what she wore to premieres and parties, and in her mid-fifties the naturally silver-haired, tall and stately Julia frequently stole the show from ladies who were far younger.

"You realize, Allyn, pet, that unless I matchmake you into a divine marriage with a perfect man within the next year or so, I shall be up the proverbial 'shits creek' in the eyes of none other than my mother-in-law, my husband and your grandmother. So now that you're out of mourning for the eye doctor, how 'bout letting me get serious about putting you on the market? I know a heavenly Beverly Hills diet doctor who would adore you."

Allyn was out of bed now. She carried the phone in her left hand and with her right she held the receiver to her ear. She tugged at the cord and pulled the phone into the bathroom. She knew she'd better start getting ready while she talked, because David would be back any minute from Nate 'n' Al's with their breakfast. David. Oh, God. David. David Kane. Mrs. David Kane.

"Julia, I'm no longer interested in doctors," she said.

"Darling, this one's gorgeous. And he'd love you. After looking at blubbery overweight women all day, one look at your teensy waist and he'll propose."

"Julia." Allyn turned the water on a low stream and worked her face as she talked. "I could have stayed in Pittsburgh if I wanted to marry a doctor."

"Not the same. Not the same at all. Now. What about dinner?"

"I'd like to, Julia. I really would, but I have a feeling David's going to stay tonight, too."

"Then bring him along. Christina's making a buffet for sixteen. I'll just tell her to expect two more."

"I'd better ask David first." Allyn was brushing her long black hair. She would tell David that Julia called her right after he left. That she had called to remind Allyn of the dinner invitation for tonight that had slipped Allyn's mind. Not that she'd called Julia to tell her she'd just been laid. Laid. Oh, yes. And relaid. And laid again. Royally. Regally. Laid.

"That's fine," Julia said. "Then I will speak to you later, love."

Allyn turned the water on in the tub. Maybe if she hurried she'd have enough time for a bath. David. Sweet David. What a delicious lover. His beautiful body was so golden and hard. And he knew just how to touch her to make her crazy. But the best part was the words.

"You're so beautiful, baby. We're perfect together," he said, nibbling, nuzzling.

Allyn stepped into the tub and as she sat in the hot water, her nipples hardened and she touched them, remembering last night.

"Get used to this, Allyn," he had said. "Get used to it, because you're going to have a real hard time getting rid of me." Oh, how she loved hearing that.

Maybe he meant it. Maybe they would have a love affair. With romantic phone calls and weekends away, and . . . He was so young, but he was bright and sexy and fun and he knew what to say in bed. Maybe it could work out.

Allyn got out of the tub and wrapped herself in a big white bath towel. She'd dress casually. Jeans and a T-shirt. She opened the bathroom door just as David walked into the apartment carrying the bag from Nate 'n' Al's. He looked in at her and they both smiled.

"I'll make a deal with you," he said. "I'll drop the bag if you drop your towel."

"Sounds reasonable."

David put the grocery bag on the coffee table.

Allyn dropped the towel.

"I'm not that hungry anyway," David said, walking toward her. "At least not for breakfast."

fifteen

David had gone to a private school in Beverly Hills. His childhood friends were the children of movie stars and of producers and directors of great importance. He'd been in many elaborate and expensive homes. But even as the electric gate opened and he drove up the long driveway with Allyn toward the Greenfields' mansion, he knew he'd never seen anything like it. The lawns were exquisitely groomed and the lush shrubs and trees were accented with the colors of every imaginable kind of flower.

As he pulled his Falcon in among the Rolls-Royces, Mercedeses and Cadillacs, David realized he was trembling. Allyn mustn't see. He had to look casual. Not blow it. He'd been so cool when she told him she wanted to take him to the Greenfields' for dinner. Now he knew his scheme was working perfectly. She wanted to prove that she trusted him.

When they got out of bed and got dressed and she was padding around the kitchen cleaning up some of the dinner things, setting up the breakfast things, she'd asked him to please join her that evening. "Oh, c'mon, David. Won't you?" So sexy in her jeans and T-shirt. She reminded him for a minute of Marlene. Marlene would have said, "Go, Davey. Go to the Greenfields' and take them all by storm." That's what she always told him when he was feeling nervous or inadequate. "Look at you, you gorgeous thing," she'd say, "and you're brilliant, too. Who could resist you?" Marlene. He missed her so much.

Allyn rang the Greenfields' bell and the enormous front door opened almost immediately. A Negro maid in uniform smiled broadly. "Miss Allyn," she said, "welcome, honey. Good to see you."

"Hi, Emma," Allyn said. "This is David Kane."

"How do you do?" Emma smiled at David, then back at Allyn approvingly. Allyn grinned. "They're all out back," Emma said.

Allyn held David's hand. He took a deep breath. He was sure he looked good. He'd gone back to his apartment late in the afternoon to change, and picked out just the right tie and jacket and pants. Allyn obviously knew her way around the Greenfield house. She led him through high-beamed ceilinged rooms, long hallways and then into a kind of playroom, furnished with a jukebox, an antique pool table and several pinball machines and out the door toward the pool area.

It looked like a set. A set in a movie about royalty. Kings and queens. Not just some successful movie mogul. There were a few people standing at an outdoor bar as they arrived.

"Allyn, precious," came a voice.

A tall gray-haired woman was heading their way.

"Hi, Julia." Allyn embraced the woman, who in turn kissed the air beside Allyn's face on each side. Then she looked at David.

"This is David Kane," Allyn told her.

"Hmmmm," she said. And that was all. "Come have some wine."

David walked next to Allyn as they approached the bar. She looked beautiful in a short white dress, and two of the men who were at the bar having a conversation looked at her long tanned legs instead of at one another. Julia ordered wine and, as the bartender poured, David saw Harold Greenfield approach.

"Young lady," he said, giving Allyn a big hug and a peck on the cheek. "And David Kane," he said, shaking David's hand heartily. "Nice to have you here. Both of you."

David only smiled but said nothing. To begin with, he didn't know what to call Greenfield. "Sir" and "Mr. Greenfield" sounded childish, and calling him "Harold" would be presumptuous at this point. But there was something else bothering David. Some flicker he saw move quickly across Greenfield's face just then that made him uncomfortable. It was as if Greenfield was surprised to see him there. Surprised in the bad sense. As if maybe David shouldn't be there. No. That couldn't be. Marlene would call what he was having "the old South Beverly Hills inferiority complex."

Everyone knew the rules of Beverly Hills. The best homes were north of Sunset, the good homes were north of Santa Monica, and the not-so-hot homes and, worse yet, apartment buildings and duplexes, were south of Wilshire Boulevard. Homes and apartments and duplexes that anywhere else or on any other standard would be considered well made and desirable, on the Beverly Hills scale were just so-so. And all of the kids from every section socialized together, converged at the same private high schools or at Beverly Hills High. It was a cold fact that within days of a new student's arrival, everyone knew exactly where he or she lived. David and Marlene's apartment was south.

"You have a beautiful place here," David managed to say to Greenfield.

"Thank you, Kane." Greenfield turned to Allyn. "Talked to your grandmother today," he said, "she was at my mother's for dinner and Mah-Jongg. I would have asked her for a message for you, but Julia didn't tell me you were coming tonight."

Maybe that was it. What David saw. Greenfield didn't expect them.

"Want to shoot some pool?" Greenfield asked them. Allyn nodded happily.

"You'd better watch out, Kane. This girl's my protégée."

"Oh, Harold," Allyn said. "You shouldn't have told. I was going to play 'poor-little-me-I-don't-know-how-to-hold-the-cue,' and hustle him for money."

Greenfield laughed.

They carried their wineglasses into the playroom, and Harold took three pool cues down.

He wasn't joking. Allyn was a great pool player. As good as Greenfield was, she could still beat him. David had shot pool in high school a few times, but he wasn't in their league. And it felt funny. A woman beating him. A great-looking woman who was bending over the table, with her white dress hiking up just to underneath her ass, and beating the head of Hemisphere Studios, too. And Greenfield was laughing. A few other people wandered in to watch. Greenfield told jokes, called for a servant to bring more wine and rolled up his sleeves.

"Don't tell this to any of your friends in the mail room," he said. "Or my reputation as invincible is shot."

David laughed.

"I won't tell she beat you, if you won't tell she beat me."

"Don't worry, Kane," Harold said, "we'll get together when she's not around. Under my tutelage you can learn plenty."

David grinned. If only Greenfield was talking about business and not pool, he thought. Maybe after the game they'd talk more. Sit down, away from the others, and talk. And David could tell him then, come right out and tell him, Give me a job as your assistant. He even knew what he would say if Greenfield told him, I don't have an assistant. I never have. I don't believe in it. Which is what David had heard about him.

Don't pay me, David would say. Let me just be there for six weeks or two months without a salary, and you'll see. I'll be so invaluable you won't want to let me go.

The game was over. Allyn won.

"You're a monster," Greenfield said to her. "I've created a monster."

"Allyn," Julia's voice rang out from the pool area.

"Coming, Julia," Allyn ran out the door. The other people had drifted through toward the house. David was alone with Greenfield, who was rolling his sleeves down, and shaking his head.

"She's some girl," he said.

"Yes, she is," David agreed.

"I know her grandmother."

"I know."

"Nice family."

"Mr. Greenfield." It was the safest choice.

Harold Greenfield looked at him.

"I know this isn't the best time, sir." Shit, he wasn't exactly taking Greenfield by storm. "But do you think we could sit down and have a talk soon?"

"About Allyn?" Greenfield asked. It was odd, because from everything David had ever seen or heard about Harold Greenfield, the man was never less than ten jumps ahead of everyone. How could he think it was Allyn David wanted to talk about?

"No. About a job."

"Oh. Yes. Of course. We'll do it next week at the studio. Call my secretary."

David felt the words in his chest. Chilly brush-off words. He had to say it. Now. Say that he wanted a job to get him out of the mail room. That he hated it there, and that he'd tried to get to Greenfield for help before, but that Greenfield's bitch secretary never let him through, and he didn't want to wait anymore. He'd say it all now. Greenfield's face broke into a smile. But he was looking past David at whoever was entering the room.

"Charlie, me boy," Greenfield said warmly.

David turned. Some people had come in. A pretty dark-haired woman and a man. The man looked— Oh, Christ. Oh, Christ. The man Greenfield was putting his arms around was Charles Wolfson. Next to him was the woman David had seen in the photographs. Diane. Wolfson's wife. Wolfson looked at David blankly, and David watched as the recognition slowly came into his eyes.

"Hello," Wolfson said, smiling at David coldly.

David nodded. So this is how Wolfson got him the job. Of course. He was friends with Greenfield. Wolfson. That fucking monster. And his wife. David wanted to run up the stairs and out the door and get into the Falcon. Marlene's Falcon. And drive away, but he knew he couldn't. Greenfield was standing right next to him. What had Wolfson told Greenfield about David? About how he knew him? Who did he say David was?

"And Paris was perfect," Diane Wolfson was saying to Greenfield. "Charlie needed a vacation so badly. Didn't you, darling?"

Wolfson smiled. Greenfield smiled. David was definitely an intruder, but he couldn't move. There was something fascinating about standing there looking at the man who was his mother's married lover, and murderer, and the man's wife, that kept David glued to the spot.

"I like the Plaza Athénée. Charlie doesn't," Diane went on. "Well, I think I'll go out and see Julia," she said. "I brought her back a bauble I know she'll adore." She brushed past David, pushed open the door to outside and was gone.

Charles Wolfson. Harold Greenfield. David's head was spinning.

"So, how's the tennis game, C.W.?" Harold asked.

"Pretty good," Wolfson said. "Played with Marty Ransohoff last week. Beat his ass."

"No kidding?" Greenfield said. "I saw Marty at lunch on Friday. He didn't mention it." They both laughed.

Wolfson said, "The figures for *Americanization of Emily* were real good."

They were talking as if David weren't in the room. They were facing one another and neither of them even glanced at him.

"Still reading the trades, huh, Charlie?" Greenfield teased. "Why don't you break down and admit you want to be in show business?"

Wolfson grinned. "Greenie," he said, "how many times must I tell you, being in the banking business *is* being in show business." They laughed.

"I'm sure . . ."

Wolfson was being playful. David had never seen him that way. He hated him. Hated the fucker. Hated him because he was alive and Marlene was dead. And now he was ignoring David. Acting as if he weren't there.

I'll take care of everything. Including you. That's what he'd said to David that morning in the poolhouse when David should have killed him. Wanted to kill the son of a bitch. Talking to Greenfield as if David weren't there. If Greenfield only knew that Wolfson was a killer. Greenfield was so fatherly and upstanding. Marlene would have jokingly called him "a pillow of the community." Take care of everything. Including you. Bullshit. All Wolfson ever did was get him the lousy job in the mail room. And then he disappeared out of his life. Well, it wasn't over. Wolfson was going to do more for David. He owed it to him. And to Marlene. Maybe it was providence that brought David to Allyn Grant and then Greenfield and now Wolfson.

David heard the sound of voices approaching from inside the house.

"Harold. Charlie. Hey. How's the tennis? How was Paris? Where's Diane? I'm afraid to find out what Julia's serving for dinner tonight. I'm starving. I'm on a diet."

David used the confusion to move toward the door to outside. He would wait for an opening and talk to Wolfson later. As he pushed the door open, he could feel someone directly behind him.

"Davey."

Wolfson was walking beside him.

"Yeah."

"Why don't we take a little walk together, Davey. The Greenfields have some nice gardens," he said. "We can talk."

"Sure." What was this about? That prick. David was the one who should be asking to talk. What did Wolfson want from him?

"Hiya, Red." Both David and Wolfson were startled. It was Allyn. She gave David a kiss on the cheek. "Having a good time?"

"Yeah," David managed. "Have you met—" he began.

"Sure. Hi, Charlie," she said sweetly.

"Hello, Allyn," Charlie said.

David felt his stomach tense when he saw Charlie's eyes scan Allyn's body.

"I'm on my way to tell Emma Julia wants dinner to be served right away," she said. "Be back soon."

She never asked how David knew Wolfson. She probably assumed they'd just met.

Wolfson and David started off in the direction of Greenfield's gardens. Trees and shrubs that looked to David like a maze in a children's book. They were both quiet for a long time. David could taste the anger in his mouth.

"What are you doing here?" Wolfson said to him finally, breaking the silence. They stopped walking and looked at one another.

"Is this some kind of blackmail?" he asked. "You being here with that girl Allyn? What do you want? I got you the job in the mail room by telling Harold you were a boy whose family I'd known for years. And he believed that."

"Don't worry," David said, trying to keep his voice steady. "I'm not going to tell Harold anything." He used Greenfield's first name on purpose. "Allyn and I are seeing one another and she wanted me to get to know the Greenfields because they're like parents to her."

Wolfson's eyes narrowed. David was feeling stronger.

"You know about parents, Charlie. They protect their young. Like you did. When you couldn't leave your children to marry my mother."

David didn't believe his own voice. He sounded eerie to himself. Crazy. Threatening. But he despised this man. Motherfucker. Yes. That's what he was. Only the mother was Marlene. David's mother, and his anger was getting stronger as it moved into his throat.

"I should have killed you, Charlie," he said. "But maybe it was good I didn't, because now you can tell Harold Greenfield to make me his assistant. That's the answer to your question. That's what I want."

"You're a greedy little bastard, aren't you?" Wolfson asked. His face was cool, but David could see what he knew was uncertainty in the man's eyes.

"Why not? It's easy for you."

"And if I say no."

"I tell your wife about Marlene. My mother. In fact, I'll tell Greenfield. I'll tell him you don't belong in this upper-echelon high-society set because you're a cheating lying low-life." David was afraid of starting to cry. Afraid he'd fall apart.

Wolfson's jaw was clenched. If only David would stay calm until he answered. Wolfson took a deep breath.

"I'll take care of it," Wolfson said.

"You said that before. Said you'd take care of everything."

"This time I mean it."

The two men turned silently and walked back toward the house. They emerged from the gardens just in time for dinner.

sixteen

Barry had been trying to write a letter home all week long. It was more than a year since he arrived in California, and in all that time he'd had no communication with his parents. Sometimes he had a fantasy that his uncle Mashe would die, and the lawyers would look at the will and discover that despite what had gone on between them Mashe had left everything to Barry anyway, and that Barry was the head of Eldor. And they would locate him in Hollywood and tell him he was now a millionaire. The next part of the fantasy was that his mother would call him and Andy would call him and they would each beg his forgiveness, and he would tell them that now that he owned Eldor he was going to sell it, because he wanted to stay in California and be with Harley Ellis, his lover. That would kill them both.

Dear Mah. Maybe he should make the letter to his dad, too. His poor dull dad who hadn't even been able to face him the day Mashe broke the news about Andy. Dear Mah and Dad, I am living in Hollywood now and I have a good job and—and what? And a lover who is a boy? So tell Mashe he was right because I am a fairy? No. Jesus. Dear Dad and Mah, I hope that you will be glad that I am writing this, because, after all, I am still your son, the only child you ever had, and I would hope that now that a year has gone by since I left that you will have forgiven me for hurting you by— No. They were wrong to be hurt. It was his life.

"Trying to write a letter again?" Harley asked. Barry nodded. Harley was sitting on the living-room floor with his guitar, trying to pick out a new tune.

"Why don't you just call them?" he asked Barry.

"Because I'm afraid."

Harley shook his head. He couldn't understand.

To Harley, Barry was strong and smart about nearly everything. How could he be so dumb about just calling his folks? No one was saying he had to tell them who he was sleeping with.

Jesus. When it came to understanding all those full-of-shit guys at the record company, and all the stuff they were talking about, Barry was a whiz. That's why Harley took him along to meetings, so afterward Barry could explain it all to him.

Harley had a five-year contract with Rainbow Records. He'd been discovered by Jim Garland, one of Rainbow's in-house producers, when Garland came to a Monday "hoot night" at the Troubador.

Garland liked the way Harley looked, and the way he sang and he thought the kid's music had great potential. So on Tuesday morning Garland hustled Harley over to Rainbow's offices and into a meeting with Bob Frank, the president of Rainbow Records, Nick Jonas, an executive vice-president of Rainbow Records and the head of artist relations, and Garland, that lasted so long the four of them had two meals brought in while they sat there talking. First they talked about Harley's music, and how his songs were better than the Lovin' Spoonful's, or Simon and Garfunkel's, and how the soft sound was really what was happening in rock, and even the Beatles had proven it with the *Rubber Soul* album. And that was the only part of the entire conversation that Harley understood, so after a while he tuned out.

The others talked about studio time and master tapes and marketing and A&R and occasionally Harley would tune back in and listen to what they were saying, and he realized that something big was happening that he wasn't sure he could handle. Especially the part about signing a contract with Rainbow for five years. In five years. Oh, man. He'd be twenty-four. Old.

It was Marty Baker who sent Harley to Jay Cooper, a Beverly Hills attorney. Jay had been a saxophone player with the big bands, and then he moved to California to become a lawyer. He was tall, sinewy slim and balding and he looked like a French movie actor. Marty told Harley that Jay was respected by everyone in the music business. When Jay said the contract looked good to him, Marty told Harley to grab the deal. But after that one meeting with Jay Cooper, Harley was pretty much on his own, so he was glad to have Barry hanging around with him now. Barry came to recording sessions with him. The three of them that followed the cutting of "The Rain Is Like My Tears." And to lots of meetings. Rainbow had released "The Rain Is Like My Tears" as a single immediately, and now they were cutting an album "to go around it," as Garland put it.

Frank and Jonas and Garland were always uncomfortable having Barry at their meetings because he never said a word. And they weren't quite sure who he was in Harley's life. He wasn't a relative. He looked too Jewish. Was Harley a faggot? Nah. He wasn't the least bit swishy. Neither was the other kid. They all wondered who that short little putz was. But "The Rain Is Like My Tears" was climbing on the charts, so the three of them decided not to ask.

"Probably his best friend," one of the guys speculated after seeing Barry with Harley for the fifth or sixth time. "You know how kids are."

"I don't know what to say to them," Barry said, crumbling up his most recent attempt at the letter. He was really depressed. "Dear Mom and Dad, don't worry about me because I'm a mail boy in a big studio. I can hear it now. My mother will say, 'Oy vay. A mail boy. He could have gone to college. He could have been a big shot. He could have owned Eldor Dresses someday. And he's a mail boy. Oy vay.'"

Harley was laughing at Barry's imitation. And Barry laughed, too.

"Why don't you tell them you're my manager?" Harley asked.

"Sure," Barry said.

"And why don't I tell them I fuck girls, too, and I'm going to marry one? I don't want to lie. That's why I haven't written to them. Because I don't want to lie." He felt helpless. Young and afraid and lonely for his family. "And I know they can't accept the truth."

"Why don't you become my manager?" Harley asked. "Then it won't be a lie."

"Because I don't know shit about managing or the music business," Barry said. "And you've already got a good start. I'd end up managing you right into the toilet."

"What do you think your friend Stan Rose knew about the music business?"

"Nothing."

The next morning Barry stopped by Henry Shmidt's office. He had tried calling Shmidt a few times but could never get through. Shmidt's secretary was away from her desk and the door to his office was open and Shmidt was bellowing at someone on the telephone. Barry listened.

"That cunt. She should go down on Godzilla for a chance to play that room. Who the fuck does she think she is?"

Barry smiled. He loved the image.

"Get back to me," Shmidt said into the phone and slammed it down. Now Barry could wait until the secretary got back from the ladies' room or wherever it was secretaries went, and ask if he could see Shmidt, or he could just stick his head around the corner into Shmidt's office.

"Mr. Shmidt," Barry said. Shmidt was sitting at his desk, deep in thought and picking his nose. When he saw Barry standing there he stopped picking.

"Yeah?"

"I'm Barry Golden. I work in the mail room."

"Yeah?"

"And I want a job at World Records." Now Barry was standing in the office in front of Shmidt's desk. Jesus, was that a picture of Shmidt in a Nazi uniform?

Shmidt looked at him for what seemed like forever, not saying a word. Maybe he was supposed to go on. Maybe he should be telling Shmidt why he wanted the job. Not the part about how he was embarrassed to tell his parents he was a mail boy, and not that he wished he knew more so he could be a hotshot and help Harley. But the part he'd made up last night after Harley fell asleep. Well, not made up, but decided on as what he'd tell Shmidt when Shmidt asked him why he should give him a job. Barry steeled himself. What was the worst thing that could happen? Shmidt would throw him out.

"Mr. Shmidt, I know I may seem young to you." Was Shmidt smirking? "But I think my youth could be an asset to World Records. You see, I have a feeling that there are a lot of important changes going on in the record business and that World Records should get in on them. And I'd like to work here to help that happen."

Shmidt still didn't say a word. Of course not. That was probably a real dumb thing to have said, because it was like saying I know more about what's going on than you do, just because I'm younger. God, Barry felt like a jerk. Why had that seemed like such a good thing to say when he thought about it last night? He should have tried it out on Harley first.

"You're right," Shmidt said, still looking as if he was deep in thought. "Right. World Records is M.O.R. and everybody wants folk, or rock, or folk rock or whatever the fuck it is."

M.O.R. Middle-of-the-road. Barry had heard the reference before. At Rainbow. In meetings with Harley and Frank and Jonas and Garland. It was looked down on by those guys. M.O.R. was old. Not contemporary. That was a good word. He'd try that one. He was feeling braver now.

"World Records ought to be exploring the contemporary market," he said, watching Shmidt's face. Shmidt seemed to snap out of his reverie.

"Shit, yes," he said. "This operation's going to be on its ass unless that happens." Then he looked at Barry again as if he were sorry he'd blurted that information out to some mail room kid.

"So here you are," he said to Barry. But now his tune had changed. He sounded like Mashe talking to the underlings at Eldor, when he knew they had to treat him with respect because he had the power. "And you think you can change it?" Shmidt asked. "How?"

"Put me in A&R," Barry said. He'd met some artists and repertoire men who worked for Rainbow. They'd been at Harley's recording sessions and occasionally one would be asked to sit in on a meeting. It seemed to Barry that they were hand-holders. It was up to them to make sure an act was happy with the job the record company was doing on its behalf. But the A&R men had another job, too. And that was to keep an eye out for new acts to sign. That was exciting.

"A&R?" Shmidt asked. "Who you gonna service? Jerry Wayne?" Jerry Wayne was an Italian crooner whose love songs were World's biggest sellers in the early sixties. "He'd laugh at me," Shmidt said. "He's got neckties older than you are." Shmidt laughed. Either at his own dumb joke or at the image of Barry with Jerry Wayne.

"I'll service whoever there is," Barry said. "And I'll help you find new acts. I go to the Troubador every Monday night," he told Shmidt. He was giving away a secret. Now Shmidt could go to the Troubador on Monday nights and not need him. "And other places," he added hastily, "and I'm hip to what's going on." Okay, so that was stretching the point. But, shit, it felt like Shmidt was kind of interested, and Barry was going to keep talking until he said yes. Or no. Or something definite.

When he'd imagined this moment on his way into work this morning, he had delivered his speech and afterward in the fantasy Shmidt said, "Barry, with your newfound knowledge of the contemporary scene and my business acumen, we'll make an impact on the music industry that will stand them all on their ears."

Instead of that, Shmidt turned a little in his chair, looked at Barry closely and spoke. "Kid," he said, "I'm so far in the crapper already one more employee can't make it much worse. You got a gig."

seventeen

"First he said he'd tell Diane. What do you think?"

"I think he's bluffing."

"*Then* he said he'd tell you."

"He's afraid to talk to me, Charlie. I'm the big boss. I can see it all over him. I'm telling you. You're safe," Greenfield said. "How many years have you been keeping *my* secrets, for Christ's sake?" he added.

Greenfield was on the private phone in his office in the gold building, talking to Wolfson on the private phone in Wolfson's office at the bank.

Charles Wolfson was tapping his fingers nervously on his desk. Maybe Greenfield was right. Maybe the sick feeling in his stomach didn't have to be there. David Kane was just a desperate little bastard.

"Let's see," Charlie said, smiling now. "About thirty-some-odd years." The two men had been roommates in college. "Since the time I came back to Pittsburgh with you that summer, and we watched the girl in the house next to your mother's house on . . . don't tell me . . . McElvey Street—"

"That's right—"

"—take off her clothes."

Both men laughed.

Charlie didn't even mention the obvious. Tomiko, the gorgeous Japanese girl Greenfield had been keeping for ten years, since she was not much more than a child, and who sometimes entertained the two of them in her elaborate Hollywood apartment when neither of them wanted to go home. She would serve the two of them dinner, sometimes wearing only a tiny apron that tied around her waist and left "the best parts," as Greenfield called them, to show. After dinner she would put on records and dance for them, and then Charlie would leave, to see Marlene, or, since her death, to go home. It wasn't until recently he found out that shortly after he would leave Tomiko's apartment, Harold would leave, too. Harold never touched Tomiko, only sat and watched her with and without her clothes on, and talked to her. About nearly everything. Business, politics, his friends, his past. And she would rub his back or his feet and nod and smile. The only important thing in Harold's life he didn't discuss with

Tomiko was Julia. That was separate. Other than that, Tomiko knew everything about him. Probably more than Julia did.

"Charlie, what do you want me to do?" Greenfield asked. "You know I'll do whatever you say."

"Kick the little bastard off the lot. Maybe that'll keep him away from Allyn Grant. Jesus, Greenie, he's liable to talk about me to her, and she'll tell Julia and—"

"Charlie. Charlie. Don't even finish the story," Harold said. "It's done."

Charlie was still unnerved from his confrontation with Kane the day before. The little bastard. That smug baby face looking up at him, threatening to pull his life apart. The kid was no good to begin with. He really would have used that goddamned gun in the pool-house that day. After that he should have had the kid locked up instead of opening himself up to this, by making the funeral, and getting him the goddamned job at Hemisphere. Thank God Harold knew everything about his affair with Marlene.

Once he had taken Marlene to dinner with Harold and Tomiko at Tomiko's apartment. Tomiko was dressed in a silk kimono and she made sukiyaki for the four of them and they drank sake and Marlene got a little drunk and kind of teary-eyed, and right after dinner she asked Charlie to take her home. He was disappointed. He was having a great time. Now he remembered it clearly. In the car just as he was making a left from Fountain to La Cienega, Marlene said, "How in God's name could you take me there, Charlie?" He didn't even have to hear the rest. He knew what she meant.

"She's his whore. His mistress. Is that what I am to you? Is that why you got us together? Two big-time moguls, on their night off from their wives, have dinner with their whores?"

Her voice was choked with rage.

"Is that the case, Charlie?" she asked. "'Cause if it is, I want what she gets. I want the advantages that a whore has. I want you to pay my rent, and buy me furs and jewelry, and give me a gift everytime I fuck you. Let me do it for the money, Charlie, as long as you think of me like that anyway."

That night, after Tomiko's, was the night he told Marlene he'd leave Diane. He loved Marlene. God, he loved her. So desperately. When he drove up to her building, she was sobbing.

"Marlene, don't. Please, baby. Don't," he begged. He turned off the motor. Davey's car wasn't there. Maybe the kid was out for the evening and he could get Marlene into bed. He would kiss her eyes

and slowly unbutton her dress and caress her till she wanted him inside her, thrusting, telling her he loved her, and once he was making
love to her, whispering how he couldn't live without her, it would all
be okay.

"Don't get out of the car, Charlie," she said. "I'm going up
alone."

"Marlene, please, let me explain about tonight."

"No. It's not tonight. It's not Tomiko or Harold or any of that.
That's just what set me off. I decided a long time ago that one day
I'd have the balls to tell you to get out of my life. And this is it."

"Stop this, Mar."

"No, Charlie. I won't stop this. The only thing I'll stop is com-
promising my life and not being able to have the man I love spend
one whole night with me unless he's away on what his wife thinks is a
business trip. And not being able to be with him on holidays and
weekends. And not being able to call him in the middle of the night
if I need him and want him." She was choking on her tears.

"I'll leave her, Marlene," he said. "I'll tell her next week."

"Bullshit."

"I swear to God, Marlene. I only took you to Tomiko's tonight
because I wanted Harold to get a chance to know you because he's
my close friend and he's known about you for years and how much I
love you."

There was a long silence. Punctuated only by Marlene's sniffles.

"Really?" she asked finally.

"Of course." It was a lie. Harold thought Marlene was the same as
Tomiko. She had assessed it perfectly. "And you know I want to
leave Diane. It's not the same. Harold never had any intention of
leaving Julia. Oh, honey. It's not the same. Don't do that to yourself.
Don't."

She seemed to be calmer.

"Mar. I love you."

"And I love you," she answered, sliding over to where he sat
behind the wheel. He kissed her and they began to kiss and touch
one another.

"Like teenagers," Marlene giggled.

"Let's go upstairs," he said. As usual he couldn't wait to have her.

"Yes."

They fell into bed as soon as they locked the bedroom door.
Marlene's lashes were still wet when he kissed them.

"My sweet girl," he said. "My beautiful sweet girl."

"Yes," she said. "Promise me, Charlie."

"I swear," he said, pulling at the buttons on her dress. Those breasts. Her beautiful softly freckled body. "I swear. Oh, God, baby. Yes. I swear. I'll do anything for you. Oh, yes."

Afterward they were lying together in a heap, and he remembered now what she said.

"Shit."

"Hmm."

"I forgot to use the goddamned diaphragm."

"I love you," he said, kissing her. And he did. He did really and truly love her.

"I love you." And she was kissing him again. My God, he was getting hard again. She made him feel like he was . . . How would he ever tell Diane? No, he couldn't do that. Diane. Twenty years. His beautiful Diane. His bride.

"Marlene. Baby. I hate to say it, honey, but I—"

"I know. You have to go." She was getting teary-eyed again.

"But I'll change that soon," he said. "I will."

He dressed and Marlene put on a robe and walked him to the door of the apartment.

"Promise me, Charlie," she said. "Say it."

"I'll marry you, Mar. I will. I'll leave Diane and marry you."

Her eyes were bright and she pressed against him one last time.

Why had he told her that? How could he face her after that if he didn't? How much longer could he hold her off? Just the thought of giving her up made him ache. But she said she'd stop seeing him if he didn't leave Diane. Oh, shit.

But then somehow he managed to stall her. Stall her for months. With gifts and promises and even a weekend in Big Sur, because he knew none of his or Diane's friends would go there. And Diane thought he was going to San Francisco on business.

And then Marlene died. Oh, God. And that fucking kid of hers looked at him as if he had killed her. Killed her. My God. He didn't even know she was pregnant. She never told him. Marlene. If Diane knew, even thought there was someone else, he'd lose her, too. She'd hate him. Wouldn't trust him again. Leave him. He promised her he'd never be with another woman. Swore it to her. Denounced all of his friends who cheated as dishonorable vermin, even on nights when he had just returned with the taste of Marlene still fresh in his mouth.

No, David Kane had to be out of the way. Even if he never told anyone about Charlie and Marlene, he served as too strong a reminder to Charlie of the hypocrisy of his affair with Marlene and the pain he'd suffered by losing her.

"Thanks, Greenie," Wolfson said into the phone to Harold. "I appreciate it. And I'll make it up to you."

Greenfield scoffed. "Charlie, it's nothing. *He's* nothing. What else is new?"

eighteen

Stan Rose stood in the lobby of the Santa Monica Civic auditorium, trying to be calm. It wasn't easy. This was the most exciting night of his whole life. Maybe he'd just walk outside one more time. He liked standing in front of the building in a feigned casual pose, and then looking slowly up at the big marquee that told the whole world his message. TONIGHT. THE ETOILES. A ROSE AND BARTON PRODUCTION. It was fabulous.

Kids, black ones, white ones, were standing in line waiting to get in. The tickets were sold out. Had been snapped up in just a few days. The kids loved the Etoiles. Four gorgeous black girls with a soft sexy singing style that made each single they cut an instant hit. First "Got to Have Ya, Baby," then "Give It to Me," and after that "I Got My Heart on My Sleeve." Songs with double-entendre messages that drove the teenagers wild.

Annie Jordan, the lead singer, was skinny and waiflike and she had huge sad eyes and everyone fell in love with her when she held her arms out, reaching for her imaginary lover, and begged.

> Oh, baby, give it to me
> How I need it
> Give it to me
> I need your love so bad.

Stan saw a few of the young girls enter the auditorium carrying autograph books in their hands. Later they would storm the backstage entrance waiting to catch one glimpse of Annie Jordan. "Oh, please, give us Annie. We just want to touch Annie. Please," they would cry.

"Uh . . . Mr. Rose?" Stan's thoughts were interrupted by Art Huff, general manager of the auditorium. Huff was tall and thin and seemed very nervous the day Stan had given him the deposit from Rose and Barton for the Etoiles concert. At first Stan thought the nervousness was because Huff felt tentative about doing business with a brand-new company, but now as he looked at him he thought this was probably the way Huff always was.

"Ahem, would you, uh . . . uh, mind coming backstage, there, uh, Mr. Rose?" he asked.

Stan noticed that Huff's nails were chewed down to the quick.

"Uh . . . there seems to be some trouble."

How could there be trouble already? The act was in the dressing room, the audience was filing in calmly, the show was sold out.

"Sure, Art," Stan said. "What is it?"

"It's that girl," he said. "Annie. She's acting real crazy. I could hear her from my office."

Stan followed Huff through the office of the building on the side of the auditorium and through the cold gray backstage area. Acting crazy? Annie Jordan was very quiet earlier this evening when she arrived with the other girls and their entourage. Family members, boy friends, bodyguards. Stan had hired a caterer to set up a buffet in one of the unused dressing rooms for the whole group, and the entourage fell on it hungrily as the group went to get dressed. It was an idea Stan got from going to the set of Barton's show. Rose and Barton could use the same caterers who did the *Give 'em the Hook* buffets, which always looked lavish and created a party atmosphere. Stan heard screams as he and Art Huff got closer to Annie Jordan's dressing room.

"You gonna ruin this act, bitch?" a woman yelled out angrily. "And where we gonna be? Nowhere. You hear me?"

"Nooooo. I ain't goin' on," an unearthly voice cried.

Stan knocked on the door. "I ain't!" They didn't hear the knock. Stan knocked again.

"Shhh," from inside.

"Who is it?"

"Stan Rose. The promoter." Stan looked at his watch. Jesus Christ. There was no opening act. These girls were it. The whole show. And they were supposed to be onstage at eight o'clock. And there was trouble. It was five minutes to eight. Stan could hear a lot of whispering going on behind the door, and people moving around. He knocked again.

"Just a second," a voice dripping with phony cheer answered.

Stan looked at Huff, who shrugged.

"I just came to get you because I heard the screaming and moaning and I figured, hell, I just make sure the place is tidy. I don't get into any . . . uh . . . personalities." Huff laughed a forced laugh and the door to the dressing room opened.

Arlene Warren stood in the doorway. After Annie, Arlene was the second most loved Etoile. She was full-figured and tall and much prettier than Annie. "Hi," she said, flashing perfect teeth.

"Anything wrong?" Stan asked.

"Oh, no," Arlene said. She moved away from the door and gestured for him to look at the room with the same flourish Betty Furness used to use to show refrigerators.

Everyone in the room—the other two Etoiles, whose names no one could ever remember, and Annie—stood stiffly composed and smiling. The others wore their bouffant wigs, but Annie held her wig in her hands. Her own hair was pulled tightly to her head in corn braids.

Stan looked at her carefully. The famous big eyes were even bigger.

"How do you feel, Annie?" he asked.

He remembered when he was at Hemisphere meeting the agents and managers of some of the big Hollywood stars. Stan always thought that agents had a strange profession. Business people who controlled the lives of creative people for a percentage of the creative people's salary. And then became dependent on the creative people's success for their own success, so the creative people's well-being became crucial to them. It always made Stan chuckle to hear an agent asking his highly paid client, "How do you feel, Cary?" "How do you feel, Elizabeth?" Not how are you, but how do you feel. Because implied, of course, was, If *you're* not well, neither am I.

And now *he* was doing it. His livelihood depended on that bony little black girl. His first concert could be a disaster if something was wrong with her.

"Hey. I'm okay," she said. "No kiddin'. I'm great." She was lying.

"Good," Stan said. "Show starts in about four minutes." He would have gone out to look for Walter until he saw the smile on Annie Jordan's face fall and she ran to him and grabbed him by the arms. She was panicky and shaking.

"Wait. I can't. I can't go out there. I'm scared. I can't. Tell the people to go away."

Stan put his hands on Annie Jordan's sticklike arms. Just by touching her he could feel her terror.

"Please. I can't," she begged. "I can't."

"Ahhh, shit," Arlene Warren said. "That crazy bitch's gonna put us right outta the business."

"Please, mister," Annie begged Stan, "don't make me go out there. You go and tell the kids I don't feel good. They'll understand."

Stan was weak. This must be a nightmare. Stanley Rose from Miami, Florida, and Annie Jordan, the star, standing in the open door of a dressing room at Santa Monica Civic, with her wailing for

God only knows what reason, and behind him the sounds of an
eagerly expectant audience. He could see the curious stagehands
buzzing around, wanting to know what was happening yet keeping
their distance. What in God's name could he do?

"Ooooh, please. I can't," Annie wailed again.

Stan saw someone moving toward them through the darkness of
backstage. It was Walter Barton. Barton had told Stan he'd be late
for the concert because he was shooting *Give 'em the Hook*. Thank
heaven he was here now.

"What's going on?" Barton said.

"Oooh," Annie moaned.

"Annie's not feeling well," Stan said. Now the tiny girl was hanging on to him for support. Barton would straighten it all out. That's
why there were senior partners. He would know just what to say to
get poor Annie feeling well and onstage. Stan glanced at his watch.
It was eight o'clock. He looked at Barton, who was looking at Annie.

"Okay, you nigger bitch," Barton said. "You get your pickaninny
ass onstage or you'll be back in the ghetto by midnight."

Stan felt Annie's hold on him stiffen.

"Walter . . ." Stan had to stop him.

"You hear me, little mamma?" Walter asked in some version of
jive talk he'd fallen into. "I'm gonna have your black ass in a fuckin'
sling if you doesn't go out dere right now. You won't want me to put
in da trade papers dat niggers is unreliable folks? Dat Annie Jordan
is poison to promote 'cause she's so doped out she can't do no
show?"

Stan was nauseated. This man was his partner. Representing his
brand-new company. The girl, in the meantime, hung on to Stan like
a cat in a tree.

"Walter. Hold it," Stan said.

"Shut up, kid," Barton snapped at him.

Stan blinked as though he'd been slapped. This was a man he'd
spent hours with. Talking about the business, excitedly planning the
future of their company together. And this was the man who was
paying him a salary, too. Who could take it all away right now.

Stan flashed on his last day in the mail room. Mickey, David and
Barry took him to DuPar's for a goodbye lunch.

"This is it, Jug," Mickey said to him. "You'll probably be a zil-
lionaire in the next five years." The mail room had been fun for Stan
but he was excited to leave, to move on to a position of importance
in the real world of the business. Now he wished he were back there.

He was afraid. If he spoke up, Barton could get angry and take it all away.

"You can't go on?" Barton said tauntingly to Annie. "Then how 'bout comin' to my place on Tuesdays and Thursdays and cleanin' up after white folk, which is what you should be doin' to begin with?"

"Walter," Stan said. This was too much. "I won't shut up. What you're saying makes me sick."

Stan looked down at Annie. She was wild-eyed. Before Barton could say another word, he moved her toward the dressing room. "Come inside, Annie," he said, and he walked the girl inside and slammed the door in Barton's angry face.

"Now," Stan said quietly to her. "What is it? Tell me what's bothering you? I mean besides that asshole," he said, gesturing to the door.

"Ah, she's so full of shit," one of the girls volunteered, but Stan stopped her with a look.

Annie looked like a child about to recite in class as she pulled herself together to explain. "Well," she said sadly, "me and my boy friend, we had this here fight. See? And he's got a new woman and he's not here tonight, so I can't go out there." The last few words were said in tears. "Because I feel so bad." She was crying now. The other three girls looked disgusted.

"Annie," Stan said. "You know what I think?" Christ, he thought to himself. What *do* I think? What could he tell her?

"I think you're a fabulous singer and a very big star, and that's something really remarkable that you've achieved all on your own at a very young age."

Annie looked down at the floor shyly. Stan knew he had to get her out on that stage. But he also knew he had to do it with the truth.

"And I think that those things make you a very worthwhile person," Stan went on, "who doesn't have to live or die or rise and fall based on how some boy friend is treating her. Do you understand what I'm saying?" He meant it. He really did and she knew it, and the sad downcast face looked at him and slowly brightened until she was grinning happily and she hugged him, laughing.

Stan was laughing, too. So were the Etoiles.

Then Annie stopped for a moment as if maybe she'd believed him too quickly and wasn't sure she should have and looked deep into Stan Rose's eyes.

"No shit?" she asked.

Stan smiled warmly at her. "No shit," he promised.

Annie Jordan walked to the mirror and carefully put on the bouffant wig she'd been clutching in her tiny hand. Then she nodded to the others. Arlene Warren opened the door and the four of them walked toward the stage. The lighting man saw them coming and dimmed the houselights, and a squeal went up from the crowd.

Barton stood in the wings next to a live microphone. He looked at the four girls as they touched hands and wished each other "good show," and then at Stan Rose, who was trying to peek around the curtain and count the people in the house. Then, with his best disc-jockey voice, Barton spoke into the microphone.

"Ladies and gentlemen," he said, "Rose and Barton Concerts is proud to bring you"—beat, beat, beat—"the fabulous Etoiles."

A multivoiced scream filled the air, the girls ran onto the stage and the first Rose and Barton concert had begun.

nineteen

It was eleven thirty in the morning and Mickey was bored. He had read *Variety* and the *Reporter,* done his morning mail run and reread *Variety* and the *Reporter*. Then he read the *L.A. Times* and went back and did the crossword puzzle in *Variety* when the mail room phone rang.

"Ashman?"

"Yeah?"

"Don Morgan."

Don Morgan was the head of personnel. He probably was all ready with a new kid to replace Stan Rose.

"Hey, Don."

"Can I see you in my office?"

"Yeah. Sure."

Mickey was glad to have any change of pace. Even a visit with the skinny and pimpled Don Morgan broke up the boredom of the day. As unattractive as he was, Morgan fancied himself a ladies' man and he loved to tell stories about his sexual conquests that Mickey was sure were lies. Mickey looked at the dilapidated bicycles lined up in the parking lot and decided to walk to Morgan's office. It was a beautiful day.

The lot was buzzing with tourists in groups being led on foot by uniformed guides. Mickey noticed that the anxious people in those groups always looked carefully at every passing face, hoping to spot a star who was on the way to lunch. More than once, as Mickey walked around the lot, someone from a tour group had stepped out and stopped him to ask, "Are you anybody?" That was a question it was getting harder for him to answer.

Don Morgan's office was in one of the small pink bungalows, or casitas, which used to house the producers' offices. In fact, Mickey noticed it was located in the building where casting used to be. The one where he'd come to see Tom Rich so long ago.

"Hi. Mickey Ashman to see Don Morgan."

Morgan opened his office door before the secretary could buzz him. He was grinning.

"Oh, Ashman, come in here," he said, pulling Mickey into his office by the arm. And closing the door.

"You wanna see pussy?" he asked. "I'll show you pussy, Ashman. Like pussy you've never seen."

"You been to Sweden, Morgan?" Mickey joked, knowing that before Don Morgan told him why he'd called him there he'd have to put up with some bullshit.

"Not *my* pussy, asshole. Her."

From his top desk drawer Morgan extracted a recent issue of a pulp magazine containing a photo of a girl lying on a bed spread-eagled.

"I fucked her last night," Morgan said.

"Yeah," Mickey said. "That girl in the magazine?"

"Yeah, Ashman," Don Morgan said. "And she said I was the best fuck she ever had."

"Great," Mickey said. "Where'd you meet her?" Why did he ask Morgan that? The lying bastard would keep him there forever now with some bullshit story.

"Through friends," Morgan said.

"Hmm. Great."

"She loves me, man," Morgan said, lowering his voice. "Begged me to come over again to fuck her tonight. But I can't. I'm too busy."

"Right. So what did you want?"

"I just wanted to fuck her once and forget her," Morgan said.

"I mean from me."

"Huh?"

"I mean how come you called me over here, Morgan?"

There was a silence while Don Morgan tried to remember the answer to the question.

"Oh, yeah," he said, remembering. "Fire Kane."

"Huh?"

"David Kane. You know, the red-haired kid?"

"Yeah," Mickey said. "I know what color his hair is. But what do you mean fire him, Morgan? Nobody ever gets fired from the mail room. People quit, move up, people die of boredom, but nobody gets fired. What's the problem?"

"He's too aggressive."

"What are you talking about?"

"He gets on people's nerves."

"How?"

"He's pushy, a pain in the ass, always looking to move out of the mail room, and people on the lot don't like it. Hey, I could maybe get her to put out for you," Don Morgan said, holding up the picture again.

"Morgan," Mickey said. What was this ugly sex-starved bastard trying to prove? "The purpose of the mail room is for young guys like Kane and the rest of us to learn about the business, and what's going on on this lot so we *can* move up and get other jobs. That's what he's doing here to begin with. You can't fire him for that."

"Don't tell me my job, Ashman. He's fired. I called you in here so you could tell him. You don't want to? Then I'll do it."

"No, I don't want to. And I don't want you to. Kane does his job just fine. This is wrong."

"Ashman, get out of my office. The son of a bitch is fired whether you like it or not."

"Whose decision was this, Morgan?" Mickey asked. Morgan was an underling. A low-on-the-totem pole nobody personnel guy who could never be responsible for firing somebody.

"Mine," Morgan snapped. "It was mine and I made it after hearing those things about him all over this lot, and I don't give a shit if you like it or not, Ashman. So get your ass back to the mail room and tell that hotshot Kane he's out, or maybe I'll just decide you're out too."

"You know what, Morgan?" Mickey said. "I don't believe you decided this at all."

"Get out," Morgan sneered.

"You bet I will." Mickey walked to the door. "And I also don't believe that any girl who looks like that would ever be in the same room with you, let alone allow you to fuck her." Mickey left Don Morgan's office and headed back to the mail room.

How the hell could he tell Kane, poor old motherless fatherless Kane, that now he didn't even have a job? How did it happen? Kane was so good-looking and so bright. He knew everything that was going on in the business, and he had that great aloof attitude that made people want to find out what he was thinking. He should be a regular big-time executive. Not getting fired.

He was already a killer. Shit. Every piece of tail on the lot drooled over him. Not just Allyn Grant, but every secretary, every waitress in the commissary, wanted his ass in bed. Maybe that was it. Maybe that jerk Morgan did decide to do it himself, 'cause he was afraid Kane was getting more pussy than he was. Maybe. Oh, Christ. Whatever it was, Mickey couldn't stand the thought of looking at Kane's face when he told him the news.

When he got back to the mail room, Barry was on his way to lunch. "Kane never made it in this morning," he said, "and he just called in. Says he's sick."

Mickey took a deep breath. He was relieved. At least he could wait a day.

twenty

David looked at the clock on the night table beside his bed. It was seven in the morning and he had looked at the clock nearly every five minutes all night long, waiting for the day to break. Maybe he had slept. He wasn't sure. If he had, it was just for a short while. He was afraid.

It was only a few days since the Greenfields' party. The first day, Monday, he'd stayed at home after calling in sick to the mail room. Feeling as if he could never go to the Hemisphere lot again. Knowing that he could never do what he'd threatened. On the morning of the second day he got into the Falcon and drove toward Hollywood, planning to get on the Hollywood Freeway to the Ventura Freeway to the studio. But once he was on the Ventura Freeway, he got nervous. So he kept driving, and within a half hour he was in Malibu Canyon heading toward the Coast Highway. By ten thirty he was walking on the beach in Santa Barbara. It was a weekday and the beach was deserted. There was something about the vastness of the ocean, as David looked out over it, that made him feel even more lonely than before.

Maybe he shoudn't have said those things to Charlie Wolfson. Maybe he should have just acted nice to Wolfson at the party, and called him the next day at the bank in a friendly way and asked him to call Greenfield. It was all that venom inside him that had been stored up since Marlene's death. Since before Marlene's death. Ahhh, fuck. Maybe since the day his father walked out, if he believed that Freudian shit. He was going to have to learn how to control those feelings. Otherwise he'd blow up again. Act on the threat he'd made. He drove home from Santa Barbara promising himself he'd go to work the next day, which was today. Wednesday. But now he was looking at the clock and he knew he couldn't go in to the studio anymore. Maybe he'd just not even go back. He'd get a job in sales somewhere. The mail room salary was rotten anyway.

The phone rang. No one called this early. Allyn? He hadn't spoken to her since he took her back to her apartment Sunday night. She'd been disappointed that he didn't come in, but he was shaking by the time they got into the Falcon outside the Greenfields', and she slid over next to him to kiss him.

"Have a good time?" she asked.

But all he could think about was Wolfson. And the conversation they had earlier, and the way even though Wolfson and his wife were at the same buffet table, and then eating dinner in another part of the same room David and Allyn were in, Wolfson never said another word to either of them all evening. Well, shit. Why should he? David had threatened to blackmail him. Blackmail. Oh, God.

The phone rang again.

"Hello."

"Kane?" It was Mickey Ashman.

"Yeah."

"Uh, how're you feeling?" Ashman asked.

"I'm okay," David said. Ashman was such a boring asshole. What did he want at seven in the morning?

"Hey, listen," Ashman said. "I need to talk to you. Can I come over? Or meet you for breakfast?" he asked.

What in the hell did Ashman want from him?

Breakfast. At the mention of it, David realized he hadn't eaten in two days.

"Yeah. DuPar's. About an hour," he said.

"See you there."

The bacon and eggs sat uneaten and cold on his plate and David was staring at Mickey Ashman.

"Look, Arch," Mickey said. "I think my guess is right. I think that putz Don Morgan is jealous of you and he doesn't want you around. Maybe if you stopped into his office and just—"

David shook his head. There was no point trying to explain to Ashman that Don Morgan was just doing his job and that the firing was really being done by a much higher power. Harold Greenfield. The highest-powered man at Hemisphere Studios. Maybe the highest-powered man in Hollywood. What had Wolfson told Greenfield? The truth? Never.

"I'm sorry," Mickey said, and David could see it in his eyes. Ashman *was* sorry. He'd never treated Ashman very well at all, and the dumb clown was sorry to see him go. What a schmuck.

In DuPar's parking lot, Mickey shook David's hand.

"I hope you get another job soon, Kane."

"Thanks, Ashman. Thanks a lot."

David got into the Falcon, and turned the key. The car didn't start. Even *that* wasn't working for him. What in the hell could he do now? Ashman said he'd try to get Don Morgan to give David a few weeks' pay, and there was always the Social Security check. He tried the car again. Nothing.

Wolfson. That killer had gotten him again. Shit. God damn it. Everyone. All of it. He had nothing. No one. His stomach hurt and he was sweating when he got out of the car and walked to the phone booth to call the auto club. Their road-service line rang twenty times before he got a recorded message. All our lines are busy now but . . .

When he finally got through, the woman at the road-service switchboard said it would be at least half an hour before the tow truck got there. David sighed, trying to pull himself together. He would have to get a job right away.

He dropped another dime in the phone and dialed.

"Hemisphere Studios."

"Jack Shear's office, please."

"Thank you."

"Jack Shear's office."

"Allyn?"

"Pardon me?"

"It's David."

"Are you calling Jack Shear?"

"No, I'm calling his secretary. Allyn Grant."

"Oh. Miss Grant no longer works for Mr. Shear," the woman said.

Fired. My God. It was a pogrom. Just to save Wolfson's ass. Greenfield fired him and now her. Even the relationship between her grandmother and Greenfield's mother couldn't save her.

"She works for Mr. Greenfield now."

"What? She's Greenfield's secretary?"

"No, sir," the voice said. "On Monday Mr. Greenfield made Miss Grant his assistant."

David hung up the phone slowly. Then he left the phone booth and got into the Falcon to wait.

twenty-one

Stan chose the new Rose and Barton offices his first day out. The building was two stories. On Ventura Boulevard in the Valley. Barton had given Stan a big enough budget to take an office in Hollywood, but Stan wanted to be frugal. To spend the money on the concerts. Showy offices were unimportant. The day the phone was hooked up he started making calls. Agents at William Morris who represented rock acts. Agents at GAC and at CMA. And Joe Rio in New York.

Joe Rio was the Howard Hughes of rock 'n' roll. Stan knew that just from reading the trades. And from stories Barton told him. Rio was the agent for six of the biggest rock 'n' roll acts in the business. And all the up-and-coming acts wanted him to represent them.

He was rich and eccentric and no one ever knew where to find him. He seldom arrived in his Manhattan office from his Chappaqua home before six in the evening. One rumor had it that he didn't want to be seen by anyone because he had a terrible weight problem and was self-conscious about his size. Another rumor was about his baldness. They said it took him all day to take that one very long hair that he'd grown, and string it around and around over the top of his head just right, to make it look as if he had more.

Stan Rose put in a call to Rio one day in August, shortly after the Beatles concert. The call wasn't returned until October. In fact before the actual call he got a call to tell him the call was coming.

"Rose and Barton Concerts."

"Mr. Rose?"

Shit. He was going to have to break down and get a secretary to answer the phone.

"Uh . . . yeah. This is Mr. Rose."

"This is Joe Rio's office."

Joe Rio's office. Joe Rio, the legerd, was calling him.

"Yeah?" Stan said nervously into the phone.

"Mr. Rio would like to speak to you."

"Great!" Stan thought.

"At six o'clock this evening, Los Angeles time," the voice went on. "Will you be in your office?"

"You bet," Stan said.

It was lunchtime but Stan wouldn't leave the office. What if Rio decided to call him earlier than six? Why had it taken Rio so long to call back? Stan went over and over in his mind the things he would say to Rio. Joe, I want to come to New York and meet you. I'd like to sit down with you and talk about the way Rose and Barton promotes a show and why you ought to work with us. I'll meet with you at your convenience. Shit, it was only one o'clock. Stan called a chicken place that delivered and asked them to bring some lunch. Thank God he had three telephone lines on a rotary so Rio could get through even if Stan was talking.

Stan made a call to see how ticket sales were going for Butterscotch, a folk-rock group, who were such hot album sellers, Stan and Walter agreed to try to promote them at the new twenty-thousand-seat Colossus, a giant amphitheater in downtown Los Angeles.

Then he called to set up a meeting with the manager of Clowns, a new group whose manager wanted Rose and Barton to use them as an opening act. Then he called to arrange for the catering company to bring a cake to the Butterscotch concert because the day of the concert was the lead guitarist's birthday. Then he called Barton on the set of *Give 'em the Hook* to remind him that the Butterscotch concert was next Monday night and to tell him he was waiting to hear from Joe Rio.

"No shit!" Barton said. He was genuinely pleased. "The weirdo is finally going to return your fucking call."

"I've got my whole speech planned," Stan said. "I'm going to ask him if I can come to New York and see him."

"You'd better wear the ruby slippers on the trip, pal. The man never sees anybody."

Stan didn't want to hear that. Rio had to see him.

"I'm telling you, Stanley. All he's doing is calling to find out what you wanted. Don't be surprised if it turns out just to be his secretary who calls," Barton said. "I'll be at home at about nine tonight. Let me know."

At nine that night Stan was on a plane to New York. He had struggled to keep busy all day. But when he ran out of calls to make he fell asleep on the sofa in his office. The phone rang exactly at six.

"Rose and Barton Concerts," Stan said, trying to sound awake.

"I like it that you answer your own phone."

"Uh . . . who is this?"

"It's Joe Rio, Stan."

Stan tried to hold in his excitement. Now he was awake. Joe Rio. Joe fucking Rio. Rio's voice was higher than Stan imagined it would be, and he sounded very mellow and soft-spoken. Not like Oz the great and terrible, the way Barton described it.

"How 'bout a meeting?" Rio said.

"Uh . . . great. Sure. A meeting," Stan replied. "Where?"

"Tomorrow. My house. Come in tonight. Check into a hotel. Take the ten-thirty train from Manhattan to Chappaqua tomorrow and I'll meet you at the platform. Later I'll take you back to the city."

It sounded like instructions from one spy to another. It was all Stan could do not to jump up and down and cheer. Joe Rio was going to see him.

The man in the vicuña coat stood alone on the Chappaqua platform so Stan figured it had to be Joe Rio. He couldn't look for a clue like the infamous piece of hair that wound around Rio's head, because the man was also wearing an alpine hat.

Several passengers got off the train at Chappaqua, but the man in the vicuña coat and alpine hat walked directly to Stan and offered his hand to shake.

"Joe Rio."

"Stan Rose."

Rio took Stan's arm as if Stan were a little boy and walked him down the steps to the street, where a limousine was waiting.

"I don't drive," Rio said as the two men got into the back of the car, and the driver set off through the woodsy Chappaqua roads. Rio's home looked like a farmhouse, and it had huge windows overlooking the dozens of acres which were his back yard.

Rio took Stan into a wood-paneled den where framed photographs of Rio and his rock groups covered the walls. A fire was already burning in the floor-to-ceiling brick fireplace, and a pot of hot tea had been mysteriously placed on a table in front of the fire.

Rio had said nothing to Stan all the way to the house from the train. Stan wasn't a fan of small talk himself, so he was comfortable with the silence. After Rio hung their coats up and sat down across the table from Stan for tea, he finally spoke. Again his voice was soft and his manner very gentle.

"I know a lot about you. I had to find out before I called you. About your father and your polio and your work at the television station in Florida. Also about your time in the mail room at Hemisphere Studios. People like you. They trust you and respect you and that's rare. I want to do business with you."

Stan was flabbergasted. He remembered the time in the commissary at Hemisphere when Harold Greenfield asked him a question about why he wasn't going to Florida for homecoming, and he had been surprised that Greenfield knew where he'd gone to school. But Greenfield owned Hemisphere and Stan worked at Hemisphere and had filled out countless forms his first week on the job. Forms that contained revealing information. So that was explainable. But this. For Joe Rio to know all of that about him, and to tell Stan he wanted to do business with him when his business was so new. This was too much. Too good.

"Why?" he blurted out.

"There's not a promoter I trust to make sure my acts get the kind of treatment they need. I think you're different. Tell me about Barton."

Stan had a funny feeling Rio already knew everything about Barton.

"He's a sweet man," Stan said. "Sometimes he has a bad temper. But he's bright and energetic and basically good-hearted."

Rio sipped his tea.

"Do you want cookies?" he asked. "I didn't put any out because I'm dieting." He was very round.

"No, thanks," Stan said. Rio didn't comment on Stan's description of Barton. In fact, it seemed as though he deliberately chose not to.

"How was your flight?" he asked instead.

The rest of the day was filled with the two men talking. They took a long walk on the grounds of Rio's estate, ate an elegant lunch, from which Mrs. Rio was absent because, as Rio explained, she was "detained in the city," and Rio told Stan stories about his youth.

"I was a tenor," Rio said. "A little chubby boy with a gorgeous voice. First I sang in church and everyone cried and filled the collection plate. And then I sang at my parents' parties when anybody asked me to. And people would give me a dollar here. A dollar there. Well, finally my dad, who was nobody's fool, realized he could turn me into an attraction. You know? An act. So he invested in a couple of little suits for me, with dress shirts, little ties and everything, and before I knew what was happening I was singing at other people's parties. For money. Ten dollars a night sometimes. My father was an alcoholic," Rio said, "and he was spending all of the money to buy himself booze, but I didn't know it. I was too young. What I *did* know was that I was working for the money and not getting it. So one day I asked him where it was and he said, 'You're going to get the money, Joey. But right now you're still paying me off for the suits.'"

Stan laughed and Rio laughed softly, too.

Stan thought about Rio's Wizard of Oz image. The man was gentle and vulnerable.

"I paid him off for the suits for ten years," Rio said, still smiling. "And then I was sixteen and I wanted to buy myself a car. I'd been working my tail off singing two or three parties a weekend and learning new music and I realized there was no money for me for a car or anything else. He had spent all of it."

Rio looked into the fire probably remembering what happened next, but he never told Stan what it was.

It had begun to rain outside and as Stan looked out the window he saw the limousine pull up in front of the house. Rio got to his feet. "I'll ride into Manhattan," he said, and got their coats. Stan looked at his watch. It was ten after five. If they left now, Rio would get to his Manhattan office at 6 P.M. That part of the legend was true.

The driver pulled up outside the Warwick, where Stan had checked in last night, and Stan thanked Rio for seeing him.

Rio patted Stan warmly on the back and looked at him for a long moment, even though the doorman at the Warwick was holding the car door open waiting for Stan to get out.

"I'll return your calls much more quickly than I did the last one," Rio said. There was no smile. But there was a twinkle in his eyes. Then his face changed. "Be wary of your partner," he said finally. Stan didn't know what to say and Rio nodded as if to tell him to get out of the car. He did.

He ran to his room to call Walter. When he got there the red message light on his phone was blinking and he called the message operator. Walter had called him. He returned the call right away. It was three o'clock in Los Angeles. Maybe Walter was at the studio. Stan couldn't wait to tell him everything. Everything but the last thing Rio said to him in the car. It seemed so strange. Walter was out. Stan called the airlines to make a reservation back. He'd go right away. There was so much to do. The Butterscotch concert was in three days.

The backstage area at the Colossus was enormous. There was an elaborate lighting booth near the stage and down a hallway were dozens of large mirrored dressing rooms with full baths and showers and well-lit dressing tables. The acts loved to work there. Butterscotch was scheduled to come over from the downtown Los Angeles Holiday Inn right after the opening act went on, and the opening act, Lita Collins, was in her dressing room vocalizing. It was very professional. By seven o'clock Stan had been all over the place. Meeting with the box office manager, talking to the caterer and looking over the spread of treats the group would indulge in after the show. Stan even sampled the popcorn at one of the concession stands in the lobby.

Walter was already there, too. Stan had seen him earlier wandering around the building. *Give 'em the Hook* was on a hiatus so he'd been in the office with Stan for the last three days, talking about the future, and talking about which of Rio's acts they should try to book while Rio was feeling so good about his visit with Stan. He also helped Stan field the dozens of phone calls that came in. Last-minute people hearing the show was sold out, asking for tickets and wanting backstage passes.

The crowd backstage seemed to get bigger at every concert. Each act's entourage, and soon the entourages had their entourages. Hangers-on and groupies. Groupies were unbelievable. Little girls. Really young. Wearing revealing sexy outfits and outrageous makeup and unabashedly puffing on joints and being generally brazen. They approached everyone. Not just the acts. "How 'bout a blow job, Mr. Rose?" Dinny asked him at every concert. Dinny had the body of a ten-year-old boy. For a long time Stan thought she *was* a ten-year-old boy, till she wore a dress and high heels to one of the shows.

"I can't, Dinny," Stan quipped. "I just gave away three and I don't have any left."

Everything was right on schedule. Stan decided to walk down to Lita Collins' dressing room, to see if Lita's people knew where the buffet room was. Stan started down the hallway. He thought it was the one on the end of the hall to the left. He knocked lightly. There was no answer. Maybe she was in the john. He knocked again. Nothing. Stan turned the knob and opened the door and stopped to stare in surprise.

Walter Barton stood, naked from the waist down to his ankles, where his trousers were bunched around his feet. And a girl Stan recognized as Honey, one of the groupies, was completely naked, on her knees sucking Barton's cock. The girl was obviously doing the trick that gave her her name. She had gobs of gooey honey all over her hands that she was spreading on Barton's cock and belly and thighs and then gobbling it off while she moaned. Barton was moaning, too.

The little girl was nubile and pink and her straight long blond hair tossed from side to side as she went at Barton's body hungrily. The strangest part of the whole scene was the way it was reflected in every mirror. Dozens of tiny blond Honeys. A chorus of them. Now she was rubbing the honey on her breasts and pulling Barton's hands down to feel the gooey little girl body. And all the Honeys in the mirror were doing that. And all the Bartons were saying, "Oh, yeah, doll. Suck me off good."

Stan knew he had to close the door. Yes, close the door. Why hadn't Barton locked the fucking door? But it was too late. Barton saw him. He opened his eyes just as Stan was about to close the door and saw him there. Watching him. Watching it all. Stan's heart was pounding. He was excited by the scene and afraid of what Barton would feel if he saw him. But Barton just smiled slightly and nodded to Stan as if to say, "Be with you in a minute," and the girl, Honey, kept on sucking and moaning. Stan closed the door and walked out to the backstage area.

"Hah, there, Rose." Stan jumped. It was Arthur D. Blake, the man who'd built the Colossus and was its owner. Blake was a multimillionaire from Texas who had financial interest in several athletic teams and thought there wasn't a "decent goddamn facility" in Los Angeles, so ten years before he'd hired a well-known architect to design "a place that's fit for my boys to play." And within a year the majestic Colossus was standing.

Blake was one of the first people Stan called to get the business underway. Blake met him for lunch at the Colossus Colonnade, a private membership dining club that was on the first floor of the Colossus. As Stan walked into the club with Blake, the maître d' and the waiters and the bartenders had all greeted Blake warmly.

"Hah, boys," he said to them with his Texas drawl. And in a flash a drink was in front of him, and a salad was being mixed for the two of them, and even though Stan had been thinking about eggs all that morning, he let the maître d' put the salad at his place and the ground pepper on the salad, and ate it without objecting. Blake was talking about his policy at the Colossus.

". . . and I like to help out you young guys. And you'll be helpin' me out. I think we have a lot to offer each other. But I'm telling you right here in this first meeting, I run a clean place here. I'm a God-fearin' man and I don't have any interests in no weirdos runnin' wild and rippin' my place apart. No, sir."

The ground pepper was stuck in Stan's throat and his eyes were watering. But Blake thought he was upset. "Now, now," he said, "I know *you're* not like that, Rose. But I do know from experience there's a lot of Looney Tunes people out there."

And now, there he was at the Butterscotch show. Arthur D. Blake. Wandering around backstage. And he could have been the one who opened the door and saw Barton getting sucked off by Honey. With honey. Oh, Jesus.

"Arthur," Stan said, extending his hand.

"All sold out, buddy," Blake said grinning. "All sold out," he repeated. Stan started moving toward the gate that led into the arena as he talked, knowing Blake would walk along with him and be farther from the dressing-room area.

"Yes. Yes. We're sold out." He was stalling, and over Blake's shoulder he saw Walter, fully clothed, walking toward them.

"And it's going to be a great show," Stan promised Blake. "Lita Collins is a doll, and the boys are terrific."

"Arthur!" Barton said warmly as he approached. Stan couldn't help but marvel at Walter's composed condition.

"Hello, Big Wally," Arthur said, slapping Walter on the back. "Ah remember when this fella here was Big Wally," Blake laughed, "with his sidekick Animal! Tell the truth. Was that you doin' the voice of Animal?" Blake asked.

Out of the corner of his eye Stan saw Honey coming down the hallway dressed in jeans and a sequined bandeau top. She stopped to talk to some of the other girls and never looked in the direction where Stan and Barton and Blake stood. Blake looked at his watch.

"Well, there's no business like show business," he said, "so I'm gonna go find me a seat out there and watch. See ya both later!" he said. And walked out into the house. Stan watched Blake go because he couldn't look at Barton, but Barton walked up next to him and stood looking after Blake.

"That son of a bitch Blake loves us, Stanley," Barton said. "You and me are gonna be real real big in the music business. Real real big."

twenty-two

Stan Rose was the one who suggested that David go to see Chuck Larson for a job. Stan called David the night he heard he was fired, which was after Mickey called the Rose and Barton office to tell Stan.

"I don't want to work for an agent," David said.

"But Larson's not like an agent, Arch," Stan said. "He's not short, he doesn't smoke cigars and I'll bet you anything he never said the words sweetie, chickie or baby in his life."

David smiled. He'd been sitting in the apartment that day after he put a new battery in the Falcon, trying to decide what to do. Rose was an okay guy. He didn't have to call like this to help him. And Rose was right. Chuck Larson was bigtime. He only had twelve clients and every one of them was a major star.

"I'm telling you, Arch. I've heard he's looking for help and it beats the hell out of being part of the crowd at William Morris, or GAC. You know?"

Chuck Larson *was* looking for help, but it wasn't the way David thought it would be. And when he told Larson yes, he'd take the job, he had a nagging feeling that it wouldn't work out. Maybe it was because as lowly a job as he thought mail boy was, in his mind secretary was lower. And that was the job Chuck Larson offered him. Secretary. Women and fags had that job.

Sure David could type. He'd learned in high school so he could do his term papers. And answering the phone was okay. But making the goddamned coffee in the morning. And serving coffee to people who came in to have meetings in Larson's Beverly Hills office. That was the fucking lowest.

Chuck Larson wore a three-piece suit and a tie every day to work. He was tall, with coal-black hair and gray-green eyes. And he looked as though he were a star himself rather than an agent for stars.

David liked being around Larson and watching him operate. He was amazed that no matter what happened Larson never raised his voice. The agent's tone was always even, despite the fact that the words he was saying were tough. David would hear Larson negotiating for an actor.

"Yes. He's available. Make an offer," he would say sweetly. Then he would listen. "Mmm. Mmm. Hmm." He jotted some numbers on a pad.

"Sorry," David heard him say sometimes, with a smile in his voice. "But I won't even address myself to that offer. Maybe you should think it over and call me some other time."

Larson was known for his soft style, the spectacular deals he made for his clients and, above all, the way he pampered the clients, all of whom had been with him for years. None of his stars ever arrived at an airport anywhere in the world without being picked up by a driver with a limousine. Not one of them could even have a cold without Larson personally delivering a gallon of chicken soup to them from Nate 'n' Al's deli. Frequently the soup was accompanied by a puppet or a doll or a battery-operated car, or a stack of books from Hunter's, or even a print of a not-yet-released film, which the poor sick client could watch in the privacy of his or her own projection room, so as not to spread the cold germs.

Larson's days were very full. He started early, having breakfast meetings with producers at the Polo Lounge, after which he made stops at the various studios to visit with clients who were working. Then he had lunch with clients who weren't. His afternoons were spent meeting with writers, discussing potential projects for his actors, and late in the day he came back to the office to return phone calls and set up meetings for the next few weeks.

David was required to stay in the office from eight thirty in the morning until seven thirty at night. He was allowed to leave from one o'clock to two o'clock to have lunch, and have the answering service take the phone calls, but there was no one for him to eat lunch with, so usually he had a sandwich sent up from a nearby coffee shop instead.

By the time he got out of work at night, he would have just enough energy left to do errands, like grocery shopping, or picking up his clothes at Holloway Cleaners, which he used because they stayed open late, have a thrown-together dinner and get into bed with a couple of scripts. He started reading scripts right after the conversation he had with Larson.

"Good properties, David, are what this whole business is based on," Larson said. "They're hard to find, but it's worth the search, because one good one can make even a so-so actor into a giant star. If you want to get ahead, you should read. Read. Everything you can get your hands on. You'll have to wade through a lot of mundane shit, but that's how you learn what the valuable material is, and how to assess it." Then Larson picked up the scripts that were on his desk, and David realized he had seen Larson take home a big pile of scripts every night. Maybe if *he* took home scripts, too, and read them, and then discussed them with Larson and proved that he was bright, Larson would think of him as more than a secretary. Move him up. There were always dozens of scripts coming in the mail. Literary agents sending scripts with the hopes of getting them to Larson's stars. Writers sending their own scripts to the star clients in care of Larson. Yes. He would read. Every one of them, and then maybe he could get Larson to make him his assistant. Call him his assistant. Assistant. In reality it was probably the same job as secretary. It just sounded better. More important.

Allyn Grant was an assistant. Harold Greenfield's assistant. Jesus Christ. David hadn't even been able to call her after he heard that. And after he let week after week go by without calling to tell her he no longer worked at Hemisphere, and she didn't call him, he figured she knew he'd been fired. Maybe even that he was a blackmailer. Or that once he nearly shot a man. She probably knew all of that and thought he was the lowest. So what? He didn't care about her. He just used her to get to Greenfield. Didn't he?

But she was soft in bed that night they had been together. And even with the bedroom in darkness, the light from the street came through the window and the sight of her beautiful body made him wish he could fuck her a hundred times. Be inside her, outside her, touching her, drinking her up. He remembered looking down at her pretty face sucking his cock, and the long thick black hair was spread on her naked back. He remembered touching her hair while she sucked him. Feeling hotter and harder. And feeling he would come as she took his hand and sucked his fingers and then his cock and then teased him more by stopping and starting again. She was so incredibly good at it.

David was getting hard remembering. Maybe he should try to see her tonight. Or on the weekend. No, he wouldn't call her. She was an assistant. He was only a secretary.

It was six thirty and the phones had stopped for the day. David was reading scripts in the office during his quiet times there as well as at home now, and when he finished the last page of a script called *Wild Ride,* his mind began to race. Rue. Yes. It was a perfect script for Rue McMillan. And David would tell Larson. Larson couldn't have read it himself yet because it just came in the mail this morning.

Rue McMillan was a superstar. He was a well-loved tough guy

whose films were box-office gold. He'd started out playing heavies on television cowboy shows, always too sinister to play the leading man. But when he was cast in a low-budget feature called *Bad Joe* where the leading role happened to be the role of a heavy, Rue emerged as a charismatic screen idol. And Chuck Larson represented him.

Larson would be back in the office any minute and David would run into his office waving the script of *Wild Ride*. No.

That wasn't the way to do it at all. He'd go over the script again. Carefully. And make notes. Then he'd type up the notes very neatly. He'd capsulize the story of the script so that Larson wouldn't even have to read it if he didn't want to. Then he'd describe the character that he thought Rue should play in detail. Then he'd give reasons why this would be a good part for Rue to do, for his image, etc., and then he'd give the script to Larson.

Larson came in to return calls and by seven thirty that night, as he was about to leave for the night, David handed him the three-page synopsis he'd just typed up about *Wild Ride*. Larson looked at it closely while David stood in front of his desk. It didn't take him long to read it and when he had, he looked up.

"Wild Ride," he said. "Sounds good. I'll read it."

And that was it. No assistantship. No "Great job, well-done, Kane." No "Wait until Rue sees this." Larson just took the script home and David never heard another word about it. Shit.

But he continued to read himself to sleep every night, and rush into the office and read some more, and type all of Larson's correspondence, and make sure Larson had a daily schedule of which client was where, doing what, and take all of the phone calls that came in.

"Chuck Larson's office."

"Is Mr. Larson in, please?"

"Who's calling?"

"This is Allyn Grant in Harold Greenfield's office."

David froze. He was positive she didn't know it was him. Yet.

"He's not here right now," he said nervously. Good Christ. Maybe she did know it was him. Maybe the word was out that he was a secretary. Maybe Ashman had seen her and told her.

"Allyn, this is David Kane."

There was a long silence.

"What?"

"It's David."

"David, my God. What are you doing there?"

She didn't know. Her surprise was real. Or if it wasn't, she was a good actress.

"You didn't expect me to stay in the mail room forever, did you?" he said, hoping he sounded jovial.

"Well, of course not," she said. "But I guess I thought you'd get a job at Hemisphere." She didn't know. "Oh, David, I've been wondering where you were. I'm really glad to hear your voice."

"Yeah," he said, trying to sound casual. "I'm having a great time over here working with Chuck." He deliberately said with instead of for. Maybe she wouldn't ask what his job was.

"What's your job?" she asked.

"Uh . . . I'm his assistant," he lied.

"Great!" she said. "And I'm Harold's. Isn't that marvelous?"

"Yeah. Marvelous," David said.

"The head honcho's out somewhere," David said, "anything I can handle?" Christ. If Larson heard him.

"I think Harold wants to talk to him about Doug Hart doing a cameo in a feature. It must be important or Harold would have had the producer call. Do you think Hart would do it?"

David had not only not met the young TV star Doug Hart in person, he'd never even taken a phone message for him, because Hart was constantly working and never in need of advice or encouragement from Larson.

"Could be," David said, "could be. Why don't I toss it out to Chuck and have him get back to you?"

"Great," she said.

David was already wondering how he'd explain to Larson why he had the information about what Greenfield wanted, when his job was merely to write down the names of the people who called. He hadn't figured it out yet when Larson burst in the door, very preoccupied.

"Who called?" he said as he walked straight into his office.

David nervously rattled off the list of names to him. Harold Greenfield's office was last. Larson usually left the door to his office open when he made his outgoing calls, but he got up and walked toward the door to the reception area and closed it.

David was worried. Larson would call and speak to Allyn Grant. He'd say my secretary told me you called, and she'd say, but I spoke to your assistant, David Kane, and David said he'd discuss the Doug Hart thing with you. And Larson would say, Why would I discuss anything with him? My secretary. Did he tell you he was my assistant? Yes, he did. And Larson would fire him.

No, that was crazy. Anyway, assistant and secretary. They were both the same. Larson couldn't be angry at him for something that small. But what if he was?

David watched the clock nervously. Larson was very precise. At 8 P.M. he left the office no matter what.

The door opened. Larson emerged.

"Night," he said to David and disappeared out the front door.

David sighed. Everything was okay.

A few weeks passed and David noticed an item in the trades that said Doug Hart was doing a cameo in a Hemisphere film. Greenfield and Larson had come to some kind of deal. And David still had his job. So the lie he told probably never even came up. That must have made him braver because after that he tried the word assistant out on a few more people. Once he even told someone he was Larson's "associate."

He was deeply involved in reading a new script that just came in the mail, when the front office door opened.

"All right, Chuck, you tough ten percent son of a bitch," the man in the doorway said, "come out fightin'!"

It was Rue McMillan. His big body filled the doorway.

"He's not here," David said.

Rue McMillan. Oh, man. David had seen plenty of stars on the Hemisphere lot. Even Frank Sinatra that day in the commissary. And all his life at friends' houses, or just shopping in Beverly Hills, he had seen celebrities. But there wasn't anybody like Rue McMillan. Now David knew where the expression "bigger than life" came from.

"Ahhhh," Rue said, disappointed. "Fuck him."

Rue had been drinking.

"I was gonna surprise him," Rue said. "'Cause I was down the street lookin' for a new car, and I thought seein' I was around, hell, I'd come up and visit the bastard. When's he due back?"

"Usually at six thirty."

Rue looked at his watch.

"It's three thirty. I'll wait."

He was a little tipsy, but still coherent. And smart. And very funny and he and David talked about everything. Television, women, films, sports. David couldn't believe it. Rue McMillan was actually sitting on the sofa across from him, telling him jokes, and swapping stories with him about boyhood, and David was calling him Rue, as if they were old friends. It was wonderful. It made David feel good about himself. Important. Rue McMillan liked him. He could tell. Now they were talking about movies.

"According to that deal I made with them," Rue said, talking about one of the studios, "I still owe them a picture. Maybe two pictures. I'll ask Chuck. If the son of a bitch ever gets here."

"I have one for you," David said. He did. *Wild Ride*. It had been a while since he'd read it, but he remembered very clearly thinking how perfect it was for Rue.

"What is it?" Rue asked.

"It's called *Wild Ride*. It's by some new young writer. I gave it to Chuck to read—but he never said anything to me about how he liked it."

Larson never told David how he liked anything. But David didn't say that. He was too high. Too caught up in the excitement of meeting Rue McMillan. Trying to find something that would create a bond between them.

"I'll look for it," he said, going into Larson's office.

One entire wall in Chuck Larson's office was nothing but bookshelves containing scripts that had already been read. Part of David's job was to make sure the scripts were shelved properly, so he knew just where *Wild Ride* would be.

"Here," he said, offering it to Rue. "You'll love it." Rue took the script, leafed through it, promised to read it that night, and the two men continued their conversation.

When seven o'clock rolled around and Larson wasn't back yet, Rue was getting restless.

"I better run, ol' boy," he said to David. "You tell Chuckie I was here, and I'll stop by another day, but I sure did enjoy meetin' you, my friend." He shook David's hand.

"Same here," David said, getting up. Rue McMillan had to be six foot five. "Hope to see you again."

David's head was still spinning a half hour later when Chuck Larson got back. He read Larson the list of calls, then casually told him that Rue McMillan stopped by to say hello.

Larson nodded and got on the phone.

The next day David had lots of correspondence to take care of. It was work he was supposed to be doing when McMillan was there the day before, and when he finished that, he started reading a pilot script someone had submitted for Carol Denning, a young television actress who was represented by the Larson office. David had just opened an envelope from Paramount when Larson came in. He was about to read Larson the list of calls when Larson said, "David, will you come into my office, please?"

David recognized the tone. He'd heard Larson use it many times. It was his sweet-killer voice.

It was the voice David heard him use when he was very angry but refused to show it. David got up and walked into the office.

"Sit down," Larson said. Larson was smiling. It was strange. David sat in the Eames chair across from Larson's desk. He was nervous.

"David," Larson began. "You're a very ambitious boy. Lean and hungry, as Shakespeare so aptly put it. And I respect your ambition, even though I'm aware that it sometimes causes you to stretch the truth by trying to better your position in the eyes of the people who telephone me."

Larson paused as if he were waiting for David to understand what he'd just said. David was silent.

"But that's not what I want to discuss. Why did you give Rue McMillan a script?"

"Because it was a great idea for him and I—"

"Listen to me, David," Larson said. He was still smiling. "As Rue's representative, I feel it's important for me to be the one who decides what's good for him and what isn't. So from now on, I'll do my job and you do yours. Okay?"

"Okay."

"Promise?"

"Promise."

This was ugly. It was all being said softly but it was ugly.

"I managed to convince Rue when I saw him today that the script you showed him called *Wild Ride* was no good, despite what you said."

David was getting angry.

"But it *was* good and I—"

"David," Larson said, "you're a very young man to already have enemies in this business. I hired you in spite of that. Don't make *me* your enemy, too."

Larson knew. He must have called Greenfield before he hired David and now he knew something. Whatever bad thing Greenfield said. And he knew about the lies, too. Assistant. Associate. David wanted to run out of the room.

"If you do as I say, Kane," Larson went on, "and you learn to behave, maybe someday you won't have to lie about your job. I'll make you my associate."

"I'm sorry, Chuck," David said, smiling humbly. "I'm sorry if I was out of line." He thanked Larson for showing him what he'd done wrong. But inside he was screaming. From his guts he was screaming.

Don't hold your breath, Larson, you shit-heel, because being your associate is not what I'm after. One of these days I'll be so fucking big I won't even know who you are.

twenty-three

"Would you care to purchase a cocktail, sir?"

"Huh?" Barry was on the seven o'clock PSA flight from Holly-wood-Burbank to Las Vegas. "No, thanks!"

The stewardess smiled at him. It was the man next to Barry she was asking.

"How 'bout a Coke for you, honey?" she said to Barry.

"Uh . . . sure," Barry answered, lowering his voice a little.

This was his third trip to Las Vegas in three weeks. The first time Shmidt sent him to service Gigi Boyd who billed herself as peppy, perky Gigi Boyd, and referred to herself as a girl singer even though she was at least fifty. In her act she not only sang in her own voice, she did impersonations of other women singers, ending one medley by doing her version of Peggy Lee, which sounded more to Barry like a bad James Cagney. Afterwards, when Barry went to her dressing room to introduce himself, which was the way World Records made sure the act knew that someone had been there, caring, Gigi was all alone. She smoked a cigarette in a long black cigarette holder and wore a chenille robe, and a blond wig. She had false black eyelashes that looked okay from the stage, but now, up close, they were bizarre.

"How's Henry, that old doll?" she asked.

An old doll was hardly the way Barry ever imagined anybody thinking of Henry Shmidt.

"Great," Barry said. "He's just fine, Gigi."

"I used to be in love with him," she said. "He's my type. Yeah. Henry is definitely my type."

"Yeah," Barry said. "Well . . . he's just fine."

Gigi put the remainder of her cigarette out in an ashtray that was on her dressing table and inserted another cigarette in the holder.

"I really liked your act," Barry said. God would forgive him for that lie. This was business.

"Yeah?" she said. "Well, you got good taste." She laughed at her own joke and lit her cigarette with a gold lighter. "I'm gonna record two of those new tunes. Tell Henry to set some studio time for me. I'm really ready to do another album."

"That's true," Barry said. "You really are." He was nodding a lot. He realized now he had been nodding since the minute he walked in the door. Probably because Shmidt's instructions were "Be positive. That's A&R's job. Get them to trust you. Get them to like you."

"Hey, listen," Gigi said, standing. "I got a great idea." She was much taller than Barry. "Why don't you come over to my place for a nightcap?" Barry didn't answer. He couldn't think fast enough. He hadn't planned to get her to like him *that* much.

"Well, I—"

"C'mon, cutie," she said. "You're my type, you know. You're definitely my type."

Barry smiled a very stiff smile. That was supposed to be flattering, what she just said.

"Gigi," he said, and the words raced through his head. Am I a fool without a mind or have I merely been too blind to realize. No. That wasn't what he wanted to say. "I have some people waiting for me or I would love to. I would. Honestly. Love to. You're really great. Really. I'll tell Henry you send your love." He was edging toward the door. "And we'll book some studio time. Right?" She looked disappointed. She was bad enough looking when she was smiling, but now with that scowl on her face. Ugly. Unequivocally ugly. " 'Bye."

Barry walked through the corridor, out into the empty showroom and through the casino holding his breath. He didn't even sigh with relief until the elevator door opened and he was safe inside and on his way to his room.

His second visit to Las Vegas was better. After Harley and Yona and Marty heard the story of the first trip, they decided they wanted to join him. Yona packed sandwiches that she brought along to eat on the plane.

"My woman has to have something on her person to eat at all times," Marty snickered as they headed for the gate.

"Eat *this,* you critical cocksucker!" she snapped at Marty, and she did a little bump for punctuation. "No offense, boys," she said to Barry and Harley. "Neither of *you* two is critical," and the four of them laughed. They laughed at everything that day. And they hadn't smoked a thing. There was just something about the whole Las Vegas scene that seemed outrageously funny to them. Yona and Marty's room in the hotel was wallpapered with bright red flocking, which opened a whole world of jokes for them.

"Hello, front desk," Marty said, picking up an imaginary phone. "My wife isn't happy with our flocking!"

"Well," he answered in a different voice, "maybe you should try a vibrator."

"Room service, room service," Yona said, picking up another imaginary phone. "Send me up some coffee."

"Yes, ma'am," she answered herself. "What room are you in?"

"The one with flocking," she said.

"Oh, lady," she answered, "in this hotel everyone's doing that!"

On that trip Barry was in Las Vegas to service the Barones. Three pudgy look-alike sisters who sang in close harmony, and whose career outside of Las Vegas included a yearly Christmas special on television. Before he left Los Angeles, Barry called the William Morris Agency and asked to have a table for four. The table was right down front.

When the Barone Sisters came on, Barry was afraid to look at Yona because he knew she would start to laugh and make him laugh, and the Barones were singing "May You Always," which was a very serious song. So he just looked at the stage. He watched the Barones dance and jiggle as they sang "La Bamba," and then from offstage someone threw them straw hats and canes and they did a medley about vaudeville, and then while the other two hummed "Tarantella" in the background, one of the sisters talked about what it was like to grow up in an Italian family, and then they all sang "That's Amore," and then one of the other sisters said, "We'd like to do a little change of pace for you now and sing our version of a tune we're sure you've heard on the radio," and they started singing Harley's song "The Rain Is Like My Tears." They were slaughtering it. In fact, they were already halfway through it by the time Barry realized what it was. And when he turned to look at Marty and Yona and Harley, the three of them were laughing so hard that Marty had his face down on the table and Yona had to get up and run out of the showroom.

Afterwards the four of them were in the casino.

"I have to go backstage," Barry said. What if they recognized him? What if they knew he was at the table where the woman ran out and the three guys were laughing so much their drinks were spilling. Yona was still giggling.

"Don't go," she said, "those three porkers are a waste of time."

"Yona," Barry said. "It's my job to go backstage. Remember?"

"Take Harley," Marty said. "Tell them who he is. They'll shit."

"Why don't you send Harley into their dressing room and have him pretend he's you?" Yona told him. "They won't know the difference."

They were all laughing again.

"This is my *job,*" Barry said, "not a practical joke." But he had to laugh.

"You chickenshit putz," Yona said. "Where's your balls?"

"C'mon," Harley said with the nerve he'd summoned to try something silly. "Let's try it."

"I'll walk you over there," Barry said to him.

Later, when they were sitting on the floor in Yona and Marty's room, passing a joint, Harley told them the story. The Barones would never know who it was who came to see them. He had said "Barry Golden, World Records" when he came into the dressing room and none of them looked up. They were sitting at three identical dressing tables in their identical bathrobes taking off their makeup, and close up, without the sequined dresses, they looked like Buddy Hackett, Lou Costello and Jackie Gleason.

"Whaddya say?" one of them asked. She might have glanced at his reflection briefly in her mirror.

"Great show, ladies," Harley said, trying to imitate people who said bullshit things like that to him all the time.

"Betchyerass," the one who looked like Lou Costello said.

"Nice choice of material," Harley said. Maybe that wasn't what you said to Vegas acts. But Barry told him to butter them up.

"Except for that one shit song," another Barone Sister muttered. Harley bit the inside of his cheek. He was afraid to ask.

"That rain number. It really sucks. And we're cutting it from the show."

"Good idea," Harley said, trying not to laugh.

"You know, they just don't write 'em like they used to," the Jackie Gleason sister mused.

"That's true," said Harley, and he practically ran back to the casino to meet the others. He was laughing so hard people were turning to look and see what was so funny.

"Let's go upstairs and order munchies," Yona said. They stayed up all night and at six thirty in the morning, when the sun was coming up and they were ripped, Yona and Marty and Barry did their version of the Barones doing their version of "The Rain Is Like My Tears," and didn't stop until the hotel manager called to tell them someone on their floor called him to complain that they were too loud.

This time Barry was doing the trip alone again. To see Jerry Wayne. A white-haired ballad singer who'd been around the business for what seemed like a million years. Most of Wayne's money was earned as a Vegas act, but there was a large group of middle-aged women across the country who were mad about his albums, so year after year World Records continued to record him. The flight was bumpy and Barry was nervous. He hated Las Vegas and these old-fart acts he had to bullshit with there. This wasn't his idea of what it should be like in A&R. He told Shmidt that on the first day. He wanted to bring what he was learning about rock 'n' roll to World Records. He knew what the figures were, and what it could do for the image of the company, but Shmidt didn't even try to understand that. Didn't want to talk about it. Several times Barry asked Shmidt to come to a club with him where new acts were playing.

"Nah, I got a poker game tonight," Shmidt told him. Or sometimes he'd just say, "Can't, Golden. I'm busy."

Maybe Barry should try to get a job at Rainbow. Oh, sure. Fat chance. He could say, "I want a job here. I've had lots of experience. I worked at World Records once for six weeks." Big deal. Of course, Harley could get him a job at Rainbow. Harley's album was coming out this month and everyone was predicting major stardom for him. Never. Barry would never even mention it to Harley.

Jerry Wayne had a beautiful voice. And the room was filled with middle-aged couples who shouted "Bravo!" after every song he sang. Barry sat alone at a small table in the back, and when Jerry Wayne sang "The Anniversary Waltz," Barry began to cry. He thought about his mother and how she used to sing that song to his father every year on their anniversary, and then make his father dance with her, waltz with her while she sang: " 'Oh how we danced on the night we were wed. . . .' "

Barry's father would be embarrassed and she would taunt him. "What are you? An alter kocker or something? This is romantic," she would say.

Mah, Barry thought. Mah. I want to come home.

Jerry Wayne's dressing room was very large and filled with people and the attitude was festive. Several of them talked to one another while others stood waiting in line to talk to Jerry Wayne. Barry spotted someone ahead of him in the line who looked kind of like himself. The fellow spotted him, too, and extended a hand past the people who were in line between them.

"Larry Levy. William Morris," he said.

"Barry Golden. World Records."

Barry flew back on the plane with Levy the next morning.

"I begged the Morris office to put me in rock 'n' roll," Larry Levy told Barry. "And you know what they said about servicing Jerry Wayne?" he asked. "It's an ugly job, but somebody has to do it."

Barry laughed.

He was really depressed.

When he got home from the airport he bumped into Harley on the stairs.

"Hey, man," Harley said. "Remember Danny Kyle, the drummer from Flight?"

Barry remembered.

"He called today. He's started a new group and asked me if I'd come and listen. Want to come along?" Barry nodded. Harley came back up to the apartment with him and waited while he unpacked.

"How was it?" Harley asked.

"The same," Barry said. "I had a rotten flight up. My room looked like a whorehouse, I had dinner alone. My table stunk. Wayne has a good voice but the act is boring. I went to meet him afterward in the dressing room and he looked right through me. Last night there was a drunk in the room next to mine throwing up and moaning till four in the morning. My plane back from Vegas was late leaving and then had to circle here for an hour because of fog."

"Jesus," Harley said, shaking his head. "Why don't you quit that fucking job?"

"What?" Barry said, grinning. "And leave show business?"

Harley laughed. It was a joke they used every time something bad happened.

"I'll drive," he said.

Harley had a new Mustang convertible, and even though it was kind of chilly, they put the top down and drove out to the Valley, where Danny Kyle's act was performing.

It was a high school auditorium and by the time they arrived, there were teenaged kids pouring in to fill the three or four hundred seats.

"I guess this is some kind of showcase," Harley said.

Barry wondered what these kids would do if they knew this slight timid boy he was with was Harley "The Rain Is Like My Tears" Ellis. Harley had only done a few personal appearances and was pretty anonymous.

There was no announcer. The first act was two brothers who dressed alike and tried to sound like Simon and Garfunkel. They sang three songs and received polite applause for each one.

The second act was a girl with long blond hair who played the piano and sang Beatles tunes. Harley's friend Danny Kyle's group was third. It took them a while to set up, and the kids were getting restless and talking loud. The lead guitarist did a quick sound check. "The group's called Heaven," Harley told Barry. "Dawson, the lead guitarist, writes the tunes."

Heaven's first song was well done. It was about how difficult it was to write gentle music in a world that was full of anger and killing. There were one or two places in the song where people in the audience yelled out "Yeah." And, at the end, the ovation was very enthusiastic.

"That's really good," Barry said.

Harley nodded in agreement.

The second song was called "Where Do I Belong?" about coming to Los Angeles from New York and how different the life-style is. Barry laughed out loud at some of the lyrics. The melody was great, too.

Heaven did two more numbers. They were as impressive as the first two. When the group finished playing, Harley nodded to Barry and they left the auditorium through a side door.

On the way home, Barry's mind was racing.

"How well do you know Kyle?" he asked Harley.

"We went to high school together."

"Does the group have a deal with any label?"

"Don't know."

"Find out. Okay?"

"Sure. You want to get Shmidt to sign them to World?"

"Why not?"

On Monday morning Harley called Danny Kyle. Kyle said, "No, man, we don't have a record deal. Why?"

"Just asking."

When Barry got to the office, he called Shmidt's office. The secretary said Shmidt was on another line.

"He'll call you right back."

Barry wanted to get Shmidt to listen to Heaven. They were really good. Maybe the best group Barry had ever heard. He would convince Shmidt to sign them and he'd be their A&R man. Then he'd get them a really hip independent producer and cut some of their tunes. They would be World Records' first venture into rock 'n' roll.

Barry waited two days before he called Shmidt's office a second time.

"Oh, yes, Mr. Golden. He's out of town."

"What?"

"He left on Monday right after lunch so he never had a chance to return your call that day. You see, he only came in on Monday morning to finish up a few things, then he and Mrs. Shmidt left for Hawaii."

"When will he be back?" Barry asked.

God damn it. He didn't want to wait. He wanted to bring the group in and have Shmidt hear them immediately. Before someone else grabbed them. They were a great find. Why couldn't Shmidt have taken five minutes out on Monday and called him back? Maybe he could have given Barry some kind of authority to take a preliminary step toward getting the group to sign with World. Shit.

"They're going on to Hong Kong, Mr. Golden," the secretary said. "It'll be about two weeks."

"Thanks." Barry slammed down the phone impatiently, and looked around the tiny cubicle that was his office. It wasn't very far from the mail room—just two flights up in the gold building. And it was painted the same dull gray as the mail room. The mail room. He was beginning to wish he'd stayed there. Or at Eldor. Fuck. He'd go over to the commissary and get some breakfast. He'd sit at the counter alone and read the trades, and then maybe he'd feel better.

The Hemisphere lot always made Barry think of the college campuses he'd seen in old musicals. People walking by in groups, chatting, waving at one another, sitting at lunch with a whole gang, laughing. He stopped to buy a copy of *Variety* from the old blind man who sold papers just outside the commissary door, and then walked inside.

"Hi, Barry," a voice said.

It was Allyn Grant. She was standing with a few executives from the gold building. One of the men was Harold Greenfield.

"Hi, Allyn," Barry said. She was Greenfield's assistant now. How in the hell did a woman ever get that job?

"How's it going?" she asked. She didn't leave the circle of people she was with to come over to talk to Barry, but she nodded as though she wanted him to come over to where her group was standing. He did. Greenfield was deep in conversation.

"It's okay, I guess," Barry said to Allyn. What was the answer to a question like that? Did people expect you to tell them the truth? That the president of the record company owned by Hemisphere Studios had no clue about what was happening in the music business, and working there was a fucking bore?

The men Greenfield was talking to were saying goodbye. "We'll close it up next week, boys," Barry heard Greenfield say to the men. The men seemed pleased. All of them were smiling as they left the commissary. Greenfield turned to where Allyn and Barry stood. He was smiling, too.

"I'll leave for New York next Thursday to handle that. Hello, Golden!"

"Hello, Mr. Greenfield," Barry said.

"Want to join us for lunch?" he asked.

"Sure," Barry said. What a surprise. Barry couldn't believe it. He thought of all the times he'd watched Harold Greenfield walking through the commissary toward the booth in the back, with heads of other studios, or big movie stars, or some famous director. And now Barry was walking along behind him. Well, actually behind Allyn Grant, who was behind Greenfield, on their way to that very booth.

A commissary waitress appeared instantly. "What can I get you today, Mr. Greenfield?" Barry recognized her as the same waitress who had spilled Green Goddess dressing on his jacket once last year. The jacket had been next to him on the seat. When he pointed the spilled dressing out to her she said, "Oh, yeah. Sorry, hon."

Today she didn't even look at him until she took his order, and then she called him sir. He was sure she didn't put him together with the Green Goddess dressing incident.

"Seen any of your old mail room pals?" Allyn asked him.

"No," Barry said. He hadn't. He knew she was asking about David Kane and he wished he had a more interesting answer. Even if it was just so Greenfield wouldn't think he was dull.

"How are things at World Records?" Greenfield asked. The waitress was already serving Greenfield his soup. "Is Henry Shmidt treating you all right, Golden?"

"Uh . . . yeah," Barry said. "Mr. Shmidt's an okay guy." Barry looked up and took in the view across the commissary from Harold Greenfield's booth. It was a remarkable vantage point. Barry noticed now that the booth was slightly elevated, built on a platform maybe, and from it there was a clear line of sight to every other booth in the room. At the far end of the commissary was the booth he'd sat in with Stan and David and Mickey. The mail room seemed like ages ago for Barry. My God. He was having lunch with Harold Greenfield.

"Then you're happy there?" Greenfield asked. Barry looked at

Greenfield's face. The expression on it reminded him of the one his mother used to have when she asked him a question to which she already knew the answer.

"No, sir," he said. "I'm not."

Greenfield just nodded.

"After lunch you'll come to my office and we'll talk about it."

Barry ordered a salad, but he barely touched it. Allyn said she'd been to the Butterscotch concert and stopped backstage afterward to see Stan Rose and he'd been glowing with success. When the three of them finished, the waitress gave Greenfield a pen and he signed the check. When they walked back through the commissary, Barry felt everyone's eyes on them. And even though he knew Shmidt was out of town, he was sure when the old doll, as Gigi Boyd called him, got back to town, one of the other A&R men would tell him Barry had been with Greenfield at lunch.

Greenfield's office was cool and all of the furniture was antique and beautiful. Allyn made coffee and the three of them sat at a table by a window overlooking the lot.

Barry was nervous. Why did Greenfield care about his opinion? Maybe he needed to have some goods on Shmidt in order to fire him. No. That wasn't right. Harold Greenfield could fire anyone he wanted to.

"I wanted an assessment of the situation at World from the inside," Greenfield said. "I can talk to my business people until I'm blue in the face. And to Shmidt. But I'm curious to know what you think."

Barry took a deep breath. What the hell. He'd say it all. The worst thing that could happen is that Shmidt would come to his house in a storm trooper's uniform and goose-step all over his face.

"Here's what I think," Barry began, and then he said everything he'd been thinking for weeks. About how the music business was totally changed, and how World Records had to keep up or not make it, and how rock music wasn't just a trend but a total change of style. He told Greenfield about the new groups he'd heard, specifically Heaven, who didn't have a record deal yet, and how he'd met them through Harley Ellis, who was his friend. And how he'd been to Harley's recording sessions and watched Jim Garland work. And Greenfield listened carefully and finally asked:

"Can we hear them tonight?"

"Heaven?"

"Yes."

"Maybe. I'll get Danny Kyle's number."

"I'll call down and get us a room on the lot," Allyn said.

The room was a rehearsal hall that was next to stage 4.

Barry brought Harley and Marty and Yona. Allyn Grant came with Harold Greenfield and his wife, Julia. Danny Kyle was a little nervous and he and the other guys brought their women with them. There were two sound men.

Barry had gone home right after his afternoon meeting with Greenfield to tell Harley the news and to change for the audition. All the way back to the studio in the Mustang, Harley tried to reassure him that everything would be fine.

"Jesus, Harley. My ass is on the line. I've gone over Shmidt's head to the biggest person at Hemisphere," Barry said. "If this doesn't work out, Greenfield will think I'm a putz. If it does, Shmidt will have me killed."

Harley laughed.

"Easy for you to laugh," Barry said. But he was laughing, too. He couldn't believe this whole turn of events.

"You heard the group," Harley told him. "You know they're great."

"What do *I* know?" Barry said.

"A lot, man. I swear to God. You know a lot," Harley promised.

Now Dawson was tuning his guitar, and they would begin any second. Everyone sat in folding chairs watching the boys expectantly. Everyone but Barry. He stood in the back of the room leaning against the wall. He wanted desperately to look calm. But his stomach hurt, and he was a little queasy. Why the fuck didn't they start already? Dawson strummed a chord. Thank God. Harley's advice to the group had been not to talk. Just to play. Of course that was Harley's style because he was always too shy to talk, but it seemed to be a good idea.

They opened with "Where Do I Belong?" and Barry was sorry he was standing in the back, because he wanted to see Greenfield's face. The music was as good as he had remembered it, and his stomach was starting to feel better. Dawson was charming. He had a sweet voice. The tunes were good.

Barry could see the back of Harley's head. It was nodding to the rhythm of the song. He loved Harley so much. He never knew he could feel as peaceful with another person as he did with Harley. In fact, when he thought back on his life he didn't ever remember there being any peaceful moments like there were now. Always it had been his mother complaining, or his father worrying, and later there was Mashe's bullying.

At the end of "Where Do I Belong?" the enthusiastic applause from the small group echoed through the big room. Now the group began another song. One Barry hadn't heard. Very up-tempo, and Barry started to worry again that Greenfield wouldn't like it, but when he looked at everyone, they were all moving to the beat, including Greenfield. And then someone, it must have been one of the girl friends of the group, started clapping out the rhythm, and then everyone else joined in. Greenfield and his wife, and Allyn Grant. Dawson was grinning while he sang. He knew his songs were a hit. Barry grinned, too.

After the third song, before the group could begin again, Greenfield stood. A second later, Mrs. Greenfield stood and then Allyn Grant.

"Boys," Greenfield said to the band. "Be in my office on Friday morning."

Barry and Harley stopped to pick up four large pizzas and a bunch of six-packs and everyone in the group met them back at Barry's apartment.

"Hey, listen," Kyle said. "We gotta do some serious thinking between now and Friday about what we're gonna ask for if we make this deal. You know?"

"It's simple," Barry said. "I'll tell you what you ask for. To begin with, you want a twenty-five-thousand-dollar advance. Then you want the right to do two albums a year for five years. You want promotion money for a tour, say twenty-five thousand, and ten thousand for instruments. You also ask for ten percent of retail for royalties."

"Is that what Harley gets at Rainbow?" Dawson asked.

"It's better than Harley gets."

Harley laughed.

"Think World will give us that? Shit, we don't even have a goddamned agent."

There was a long silence. Barry picked a cold mushroom from a leftover piece of pizza and put it in his mouth. He looked at Harley, who was looking at him.

"Let's talk about that," Barry said.

* * *

The next morning Barry sat in his gray cubicle thinking about how he would handle the situation. Several times he reached for the phone and then stopped himself. Fuck. He'd sit here all day if he didn't do it now.

"Harold Greenfield's office."

"Allyn?"

"No. Did you wish to speak to Miss Grant?"

Jesus. She doesn't even have to answer the phone.

"No," he said bravely. "I wish to speak to Mr. Greenfield."

"Who's calling, please?"

"Barry Golden."

She clicked off for a moment. Then back on.

"Mr. Golden? Mr. Greenfield asked that you come up here. Is that all right?"

"Yes," Barry said, and hung up the phone.

The secretary ushered him right in to Greenfield's office. Allyn was already there. Fresh. Pretty. Bearing coffee. Barry's stomach was hurting again.

"Golden," Greenfield said, gesturing to Barry to sit. "You beat me to the punch. I was just calling you when you called."

Yeah. Yeah. Sure.

"I liked the group, Golden. It was nice to meet them, and to meet your friend Ellis. I'd like to sign Heaven. Actually, I'd like you to sign them. And then we can talk about what position you'd like to hold at World Records. Oh, and don't worry about Henry Shmidt. I'll take care of that, and make sure he doesn't get upset by all this."

"Harold," Barry said. Jesus Christ. He called him Harold. "I'm leaving World Records. That's what I called to tell you."

Greenfield was silent, waiting to hear the rest.

"I'm a manager now. I represent Harley Ellis and I also represent Heaven."

A smile played on Harold Greenfield's lips. Then he laughed out loud. The laugh was sincere.

"Well, isn't that nice," he said. "Isn't that nice."

Allyn stood and shook Barry's hand.

"That's wonderful for you, Barry," she said. "Congratulations."

"Well, then," Greenfield said. "Well, then. I guess I'll be making my record deal for the group with you."

"I guess so," Barry said. "Provided you're willing to come up with what we want."

Greenfield smiled again and shook his head.

"You're on your way, Golden. Yes, you are. I think you're on your way to being very important in this town."

twenty-four

Mickey lifted the large canvas bag containing the morning mail, slung it over his shoulder and left the post office. He knew he could have sent one of the new boys over to make the pickup, but there was something he liked about this trip back and forth. Maybe it was that he needed to get away from the new boys. Just their presence, their young smug attitudes, made him uncomfortable.

One of them, Josh Crane, looked as if he were twelve years old. And he had a master's degree in cinema from U.S.C. One of the others, Burt Dubin, looked as if he'd just stepped out off the pages of *Gentlemen's Quarterly*. Pedaling around on a two-wheeler wearing those dress pants. Mickey told him he was crazy to wear good stuff like that to work, and the kid, Burt, only laughed. The worst of it was that even when Dubin ran the mail to transportation and places far across the lot, he'd come back and his dress pants wouldn't have one wrinkle. Little bastard.

And the third guy. Peter Daimler. He was like a Nazi, for Christ's sake. Real efficient. Always calling Mickey on mistakes, or bugging him about sitting around reading the trades. Maybe Daimler would get a job soon and get out of Mickey's hair.

A job. Mickey needed a fucking job. Here he was. Still running the mail. He had been in the mail room before Kane, and Golden and Rose. With Ned Carr, and Andy Solari. And now all those guys were gone. Of course, none of them were actors, and it was harder for an actor to get a break. Too many factors had to fall into place. The way a guy looked, experience, the right part. That's why it was taking him so long to get out of the mail room. Well, maybe it wasn't so bad. Most actors had a hard time finding jobs outside the acting profession to support themselves during the lean times. And this job not only paid his rent but allowed him to be where the action was in the industry. And it wasn't a hard job, like digging ditches or anything. It was pretty easy. Especially after all these years because he really had it down. It was serving his purpose because eventually someone would notice him and give him a few lines in something and then, look out. Shit, he'd had dinner at Jackie Levitz's house last week, and Levitz promised Mickey the workshop was going to put on a showcase production for agents within the next year.

"That'll do it for you, kid," Levitz promised. "That'll be the night that puts you on the map."

The three new boys were waiting when Mickey got back.

"Hey, Mick. Don Morgan called you," Josh Crane said.

"Okay."

While the three boys set on the large canvas bag to sort, Mickey dialed Don Morgan's office.

"Don Morgan's office."

"Mickey Ashman here."

"Oh, yes, Mr. Ashman. He'd like to see you in his office at ten."

"Yeah." Mickey hung up. What did Morgan want now? Maybe to tell him to fire Daimler. Mickey took a handful of mail and began sorting. He was very fast at it because he knew where each of the boxes was by memory.

"Look at that," Burt Dubin said, emitting a whistle at Mickey's style.

Mickey took another handful of letters. He loved having an audience. Now he would back up and spin letters into their boxes from a distance. Then he would send two at a time off in different directions. The three boys were loving the show. When he finished the third handful, Mickey bowed.

"Unreal!" Josh Crane exclaimed.

"Obviously the result of many years of practice," Peter Daimler said with a slight smile.

Mickey pulled a copy of *Variety* out of the mailbag and sat down at the table to read while the others finished sorting.

Don Morgan had a new secretary about once every three months. Stan Rose noticed that a long time ago and called it to the attention of the others. Mickey imagined it was probably because the ugly son of a bitch Morgan was always trying to grab the secretaries and they'd beg to be transferred somewhere else. The new girl was very ugly, which Mickey figured meant she'd have longevity. Either because Don Morgan wouldn't touch her or because if he did she'd be thrilled. She told Mickey to go right in. Don Morgan was on the phone. He motioned Mickey to sit down.

"Don't worry about me, baby," Don Morgan was saying into the phone. He winked at Mickey and made a gesture as if he was jerking off. The thought of Don Morgan jerking off turned Mickey's stomach.

"I'll be there. In a few hours I'll be there to lick your sweet thighs," Don Morgan laughed.

Mickey tried to look as though he hadn't heard that.

" 'Bye," Don Morgan said into the phone and hung up.

Mickey braced himself for one of Don Morgan's graphic descriptions of the girl last night, or the girl on the phone, but Don Morgan's expression had already changed since hanging up the phone. He looked very serious.

"Ashman," he said. "I called you here to tell you that you're no longer head of the mail room."

A promotion. Somehow he was getting a promotion. How great. And he hadn't even kissed anybody's ass to get it. Where could they be sending him? he wondered. Maybe casting. An assistant in the casting department. That would be great. He could see all the scripts and submit himself for the good parts.

"Okay," Mickey said.

"From now on the head of the mail room is going to be Hal Bradford," Don Morgan said, and then he turned his chair and opened his desk drawer. Mickey waited for him to go on. Instead he pulled out an eight-by-ten glossy photograph of a naked girl with very big breasts who was sitting on the hood of a car smiling.

"Actress," he said, "loves me. The girl on the phone. Gives blow jobs like you can't believe. Swallows, too."

Mickey was annoyed.

"Morgan, where am I going?"

"Huh?"

"Where are they sending me?"

"Who?"

"The studio, Morgan," Mickey said. "If I'm not the head of the mail room anymore. What am I?"

"I don't know," Morgan said. "I guess you're in the mail room again. Like the old days."

"What?"

"Ashman, give me a break," Don Morgan said. "This one was forced on me. I'd much rather see you keep the job. I like you, Ashman, you know I don't give a shit about hiring some nigger. But they have to. Hemisphere has to. Otherwise there'll be spooks all over the place picketing. You know what I mean?"

Mickey was on his feet now.

"You're saying they're giving some black guy my job?"

"Sorry, pal."

"But I can't go back to just being one of the boys. What do I do?"

Don Morgan snapped. "Maybe you could get a job in operations or scheduling," he said. "That would be okay."

"What?" Guys in operations and scheduling were little machine-like boring men, and most of them had been in those jobs for fifteen or twenty years. It was a dead end.

"I don't want that."

Don Morgan was silent. He had nothing more to offer.

"I quit, Morgan," Mickey heard himself say. Maybe now Morgan would come up with something.

"I think it's for the best," Don Morgan said. Mickey turned and walked out of Don Morgan's office.

He didn't want to stop by the mail room. He couldn't bear to tell the new boys and watch Peter Daimler smirk. He hadn't left any of his things there. He'd go straight home. He'd call Jackie Levitz and start hustling some business. Some real business. Acting jobs.

This wasn't bad news. It was good news. A blessing. Now he would have his days free to spend time looking for jobs as an actor. His true profession. No more of this deliver-the-mail-to-people-who-treat-you-like-shit kind of life. Yes. Now he would use all of his energy, and God knows he had a lot of that, to get this goddamned acting career off the ground. And when he made it, every one of them would kiss his adorable ass. Mickey Ashman the star. Ha. That was what he wanted more than anything and he was going to make it happen.

twenty-five

"There's a certain kind of chemistry that occurs between two people almost immediately upon meeting that can't be denied or reversed. It's knowing instantly that another human being has the ability to make you crazy if they want to, or happy if they choose to, because your need to be with them is so great it gives them a kind of power."

Allyn Grant wrote those words on a piece of yellow legal pad that was sitting on her desk. Then she scratched out the word "it" where she'd written "it gives them a kind of power" and replaced it with the word "you" so it read "you give them a kind of power." Yes. That's what she'd done. She'd given David Kane the power to decide what would happen next with them. The night after Greenfield's party she wanted David to come into her apartment to make love to her the way he had the night before, fiercely, demanding. Moving her body down on his, gently but with some force, telling her to suck him, to take his cock in her mouth and . . . Damn him. She'd loved it with him so much, needed it all so badly. And now he was gone. He'd left the studio without a word and she had been so caught up in her move to Greenfield's office, and the dizzying possibilities the change could mean to her future, that for days she barely even thought about David. Bullshit. She thought about him constantly. "There's a certain kind of chemistry that happens between two people." God. Why was she doing this to herself? Indulging herself in the memory of that night, as if she were some hag of a spinster who was reliving her one and only sexual experience.

Every day she had made sure to be around for the mail room delivery and pickup. But it was always Mickey Ashman who was on her route, dancing in, singing songs from Broadway musicals in full voice, being so pitiful about needing to be noticed. Pitiful? *She* was the one who was pitiful. She was afraid to ask Mickey about David. Then finally, fate is so damned strange, to have to call Chuck Larson about some drippy actor and have David answer the phone. She tried to sound cool that day but she literally had to catch her breath when he said, "Allyn, this is David Kane." So casually.

Oh? Is that all? Just David Kane, the person she'd been obsessing about for weeks. There on the phone. But it was all business, that phone call. Not even the usual Hollywood bullshit of "Let's have a drink sometime." He was Chuck Larson's assistant. Larson was a good agent. Harold respected him. He had a sensational client list. David was probably meeting actress after gorgeous actress and didn't even think about her anymore. She tore the pieces of paper she'd been writing on from the legal pad, crumpled it and threw it in the wastebasket. She hated herself for getting so goon-faced about men. That's why she'd left Pittsburgh. To get away from the pain of a man who didn't want her anymore. Now she was eating her heart out over another man who didn't want her. Incredible. In her high school yearbook next to the picture of herself that she hated because she wore her hair teased at the top with the back in a ponytail, it said in italics "She walks in beauty."

Allyn laughed to herself. That was a great way to gauge her success, by what it said in her high school yearbook.

The phone rang. The secretary was out.

"Harold Greenfield's office," Allyn said.

A little tiny voice spoke. "Is Mr. Greenfield in?"

At first Allyn thought it was a child. Then she remembered.

"He's at a meeting outside the office. This is Allyn Grant, his assistant. Can I help you?" It was Tomiko. One of the secretaries who worked for Harold for years told Allyn the story about Tomiko just last week. Greenfield had a Japanese mistress. Had been keeping her for years. Allyn tried to take it as a matter-of-fact piece of news but she was genuinely surprised, and almost hurt for Julia, whom she adored.

"When do you expect him, please?" the voice asked.

"At about four."

"Thank you." Click.

God, Greenfield was strange. First she'd heard that he never hired an assistant. That his life was very private and he didn't want anyone to get that close. There was even a joke on the lot about how Greenfield never fired his secretaries. That instead he locked them in a room somewhere in the gold building and left them there until they died because they knew too much. But out of nowhere, the Monday after the party, late in the day he called Allyn into his office and told her to report to him on Tuesday instead of to Shear. Allyn immediately felt guilty about Vi, Greenfield's faithful secretary of twenty years, but Greenfield assured her he fully intended to keep Vi.

"You're a good schmoozer, Allyn," he said. "Good with people. That's what I need. A pretty, bright woman who shoots a mean game of pool, charms everyone in the room at a glance, and remembers what goes on at my meetings because I'm too rich to care," he laughed. She laughed.

"Have any eyes for a big executive job someday?" he asked.

"I don't know," Allyn said. She wished immediately her answer had been more Barbara Stanwyckish, more sophisticated woman. "I mean, it never really occurred to me. But maybe."

"Reva Barkin was a secretary here, you know," he said. Reva Barkin was one of the few women television producers. She had an office on the lot and was developing dramatic television shows. "She used to be Al Dietrich's secretary."

"I know," Allyn said.

"She was very aggressive. Wrote speculative scripts for every god-damned show on television till Rudy Daitch bought one from her. Then she wrote a pilot, and little by little she worked her way up."

Allyn looked down at her foot. She had a run starting on the ankle of her pantyhose. Not exactly executive material looking like this, she thought.

"Well—if you ever decide to go that kind of route," Harold said, "I'll certainly help out."

Why had he picked her? Why not one of the mail room boys? David. Why not David? David.

It was amazing. That moment. That wonderful moment of that powerful man offering her compliments and support was eclipsed by her thoughts of David. Did men live like this? Probably not. They weren't taught to believe that love was first. That being loved by a lover was more important than a job, a career, friends, anything.

She had to see David. This was foolish and teenaged and Pitts-burghish. She had to stop waiting and giving him the power to decide whether or not they would have a relationship. She would take a long lunch and drive over to Beverly Hills. She'd pretend she'd been shop-ping at Saks, and just casually drop by. She looked good today too, so the timing was perfect.

"Vi, I have errands in the city," she said, breezing past the recep-tion area.

Beverly Hills was bustling and as Allyn pulled her car into the parking lot on Camden she felt anxious. What if David had left for lunch already? What if he was just coming out of the office with a woman when she got there? That would be awful. Stop it. What if? What if? She wanted to see him and she would. She put the white ticket that said "We Are Not Responsible for Damage to Your Car" into her purse and watched the parking attendant get into her car and screech off to a distant space in the lot. She'd be fine.

Larson's office was at 443. Up the stairs and to the . . . Chuck Larson on the door. She opened it and smiled. David was sitting at the desk in the reception area, jacket off, tie loosened, eating a sandwich and reading. He looked up. It took a minute before the recognition came into his eyes.

"Hi," she said softly. Lip gloss. Was she wearing lip gloss?

"What are you doing here?" he asked.

Allyn started to feel afraid. Dumb. What was she doing here? That wasn't exactly a hearty welcome.

"Just in the neighborhood," she tried.

"Yeah?" a smile was starting on his face. "Great. Want half an avocado sandwich?"

"No, thanks." It was getting a little bit better.

"Uh, listen." Something was making him uncomfortable. "Maybe we should go out for coffee," he said. "I mean, do you—did you eat lunch yet?"

"No. But that's okay. We don't have to."

"Yes. Yes. Maybe we should—"

The phone rang.

"I'll get my jacket," he said. He seemed really nervous. He walked to a closet looking for his jacket, which was hanging on the back of the chair where he'd been sitting. "It's nice to see you," he said.

The phone rang again. David put his jacket on. He was very interested in getting out of there.

"Should you get that?" Allyn asked.

"No. The service will get it," he said, taking her arm and shoving her out the door.

Once they were on the street he was calmer. They walked down Camden, commenting on the people, and made a left onto Wilshire before David even mentioned food again.

"Oh! Lunch," he said. "What about it?"

"I'm not really hungry," she said.

They walked leisurely along Wilshire. It was a beautiful day. Allyn decided she wouldn't look at her watch at all. She didn't want to remind David or herself about having to go back to work. She was with him. Finally with him. She felt warm and good and panicky all at once. Panicky because she didn't want it to end. And she knew it would any minute.

"My place is right around the corner," David told her.

Allyn's heart beat a little faster. "Right," she said. "I remember your telling me that." She looked at his face. He looked at hers, and somewhere very close to the corner of Canon Drive and Wilshire Boulevard they stopped and kissed one another hungrily.

"I'll forget going back to work if you will," he said.

"Yes."

David. David. She could hardly wait until they got inside the apartment. Didn't even see the living room, dining room, whatever it was, because they were in the bedroom and on the bed in one another's arms, undressing one another, feverishly embracing, touching each other's bodies. Oh, baby. It was better than she remembered. His gorgeous body against hers. Now looking down at his thick red hair as he moved down on her and his tongue explored her cunt. Pushing her clitoris back and forth. Then he was face to face with her, and when he kissed her mouth she could taste herself on his mouth. It made her writhe with joy and toss and moan. David. He was licking her clit again. David. Now he was moving on the bed. Turning around, so his head was near her cunt but his cock was near her mouth. She knew what he wanted, and took him in her mouth and as he licked and sucked her she was sucking him. Oh, yes. Oh, baby. She felt the hot come explode in her mouth just as she came herself, and she swallowed fast. She'd never done that with Phil Gruber. David lay exhausted next to her on the bed. Slowly, she sat up to look at him. He was gorgeous. So perfect-looking.

She turned around the room. On the dresser was a picture, in color, of a beautiful woman. The woman had red hair and huge green eyes. Allyn felt a flash of jealousy.

"My mother," David said, seeing where Allyn was looking. "She's dead."

Now she remembered hearing that David had no parents, but it was something they hadn't discussed.

"I'm sorry."

"So am I," he said. He seemed to be closing up all of a sudden. The passion and the warmth he'd had for her, all the way over to the apartment seemed as if it was about to be covered over with anger.

"David." She couldn't let it. She wanted to get through to him. "David, why did you disappear out of my life after Harold and Julia's party? I loved being with you the night before at my apartment. I thought our lovemaking was wonderful and I thought you had a good time at the party, too. Was it what we talked about? Does my friendship with the Greenfields bother you?"

He didn't answer. Wouldn't say anything. Just stared up at the ceiling. She looked at him. He was breathing slowly. More relaxed now. If they got up and got dressed and he went back to work now, before she had a chance to make another date with him, made him promise to see her again, he never would. It would be like before.

"David, I really care for you," she said. "I think you're bright and attractive and I like your aggressiveness and I want to spend time with you. Lots of time. If you feel the same way about me I wish you'd tell me."

He looked at her. She went on.

"And if you don't, I wish you'd tell me that, too, so I can stop spending so much time thinking about you and hoping you'll call." She smiled.

He remembered thinking once before that she reminded him of Marlene, and now as he looked at her this time she did again. Of Marlene with no makeup on, in the days before Wolfson, when she would come home from work and sit around with David all evening. Sometimes they played cards; Marlene was a great card player. And sometimes they'd watch television all night and Marlene would make buttered popcorn, or they'd do the crossword puzzle in the *L.A. Times*. Marlene was a champ at crossword puzzles. She knew all the tricky little words and understood the clues and went through them, finishing the whole thing in minutes. Most of the time she didn't even erase. Sometimes she'd do them in ink. Marlene. It all raced through David's head. From the early days with her, to the time she met Wolfson, to her years as Wolfson's mistress. Mistress. His mother. David felt overwhelmingly sad. He closed his eyes to stop the tears he was afraid would come.

"What is it?" Allyn asked gently.

"I'll tell you what it is," he said, not sure he could even choke it out. "I'll tell you"—and he told her everything. About Charlie Wolfson and Marlene, about the abortion and Marlene's death, and how he had gone to Charlie Wolfson's that day with a gun he'd taken from his boss's desk at the Beverly Hills *Messenger,* and when he left Wolfson's house, Wolfson must have called Harold Greenfield to get David the job because by three o'clock that day Wolfson called David and told him he had the job. But David never knew it was Greenfield who was Wolfson's friend at Hemisphere. So that night at the Greenfields' party when he saw Wolfson he was surprised and nervous and wanting to be as impressive as some of those people in that crowd of high-society hotshots, and hating Wolfson for being one of them, and for being there with his wife instead of Marlene, who loved him. She did love Wolfson. Maybe for a while she loved that bastard Wolfson more than she loved her own son. So then—so then, he was living all alone and working at Hemisphere. And all that seemed to matter was getting ahead and moving up, but no matter what he tried, he couldn't. And he didn't know why. And then he saw Wolfson with Greenfield—and he figured out that maybe Wolfson told Greenfield about him—and that Greenfield was telling people not to hire him. Or that when he got fired it was because of Wolfson and Greenfield's friendship and—and—and— He was choked and tears were in his throat when he talked. And the rage and the bitterness filled the room. This room. Marlene's room. He found her in that bathroom. He pointed. Bleeding. To death.

"David."

Your mother is dead, Mr. Kane.

"David, it's okay."

Allyn was holding him. Rocking him. Kissing away his tears now.

"I'm here for you, David," she said. "I'm here."

"Mah," he sobbed, holding her. "My mah. She's gone. She left me."

"Oh, David," Allyn said, "I'm so sorry." She looked at the photograph of Marlene Kane. Poor Marlene Kane. It was getting dark outside. And the room was dark. Greenfield was in meetings all day. He wouldn't even notice she was gone. David. She pulled the covers from the bed around them. David was calmer now. His wet face was lying on her shoulder.

"I'll stay with you, David," Allyn said. "I'll stay with you, and I won't leave."

ON THEIR WAY . . .

twenty-six

Stan couldn't remember being sick like this. Since his childhood bout with polio he had never had a cold or even a headache, so when he started sneezing and coughing and getting bleary-eyed that morning, he didn't have anything in the medicine chest to take. He went to the office, but by lunchtime he was having chills and he knew he'd contracted whatever this flu was called that was going around. In the three years since Rose and Barton first went into business Stan hadn't missed one concert and he wasn't going to miss the one tonight either. It was Corpse, an acid-rock group who had a live lion in a cage which they brought onstage with them. Sometimes the lion roared so loud it blotted out the sound of the music. One critic said in a review that that was the only time the group sounded good.

Maybe Stan would stop at home. Yes. Go home from the office early and just sack out for an hour. He didn't have to be at the auditorium until seven. Which auditorium? Was it Long Beach? Jesus. He was really feeling awful. Yes. He would definitely go home, and maybe have some juice or something, and lie down. That would make him feel better.

He wasn't hungry when he got home. It was only four o'clock and he'd had some eggs for lunch, so he went into the bedroom and got undressed. Then he set the alarm clock to wake him at six. He fell asleep instantly and had a dream that someone was running after him, chasing him up a very steep hill. He wasn't wearing shoes, so his feet hurt and he kept slipping and he wanted to look back and see who was behind him, but he knew it was someone he was afraid of. When the alarm went off, his heart was pounding and he was sweating. Get up. He had to get up and get to the auditorium. When he sat at the edge of the bed, he felt weak. Oh, God. He ached. Every part of him ached. He couldn't go. He'd never be any good there even if he *did* go. He dialed Barton's number.

"Phyllis?"

"Hello, Stanley," Phyllis said. "I'll get him for you."

Stan always felt that Phyllis Barton didn't like him.

"Stanley?" It was Walter getting on the phone. "What's the haps?"

"I'm really sick," Stan said.

"No problem, buddy," Barton said. "Get some sleep and I'll take care of everything."

"You're sure?"

"Shit, yes. I did stuff like this before you were born," Barton said.

Stan went back to sleep the minute he hung up. Once a little later he woke again and looked at the clock. It was dark outside. And it was eight o'clock. For a minute he couldn't remember what day it was. Thursday. Corpse concert. I'm sick. Yes, sick. Barton is taking care of it.

The next time he opened his eyes it was ten forty-five. He still felt feverish, but a little better. His mouth was dry. He walked into the kitchen and took some orange juice out of the refrigerator. He didn't bother to pour it in a glass. Just took a long cold swig out of the plastic bottle. He had nothing to do all day tomorrow, there was no concert tomorrow night, and an easy one Sunday night that was all sold out. Great. He'd get back into bed now and sleep until Sunday.

He walked into the bedroom, still carrying the plastic orange juice bottle, and turned on the television. He was feeling pretty wide awake now. Some show was finishing up. He'd watch the news and maybe Johnny Carson and then go to sleep. The show that had been on since ten was over and Stan watched the credits roll by. He flashed on the year he spent so sick in bed watching everything, making a game for himself of learning the names of everyone involved in any way with every show. Faceless names. Now he was amazed at how many of the people on the list of names he actually knew personally because he'd met them at Hemisphere, or backstage at one of his concerts, or at some party.

There was a station break. Stan took another swig of the orange juice.

"Drug bust at rock concert tonight. Film at eleven," someone said. It was so fast Stan wasn't even sure he'd heard it. The news began.

"On the national scene," the anchorman was saying. It was a blur. Yeah? Yeah? Stan kept saying to himself. Go on. Get to the drug bust.

Then suddenly there it was. On film. Narcotics officers tonight . . . concert produced by promoters Stan Rose and Walter Barton . . . the outrageous rock group known as Corpse. One of the promoters, Walter Barton . . . radio personality "Big Wally" . . . arrested . . . charge: trafficking in narcotics . . . promoter Rose was not available for comment . . . Jesus. What the fuck was going on? Stan picked up the telephone, and sat there holding the receiver in his hand. Who could he call? He'd call Barton's house. This had to be some kind of a nightmare. Walter wouldn't have. It was pretty bad for a guy to get sucked off in the dressing room by an underage kid, but Stan had sat down with Walter and begged him to swear he'd never do that again. At least not in the building where the concert was being held. And Barton laughed and he seemed to understand why it was dangerous for the business, so there was never any behavior like that again—at least that Stan knew about. Barton's phone rang ten times. No one was there.

Marty Leff. That's who he'd try. Marty Leff was the lawyer who drew up the contracts for the forming of Rose and Barton. He was Barton's lawyer and the company had used his services a few times to check over various contracts. Stan was sure that if Walter Barton had been allowed to make one phone call after he was arrested, the way they let people do in movies, he'd call Marty Leff. Where was Leff's number? The fever was really dragging Stan down, but he went through his desk in the living room. Leff's number would be on the contract. Yes. Here. He dialed Leff's office knowing the service would pick up. Five rings. Six.

"Leff and Marcus."

"Yeah. I'm trying to reach Mr. Leff. It's an emergency, and I don't have his home phone number."

"Who's calling, please?"

"Stan Rose."

"And your phone number, Mr. Rose?"

Stan dragged the phone into the bedroom while he gave his phone number to Marty Leff's answering service.

"I'll try to reach him, Mr. Rose, and ask him to call you back."

Stan got into bed and under the covers. His teeth were chattering.

Why was he waiting for Marty Leff to tell him what to do? He knew what to do. He should go down to the county jail and see if he could bail Walter out. That's what people did in cases like this, wasn't it? After all, Walter was his partner and his friend. No. He was just his partner. But still. This was a terrible mistake. Walter and drugs? No. Did the news say trafficking?

The phone rang.

"Stanley? Marty Leff."

"Jesus, Marty," Stan said. "Is there anything I can do,"

"Sit tight," the young lawyer said. "He's downtown at Parker Center. He'll be arraigned tomorrow morning and the bail will be set at that time. I'm going to try and get him out tonight on a writ, but I don't know if I can. You'll probably have the press crawling all over your office tomorrow, so maybe you should just stay home," Leff said.

"Yeah, okay."

"I'll call you in the morning," the lawyer told him and hung up.

Stan hung up the phone and dialed his secretary Patty's number. He'd tell her to stay at home tomorrow, too. Patty wasn't home. Stan watched two old movies on television until it was four o'clock in the morning, and somewhere around then he drifted off to sleep.

At seven the ringing of the phone woke him.

"Mr. Rose?" It was his secretary, Patty. "Uh . . . I saw the, uh . . . news last night and—"

"Don't go in, Patty," he said. "I'll call you when I know more."

Now he was wide awake. The phone rang again. "Stanley!" It was Albert Rose, his father.

"Dad?"

"It was on the news this morning," he said. "Anything I can do?"

"I don't think so."

"Well, I'm here and I love you if you need me."

Stan's eyes filled with tears. He hadn't been back home once since he moved to Los Angeles. Albert came to visit him for a week right after the concert business was starting to become successful, and Stan was so busy running off to meetings and coordinating the shows that his father had to spend a lot of the time alone. On Albert's next visit, last year, he had brought Stan's sister, Bonny. Bonny was in her early twenties now and deeply involved with some long-haired guru in Florida, and even though she got to have front-row seats at a Rose and Barton concert, which she loved, she was in a hurry to get back.

"What do you think of your sister?" Dr. Rose asked Stan. Bonny was a hippie. There was no doubt. She was using all the vocabulary and wearing all the outfits to try to look as if she were from Haight-Ashbury.

Stan had shrugged. It wasn't his problem. Now he felt terrible about that. Members of a family should help each other. Albert had nursed Stan every day and cured him of polio. Nursed his mother, too . . . Stan should have said about Bonny, "I'll talk to her, Dad." But he didn't. And now Bonny had moved out of Albert's house and was living in a commune somewhere and Albert worried about her constantly.

"Thanks, Dad," Stan said into the phone now. "I love you, too."

When Stan and his father hung up the phone, it rang again. It was the Rose and Barton answering service.

"Mr. Rose? We have Arthur D. Blake's office on the line. Can we cross-connect?"

"Yes." Oh, Christ. There was a silence. Some clicks.

"Go ahead, please."

"Mr. Rose?"

It was Blake's secretary. "I'm calling for Mr. Blake," she said. "He asked me to tell you that he wished to cancel the two Rose and Barton upcoming dates at Colossus. There will be correspondence from our lawyers to follow, but Mr. Blake wanted you to know right away."

"No," Stan said. "Wait a minute. We have contracts."

"Mr. Blake asked me to remind you about the morals clauses contained in those contracts, Mr. Rose," she said icily.

"But—"

There was a click. The concerts. Canceled. Big ones. Shriek and Joyride. Both Joe Rio acts. How could he tell Rio what had happened? Jesus. Joe Rio, who warned him. Three years ago, and Stan had never stopped worrying about why. And always when Rio called the Rose and Barton offices, if Stan was out and Barton was in, Rio's secretary would say, "Have Mr. Rose call Mr. Rio back." Rio never spoke to Barton. He must know about the arrest already. Albert knew in Florida. It was probably in the trades today.

Seven thirty. Ten thirty in New York. Rio would be up. Not in the office yet, but Stan had the number in Chappaqua.

"Rio residence."

"This is Stan Rose calling Mr. Rio."

"One moment."

It was strange. Whoever answered the phone must have just laid it down because it wasn't on a hold button. Stan waited for fifteen minutes. Sometimes he heard voices as though there were people in the room where the phone was, but no one picked it up. Finally he hung up and called the Chappaqua number back. The line was busy.

He should get up. Do something. Get showered. Dressed. Something. He was still so achey. He dialed Joe Rio's Chappaqua number again. Still busy. He dialed Rio's office in New York.

"Joe Rio Enterprises."

"Can I speak to Mr. Rio's secretary?"

"Who's calling?"

"Stan Rose."

"One moment."

Long silence. Long. Stan decided to time it. He looked at the clock on his night table. He knew Rio's secretary pretty well. He had taken her out to supper once when he was in New York for a meeting with Rio and Rio was two hours late. One minute. Surely Rio would be on his side. Would understand that whatever happened with Barton had nothing to do with him, and the act would go on. Stan would have Marty Leff fight for this. And Rio would be behind him, because Rio knew what kind of a guy he was. Always told Stan he trusted him. They had become friends. Sort of. Oh, God. Walter was on the news last night. Getting into that police car. Big Wally. Trafficking in drugs. Promoter Rose unavailable for comment. Thank God Stan's phone was unlisted. Three minutes.

"Mr. Rose." It was still the receptionist. "She'll have to call you back."

"Thank you." Stan sighed and hung the phone up and it rang.

"Hello."

"Marty Leff here, Stanley."

"Marty. What's going on?"

"Well—it looks like the bail is going to be somewhere around a million dollars."

"What? Jesus, Marty. What happened? I don't know anything. I was here. Sick in bed. What are the charges?"

"Apparently they've been watching him for months, Stan," Marty said. "Based on information they got from what they call an unidentified informer. I guess they must have decided last night was the night to close in, because they hit his house with a search warrant at about the same time they hit the auditorium. An undercover agent made a cocaine buy from Walter, and agents found a stash at the safe in his house with a street value of five million bucks."

"What?"

Stan was shocked. He knew Barton seemed a little shady, sometimes mysterious about phone calls he got, which Stan always assumed were his extracurricular girl friends. But this? This was major crime.

"It's big," Marty said, as if reading Stan's mind. "Big-time deep shit, and I need your help."

"Of course," Stan blurted out, wondering immediately if he hadn't blurted it out too soon.

"I know you guys have a few business bank accounts. Barton needs a hundred thousand as a down payment to a bail bondsman who will underwrite the million-dollar bail. I need you to get the hundred to me, now. This morning."

"But I—"

"Walter needs you, too, Stan."

"Sure," Stan said.

"Banks open at nine," Leff told him. "I'll be in my office waiting."

Stan hung up the phone, and touched his own forehead, the way Albert used to touch it when Stan was a very little boy, to see if there was a fever. He was burning hot. It was fate. This flu. This fever. It kept him from going to the concert or the police might have taken him to jail, too. Jail. Prison. Good God. Fever or not, he had to get up. He would go to the bank and get the hundred thousand to Leff, and he'd worry about the company later. And Arthur D. Blake and Joe Rio. Rose and Barton Concerts. Jesus. Maybe now there wouldn't be any more Rose and Barton Concerts.

When Stan left Marty Leff's office after dropping off the money, it was raining. Hard. Stan stayed in bed for three days, getting up only to have an occasional light meal. He had been certain the phone would ring constantly the way it had earlier that day, but no one called, and by Monday he was feeling stronger and at nine o'clock he got up and dressed and went to the office. Patty was already there.

"Joe Rio's secretary called from New York," she said. "And a Mr. Leff called to say Mr. Barton is staying at Mrs. Barton's sister's house to avoid reporters. And a Mr. Ashman called. Said he just wanted to see if you were all right, and some letters came by messenger from Arthur D. Blake's office."

"Get Joe Rio's secretary for me, Patty."

Stan sat down at his desk. He would handle this. He had to handle this. He wasn't going to let this destroy all the things he'd been working so hard for. Ashman had called to see if he was okay. That Ashman! He was a sweet guy.

"Rio's secretary on line one," Patty said.

"Sheryl," Stan said into the phone.

"Hello, Stan," she said. "How's it going? We heard the news. My goodness. Five-million-dollar street value. With a load like that, why even bother with the music business, huh?"

"Look, Sheryl," Stan said. "I have to talk to Joe."

Silence.

"I have to discuss the Shriek and Joyride dates with him. Arthur D. Blake is trying to pull the dates from us because of this and the tickets are already on sale. So ask Joe if he'll—"

"It's just as well, Stan," she replied. "Joe told me to tell you we're pulling the acts because of illness."

"What?" Stan said. *"Who's* ill?"

"Just call the trades, Stan," she said. "Tell them the shows are off."

"Wait a minute," Stan said. "Who's ill, Sheryl?" He was talking very loud into the phone. That wasn't the way he liked to do business, but he was furious.

"Let's say the groups aren't feeling up to playing Los Angeles, Stan. Okay?"

"Not okay," he said.

"Cancel the dates, Stan," she said. She sounded very firm and sure of herself. Not like the demure girl who had taught him how to use chopsticks that night in the Chinese restaurant near Rio's office. "Or let me put it another way. They're canceled." She hung up.

The envelope from Blake's office contained the letters Blake's secretary had said she would send.

"Get me Marty Leff," Stan said. God damn this whole fucking thing.

Marty Leff told him to call the trades and announce the cancellation of the dates.

"Everyone will understand," he said. "Call the ticket agencies and tell them the same, and don't talk to the press."

For the next three work weeks, Monday through Friday, fifteen work days, the Rose and Barton phones didn't ring. Stan and Patty played darts, ordered fried chicken to be delivered for lunch, and watched soap operas on a portable television Patty brought to the office. Stan got one phone call at home from Walter.

"Stanley," he said.

"Walter," Stan asked. "Are you okay?" In his whole life Stan never knew anyone who'd ever been in jail. And this was his partner.

"Okay," Walter repeated. "I'm in big-time deep shit, kid," he said. Stan recognized that expression as Marty Leff's. "I want you to know, Stanley," Barton went on, "I'm sorry for what I did to you."

"Walter . . ." Stan didn't know what to say. He wished he could say it's okay. Or don't worry about me. I'll be fine. But he couldn't. Walter had fucked him over and had a good reason to be more than just sorry. Besides, never mind what he'd done to Stan. The man had been selling drugs to kids, for God's sake.

"I'll make it up to you," Barton mumbled, or at least it was something that sounded like that. And then he hung up.

By the fourth week, Stan hated to even go into the office. No one he tried to reach would take his calls, and no one called him. When he arrived that Monday, the phone was ringing and Patty wasn't there yet.

"Stan? It's Barry Golden."

Jesus. Barry Golden. Stan had tried him a few times but the secretary said he was in Europe. Stan was sure she was telling a lie.

"I just got back from Europe last night," Barry said. Now Stan knew it was true.

"What can I do?" Golden asked. "I know you're being frozen out," he said. "Maybe I can help."

Golden. That frenetic little hustler was a multimillionaire. And he was twenty-two years old.

"I don't know," Stan said. He remembered reading some play by Tennessee Williams once where these two guys kept talking about how much they had in common because they'd been army buddies. Maybe being in the mail room together was like being army buddies. Stan hadn't gone to the army because he had flat feet. And Golden. Golden was a fag. Gay. A homosexual. Stan remembered being surprised when he found that out. He was so naïve about that kind of stuff. He always thought the only guys who were real homosexuals were the ones who wore eye makeup and walked around on Sunset Strip. Golden looked to Stan like every kid he knew in Florida. But Barry Golden and Harley Ellis were lovers. Had been for years. Everyone knew that. And they were very cool about it. Out-of-the-closet cool. They had a really neat house in Malibu, and they gave great parties. Parties that only two millionaires like that could give.

Jesus. What a nervous little punk Golden was in the mail room. Then he was at World Records for a short time and then all of a sudden, out of nowhere, there was Barry Golden Management. With two huge acts. Harley Ellis and Heaven. Well, it was Golden who really made Heaven a big act. He even signed them to World, in spite of the fact that World's artists were all M.O.R. up until then. Then he totally turned World around. Made it one of the biggest labels with his acts. New acts that came to him to get him to do for them what he'd done for Heaven. And he did. And Harley was a superstar. His albums shipped platinum. He was the most successful male singer today. And even with the articles that flared up occasionally in the fan magazines implying that Harley Ellis had a male lover, the poster bearing his gentle, little-boy face adorned the bedroom walls of millions of teenaged girls.

"Har-leee," they would scream when he sang. And the royalties came pouring in.

"Harley's going to do some dates," Barry said. "I want you to promote them."

Rose and Barton had promoted Harley during the first few years when he was rising. But now Stan was afraid that none of the auditoriums would accept them as the promoters of anything. Barton's arrest and the cocaine sales were still the biggest news in the music business. Every day there was something in the trades about parents who said their kids had bought cocaine from Barton, and they were suing the company.

"Rose and Barton is poison in this town, Golden," Stan said.

"Wrong," Barry answered. "Walter Barton is poison. Stan Rose is just fine."

"You sure?" Stan asked. He had been convinced for the last few weeks when the phone didn't ring that he had nothing left. That all the connections he'd taken so long to build were shot. Gone.

"Change the company to Stan Rose Presents. Today. I have lawyers who can do it for you fast."

"I have plenty of lawyers," Stan said, "but I don't know if I can—"

"Rose," Barry Golden said. "Save your ass. The time is now. Harley's name can open the doors for you. Let us help you."

Stan was confused. Barton was his financial backer. The one hundred thousand dollars that came out of the Rose and Barton account for Barton's bail would never have been there if Barton hadn't started the company off with his cash. Cash that Stan needed to make deposits to the groups, to the auditoriums. Without Barton he had no money either. Barry must have read his thoughts.

"I'll put the deposit down on the Colossus," he said, "and we'll give you some percentage we can all live with."

"But Blake won't—" Stan began.

"Blake won't what?" Barry interrupted. "Do a Harley Ellis show? Maybe three nights sold out? You think he wants us to go to the Forum or Anaheim?"

"They won't do business with me either," Stan said.

"You asshole," Golden bellowed. Golden had become known for bellowing in the last few years. It was as if he had stored it up for so long, being timid, and short and shit on, that now he'd let it all come out. "If I tell them to, they will."

That was true. Golden did have that kind of power. Now. He was big. One of his female stars, a folk singer named Minnie Kahn, wrote and recorded a hit song called "Brooklyn Boy," and it was the story of Golden's life. Everyone in the business knew him. He was a kind of a star in his own right.

"Now do we do these dates as partners or not, Rose?" he said, still bellowing.

Barry Golden saving his career. That was something Stan never imagined could happen. But then there were lots of things happening now that he never imagined could happen. He'd call Marty Leff immediately. They'd work out something fair with Barton, and Stan would find some way to capitalize the rest of his shows. Some backer who would look at his record as separate from Barton's. And he'd go on.

"Yeah, we do them, Golden," he said. "We do them. And I appreciate it."

"Call you later."

Stan's secretary, Patty, walked in just as Stan hung the phone up.

"I brought my Scrabble board," she said. "Thought maybe we'd play."

"No more playing, Patty," Stan said.

"Huh?" When she looked into the office, Stan Rose's secretary saw him sitting back in the leather armchair with his sneaker-clad feet up on his desk, the way he had sat when Rose and Barton was thriving. There was a toothy smile on his face that she hadn't seen in a long time.

"We're doing three days of Harley Ellis at the Colossus," he said happily.

twenty-seven

Mickey was still thinking about his brother Harvey's wedding while he drove to work on Monday morning. The weekend in Chicago had started out as a good time on Thursday but began to deteriorate on Friday when Mickey's mother said, "What do I tell my friends you do for a living if they should ask?"

"I'm an actor," Mickey said, hoping that would end the discussion.

"Oh?" was what she said next. "I always thought actors acted."

"Mother."

"It's all right. I'll say you're in the furniture business."

That was sort of true. Mickey had a full-time job now at a waterbed store in the Valley called Water, Baby! He worked on commission selling platform waterbeds with double-ply rubber lining, and punctureproof water mattresses, and satin-fitted sheets in every color with the top sheet attached at the bottom to the fitted sheet so it wouldn't slide out, and Day-Glo colored velveteen-fitted spreads and pillow shams. Water, Baby! What a shit-hole. The building used to be a Mercedes dealership.

Mickey stopped at the newsstand on the corner of Ventura and Van Nuys to buy the trades. The guy at the newsstand nodded as Mickey picked up the two papers and left the change on the pile of wooden crates. He was a few minutes early for work, so he sat in his car in the parking lot at Water, Baby! and leafed through *Variety*. Jesus. A two-page ad. Stan Rose presents Harley Ellis in concert at Colossus. April 3rd, 4th and 5th sold out. Management: Barry Golden.

Rose and Golden. Working together. Mickey smiled. Those two mild-mannered guys. Well, Golden was a faggot. That's why he was mild-mannered. But Rose was always—what was the word Mickey's mother would use? Genteel. His mother. She'd practically ignored him all weekend.

"My Harvey is an attorney," she told some of her friends, "and so is his bride-to-be, Libby. Of course she'll give it up now and have some grandchildren for me." Then she laughed and Mickey hated her. Harvey's wife was nice to him, though. Mickey had the feeling that maybe Harvey warned her to be nice to Mickey, but she seemed sincere and very smart and she told Mickey she remembered him as

Mr. Chunky. She said she felt the Mr. Chunky commercial had been a particularly impressive one in an era when the commercial was becoming an art form in itself. She was nice. But very unattractive. She was also polite enough not to mention that it had been four years since the Mr. Chunky commercial was on the air, and that Mickey hadn't been seen in anything since.

Maybe something would happen this week. The hiatus was coming to an end, and maybe today he would get a call for an interview. Maybe. Maybe not. His agent, Milt, was out of it. He had a wonderful spiel that he repeated over and over to Mickey about, "It's slow now, don't worry, you'll work," but it was waterbeds, not Milt Stiener's promises that were paying Mickey's rent.

Mickey looked at the ad again. Rose and Golden. He shook his head. Rose and Golden and Kane and Ashman. Mickey heard recently that those four names were legendary now with all of the new mail room groups, because the story of the Pinsky Caper had been told and retold since they left.

Kane was living with Allyn Grant. And he was still working for Chuck Larson. Larson had trained him well. Kane already had a reputation as a tough deal-maker, and he'd only been a full-fledged deal-making agent for a few years. Stan Rose told Mickey that he bumped into Kane one night at Musso and Frank's, and that Kane was with Rue McMillan. Rue McMillan. Christ. Old Arch Andrews was hanging around with some biggies.

Maybe Mickey should call Kane. Maybe Kane would remember the time Mickey got the waitresses to sing "Happy Birthday" to him in the commissary and Mia Farrow and Frank Sinatra were there. Shit, maybe Kane thought he was an asshole for doing that. No. He'd call him later today. What the hell. Mickey got out of the car and walked into the delivery entrance of Water, Baby! to start his day.

He didn't think about calling David Kane again until twelve thirty and then he was sure David would be at lunch. No one in the business answered the phone between twelve thirty and two. Maybe he should call Stan Rose and get tickets for the Harley Ellis concert. Sold out. Oh, that was always bullshit. Stan Rose was sure to be holding some tickets for friends. He'd call and leave a message on the service for Rose to call him back.

"Stan Rose Presents."

The voice sounded familiar.

"Stan?"

"Yeah."

"Mickey Ashman."

"Aaay—Ashman." Rose sounded glad to hear his voice.

"What are you doing there?" Mickey asked.

"Well, if I wasn't here I would have missed your call," Stan teased.

"Yeah. Say, listen . . ." Suddenly Mickey felt like what Barry Golden would have called a schnorrer. A person who was always looking for a handout. Maybe he would just say he called to say hello.

"How's two in row three on opening night?" Stan said before Mickey even had a chance to ask. Mickey smiled.

"Great," he said.

"I'll leave the tickets at 'will call' for you, and a couple of back-stage passes, too. Okay?"

"Okay."

"See ya, Reg!" Stan Rose said.

He remembered the nicknames. Mickey opened the paper bag with the lunch he'd packed for himself. A bologna sandwich. Crap. He should walk over to Denny's and get a hamburger and fries. He could afford that. Then he'd call David Kane. By then Kane would be back from lunch. Arch. Mickey was glad that Stan remembered to call him Reg. Remembered the nicknames. Stan was his friend. A good friend. They were all friends, David would be glad to hear from him. There was a young couple looking at a bed out front. He'd go give 'em the old charm, then he'd go to Denny's and come back and call Kane.

"Mr. Kane's in a meeting, Mr. Ashman. Will he know what this is regarding?"

"It's a personal call."

"Will he know your name when I mention it to him?"

"Yeah."

"Is there a number where you can be—"

"Never mind." He hung up.

Jeez. Arch was getting big. In a meeting. Like Lowell Spears. Next he'd hear Kane went to New York for a few days, or Europe. Well, Kane was aggressive. Too aggressive. Isn't that what Don Morgan said? Don Morgan was so jealous of Kane. Kane lived with Allyn Grant now. Boy, that was to be jealous of. She was a doll. And making a few bucks herself now. She had some kind of a job in develop-ment at Hemisphere. Mickey saw it in the trades. The trades. He was reading the trades every day, watching the lives of his friends move up the show business ladder, and his name, Mickey Ashman, had never, not once, been in the trades, except for the time they put the obituary for Pinsky in *Variety*. And then it was only Mickey, his first name. He never even had a reason to take out an ad. One of those little ones with his picture in it saying, Tonight see Mickey Ashman on *Hawaii Five-O*. Because he'd never done an episode of *Hawaii Five-O*. Or anything else.

Now Mickey felt like a jerk. Why had he called Kane anyway? He'd only seen him twice in years and one of the times was at DuPar's when he had to tell him he was fired. Maybe Kane thought Mickey was responsible for his getting fired. Or maybe now that Kane was hanging out with Rue McMillan, he didn't give a shit about a waterbed salesman from the Valley. The furniture business. An out-of-work actor. What was lower? To a big agent? But that was the point. Kane was a big agent now. He could help. Should help him. He'd try Kane again in the morning.

"Chuck Larson and Associates."

"This is Mickey Ashman calling David Kane."

"One moment."

"David Kane's office."

"Yeah, this is Mickey Ashman calling him."

"Oh, yes. Just a minute."

Mickey doodled with a pencil in a brochure that contained pictures of the bedspreads that came free with the deluxe Water, Baby! bed.

"Hello." It was Kane. Maybe he wouldn't like it if Mickey called him Arch now.

"Hiya, David, it's Mickey Ashman."

"Hey, Reggie," David said.

Relief flooded Mickey's chest. Kane was feeling friendly.

"Seen the ad in yesterday's trades?" Mickey asked him.

"Golden and Rose's ad? Sure. Well, Allyn saw it first and she called me. We're going to the opening show."

"Yeah. Rose is holding a pair of tickets for me. Listen, Arch, I'd like to see you."

"I'd like to see you, too, pal. We'll be at the concert. I'm sure I'll see you there. Boy, oh, boy, Golden really went out on a limb for Rose. I hope this isn't Rose's swan song."

"Whaddya mean?"

"Well, he can't make a business out of only doing Golden's acts. He's gotta get other acts, too."

"Say, listen, Arch. What I actually wanted to do was to like . . . just sit and talk to you. You know? And I don't think we'd be able to—"

"Ohhh. A meeting?" David said. "You mean you want to talk business?" His tone was slightly mocking, but Mickey didn't care.

"Yeah, business," Mickey replied.

"How 'bout tomorrow?" David said. "In my office around six thirty."

That night Mickey went home and looked through his closet. He decided that maybe it would be good to wear a suit when he went to see Kane, probably because he remembered once hearing his father tell Harvey that a man wears a suit to let people know he's serious. He looked carefully at the suit he'd worn to the rehearsal dinner for Harvey and Libby's wedding. It was new and he looked very smart wearing it. So smart that Libby's aunt, who was pretty and was Libby's mother's younger sister, kept giving him the eye that night. The suit was wrinkled now. Probably from a combination of being worn once and being folded in the Val-pack on the trip back, but he could put it in the bathroom and run the hot water and close the door and maybe it would steam out. He'd have to iron the shirt.

The next morning Mickey dressed carefully. He hated to wear the suit to the fucking waterbed store, but he had no choice. He didn't get out of work until six, so he'd have to race right over to Coldwater Canyon to get to Kane's office at six thirty. Everyone at work teased him all day about the way he looked and about how he wouldn't sit down even to eat the sandwich he brought, because he was afraid of getting wrinkled. At four o'clock one of the girls who worked in the waterbed store offered Mickey a donut and he panicked when some confectioner's sugar spilled on the lapel of his jacket, but it came right out.

There was a lot of traffic going over Coldwater and Mickey looked at his watch. Perfect. He'd get there exactly on time. He looked for a space on the street on Camden, but he couldn't find one. The pay lots could break you. What the hell. He'd splurge. Maybe Chuck Larson validated. No. Why would he? Most of the people who came there were giant stars. What did three dollars for parking mean to them?

Up the stairs and to the left. Chuck Larson and Associates. Wow.

Pretty soon Arch would probably have his name on the door. The receptionist was pretty.

"Help you?"

"I'm Mickey Ashman, to see David Kane."

"Yes. Have a seat, won't you?"

She respected him. It was the suit.

Mickey sat down and realized that the door to David's office was open. David was on the phone. His shirt collar was open and he was talking animatedly. The receptionist handed him a note which he glanced at, then continued talking. The receptionist came out and sat back down at her desk.

"He knows you're here," she said to Mickey.

"Thank you."

Mickey couldn't stop looking into David's office. David may have known he was out there, but he never looked at him, so for Mickey it was like watching a movie that was starring someone he knew. David's office was beautiful. It had Mediterranean furniture, and brightly colored wall hangings, and a large ficus tree growing in a pot right behind the desk. The desk was large and made of wood that was stained very dark, and it was covered with piles of scripts. David looked like a real agent. He *was* a real agent. Why was it so hard for Mickey to believe that? He felt as if he were a boy and that everyone who had been a boy with him had grown up, like David in there, but that he continued to remain a boy. It might be because David was an agent, and Mickey had had it up to his ears with agents. He'd made a list of how many agents he'd seen before Milt Stiener agreed to sign him. Thirty-two. That's how many agents he'd seen. Thirty-two fucking agents. And every one of them had some bullshit cockamamie reason for not signing him. Signing him. What was it? The Screen Actors Guild contract said if you didn't have at least five days' work during a three-month period with an agent, the contract didn't matter anyway. Somebody in Jackie Levitz's group pointed that out to Mickey one night when he was complaining about Milt Stiener never sending him on interviews. That was the killer. All Milt Stiener had to do, all any actor's agent had to do, was just get him the goddamned fucking appointment with the casting people. He'd do the rest himself. He'd be brilliant. He *was* brilliant. In the Levitz workshop production he had been the best one. And everyone came. He sang "Nepotism," the special material song he'd written, he did the blackouts that were spoofs of old movies and he got huge laughs and applause. Stan Rose came with his secretary Patty, and Barry and

Harley came, and David and Allyn were there and there were people from the business who came out of respect for Jackie Levitz. It was big. There were agents and casting people, and someone even said they'd heard Carl Reiner was out there. Afterwards a lot of people came backstage. Some of the agents who were there represented people who were in the show. Beans and Mitzi Cass were with William Morris and their agent told Mickey he was "a fabulous entertainer." Fabulous. And so Mickey called him the next day. And on the phone the guy didn't remember who he was. When Mickey reminded him, the guy said, "Oh, yeah. You're great. But you're not commercial at all. Hey, thanks for calling." Fuck.

By the time he met old, slightly hunched-over white-haired Milt Stiener, Mickey was so defeated that even though he recognized that all Stiener had left was stories about the days of Hollywood long ago, and about how he knew "Jolie" personally very well, and the Gumm sisters when little Frances was just a baby; "And that girl became Judy Garland" was always the last line of Milt's story, as he peered over his glasses at the listener. Mickey had been the listener to the Frances Gumm story at least six times. And he knew Milt had a very good heart, but sometimes he was sure Milt didn't even know who he was. And that he signed anybody who walked in. Why not?

David Kane hung up the phone.

"Ashman," he yelled. "Get in here."

He sounded like he was in a good mood.

David stood to shake Mickey's hand.

Mickey felt nervous. He was scared. How could he be scared? This was Kane.

"Jesus," Kane said smiling. "A suit. How come you're wearing a suit, Ash? Who died?"

Mickey was embarrassed. He felt caught. He couldn't tell David the thing about suits being serious. He needed David to help him. Not to think he was foolish. David *had* to help him. He'd smile and not answer about the suit.

"Arch," he said. "I'm having a hard time getting work," he said. "Getting anything. I can't seem to beat the system. I mean you saw my work that night last year. In the Jackie Levitz thing."

"Yeah," David said. "You were pretty good."

"Well, I'm still with Milt Stiener. And he's not doing anything for me."

David smiled when Mickey mentioned Milt Stiener.

"Milt's cute," David said, "but he's so senile he tells me the same story every time I see him."

"Frances Gumm?" Mickey asked. Mickey could feel his heart beating in his chest. He was feeling a stage-fright kind of nervousness.

"Yes," David said laughing. "Frances Gumm. That's the story. He always wears those little glasses and says, 'I knew the Gumm sisters.'" David kept laughing. And pushed a buzzer on the phone, and spoke into the receiver.

"Remember the day we were trying to remember what story it is old Milt Stiener always repeats over and over? It's about Frances Gumm." Mickey figured David must be talking to Chuck Larson. Mickey had noticed that the door to Larson's office was closed. David was really laughing hard now, and the person on the phone was laughing hard too.

"A guy who was in the mail room with me," David said into the phone. "Stiener's his agent."

Chuck Larson, or whoever David was talking to, must have said something really funny then, because David was laughing very hard now. His face got really red, like his hair.

"Yeah," he said into the phone. "Yeah, I know." He wiped his eyes. "Okay, I'll be in in a minute."

Mickey felt a heaviness in his chest. David put the phone down. He was still flushed from the laughter. Why had he told Larson he'd be in in a minute? Mickey needed to talk to him.

"Oh, Christ, that's funny," David Kane said. "Frances Gumm." He giggled again. "I'm sorry, Reg, go ahead. You were saying?"

Mickey was afraid he couldn't talk now. He didn't know what to say. He had always been embarrassed by the fact that he couldn't get an agent who was better than Milt Stiener, but now he felt humiliated. Foolish. Like a person who was pretending to be in show business but who was really kidding himself. He was kidding himself. What did it matter what he said to Kane now? Kane knew exactly who he was. Just like his mother knew. A waterbed salesman.

"I want you and Larson to represent me," he said. Now his heart was really pounding. Why the fuck did he say that? Because he'd been practicing it since yesterday when Kane agreed to see him? Because it seemed like something out of an old movie, where now Kane was supposed to say, "Of course, Mickey, I know of three parts you should be submitted for right now," and then Kane would pick up the phone and call Larson in, and the two of them would make phone calls that could change Mickey's life? Yes. David Kane had the power to change Mickey's life and he had to do it for him.

He was laughing again.

"No, really, Reggie," he said. "What did you *really* want to talk about?"

Oh, Jesus. Kane thought it was a joke. He thought Mickey was trying to make him laugh the way he had when he mentioned Milt Stiener.

"That's it, Arch," Mickey said. "That's what I really want."

Kane's face sobered slowly.

"Mickey," he said. "Do you know who we handle?" he asked. He looked to Mickey now as if he wanted to laugh but was keeping it inside to be polite. "Do you?"

"Yeah," Mickey said softly. "Some of them."

"Mickey, every one of them is a big star! We have Rue McMillan and Carol Denning and Beau Daniels and Doug Hart. Big giant motherfucking stars. We don't handle anybody who's new."

"But everybody has to start somewhere," Mickey said.

"Maybe so," Kane replied, "but not with us. Shit, Ashman, I don't even deal with the people you should be working with. Casting directors of episodic television. I only talk to producers and studio heads. My people are all names."

Mickey was quiet. He'd go. God, he was a schmuck.

"I'm working in a waterbed store," he said quietly.

"That's a shame," David said. Mickey knew Kane didn't give a shit. "You *should* get someone better than Stiener though. Maybe you should try to meet an agent like Mike Amos," he offered.

"I did. He turned me down."

"How 'bout Anne Corey? She's very—"

"She turned me down."

"John Marks is good. He's a—"

"He turned me down."

"Well, maybe you should keep selling waterbeds," Kane said, smiling. He meant it as a joke, but Mickey had to grasp the arm of the chair he was holding very tightly to keep from getting up and grabbing Kane by the fucking shirt.

"Yeah," he said instead. "Maybe I should."

Mickey got out of his chair slowly and left.

twenty-eight

Beau Daniels wore a pink-satin mask over her eyes when she slept. She told everyone it was because even the smallest drop of light in the bedroom kept her awake. And that really *was* one of the reasons. The other reason was that somewhere along the line, while Beau was growing up and deciding she wanted to be a famous star, she imagined that when she *was,* she would sleep wearing a pink-satin mask. Beau's four-poster bed with the canopy, and her slinky nightgowns and the huge bedroom with French doors opening to the pool and grounds of her immense Bel Air estate were also part of the how-a-star-sleeps fantasy. Being in the bed alone, however, was not part of the fantasy. The house would be shared with her dream man, handsome, strong and sexy, who would make love to her passionately, then cuddle her lovingly and chuckle understandingly as she donned the pink-satin mask and settled in for her beauty sleep. Unfortunately, instead of having that man, Beau had Benny. Benny Daniels, her husband and Svengali. That son of a bitch. Where the fuck was the bastard anyway?

Night after night he didn't come home. Not that he slept in the bedroom with her when he *did* come home. Benny had his own suite on the other side of the Daniels mansion. At first he told Beau he wanted to use the bedroom in the east wing so she would be able to get her sleep on the nights before she shot her television show. After all, he was so hyper and nervous with all the details of being the show's producer that he'd be pacing and talking on the phone, and that would only keep her awake.

Beau knew Benny cheated on her. That any girl who would pull her pants down had been fucked by him. But she never dreamed he would fuck one of his other women at home. Or that that was just why he wanted the east wing for himself. Prick. Prick. Rotten prick. Even now, remembering, the heat ran through her veins. A Valium. A ten. Perfect. Maybe a ten plus half a ten. She'd break the second one.

She had been feeling scared one night about doing the show she was shooting the next day. She was afraid she wouldn't remember the dance steps and she woke up and walked down to Benny's room. And Rhonda, that tiny girl dancer from the show, was lying naked on Benny's bed. On the comforter Beau's mother had given them.

With Benny. He was still in his shorts and socks, that uncool asshole, sucking on Rhonda's cunt. Beau remembered screaming. Screaming and yelling and running back to her room. Swearing to God she'd leave him. Leave the show because it would be nothing without her, and the partnership. But Benny never even came to her room to apologize or explain. He just went on, as he told her later, "sucking Rhonda's delicious pussy" and making her come, Beau, honey. You know how you love it when I do it to you? Well, Rhonda loves it when I do it to her. In your house. So do Sheila, and Josie and Betty. It was the next morning when Benny told Beau that. And then he fucked her. And she wanted him to. It got her hot thinking about him with those women, and after she came and he came and he fell asleep, she hated his guts. Hated his fucking, bloody, leeching, cheating guts. But she felt stuck. Trapped. She was Beau Daniels. Where was she going to go? What was she going to do? Date? Ridiculous. Who would date her? It wasn't like Connie. Connie was Beau's secretary. She and Beau looked alike. They both had short blond curly hair and were very skinny. Sometimes if fans were waiting outside the television studio for Beau, and Connie came out, they would scream for her before they realized it wasn't Beau. No, it wasn't like Connie. Connie could date anyone she wanted. The delivery boys from ABC Messenger who dropped some scripts off. The mustached shoe salesman at Pappagallo Connie met when she went to pick up fourteen pairs of shoes for Beau to try on to see which were the best to dance in for the production numbers. But Beau was stuck. Unless she ran away to another planet where no one knew her constantly photographed face, she was stuck.

The Valium was starting to take effect. Thank heaven. Maybe she would talk to Lutz tomorrow and see if he could help her. Lutz was her psychiatrist. And the only time during the day she felt free from Benny was when she was on Lutz's couch. Mostly she was sure Lutz was crazy himself, because he was enormously fat, obese maybe, and that had to mean he couldn't even control his own eating. But at least she could tell old Humpty Dumpty Lutz—yes, that's who he looked like sitting so large in his chair—how awful her life was.

Beau was getting very sleepy now. She loved the feeling of losing herself to a deep and heavily sedated rest. It was peace. Her only peace. The dreams would take over soon. Sometimes she had wonderful Technicolor movie dreams that were like dance numbers from her show, with chiffon and sequins and glitter-covered platforms, and she was in the center, singing. Her theme song. In her dreams, "I

Am Yours." Well I Have Tried to Deny the Way I Feel For You / And I Have Tried to Ignore the Way You Love Me Too / But There's No Runnin' Away from What Is Really True / Yes, Baby, I-Am-Yours.

Once in the dream she couldn't remember the next chorus of the song and she got panicky. Very panicky, and she realized somehow in her panic that she was dreaming, not really doing the show and forgetting her words in front of an audience, but asleep, and she wouldn't wake up. She couldn't find the way back. Panic. Finally and slowly she became aware of her room and then the bedclothes around her and little by little she was awake. But tonight her dream was delicious. She was dancing, rocking with one of the boy dancers. He was behind her with his arms around her and his face in her neck. And he kissed her. Really kissed her, not just put his face there, the way those faggy boy dancers usually did. This must be someone new. She liked that he kissed her. It felt good. It tickled. His hands were on her breasts. Oh, yes. Her nipples pressed against his hands as they cupped her. "Beau," he whispered. "You're a superstar, aren't you, baby?" From behind her his hands slid down inside her gown to her crotch and inside her cunt, and it felt like there was something on his hands like lotion because they were wet and smooth, and she wondered why the director was letting this dancer do these things to her on camera but she couldn't stop to ask, didn't want to, because she was getting very hot and close to coming. Oooh, she was so aroused. Not a dream.

"Come on, Beau baby, come for me." Not a dream at all.

"Show me how you love it, let it go, baby, come on." Benny. Doing her.

"Want it, baby? Do you want it, baby?"

"Yes. Yes." She was awake now.

"Do it for us, baby," he said. "We want to watch you come. We want to see a superstar come. We want to see if you come different from real people."

We? Who was we? Beau wasn't sure but she thought she heard a giggle. God, she was hot. Coming. Coming. That's what she needed. To come. Now. Oh, Benny, baby. Oh, yes.

She pulled at the mask and saw the tall, auburn-haired woman who sat nude in the chair across from the bed, grinning.

"I'll be damned," the woman said to Benny, who sat next to the trembling Beau on the bed. "She does come just like everyone else."

"Told you," Benny laughed. Benny had an erection.

"You bastard," Beau said quietly to him.

"Yes. She does," Benny said to the woman. "But this is for you." He took his erect cock in his hand and moved his hand up and down on it slowly.

"Lucky me," the woman said, standing. She was beautiful and not the least bit self-conscious about being naked with Benny in front of Beau. "But let's do ours in private," she said, laughing.

"Okay." Benny got up and put his arm around the woman and they walked out of Beau's room while Beau lay agonized and silent on the bed.

"I can't wait to tell all of my friends about that," she heard the woman say.

A sob rose in Beau's chest and for a few minutes she could only gasp silently but finally she began to wail and cry and beat the bed with her fists. That rotten cocksucker. That filthy prick. How could he do this to her? She loved him. She supported him. She was his wife and all he cared about was cunt, cunt cunt. Pussy, pussy, pussy. Not how she wanted to have a baby with him. Not that she wanted to go away with him and try to rekindle the romance they'd had in the first few years where she was the only one for him. A roaring piece of ass, he called her. And he fucked her silly. Day and night. And then she noticed it was just night. And then every other night and then never. Or so rarely that— The lousy shithead. She reached for the telephone. She'd call Chuck Larson and tell him to tell the network that she wasn't showing up at the studio. Tomorrow or ever again. Why should she? So that little weasel Benny could get half of everything she owned? Not on his life. It was over, and she'd tell Larson right now. She dialed Larson's number in the dark and then looked at the clock on her night table. Three A.M. So what? So the fuck what? She was Beau Daniels. Her picture was on the cover of *Time* last year. Not Rue McMillan's. Hers. And Larson would answer her calls no matter what time it was. Or she'd cut him off, too. It was ringing. Kept ringing. Ringing. That's right! Shit. Larson was in New York. She slammed the phone down.

Kane. David Kane. She'd call him. The overeager little asshole. He'd probably come over right now and beat Benny up just to make her feel better. He was Larson's associate, and when he came to the studio to visit her, to pay a service call, he was all over her, fussing, bringing things, telling her that she was the boss and that the director in the booth was just a puppet they chose because it was Beau's instincts that made the show a hit. Or course he never said that stuff in front of Benny. Benny. That fucker. She was seething. And she grabbed for the phone again and dialed. It only rang twice.

"Hello." The voice was sleepy.

It was a woman. Kane's woman.

"It's Beau Daniels. I'm in trouble," Beau said.

"Just a second."

"Hello?" It was Kane.

"Benny's fucking a woman in his room. Right now. I'm gonna kill myself." It was bullshit. She wouldn't give anybody the satisfaction of her suicide. Least of all not Benny Daniels, but it always got people crazy when you told them that.

"No, Beau, hang on," David said. "I'll be right there."

"Oh, God," she wailed into the phone, and when she heard the sound of her own wail it seemed strange to her. Because even though she did mean some of it, most of it was pure drama. Nevertheless it made Kane very nervous.

"Beau, try and relax. Lock your bedroom door and pack a bag and when I get there I'll honk the horn twice and you can come here to stay at my place. You'll be fine."

She didn't say anything.

"Beau?"

"Yeah."

"Did you hear me?"

"Yeah."

"I'll be there in ten minutes tops."

Beau put down the phone. She didn't want to pack a bag and go and stay with David Kane and some girl friend of his. Maybe she could get him to stay with her at the house tonight. That would be great. And in the morning—what? She and Kane and the woman and Benny would have breakfast together? Beau laughed out loud at the thought. She would leave with Kane now, and in the morning when Benny and that big broad, who couldn't wait to tell her friends about watching Beau Daniels come, woke up, they'd hear from her lawyers. Not just no more show. No more marriage. No more Benny and Beau. A divorce. She wanted a divorce so that this was the last time she'd have to feel like this.

twenty-nine

Everything was going smoothly. The concert was scheduled to start at eight o'clock. At one minute before eight, without anyone going to the dressing room to tell him it was time to go on, Harley emerged and walked quickly down the backstage hallway, carrying his guitar, nodding and smiling at everyone, took the three steps up to the stage all at once, and stepped into the spotlight. A hush fell over the restless audience when they saw him, and he began to sing "The Rain Is Like My Tears" at exactly eight o'clock.

They loved him. They swooned over him. His sound was sweet and light and mellow and about love. And the people who knew the rumors weren't rumors at all, but the truth, knew that every song was for Barry.

Stan and Barry stood in the dark next to the stage watching the concert. Stan felt very choked up and he wasn't sure why. Maybe it was because he was so grateful to Barry and Harley for helping him back into business. Maybe he was just feeling lonely. Yes, for the last couple of days he'd been walking around with this heavy lonely feeling that wouldn't go away. As strange as Barry and Harley's love seemed to him, at least they had one another to care about. Stan had to stop using every ounce of his energy for business and have a social life. Call some girls for dates. Maybe he would find one who was special. There were lots of Dinnys and Honeys backstage he knew he could go to bed with, but he didn't want that. Not just to come and then start looking for his pants in the dark so he could go home. That was the way it always had been for him over the past years. A few girls at Hemisphere looked pretty at their desks when he asked them, "Want to go to dinner?" But later, in bed, before sex, after sex, there was never very much to say to them, and then they didn't look pretty anymore. And he wanted to get away from them. Fast.

Stan smiled to himself, remembering he'd once heard some comedian say it was easy to understand what the attraction was in being homosexual. Because after two men had sex they could turn over and talk to one another about baseball. Did Barry and Harley talk about baseball? Maybe there was a woman who could talk about baseball. Stan didn't even like baseball.

The final burst of applause broke his thoughts. And Barry gave him a nudge.

The first show was over and it had been a huge success. Harley was smiling and waving and blowing kisses and fans were throwing flowers at the stage and snapping pictures of him. He ran off the stage and Stan and Barry moved quickly with him toward the wings.

Almost instantly the backstage area was filled with record company executives, publicists, groupies, roadies and employees of Colossus, all standing in clusters laughing.

"Hi, Stan." It was Jerri Marshall, a girl who was in Artists Relations at Rainbow. Great body.

"Hi," he waved.

"Terrific show, Golden," someone said. Harley had already disappeared into the dressing room and Barry was taking the congratulations.

"He's the best," everyone agreed.

"Here's Arch," Barry said to Stan.

David Kane looked better than ever. Slim. Well dressed. His bright-red hair now in a perfect haircut. He was walking toward them and there were two women with him. Typical. One was Allyn and the other one—

"Look at that," Stan said softly to Barry. "He brought Beau Daniels."

David was grinning. Allyn looked beautiful. She was prettier than Beau Daniels, who looked tired.

"Hey, guys. You remember Allyn? And this is Beau Daniels, my client. I'd like you to meet Barry Golden and Stan Rose. The geniuses behind this night."

Beau smiled slightly at Barry and Stan.

"The old gang," Allyn said.

"Wonder where Reg is," Stan said. "He said he'd be here."

Now the backstage area was flooded with people. Faces Stan hadn't seen in a long time. Barry knew a lot of them. So did David. Everyone was chatting and it was noisy and happy. Barry was the center of attention.

"Mr. Rose?"

Stan turned.

It was Annie Jordan. She was a vision. Her hair was pulled tight and back on her head, emphasizing her huge eyes. She wore a straight-lined black Lurex dress and a big flouncy black fur stole.

"Hi," Stan said. He was surprised she remembered him. Annie left the Etoiles only one year ago to work alone and she already had movie deals and deals with the networks to do specials, and a new album that was at the top of the charts. People in the backstage crowd were looking over at her. The kind of looking over where they try to act as if they're not.

"I want you to know that I didn't forget what you did for me a few years ago," she said. The way she was speaking was different. It was slow and precise, as though she were making a very conscious effort to sound more intelligent. "I told Arthur Blake that. I called him when I saw your partner on the news gettin' busted." A momentary slip. "And I want you to promote my concerts, too. Okay?"

Stan was moved. "Okay."

Annie squeezed his hand then moved into the crowd. Stan saw her take the arm of an elegantly dressed black man and head for the door. Annie Jordan. He had helped her. Now she was helping him. She'd been talking to Blake. Jesus. No wonder Blake was apologetic for canceling those dates.

"For your own good," he'd told Stan earlier today. Stan had arrived at Colossus at noon today. Just to check. To make sure. To be there when the concessionaires arrived, and the ushering staff and the sound crew. "I hoped you would sever your connections with that no-good partner of yours." Blake added, "Now we can do business."

A funny picture in Stan's mind. Annie Jordan talking to Blake. And who had talked to Joe Rio? Joe Rio called just yesterday with a similar apology.

"If I had let you do those dates with my acts, it would have looked as if I condoned Walter Barton's actions," the soft-spoken fat man told Stan in one of his rare phone calls. Maybe the first time they'd actually communicated without secretaries as intermediaries since Stan's visit to Chappaqua. "It would have looked as if my acts condoned Barton's drug dealing, too. I couldn't have that."

"But, Joe, I called your house the day it happened to explain. You never came to the phone. Someone just put the phone down. It was strange."

Joe Rio made a sound that was cross between a giggle and a snort. "I'm a strange guy," he said.

Stan nodded vigorously. He was glad he was talking to Rio on the phone and not in person.

The crowd was beginning to thin out a little. Stan was relieved. His feet always ached after several hours of standing on concrete.

David and Allyn and Barry and Beau Daniels were standing in one group now. A lot of people were looking at Beau the way they had looked at Annie. Stan walked over to them.

"Let's all go out and get some supper," David said.

"Okay," Stan said. "But let's stop at the box office first and see what the final totals are for tonight."

"Here comes Harley," Barry said.

The enormous auditorium at the Colossus was eerie and full of echoes when it was empty. And as the group walked up the aisles they passed the late-night custodial staff, whose mops made clicking sounds against the bottoms of the metal folding chairs. They moved toward the lobby. Stan and Allyn and David and Beau, and a little bit farther behind, Barry and Harley. Stan and Barry took a quick look at the figures the box-office manager had prepared, and were satisfied. Then the group opened the heavy doors that led outside and walked toward the parking area.

"Let's all go in my car," Barry said. His dark-green Corniche was across the lot.

"Great. Sure. Okay."

As they headed toward Barry's car, they were all glad to be together. All of them feeling the kind of relief that follows a successful show. Not just for the people who produced it, but for the people who saw it as well.

Harley walked with Beau. They'd met before. They were both signed to Rainbow Records and now they were talking about a record producer they both knew and disliked. Stan was telling Barry about his conversation with Annie Jordan and David and Allyn walked with their arms around one another.

Not one of them noticed the faded blue Corvair that was parked in the far corner of the same section where Barry's Corniche was sitting. But the man who was sitting in the Corvair was watching them. He was red-faced and had a few drinks in him. It was Mickey Ashman. He'd been sitting in his car since he had paid to park in that spot tonight at seven fifteen.

He wasn't sure why, but he hadn't been able to bring himself to go in to the concert. He never even picked up his ticket. Just sat there. In the car. Watching the people stream into the building. Like ants. Then the doors closed. It didn't seem to be for more than a minute, but it must have because then the people streamed out of the building. And cars were starting. And people were laughing and people were singing. Singing. And now there they were. The others. And whoever that blonde woman was with them. But he couldn't tell them he was there. Couldn't let them see him like this.

It wasn't until after the Corniche started and its headlights went on, and it glided slowly forward and out of the parking lot and made a left turn and was out of his sight, that Mickey was able to start his own car and head back home to the Valley.

thirty

Stan drove into Westwood to Bullock's to buy himself shirts that night. He thought maybe he'd get a new robe, too. His blue one was really ratty and he'd had two different girls sleep over at his apartment last week, and both times he felt self-conscious about the ratty robe. The new robe was also blue, but navy instead of powder, and velour instead of terry cloth, and he bought four of his usual plaid shirts, laughing to himself about his Jughead image, and then walked to the Baskin-Robbins and got himself an ice cream cone. Pralines and cream. His car was in the Bullock's lot. A white Cougar. Maybe next he'd get himself a Grand Prix, he thought as he paid the parking lot attendant. It was only seven o'clock. He'd finished shopping sooner than he thought he would. Maybe when he got home he'd call up one of those girls he was with last week. He started the car, turned on the radio, and pulled out of the lot onto Weyburn. He turned the dial. Music. More music. KFWB news. "A twin-engine jet carrying rock star Harley Ellis crashed this morning in the San Bernardino Mountains. The cause of the crash was unknown, although thunderstorms and severe turbulence were reported in the course of flight. The members of Ellis's road crew and the pilot of the aircraft were also killed. The co-pilot is in critical condition with massive head injuries."

Stan made an abrupt right turn and headed west. Harley dead. They hadn't mentioned Golden. Golden said he couldn't go back East. He had to stay in town because Minnie Kahn was recording and needed him here. Stan switched the radio dial. He'd try to find out more. Golden. What about Golden? It was still rush-hour traffic on Wilshire. Bumper to bumper. Shit. He continued to turn the radio dial. Nothing. Nothing. Barry. He couldn't have been on the plane. He must be at his house in Malibu. Stan would go there. What could he say? Poor Golden. It was such a strange thing. It had always been understood. No one ever discussed it. Anywhere you saw Harley, Barry was there. And that's just how it was. Of course, Barry was Harley's manager and that could have been the reason they were always together. But no. The feeling between the two of them wasn't about business.

The traffic began moving now. Stan made a right onto San Vicente Boulevard, and took it to Seventh, made a right and followed it down to Entrada and the Coast Highway. Barry's house was in the Colony. So fucking far. Stan was speeding. It was dark outside. Maybe he should have called Golden. Of course. Golden wouldn't be at home. He'd be wherever it was people went to pick up their loved ones' remains from plane crashes. Oh, Jesus. Webb Way. A left. The Malibu Colony guard looked into the car.

"Golden," Stan said. The man nodded.

The Corniche was in Barry's open garage, but the house was dark. Someone had come to tell Barry already. To take him. Stan parked in the street and got out of the car. He could hear the ocean pounding hard on the beach in front of the house as he opened the gate and walked along the redwood deck to the front door. It was unlocked. Stan opened it.

"Barry?" he said softly. He thought he heard voices from somewhere in the house.

"Barry?" He walked into the living room and pushed a light switch on the wall. It was an outside floodlight and the surf directly behind the house was illuminated as it repeatedly pounded forward and then slid back. Stan was starting to feel foolish. He would get in his car and go home. He heard the voices again. He walked toward the steps. It was the television upstairs. "Barry." Stan walked up the stairs. The door to Barry and Harley's oceanfront bedroom was open. In the dark, Barry lay silently on the bed, looking very young and small and afraid. His eyes were open, and he was staring at the ceiling.

"Barry. It's Stan Rose. Are you all right?"

There was a long silence before Barry looked at him.

"Harley's dead," he wailed. "Oh, God," he said it out loud for probably the first time. "He's dead. He's dead. Harley's dead." And he turned over on his stomach and after a moment Stan could hear his long intakes of breath and then sobbing. Stan kneeled beside the bed so Barry would feel he was nearby, and waited for the sobbing to subside. It was slowing down.

"We loved each other," he cried.

"I know you did," Stan said. And now he was crying softly, too.

"We loved each other more than anyone else ever loved either of us in our lives," Barry spit out. His words were angry and his face was flushed and wet. He grabbed a pillow and squeezed tightly and sobbed into it.

Stan felt helpless. There was nothing he could think of to say. No words of comfort came to mind. So he sat on the floor until Barry's sobbing began to subside. Finally Barry turned a tear-filled face toward him.

"I took him home with me last summer. To New York. We had to do some business there, so I figured maybe it was time for me to try and make some contact with my family. I mean, the only contact I've had with them in five years has been two letters from my aunt Eleanor. My mother's sister." He wiped his wet face with a corner of the down comforter on the bed.

"So we stayed at the Sherry Netherland in a big suite and finally, after three days of my being nervous about it, and once deciding I couldn't even try it, I dialed my mother's number." He stopped and shook his head. Remembering.

"I hadn't spoken to her in five years. Five years. And my whole life had changed. I'd really come up from being a shmatah schlepper in my uncle's dress business, and my mother knew it, too, because I sent her the articles from *Newsweek* and some of the other articles, too. So she said, 'Hello,' and I said, 'Mah? It's me, Barry.' And she said, 'Oh, hello, Barry,' as if I had just talked to her the day before. Not excited. Nothing. After five years. So I said, 'I'm in New York, Mah, and I want to come and see you. I have a limousine and a suite at the Sherry Netherland.' You see, I thought maybe if I was rich, like Mashe and Eleanor, my aunt and uncle, she would excuse everything."

The ocean was relentless outside, and Stan was trying to put the story together in his mind. He had never even thought about Golden's family. About how middle-class Jewish parents feel knowing their son is a homosexual. At least it sounded from the story like they knew.

"And she said, 'Isn't that nice?' And I said, 'So if you want to, we can go to a play or out to dinner or something like that. Would you like to?' And she said, 'I don't think so. Your father hasn't been well, and I'm involved with the Sisterhood, and I go to dinner on Thursdays with Mashe and Eleanor . . .' and she started constructing this big phony schedule like she was trying to tell me she was too busy to see me. Her only child, so I stopped her. I said, 'Mah, I'm coming over. I'm coming to see you. Don't leave because I'm coming now. I love you and I have to see you,' and she said, 'No.' "

Stan thought about Albert and the phone call from him right after Barton was busted. I'm here if you need me, Albert said. It made a big difference in Stan's life to know that about his father. He always remembered feeling safe and protected by Albert. Maybe it was what caused the difference between his approach to things and Golden's approach to things.

"So then my mother said, 'Listen, Barry, why don't you come to see me another time? Yes, come to see me when you're in town with your wife,'" Barry remembered and propped a pillow behind him. "And she hung up. Harley made me laugh about it, though. First he said he was relieved it was canceled because he didn't have a thing to wear." Barry smiled. "But I couldn't understand. So much happened since I left home, so much changed, and still my own mother wouldn't let me see her."

"What did you do?" Stan asked.

"I had a few meetings. I made deals for my acts, and I came back here. But I felt like shit. Because I was planning to tell my mother that I am what I am. And I was going to forgive her for throwing me out the way she had. Because I was sure that for all those years she was walking around hating herself for doing it. But she wasn't. She hadn't been. She still thinks she was right, wishing me dead. I felt bad for Harley, too, because he watched me go through all that shit. But he just kidded me about it. I remember one morning we were running on the beach and I was talking about my mother and he said, 'What can you do? She just doesn't believe in fairies.'" Barry laughed remembering.

Stan laughed, too.

"I have so much to do," Barry said. "I should make calls. To see how Harley's family is. They hate my guts. And the funeral." He closed his eyes. "Oh, Christ."

"Why don't you rest now?" Stan said. "I'll try to reach your secretary and she and I can take care of a lot of those things." Stan thought to himself that he sounded like his father when he said that.

Barry seemed to accept the offer. He put his head down on the pillow and was sound asleep in minutes. Stan took Barry's leather phone book from the bedside table and went downstairs to call and make the arrangements for Harley's funeral.

thirty-one

David sat in the living room of Beau Daniels' bungalow at the Beverly Hills Hotel. It was getting late and he was supposed to meet Allyn for dinner at eight o'clock at La Scala, but Beau was in the bedroom on the telephone talking to Benny. Shouting at Benny. And she told David not to leave until she got off the phone. The network was in an uproar about her walking off the show. Benny, who had always been able to push her around, was shocked when, on the day after she moved out of the house, Beau hired a lawyer to begin divorce proceedings. And Chuck Larson had taken David aside and said in his killer voice, with a smile on his face, "David, you handle this and I'll put your name on the door." He paused for a beat and then added, "Under mine," and both men grinned.

Beau was like a petulant child. She knew she had power and money and she listened to the stories about the havoc she was creating with an excited gleam in her eye.

"Tough shit," was the comment she usually made after hearing how much her absence was costing the network. They would bar Benny from the studio and get another producer. No. They would try to find a way to defer her earnings or invest them so that Benny couldn't touch them. No! No? Then they would sue her ass. "Fuck you," was the reply.

David wished he'd counted the number of times he'd heard Beau say "Fuck you" on the telephone to someone this week. He could hear her now shrieking into the phone.

"You filthy prick. You're nothing. You snake. You're a leech, and you've been living off of my talent since you met me."

Now Benny was saying something.

"Yeah?" she said. "Well, *you* liked it for ten years, you prick. What?" Benny was talking now. "Stop it. Stop it. Don't say that!" she screamed.

David got up. Maybe he should go in and tell her to hang up. To stop exposing herself to Benny's abuse.

"Fuck you," Beau said and she slammed the phone down and walked slowly into the living room. She was wearing a white chenille bathrobe, her face was flushed and she was trembling.

"He said I have a loose cunt and that I'm rotten in bed, and I was never a good fuck. Ever. He said if it wasn't for him, I'd be sucking old guys' dicks for a living, for eight bucks a throw."

Her fury was building.

"He said if I don't stop acting like a baby, the network is going to see to it that I never work anywhere again. On any television show, or in any movie, or anyplace. That isn't true, is it?"

"Beau, what you're doing isn't right," David said, softly. He was trying to do this the way he thought Larson would. "I know you're angry at Benny, and you certainly have every right to be, but—"

"You too?" she snapped. "Now you sound like the lawyers. And Benny. That prick. That filthy son-of-a-bitch prick! It *is* right," she screamed. She picked up an ashtray and threw it at the wall. The ashtray didn't break, and the noise wasn't loud enough to be startling and that made her more angry.

"He said I was never a good fuck," she screamed. "Never. In ten years."

"Beau, he's trying to get even with you," David said.

She didn't hear him.

"That asshole."

"Beau. Please."

"Want to see what a good fuck I am?" she asked, turning to him suddenly. "Want to?"

David was afraid. Beau Daniels. Under that robe was that million-dollar body, and she was offering it to him because she was angry at her husband. A grudge fuck. It was eight fifteen. Allyn was waiting at La Scala.

"I don't think I—"

"C'mon, David," she said. "You're supposed to be cheering me up. She sat on the sofa next to him. Then she took his hand and slid it into place where her robe was slightly open on her lap. He could feel the coarse pubic hair and she pushed his fingers down and into her wet cunt. Beau Daniels' cunt.

"Maybe you can tell me if it's too big, huh?" she said.

"Beau, I'm supposed to—"

"I know. You're supposed to meet Allyn. So what? Be a little late." She was still holding his hand inside her and with her free hand she undid her robe. That body. That famous skinny body that America could see through every lacy and sequined costume she wore, bared and gorgeous, and her nipples were hard.

"You want to fuck me, David," she said. "Everyone in America wants to fuck me, so why should you be any different?"

He did want to fuck her. He wanted to fuck her hard. Jam his cock into her. Control her. Make her do what he wanted her to do. Get her in line, to prove to himself and Larson that he could do it.

I'll put your name on the door. Larson said that. Larson never said things like that lightly. She was breathing hard and rubbing against his arm.

"Yes," he said. "I want to fuck you, Beau."

As David undressed Beau took her robe off and walked into the bedroom. When he got there she was lying on the bed with her back arched and her legs spread. David almost laughed. It was as if she was posing for some magazine. No. He couldn't think like that or he'd lose interest.

"Do me, honey," she said. He lay on the bed beside her and began to caress her, stroke her body, trying to think of what he was doing instead of thinking about Allyn. Allyn who loved him. Who was waiting for him. Right now at La Scala. She wouldn't know. This wasn't about her. This was business. Beau Daniels. Fucking Beau Daniels. Well I have tried to deny the way I feel for you / And I have tried to ignore the way you love me too. The whole country watched her on television, and saw her pictures in magazines and loved her, and she wanted him to . . .

"Fuck me."

She wasn't interested in the foreplay. All she wanted was for him to put his cock inside her and to tell her what Benny said wasn't true. That her cunt wasn't loose. That she was a good fuck. Slowly he mounted her and slid his cock inside her. She began moving her hips. But it was all automatic. It didn't seem to be related to David's thrusting. Benny was right. Beau Daniels was a real boring fuck.

"Fuck me good, baby," she said in what sounded like a voice she'd heard in a porno film. David thrust and thrust again and again, amazed that he was staying hard since he felt so passionless.

"Oh, I'm close," she said as he thrust more and more.

"Come for me, baby," David said. "Come for me." Now her movement was closing in on his. Together. "Come, you bitch," he said. "Come."

She came. Moaning "Oh, yes. Oh, yes." And he thrust for another moment and then, Yes. Now. His cock exploded inside her. Gentle, he thought to himself. Be gentle. He wanted to leave. To get out. But that would be defeating his purpose. She had to do what he told her to do.

He moved his weight onto his elbows and looked at her face.

"You're fabulous," he said to her.

"Am I? Swear to God?"

"Oh, yes," he said. "I swear."

She kissed his face.

"Then stay with me. We'll fuck all night long."

"Beau—"

"Please."

Allyn at La Scala. He had left his watch on but was afraid to look at it. This was Beau Daniels.

"You can do it," she said, suddenly using a cutesy little-girl voice. "Make a phone call. Tell her you had business. *I'm* business, right? I'll order goodies for us from room service. Then I'll put your dick in my mouth and you can give me eight bucks." She really wanted him there. He had to use that to get her to listen to him. To go back to the show. It would make him a hero. To Larson. To the networks. It would be in the trades.

"Hand me the phone," he said.

It was four o'clock in the morning. All the way back to the apartment, David rehearsed the lie he would tell Allyn. He'd say he had been with Beau and Benny and the lawyers and they were trying hard to come to a settlement. But Beau was so angry she wouldn't agree to anything, so they ordered dinner from room service for all of them, and kept trying to work out a solution, and finally, at three thirty in the morning, one of the lawyers said Beau had better think about it some more, and they all left. He would tell Allyn he was sorry he called so late at La Scala, because she'd had to wait there for over an hour, but they were so heavy into the dealings that he never even looked at his watch.

Allyn was asleep. David undressed and slid into bed next to her, but he wasn't sleepy.

His mind was racing. Beau said she would think about it over the weekend, and maybe go back to the show if the network dumped Benny as the producer, and paid him off for the rest of the year, and Benny would consider that money his support from her.

David didn't think there was a prayer that Benny would go for that, but at least it was a starting point. When he told her he had to go home, she pouted and asked him to wait until she fell asleep. Then she took a pink-satin sleep mask out of the night-table drawer. "I'm glad you fucked me, David," she said. "Remember that night when you rescued me at my house and helped me check in here?

Well, I wanted to fuck you then. But I knew you had that girl friend. I'm glad to know you don't mind being unfaithful to her." She smiled. David felt an angry rush when she said that, but he didn't react; instead he watched her put the pink-satin sleep mask on, turn over on her side and fall asleep. It was the first time he'd been to bed with anyone but Allyn since they began living together.

Unfaithful. To Allyn. Pretty delicious Allyn. His woman. David looked at her sleeping profile now. So beautiful. She was so filled with love and optimism. She reminded him of Marlene. In spite of her long hours at her job in television development at Hemisphere, she still had time to stop on the way home for bunches of flowers, or surprises to brighten up the apartment. Her relationship with the Greenfields had cooled considerably since she moved in with David, and since they'd been her closest friends, now she had only him. And, now that he thought about it, he had only her. Best friends. That's what she always told him. You're my best friend. He reached over to touch her and she stirred.

"David?" she said, only half awake. Then she looked at him. And smiled. Unfaithful.

"Hi. Was it awful?" she asked. "I mean, lots of wheeling and dealing?"

He nodded.

"I love you," she said.

"I love you," he answered. He *did* love her. She looked like Marlene lying there.

"Marry me, David," she said.

Marry her. She wanted that. More than anything. She asked him all the time. Most of the time when she said that, he would kiss her and tell her that he probably would marry her someday and then he would kiss her again and touch her and make love to her and that would end the discussion for a while. He didn't want to do that tonight. Not now. Not after— He tried to block the picture out of his mind of Beau spreading her legs for him, posing on the bed for him. Putting on the sleep mask.

"Allyn, honey—"

"We'll just invite a few people and a minister, and I'll make hors d'oeuvres."

"Allyn."

"I make great hors d'oeuvres. Remember the shrimp puffs I made you on our first date?"

He laughed. She was a wonderful woman and he knew she really loved him.

"I hate shrimp," he said, teasing her.

"David."

Why did women want to get married? Why did it mean so much? He was here. Together with her. Wasn't that all that mattered? He couldn't. Didn't want to. He was young. Younger than she was. Marriage was a trap. Especially in California with community-property divorce laws. No. He wouldn't do it. She would have to understand.

"Allyn, listen, honey," he began, as he rubbed his hand against his face. He could smell Beau Daniels all over it. For a moment thinking about his sex with her was exciting. Two women. Having one. Fucking one. Like Wolfson. Being married and fucking Marlene. Sometimes in this very bed. And probably late at night when David was away at a friend's house. Probably Marlene had wanted Wolfson to marry *her*. Asked him to. And Wolfson promised her he would. She told David that. Wolfson told David that. Wolfson killed her. Killed her.

"Is it too late to leave tonight?" he said quietly.

Allyn's eyes narrowed. "Where are you going?"

"To Las Vegas," he said. "With you. To get married."

"Oh, David," she said, sitting up to embrace him. "Are you sure?"

"Yes," he said. Over Allyn's shoulder he could see the picture of Marlene on the dresser. "I'm sure, sweetheart. I'm sure."

thirty-two

Barry spent most of his time at home now instead of at his Sunset Boulevard office. He would sit on the porch staring at the ocean for hours wondering what to do. He knew he had a few million dollars. He knew he was famous. At least in the business. He knew he'd accomplished it all without help from anyone else and with great style. Big fucking deal.

It was overcast today and chilly, and he was cold. He got up to go inside and get a sweater, and as he turned toward the door, he saw the boy's reflection in the glass. He turned back quickly and looked out on the beach. The boy looked like Harley. Sort of like Harley. Barry folded his arms on his chest to protect himself from the cold, but he didn't go inside. He continued to stand there and watch the boy. The boy was probably twelve years old. He was throwing a stick for his dog, who was very mangy, into the water and watching as the dog leaped in the air, swam into the ocean to retrieve the stick, and then swam back to shore, shaking itself off and wagging its tail proudly. The boy repeated the same cycle with the dog three or four times and Barry watched them. He moved over to the edge of the deck and sat on the railing and watched them. It really was chilly. After about ten minutes, he went inside.

His white sweat shirt was hanging on the arm of the living-room sofa and he put it on. He would fix himself some lunch. No. He walked to the window. The boy and the dog were still playing the same game. Doing the same thing. Over and over. They were like a mechanical toy. Throw. Leap. Swim. Catch. Turn. Swim. Shake. Wag. Remove. Throw. Barry walked back outside, over to the gate that led to the beach and down the steps. The sand was cold under his feet. He had no idea what he would say.

"What kind of a dog is that?"

The boy didn't even look at him.

"Mutt."

"Good retriever."

"Yeah."

"You live near here?"

"Nah." The boy had smooth skin and shoulder-length brown hair. The dog was swimming toward the shore after another perfect save of the stick. When he arrived, he shook, and the water sprayed all over Barry.

"Sorry," the kid said to Barry without looking at him. Then he threw the stick again.

"Can I throw it next time?" Barry asked.

"Sure."

The boy said that he would have to remove the stick from the dog's mouth and then give it to Barry to throw, because the dog wouldn't release the stick to Barry.

"Not too far," the boy said, handing Barry the stick.

Barry threw the stick, aiming for the place in the water where the boy seemed to have thrown it each time.

"Good shot," the boy said.

Barry felt glad. He wanted very much to get it right. When the dog returned, even though Barry had thrown the stick, the dog gave it back to the boy. But this time the boy didn't throw it. He put the stick under his arm and, after a quick glance at Barry, he said, "See ya," and started walking away.

"Wait," Barry said to him. "I live in the redwood house."

The boy kept walking. Barry didn't move. He watched the back of the boy as the boy walked. And he pretended for a second that the boy was Harley. Just going for a walk down the beach. Be back soon, he used to say. Now the boy was running.

Barry walked up the beach toward the redwood house. He was shivering by the time he got to his deck. He went directly upstairs to his bathroom and took a hot shower. He didn't shave. He was starting to like the two-week-old growth on his face. He put on some clean Levi's and a sweater and a leather jacket and put his wallet in the pocket of the jacket and took his keys from the dresser and went downstairs, out to the garage.

His car. His beautiful car. He hadn't driven it in so long. Harley loved the Corniche. He had chosen the dark-green color. Sometimes, after Barry first got it, they would get in the car and Barry would drive north on the Coast Highway and Harley would sit in the back seat holding his guitar and wearing his Greek fisherman's cap, picking out tunes as they drove. Barry backed the car out of the garage, nodded at the Colony guard and headed south on the Coast Highway to Sunset.

Sunset. It was getting dark now. U.C.L.A., Beverly Hills, Sunset. He passed the building where his office was. There was always traffic around here. He looked at people looking into the Corniche. They always did. Who could afford such a car, people wondered. Past Doheny. The Strip. Slowing down. Maybe he'd stop at the Roxy. No. He drove for a few more blocks, then stopped for a red light. A kid, maybe sixteen. Very tight jeans. Silky blue turtleneck. Blond. Like a surfer. Streaks in the hair. Leaning against a telephone pole. He looked at Barry in the Corniche. Is he—did he want to—Barry wasn't sure, but it looked at though the kid nodded.

Barry made a right turn down Harper, a right turn on De Longpre, and a right turn on Sweetzer and headed up to the Strip again. The kid was still there. Barry pulled up to the corner again and the kid got in. Barry looked straight ahead so he wouldn't have to make eye contact. "A hundred bucks," the kid said. There was a mixture of defiance and fear in the demand. As though he were saying, No negotiating, because I can tell by the car that you can afford it. Barry's heart was pounding. What if someone had seen the kid get in the car? The Corniche. There were a lot of music-business people who had offices around here. And they all knew his car. They would know he picked up a kid on the Strip.

"Okay," he told the kid. "But I want to go back to my place."

"Where?"

"Malibu."

"Yeah? Far out!"

This was dangerous. Picking the kid up like this. Why was he doing it? Maybe they could find someplace where they could pull over. He could do the kid in the car. Not take him home. He couldn't believe he was thinking those thoughts. He couldn't believe any of this. He drove down Fairfax toward the Santa Monica Freeway. He would avoid Beverly Hills and Brentwood.

The ride to Malibu was made in complete silence. Barry didn't even turn on the radio. He hadn't listened to the radio at all since Harley died.

When they walked into the beach house, Barry could see in the kid's eyes that he was amazed at what he'd stumbled into.

"I turned a trick once in Zuma Beach," he said, "but this is better."

"I'm glad you like it," Barry said, then almost laughed. He sounded like his mother when she was selling Eldor dresses. Why was he trying to be so charming? He heard the kid. This was a trick. A one-hundred-dollar cocksuck. Take it out. Just take it out and let's get on with it.

"Want to go upstairs?" the kid asked.

"No." It was a sharp retort. Upstairs? This filthy hooker in Harley's bed? "Here," he said. "We'll do it here."

As he was taking his clothes off, the kid noticed the two-by-three-foot portrait over the fireplace.

"That picture looks like that, uh . . . like that singer who died. You know who I mean?" The kid had a big uncircumcised cock. "You takin' your clothes off now?" he asked.

Barry sat on the sofa looking toward the ocean, but it was dark outside so the light inside made the doors into mirrors in which he could see the reflection of himself and the naked boy. Barry reached into the poket of his leather jacket and took out his wallet.

"Here's a hundred bucks," he said. "Do me a favor—hitchhike home or find some other way out of here because I—"

The kid was already back into his shorts and pulling his jeans on.

"Oh, hey, like don't worry about me, man. I'm very cool. You know?"

Barry put the money on the table next to him and the kid took it and offered his hand for Barry to shake. Barry didn't even look up.

thirty-three

Mickey only left his house once a week now. To go and collect unemployment. The waterbed store had gone out of business. The days were very long for him and he thought about suicide all the time. He wasn't even going to Jackie Levitz's comedy workshop anymore. He couldn't take it. Long days. Turning into longer nights.

The phone rang.

"Ashman?"

"Yeah." It was Milt Stiener.

"This Ashman?" the old man asked again.

Mickey held the receiver closer to his mouth.

"Yes. This is Mickey Ashman."

"Got an address for you, Ashman. Over at Studio Center. On Radford. Know where that is?"

An interview. Finally, an interview. His last one was two months ago.

"It's the part of Larry—the brother. Twenty-five. Thinks of himself as a swinger."

Mickey could tell Stiener was reading to him from the cast breakdown.

"Can you handle that?"

"Yes," Mickey said. "When do I read?"

"You already read," Stiener said. "Few months back. But the thing got postponed."

Yes. That's right. Some pilot at CBS. The part of the brother. He remembered.

"Then this is a callback?" he asked.

"No, Ashman. You got the job," Stiener said.

Mickey let out an involuntary yelp. The job?

"Milt? Are you sure?"

"Sure I'm sure. Just got off the phone with the guy. The producer. Arlen White. Used to know his dad. A cameraman. Dead now."

Mickey had to laugh. Suddenly Milt's stories of the old days sounded funny to him. He wanted to kiss the old guy.

"Work Wednesday. Seven A.M. Stage 16. I got you fifteen hundred for the week, and if it goes to series, you'll get two thousand a show. How 'bout it? They'll probably deliver your script tomorrow."

Mickey's feet were doing a little dance around the floor. Now a waltz with the telephone as his partner. Then he stopped. God. He was much heavier two months ago or whenever it was he interviewed for this part. Maybe he'd better go out and fatten up. Yes.

"Thanks, Miltie," he said into the phone. That's what he'd do. He had barely eaten for weeks. He would take himself out to dinner. Wednesday. Seven. A job. He'd go over to the Screen Actors Guild tomorrow and take himself off of the honorary withdrawal list.

He got into the Corvair and drove up to Ventura Boulevard. The brother. What was the part like? He'd been so numb that day. It might have been right after he heard about Harley Ellis dying that he went in to read. He remembered feeling very anxious that day and not sure if he should call Golden and extend his sympathy, or if Golden would think he was mocking him and his faggot relationship. So he didn't call, and he remembered that for a few days he had this guilty feeling about the night he sat in the car outside the Colossus. As though maybe if he'd gone inside, maybe Harley wouldn't be dead.

Where could he eat? There was a Sambo's and there was DuPar's, but no. He wanted to celebrate. He pulled the Corvair up to the door at the Sportsmen's Lodge. He wanted to say, "I'm Mickey Ashman. On Wednesday I'll be playing the brother," but he didn't. In the old days he would have. But he was getting to be shy. Quieter. Sometimes he reminded himself of Mrs. Polnazy's little son, Rico. Rico Polnazy was a five-year-old boy who lived with his parents in the same apartment building as the Ashmans. Mickey's mother called Rico "a little devil." And Mickey and Harvey always egged Rico on. They would teach him dirty words to say to his parents and practical jokes to play on people in the building, and Rico would listen carefully, laughing with an excited look in his eyes, and then run off and say and do the things they'd taught him. And every single time Rico's mother would get furious and smack the shit out of him. Harvey and Mickey could hear it. Her slapping him and him screaming. And one day Mickey noticed that the excited look in Rico Polnazy's eyes was gone. The kid was only six years old but he was through. His spirit was broken and it was Mickey and Harvey's fault. Now when Mickey looked at himself in the mirror, he didn't see the old spirited Mickey looking back. As though someone had been smacking the shit out of him a lot too. Maybe God was punishing him for egging on Rico Polnazy.

The dinner was great and Mickey didn't even mind eating alone.

He had so much to think about. He felt happier than he had in months, and eating alone was only bad when it was a baloney sandwich you were eating. Not when it was a thick rare steak.

When he got back home there was a large manila envelope between his screen door and his door. CBS! It was real. He didn't imagine it. The minute he got the door open and the lights on, he tore the script out of the envelope. *I Give It Six Months.* Yes. That was the name of it. He remembered. A pilot for a situation comedy. LARRY, KAREN'S TWENTY-FIVE-YEAR-OLD BROTHER. THINKS OF HIMSELF AS A SWINGER. HE'S NOT. Cute. He liked that. Larry. Larry. Larry. He leafed through the script. A scene with Larry and Karen. Lots of lines. Lots of them.

KAREN

Well, brother dear. Where are you off to tonight?

LARRY

That, my dear Karen, is none of your business.

KAREN

Is it a blonde none of my business or a brunette none of my business?

(LARRY LOOKS OFFENDED)

This was cute. And he had two scenes. Two nice scenes. The phone was ringing.

"Hello?"

"Mr. Ashman?"

"Yes?"

"This is Donna over at wardrobe on *I Give It Six Months.* I'm really sorry to bother you at this hour, but I know you're working over here this week, so I need to get some sizes on you for shirts and pants."

"I can come in if you want," Mickey offered.

"Could you? That would be great. Tomorrow?"

"What time?"

"At your convenience."

Mickey smiled. Either they shit all over you or they treated you like a king.

"Ten," he said.

"I'll leave a drive-on for you and the guard will show you how to get to the costume department," she said.

"Great."

The next several days were a whirlwind of dreams coming true. Fittings on Tuesday morning. Script revisions arriving later that day. Learning lines. A welcome-aboard telegram from the producer, Arlen White. And at last, after a sleepless night, making the drive to the studio. A drive-on pass. A little trailer dressing room with his name on the door. So what if it was written on a piece of masking tape and then stuck on the door? It was his name. And Karen, the girl who played Karen, a knockout named Ginny McConnel, and the director, Jeff Bain, Mickey remembered him now from the reading, and Arlen White. They were all there. And a girl brought him a contract to sign. After everyone arrived, they all sat at a table. And there wasn't a camera around anywhere.

"This is a three-camera tape show," Bain said to the actors. "So we'll be rehearsing and blocking for the next few days and on Friday night we'll tape in front of a live audience. Twice. We'll bring one group in to watch our dress rehearsal and another for the actual running of the show. Then after the audience leaves we can do pickups. So let's read the thing down. See what we have, and what we need to fix, and then after lunch we'll get it on its feet."

Mickey was so happy it embarrassed him. He was afraid his excitement would make him look amateurish so he tried not to grin too broadly at anyone or laugh too loudly at the jokes. The actor who played Karen's husband was Jud Mann. He'd been on lots of television shows. He and Ginny McConnel read the opening scene. Mickey was nervous. He was in the second scene with Ginny McConnel.

(KAREN'S LIVING ROOM. A TYPICAL WORKING GIRL'S APARTMENT. KAREN IS DOING EXERCISES WHEN LARRY ENTERS FROM THE BEDROOM AND TRIES TO GET OUT THE FRONT DOOR BEFORE SHE CAN NOTICE.)

KAREN
Well, brother dear. Where are you off to tonight?

Mickey heard his own voice. The scene was on its way. He had good jokes. Better ones in the revised script than there were for Larry's character in the original. Everyone at the table laughed when he read his lines. After the first read-through Ginny McConnel smiled at him.

"You're great," she said.

Great. Great. She said he was great. One more read-through and they broke for lunch.

Ginny McConnel left with a guy who Mickey figured was probably her agent. Arlen White and Jeff Bain drove off in Arlen White's Mercedes. Mickey went into his little trailer and sat on the sofa looking at himself in the mirror for almost the whole hour. Great. Ginny McConnel said.

At two o'clock everyone was back and they blocked the scene. Then they ran through the blocking with scripts.

"Tomorrow we block cameras, people," Bain said.

Mickey went home so filled with energy that for the first time in months he cleaned the house. He scrubbed the kitchen floor, he mopped the bathroom floor, he even cleaned out his dresser drawers. Then he drove to the market and bought an entire grocery order, came home, put the groceries away, and made a spaghetti dinner for himself, which he ate while studying his lines, being careful not to spill the meat sauce on the script.

Show business. By Thursday the group was already feeling comfortable together. Joking about billing and about how they would feel about one another when the show was in its twentieth year and what the episodes would be about.

"How 'bout a story called *Larry Gets Dentures?*" Mickey said.

Everyone laughed. They decided to send someone for sandwiches instead of going out and they all had lunch together at the table. It was starting to feel to Mickey as if they were a family.

Thursday, when Mickey got home, he fixed himself a snack, then brought the phone into the kitchen, and while he was eating he dialed his parents' number in Chicago. No one was home. He dialed Harvey and Libby's. No one was there either. He was so excited he was afraid he'd never sleep tonight, and then tomorrow he'd be a mess. So he went to the La Reina theater in Sherman Oaks, where there was a James Bond movie playing. A few weeks later when someone asked what the movie was about, he didn't remember and he realized he had looked at the movie but he hadn't seen it. A live audience.

The cast call wasn't until late on Friday, but Mickey got to the studio early anyway and sat in his trailer and read a few magazines just to make sure he was there on time.

After one run-through, the cast took a break and when Mickey went back to his trailer there was a telegram waiting for him from Arlen White that said "Break a leg," and a little doll holding a card-board calendar that came with a card that said, I give it *more* than six months, I hope! Break a leg from Ginny McConnel.

Mickey opened the door of the trailer and looked out. It was al-most time for the dress rehearsal. People who had written in for tickets were already standing in line waiting to go into the studio. For the first time since he'd found out he had the part, Mickey was nerv-ous. He lay down on the sofa to relax, and he thought back over the last five years. He had paid his dues. He had been pushed around a lot by the business. But now things were going to change. No more envying everyone else. He would go to Levitz's workshop this com-ing Monday and everyone would say, "Hey, Ash. Where you been?" And he'd say—"Oh, I been workin'." "Yeah? On what?" "I played the brother in a pilot over at CBS. Worked with Ginny McConnel. She's a real doll." They'd be so impressed.

"Mr. Ashman?"

"Yeah?"

"We're ready to do your makeup now."

"The dress rehearsal was a little choppy because there were laughs in places you didn't expect them," Jeff Bain told the cast.

Mickey was numb. He picked at the between-shows cheeseburger someone handed him.

"But, all in all, it'll be perfect if you all just take your time. We'll be starting again as soon as they bring in the audience."

Jeff Bain had singled out a number of things Jud Mann did that didn't work, and a few things Ginny McConnel screwed up, but noth-ing for Mickey. That was either a very good sign or a very bad sign.

There were only a few minutes before they started the perform-ance. Mickey paced around behind the set trying to remember if he knew any prayers. Prayers. Now I lay me down to sleep. No.

"Break a leg," Ginny McConnel said to him. She looked great in her makeup and perfect hairdo.

Arlen White was doing the warm-up himself. Out front. Talking to the audience. Explaining to the audience about the monitors and the applause sign, and telling them to use their most sincere laughs, which made them laugh. And then the first scene started. Ginny and Jud were smooth and professional and the audience loved them. But there was a sound problem during the first take so they did another one, and then the crew set up Ginny's living room. Mickey's heart felt like it was in his throat. Relax. Now I lay me—"Well, brother dear . . ."

Now he was sailing. Thriving. Cooking. Joke. Laugh. Joke. Laugh. Joke. Laugh. Exit. Applause. My God. Applause on his exit. He paced as he listened to the other scenes being played. His cue. Enter. This scene played even better. Larry, the brother, was a lovable character. Mickey, the actor playing Larry, was making him Lovable. Applause.

When the taping was over, there was a curtain call. They had rehearsed it yesterday. Some of the people with very small parts came out to bow and got light applause, but when Mickey came out to bow, the rise in the volume and enthusiasm of the applause was noticeable and his heart sang.

When the audience left, Bain did a few pickup shots and when he said, "That's a wrap," everyone congratulated everyone else, and headed toward their trailers to gather their belongings and go home. Mickey walked slowly out of the studio toward his trailer to change. He didn't want it to be over. He hadn't felt so elated since that day, very long ago, when he got the message to call Lowell Spears.

"Ashman."

It was Jeff Bain coming toward him.

"You were great," Bain said, shaking Mickey's hand. "Confidentially, in fact, you were the best one."

Mickey smiled.

"Thanks, Jeff," he said.

"And I have every intention of using you again and again," Bain added. "Thank you for everything," Bain patted Mickey on the hand, then turned and walked back into the studio. Mickey changed, gathered his things and said goodbye to his trailer. Outside he pulled at the piece of masking tape that had his name on it and stuck it on the plastic duffel bag he was carrying. He wanted to keep the tape as a souvenir.

thirty-four

Barry hated the Troubador. Being there always reminded him of his desperate times. The nights when he'd sat alone at a table to watch the show, nursing a beer, hoping the waitress hadn't noticed that he'd neglected to order another. Not only because he couldn't afford another, but because two beers made him blurry. Unsure if the weakness he was feeling in his legs and the ringing he heard in his ears in those days was because he was losing his mind from loneliness, or just no good at drinking. Now he could afford the beer, he could even afford the brewery, but instead he ordered Coca-Cola. And he was alone. Just like before.

He hadn't planned to come here tonight, but Magic Hat was playing and recording a *Live from the Troubador* album, so at the last minute he decided to drive in from the beach.

"Hi, Barry. I love your beard," said a girl who was a secretary at World Records. He forced a smile. He wished the show would start. It was the waiting, when everyone saw him sitting by himself, that was hard for him. He knew they were all feeling sorry for him since Harley died. Wondering what the millionaire faggot would do now. It was enough to make him never leave his house at the beach. He was surprised that Magic Hat was doing all this business. It was probably a "freebie" night. Where the record company paid for everyone's drinks. There were some people who'd go to anything that was free.

Jim Garland. Bob Frank. Nick Jonas. Nick's girl Jerri.

"Hey, Golden." Bob Frank came over to greet him. "How ya doin'?" Barry remembered the days of sitting in on Harley's meetings with those guys and being knocked out just by the way they looked. So successful. Their shirts and their watches and their hairstyles. Now he could buy and sell them all. And they knew it. He nodded hello. These guys were okay. Barry knew they sincerely felt bad when Harley died, not just because he was the most successful artist on their label, but because he was a good person. Even in the worst disagreements, when Harley would hate the way they were promoting something of his so much that he'd storm around the house for days in anger, it was always Barry who was the bad guy to them. "It's my job," he told Harley. And now he was being the bad guy again. They wanted to release an album called *Goodbye, Harley*. It would be a combination of all of his hits, but they would promote it as the

Harley Ellis memorial album. A must buy. A cult souvenir. Barry hated it. Harley would have hated it.

Bob Frank called Barry at the beach five times a day trying to get him to change his mind and agree to it. No.

"I'm okay, Bob. Jim. Nick."

"Good to see ya," Nick Jonas said.

Sure. He wasn't even looking at Barry when he said it.

"You, too."

The four of them headed for their table.

"Hi."

Barry looked up. It was Beau Daniels. And she was with a woman who looked just like her.

"Remember me?" Beau asked. How funny. What a dumb thing to say. How could anybody not remember her? She was on the cover of *Time* magazine last year.

"Yeah."

"This is my secretary. Connie."

She had a secretary who looked just like her. How strange. The height of conceit.

"Hello, Connie."

"Can we sit with you?"

"Of course."

"Great."

Not alone. With Beau Daniels and her twin secretary. Barry was trying to think what he could talk about with Beau. He'd caught a glimpse of her at Harley's funeral, but that and the night of Harley's concert were the only real times he'd seen her. Aside from on television. The lights dimmed and the group was announced. Magic Hat. They were good. Barry looked over at Beau, who seemed to be enjoying the music. She was an amazing-looking woman. Her tiny turned-up nose was perfect. Her short curly hairdo was being copied by every woman around. Beau Daniels. She must have felt him looking at her because she looked over at him and smiled gently. The music was very loud. She reached over and touched Barry's hand. He couldn't hear her but he read her lips.

"Are you all right?" she asked him.

He nodded.

She smiled, squeezed his hand again, and looked back to the stage. She wanted to know if *he* was all right. And she was in the biggest crisis of her career. Breaking up with that asshole Benny Daniels, and trying to start a new life and a new show on her own. Barry reached out across the table and touched Beau's hand, and she looked at him.

"Are you?" he mouthed.

She shrugged lightly, and the two of them smiled. Beau Daniels. He really liked her.

When the show was over, Barry knew he should go upstairs to the dressing room, but he didn't feel like it. He saw Garland, Frank and Jonas heading for the steps.

"I know I should go up and see the guys," Beau said to her secretary, "but I don't feel like it."

Barry smiled to himself.

"Want me to go up and give them your regards?" Connie asked.

"No."

Connie looked disappointed.

"I want to get back to the hotel," Beau said.

"I'll drop you," Barry blurted out. "I mean if Connie wants to go upstairs and you need a ride," he added hastily.

"Will you?" Beau asked. "I'm at the Beverly Hills Hotel."

"Is it okay, Beau?" Connie asked. "I might stay for the second show."

"Yeah."

Barry liked the idea of being alone with Beau. Maybe they'd have a chance to talk. Barry's car was parked in the lot behind the building. As he opened the door, the burst of flashbulbs shocked him. And another burst. Dozens of photographers. Barry had been with Harley when photographers or reporters followed them, but nothing like this. There were at least twenty of them. Instinctively Barry grabbed Beau's arm to move her. Either back into the club or quickly to the parking lot and into his car. To protect her. But she wouldn't move. Instead she smiled that incredible perfect-teeth smile at them and said, "Hi, boys! This is me—having a great time."

"Hiya, Beau honey." More flashbulbs popped.

She *was* having a great time. She was more animated than Barry had ever seen her.

"That your new fella?" one of the guys asked.

Barry tried to decide whether to smile or not. He had to admit this was sort of funny.

"Uh . . . yes," Beau said, looking at Barry, and both of them laughed.

More flashbulbs. Barry couldn't stop laughing. Beau put her arm around him and kissed him on the cheek and they both laughed again. Pop. Pop. Barry noticed she was a little taller than he was.

"He's Barry Golden," she said. "But we have to go now, boys. We've got better things to do. 'Bye."

"See ya, Beau," the photographers shouted.

Barry was still laughing as Beau, who was now pulling *him,* headed for the parking lot. The attendant drove the Corniche up and Beau ran around to the far side of the car.

"Can I drive it?" she asked.

"Yes."

No one had ever driven the car but Barry. Not even Harley. But there was such a little-girl need in the question he couldn't refuse her. As they pulled out onto Doheny, she said, "I don't have a license. Benny never let me drive. He made me go everywhere in limos. Since I moved out, Connie's been driving me around. But it's a drag. This is fun."

She made a left on Sunset and they headed toward the hotel. Barry felt a tense knot starting to form in his stomach. What if she wanted him to come in to her hotel room?

"Hey, listen," she said. "Why don't I just pick some clothes up and come and stay with you tonight? Huh?"

"Uh . . . well . . ."

"It would be fun. And I'll leave a note at the desk for Connie. It'll only take me a minute." Her eagerness made him nervous.

"We could talk," she said. "Maybe smoke a joint or two. Stay up all night. Watch the sun come up. Can you watch the sun come up in Malibu or only watch it go down? I forget."

Barry felt cornered. He liked Beau, but taking her back to his house? Where would she sleep if they slept? Could he put her on the living-room sofa? He only had one bedroom. With one bed. One big bed, but—

"Please," Beau asked.

He'd work it out.

Beau drove the Corniche up Crescent Drive and made a U-turn so she wouldn't have to walk far to the bungalow to get her clothes. There were a few empty parking spaces, but she stopped the car in the middle of the street, and looked at Barry shyly.

"I never learned parking," she admitted.

Barry laughed. Tough bitch Beau Daniels.

"I'll teach you," he offered.

"No kidding, will you?" She was really excited.

"Sure," Barry said.

"Now?" she asked. Eyes enormous.

"Pull up right next to the brown Mercedes. Okay?"

"Okay."

Concentrating carefully, with her tongue sticking out of the corner of her mouth as if she were a kindergarten child doing some serious coloring, Beau pulled up next to the brown Mercedes that was in front of a parking space.

"Now put the car in reverse," Barry said, "and start backing up, and when you get about halfway back you're going to start cutting the wheel. That's it . . . halfway back. Now cut the wheel, Beau. No. No. The *other* way. The other . . . That's it. Slowly. Cut it harder. Harder. Then turn the wheel toward the curb."

"You mean now?"

"Yes. Now. Now. That's it. That's it. Uh-huh. Good."

"How am I doing?"

"Great. Great. Perfect. You're in."

Both of them sighed with relief, then looked at each other.

"Was it good for you?" she asked. They both laughed.

"Go get your stuff," Barry said. "I'll wait here."

"Oh, come with me," Beau said. "I'll just be a minute."

Beau Daniels. Was she seducing him? Maybe. He'd stay in the living room while she changed her clothes.

But Beau dragged him into the bedroom, sat him on the bed, pulled off her yellow sequined dress before he could look away, and put on jeans and a T-shirt and sneakers. She opened a shopping bag from the Right Bank Clothing Company, threw some clothes into it, then went to the night table next to the bed and pulled out something pink and shiny. She looked at it for a minute then held it up to show Barry.

"Would you think I was a total jackass if I wore this to sleep?" she asked him. It was a pink satin sleep mask.

"Uh . . . probably," Barry said.

"Good," Beau said, tossing the mask into a nearby wastebasket. "Let's go."

All the way to the beach, Beau told Barry about Benny Daniels and her love affair and marriage with him, and his involvement in her career. And at Barry's house they sat on the deck sharing a joint. Barry reminisced quietly about his relationship with Harley and how much he had learned from those years about loving and sharing.

Beau just nodded, and he realized that she had known all along that he was gay. Of course. Everyone knew.

For a quiet time they stared at the flickering reflection of the moon on the ocean and they held hands.

At six o'clock in the morning in Malibu, when the dawn was just beginning to break, Barry and Beau, both in jeans, T-shirt and bare feet ran down the beach. Both of them were laughing a laugh that was a mixture of a marijuana-high laugh, and an affirmation-that-one-can-still-feel-happiness-after-great-pain laugh.

By breakfast they had decided Beau was moving out of the Beverly Hills Hotel and in with Barry. By lunch they had decided Barry would be managing her career. And at dinner, which Beau cooked after a trip to the Colony Market, where maybe because she was wearing a big beach hat no one noticed it was her, they decided it was highly possible they were falling in love.

thirty-five

Jerri Marshall looked at her naked body in the bathroom mirror. "Hi, titties," she said out loud and then giggled. They were still good, those titties. Still plenty good. They would last her for quite a while.

She walked into the bedroom, opened the closet and looked at her clothes. Her expensive Alan Austin wardrobe looked funny jammed into the tiny space. But she had to stay here in her parents' house until she got her life together. Soon. It would have to be soon.

Actually, staying here was fun in a way. Her younger sisters and brothers idolized her and loved having her around. Some mornings her father would go late to the diner and the family would have breakfast together. Her mother did Jerri's laundry and cleaned her room for her. And late at night, which was when she got depressed about her breakup with Nick, there was always someone from the family still awake in the kitchen who would have coffee with her, and tell her she was prettier than a movie star, and she would find another man to take care of her the way Nick had. And that life was about change, and then she would be okay.

Nick Jonas had served his purpose. He was an executive vice-president and the head of artist relations at Rainbow Records, and when Jerri met him at a party she was working at an answering service, but she told him she was a secretary and he said he might know someone who was looking for a secretary, and did she want a job? And she said maybe, and he said she should give him her number and he'd call her.

He called her the next night and took her to dinner and she saw in his eyes all evening long how much he wanted her, and the way he watched her body when she got up to go to the phone to tell her mother she wouldn't be coming home that night. And in the morning, Nick said he'd fire his secretary and she could work for him. Jerri laughed when he said he didn't ever want to let her out of his sight again. She was too beautiful.

She was beautiful and she knew it. She'd made it happen. She'd worked on it. Created it. Beauty parlors, manicurists, with her last dime. And the little bit of money her mother would beg from her father, "the restaurateur," as she called him jokingly. And when there wasn't money, Jerri managed, too. Like when she was eighteen and Arnold Pierce, D.D.S., told her the caps she wanted for her teeth would cost two thousand dollars, and she looked at him sadly, and told him she wanted the caps so much, but she couldn't afford them. And wasn't there some way he could work something out, she asked, never taking her eyes from his. Knowing he would get her message. "I have to have the caps," she said.

Dr. Pierce had an erection. She reached her hand out and touched his trousers where she could feel it from the dentist's chair. "Can't I get a discount?" she said, grinning, and she and the dentist both laughed.

Dr. Pierce fucked her that day in the dentist's chair, in the reclined position, and a week later at a motel, and two weeks after that he made her meet him in Las Vegas, where he fucked her for a weekend, and she made him come while he was talking on the phone to his wife, and after the caps were ready and perfect and he put them on her, she looked at herself in the mirror he held up, smiled at him, said "Thanks, Doc," and never saw him again.

It was worth it. Nick loved her smile. And her titties and everything about her. And she became his secretary. She was a wonderful secretary. More than a secretary. She was learning the music business. She went with Nick to see new acts, she tagged along to recording sessions, she went with him to every concert of every Rainbow act. And at the end of her first year of dating Nick, of having this gorgeous music-business biggie pull up in front of her parents' tiny boxlike house in Culver City to pick her up in his red El Dorado convertible, Jerri was thrilled when he asked her to move in with him. She loved his Hollywood apartment. It had a fur bedspread, and giant mirrored closets, and a sunken tub in which she and Nick fucked countless times.

"No," her mother told her.

"Mother, I'm not asking you," Jerri said, packing her suitcase. "I'm over twenty-one years old. I'm leaving."

"You live with him and you'll be working twice for the same money."

"What?"

"If he wants you there so much, let him do something for you in return."

"Mother—"

"Men only want one thing," her mother said.

Jerri laughed. How could her mother say such a dumb-asshole old-fashioned thing? "And I'm the girl to give it to them," she said.

"Mother, I've been fucking since I was fourteen. I'm like you. I'm hot stuff."

"You're not like me. I don't want you to be like me. You're prettier and you're smarter than I was, and I don't want you to let some man run your life with his sex the way I did." Jerri had heard this story before. Her mother always liked to think of herself as that woman in the movie *A Streetcar Named Desire* who was married to Marlon Brando. Stella. With a slobby husband she only stayed with because she had to have his fucking. Jerri and her sister laughed about it all the time, the way their mother imagined Ray Marshall to be like Marlon Brando when he was really only five foot seven and skinny and not very sexy at all.

"Make him marry you. Make him give you a better job over there. Don't you want a better job?"

Jerri had thought about advancing at Rainbow. And then decided to forget it. The only job she wanted was one in Nick's department, artist relations. But there weren't any women in artist relations at any of the record companies. Besides, no one at Rainbow would ever think she could handle a job like that. Certainly not Bob Frank, the president of the company, who probably thought, who probably knew, she'd gotten the job as Nick's secretary by fucking Nick.

"Tell him no," her mother said. "Tell him no, and watch what happens."

Maybe she would try it. She could always change her mind later and say she *did* want to move in.

"C'mon, baby," Nick begged her that night. "You don't want to go home tonight. Sleep here."

"I can't, Nick," she said, feeling around in the bed, in the dark, for her bikini underpants. "I have to go home."

"Why?"

"Because people will talk if I don't," she said playfully. "They'll say you're sleeping with your secretary. If I go home they can't say that."

"Cut the shit, Jerri," he said. "What's going on?"

"Nothing," she said, pulling her boots on. She stood up to look for her jeans and pretended to look around for them even though she knew she'd thrown them on the chair, because she knew he loved to look at her dressed just in her bikini underpants and her boots.

"What do you want?" he asked.

"Nothing." She located the jeans.

"Baby . . ." he said. "I'd do anything for you."

"Would you?"

"You know I would."

"Give me a job in artist relations."

Nick was silent. He looked at the ceiling. When she realized he wasn't going to respond, Jerri pulled on her jeans and her turtleneck, and went downstairs to the lobby, and called a cab which she took all the way home to Culver City. The next day she called in sick to work. At six o'clock Nick called her mother's house.

"She's asleep," Jerri's mother told him. Jerri was sitting at the kitchen table reading *Cosmopolitan* at the time. "She's very depressed," her mother went on.

"Ask her to call me," Nick said.

"Yeah." Her mother hung the phone up.

"Trust me," she told her daughter.

On April 4, three days after she had left Nick's apartment, Jerri Marshall became the first woman to work in artist relations at Rainbow Records. Her title was director of artist relations. Incredible! Sensational. An occasion for screaming and yelling and celebrating. She was happy. At least for now.

She moved into Nick's apartment a week after her promotion. And even though she was making a decent salary, he got her a Master Charge and a BankAmericard for which he paid all the bills. Field day. Clothes shopping once a week. Sometimes with Nick picking the outfits for her. That's what she needed all along. Those clothes. The chic expensive clothes. Nick was proud of her. Proud of the way she looked and proud of the way she was becoming known right away as a "smart little cookie" around the office. Three months as director of artist relations at Rainbow, and she was getting very friendly with all of the acts, and she facilitated the signing of a new rock band that looked as if it was going to take off and be very hot. His Jerri. Why had he ever hesitated that morning, that awful morning, when she said she wanted a better job? She was a natural at it. He knew she would be. Women would be good in jobs like that, too. He wasn't angry at her anymore for leaving him that morning. Or for not taking his calls for those few days. He couldn't be angry with her. She was such a good person. In fact, now that he was supporting her, she gave her entire paycheck to her mother and Ray to help out at home.

He wouldn't even be angry at her for the night he had to go to a recording session and Jerri went with Bob Frank to hear a new group perform, and didn't get home until 3 A.M. Frank was happily married. And Jerri was hot, but she wasn't crazy.

At the end of Jerri's first year as director of artist relations, which was her second year at Rainbow, Nick was in a meeting with Bob Frank and some other executives when Bob Frank's private line rang.

"Excuse me."

The meeting went on without Bob Frank. He was red-faced and laughing quietly about something with the person on the phone. Nick, who was supposed to be running the meeting, was feeling very uneasy and he wasn't sure why. When Bob Frank got off the phone, he didn't look at Nick. In fact, he didn't look at him for the rest of the meeting.

That night when Jerri got back to the apartment, Nick was waiting for her in the living room.

"You called Bob Frank today at two o'clock, didn't you?" he said.

"What?"

"On his private line. Didn't you?" Nick got up and walked toward her.

"Nick."

"You've been fucking him, haven't you?" he asked.

"No."

"You lying piece of shit," he said, grabbing for her.

"Let go of me, you asshole," she screamed.

"Is he going to give you my job?" he asked her. "What did you say on the phone to him? Did you tell him he's a better fuck than I am and that's why he's the president of the company? Did you?" He was shaking her. "Did you?"

"You're crazy, you asshole," she said.

Nick was furious.

"I'm not fucking Bob Frank at all," she spat at him. "And I'm not fucking you anymore either. I'm moving out of your stinking apartment tonight, because you're crazy."

She ran into the bedroom and started packing.

"Jerri, I'm sorry. I—"

"Too late," she said.

Nick walked back into the living room. When she left he was sitting in a chair looking out the window.

Jerri went straight home and moved back in with her parents.

In August, Nick Jonas was fired from Rainbow Records, and in

September Jerri Marshall was made a vice-president and head of artist relations. Her family was very proud.

"Mother," she called out. "Do you think it's cold enough for me to wear my fox jacket?"

"Sure."

"Okay."

When Jerri walked out the door of her mother's house, and got into the Cadillac the company had leased for her last month, all the neighbors watched her. Later, when they saw her mother, they told her, "What a lovely daughter you have."

thirty-six

Western Sound was booked solid. In the looping studio an advertising agency was working on a series of car commercials. In the largest studio, A, they were cutting the voice for an animated television special, and in studio B Beau Daniels was laying down the last three cuts on an album she'd started making a year ago, but which had been interrupted by the problems of her television show, and more recently by the problems of her dissolving marriage.

Beau, wearing a black sweater and jeans that were so tight even she, with her skeletonish body, had had to lie down in order to zip them up, sat on a stool in the studio with headphones on. There were too many fucking people in the goddamned booth and it pissed her off. She just didn't know which of them she could throw out gracefully. Not her love, of course. Adorable delicious Barry. She was crazy about his black curly hair and his beard. He was walking around out there talking to Jim Garland and the engineer.

The key was open so Beau could hear them.

"Let Beau hear the headphone mix," Barry was saying. "Let her hear herself back with reverb."

Stan Rose, the promoter, was out there. And Bob Frank from Rainbow, and some big-boobed artist-relations woman from Rainbow, and Connie, and some guy Connie was dating named Dino, who was a drummer on Beau's show.

"Are you ready, sweetheart?" Barry asked Beau.

"I think so."

The tracks had been cut the week before. Everyone said they were great. Now all Garland had to do was lay in Beau's voice and they could get the album finished. Finally.

The music started. Beau liked the sound. She'd been rehearsing at Barry's with her accompanist from the show and a rented piano.

> *"It was a fine time*
> *It was a time and a half*
> *It was a fine time—"*

"Hold it," she said.

Garland told the engineer to stop the track.

"Something's wrong with the phone mix."

"Sorry, Beau," Garland said.

Now the key was turned off. Beau watched Jim Garland give some instructions to the engineer.

"Ready?" he asked her.

"Yeah."

Intro.

> *"It was a fine time*
> *It was a time and a half*
> *It was a fine time*
> *And you were good for a laugh—*
> *But then I looked around—"*

"Hold it."

The music stopped.

"Jim," Beau said. "It's still not right. I need to hear more piano, and more of my voice and less of that fucking drum."

"Okay," Garland answered. "I'll take the drum down. Ready?"

"Yeah."

Beau waved a little wave to Barry, who waved back. Thank you, God, for bringing me this wonderful man, she thought. Barry had simply stepped in and taken over her life. Not the way Benny had, by treating her like a child, but by being at her side when she met with the lawyers, telling her what to say, and then saying it for her when she forgot to say it at the network meetings. Even telling Larson and Kane that although he didn't plan to interfere with their agenting, he and Beau were in love and he felt an obligation to make sure everything was done right for her. And she loved seeing the look on Kane's face when he said it. Kane couldn't believe Barry was in love with a woman. Barry wasn't so sure he believed it himself. But he was. He told Beau he loved her ten times a day.

> *"It was a fine time*
> *It was a time and a half*
> *It was a fine time*
> *And you were good for a laugh—*
> *But then I looked around . . ."*

She got through the whole thing. Nicely, she thought, considering she couldn't hear the guitar. Another take or two and she'd move into the next cut.

"I don't hear the guitar at all," Beau said. She was getting antsy.

She wished she weren't sitting in here. She wished one of *them* were sitting in here instead, and that she could sit in a chair in the booth and laugh and talk and have a party in between each take. Connie and her date were smoking a joint. Jim Garland had smoked at least one box of Marlboros. And that girl with the tits, Jerri, was passing out chewing gum. Beau was getting real turned off.

"Stay relaxed, Beau," Barry said to her.

"Yeah, sure."

"More guitar," Jim Garland said. "And we're rolling."

Intro.

> *"It was a fine time*
> *It was a time and a half*
> *It was a fine time*
> *And you were good for a laugh—"*

She liked the way her voice sounded this time. It was working. She'd be home in time for the eleven o'clock news.

"Beau," Jim Garland said. "Come on in and we'll play that one back."

Beau sighed. It was a good take. She walked into the booth. It smelled like marijuana. Barry put his arm around her and kissed her cheek.

The playback was rolling and something was funny about it. Beau didn't know what. If Benny had been there, he would have been able to put his finger on what was wrong instantly. Benny. That leech. No, she wouldn't think about him.

"You're singing flat," Jim Garland said to her when the tape ended. Anger rushed through Beau's body.

"What?"

"You were flat, Beau," Garland said.

The air in the room became tense.

"Your ass I'm flat," she said. "The guitar is sharp." Beau was embarrassed and pissed and she looked around the room. At Connie. At Bob Frank. No one looked back at her. They were afraid.

"She's right," Barry said. "The guitar is sharp."

"No," Garland insisted. "The guitar is perfect. Beau is flat. Now, let's just do the song one more time. Raise the pitch and move on."

"Garland," Beau said. "Go fuck yourself," and she stormed out of the studio. Connie and Dino went after her.

Barry had been at all of the instrumental sessions. Yona and

Marty played on them. He knew Garland was right. Beau was flat.

"You're an asshole, Garland," Barry said.

Bob Frank stood.

"C'mon, Golden, let's not get into name-calling," he said. "You know Jim is right."

"He's not right," Barry said, "because what's right is to know how to talk to Beau. To any act. You don't spit in their faces and then expect to get good work in return. We won't work with you anymore, Garland," Barry said.

"What do you mean 'we,'" Garland said, standing. He was about six inches taller than Barry. "Who do you think you are, Golden, you cocksucker? You're not the act. Benny Daniels came to me when we started this album—"

"Benny Daniels is out of the picture," Barry bellowed. Stan Rose sat on a folding chair in the corner. Listening.

Bob Frank was getting red in the face.

"Golden, maybe we ought to come back tomorrow and Beau will feel—"

"I won't let Beau set foot in any studio where Garland is, after what he just did to her," Barry said.

"Golden—"

Garland was seething. "Listen, you slimy little weasel. She'd have no recording career at all if it wasn't for me. And maybe you don't know this, but I gave your precious Harley Ellis his career, too. So you can take no-talent Beau Daniels' newest album and shove it up your little faggot ass where you shove everything else." Garland stormed out the door.

"We're not renewing with you, Bob," Barry said to Bob Frank. "Her contract with Rainbow is up in two months and we're splitting." Barry left.

Only the engineer, Bob Frank, Stan Rose and Jerri Marshall remained. The room was very quiet for a moment.

"I guess this means we're not going out to celebrate," Stan Rose said.

The other three laughed.

Stan put his jacket on, said good night, and left studio B. Barry had invited Stan to this because he wanted him to see how great Beau was doing. And how happy she made him, and Stan had no plans, no concerts, no dates that night, so he had accepted.

He stopped at the men's room at the end of the hallway. He'd go home and get a bite, read the trades. It was Tuesday so all his magazines would be waiting in the mailbox. He was about to emerge from the men's room when he heard the conversation.

"You said you were going to tell her you had a late meeting and spend the evening with me," the woman said.

"I'm tired, Jerri. And I'm pissed off." It was Bob Frank. He lowered his voice, but Stan could still hear him. "If Beau Daniels leaves Rainbow, it'll cost me millions. Golden was right. Garland behaved like an asshole."

"Don't go home."

"I have a headache and I don't want to stay out."

"Okay, Bob." Jerri Marshall's voice was cold. "I understand."

"Good. See you tomorrow."

Stan waited another minute or two to be sure they were gone, then he went out to the parking lot. Jerri was getting into her Cadillac. Bob Frank was already gone.

"Good night, Stan." She spotted him.

"Night."

Stan started his car and was about to back out of the space, but when he looked in the rearview mirror he saw that Jerri Marshall had pulled her Cadillac up behind his Cougar so he couldn't back out, and she was getting out of the car. She walked over to his window, which was rolled down, and she leaned into the car. God, she was a vision.

"Want to go out for a beer?" she asked.

She was Bob Frank's girl. He knew that now. But what did he care? The street light behind her played in her blond hair.

"Sure," Stan said. "Where to?"

"Follow me," she said, and bounced back to her car.

Stan rolled up his window.

"Gladly," he said out loud to himself. "Glad-lee!"

Cyrano's was crowded and Stan saw a few people he knew. But Jerri knew many more. Stan remembered a cheerleader he'd called for a date once in high school, who he feared was out of his league because she was so popular. The girl accepted the date and all evening long he looked at her and thought, She's really here, how did this happen? She's really here! That was how he felt now about Jerri. They were talking about their childhoods.

"Your father really sounds nice," she said. "I'm close with my parents, too. In fact, I live with them." Stan was surprised.

"Well, I'm not really dating anyone now," she went on, "and I'm so busy at work, and coming home to them at night is kind of cozy. It makes me feel protected."

"Weren't you living with someone at Rainbow for a while?" Stan asked. Bad question, he thought.

"I was going out with Nick Jonas for a while, but I didn't really live with him."

Stan knew that wasn't true. He also knew she was involved with Bob Frank, but he couldn't tell her that. He was fascinated with her. She held her wineglass with both hands while she talked and she had long red fingernails.

"Do you like working at Rainbow?" he asked her.

"Oh, yes. I was always interested in the music business so I just set out to work in it. I applied for a job at Rainbow, and only started as a secretary because I was a woman. I had no choice. Unfortunately, I was assigned to Nick Jonas."

"Unfortunately?"

"Well, he wouldn't leave me alone, and he was my boss, so I was afraid to be too rude to him, but finally I said, 'Look, Nick. I'm not an object. I'm here for the same reasons you are. To get ahead in the business. And I'm going to do it because of my ability.' "

"What did he say?"

"He was insulted, but he realized I was right and he recommended me for a job as director of artist relations. Then, of course, I really was much more in my element. Then, Bob Frank saw that I was working so well with the groups—not Beau, she doesn't even talk to me. She doesn't talk to anyone—so, anyway, Bob Frank made me vice-president in charge of artist relations at Rainbow."

"Wasn't that Nick Jonas's job?" Stan asked.

"Yeah," Jerri said. "But he left."

"Why?" Stan asked her.

She smiled a very broad smile.

"Who knows?"

Stan was drinking a bullshot. Easy on the vodka. He wasn't much of a drinker, but he felt pleasantly high now. This beautiful woman. An executive.

"Know what I'd like to do?" she said.

"What?"

"I'd like to put the top down on my car and have you drive it and head for the Coast Highway, and keep going till we're both exhausted."

Stan smiled. He was trying hard to remember what his schedule

was the next morning. If he had any meetings, he'd be too tired if he
went on this late-night jaunt with her. God, he was square. Fuck the
meetings.

"Sounds great," he said, summoning the waiter to bring the check.

In the parking lot behind Cyrano's, Jerri handed Stan the car
keys, then put her arms around his neck. "Who knows?" she said.
"Maybe we'll end up in San Francisco."

Stan wished they were going to his place.

"Think you can cut it?" she said.

"What?"

"The drive. I have some coke if you want."

Cocaine. She had cocaine. Jesus.

"Uh, I'm fine," Stan said. "Let's go."

In San Luis Obispo, at the Madonna Inn, Jerri and Stan did a little
cocaine. "Just a little," she instructed him, and then turned out the
bedroom lights.

"Don't you have to call home and tell them you won't be there tonight?" he teased.

"They'll notice," she said.

Her naked body was spectacular. The best Stan had seen, and he
was flying from the cocaine. And he was embarrassed that he'd been
so unsophisticated about it. And he thought about Bob Frank and
Nick Jonas. Then Jerri put his hard cock between her breasts and in
her mouth and inside her wet pussy. And he came and a little while
later he came again and he didn't think about Jerri and other men
until the morning when he woke up to the sound of Jerri's voice. She
was on the phone in the bathroom.

"I won't be in today. None of your business where I am. Too bad.
Go home and fuck your wife."

Stan had been in a deep sleep and as he heard Jerri hang the
phone up, he rolled back over and pretended to still be asleep.

She came out of the bathroom and got back into bed, and after a
minute he felt her nakedness close to him. She kissed his back, and
he pretended to stir.

"Good morning," she whispered softly.

He turned and looked at her. God, she looked great. Even in the
morning.

"Good morning," he said. "Who am I? Where am I? What happened?" They both laughed.

"You're Stan Rose, famous concert promoter," she said. "You're in San Luis Obispo. And I think what happened is that last night we fell in love."

Stan was silent. He looked at Jerri's pretty face. A woman who could talk. Before sex, after sex. Who was a great fuck. Who looked like this. Good God. It was all there.

"You're right," he said. "I think we did."

thirty-seven

Rue McMillan sat on the diving board looking down into his Olympic pool as he talked.

"It's a toughie, Kane, old kid," he said. "I been with Larson for years. He got me the first jobs I ever had."

"That was *then,* Rhubarb. This is now. You can go on forever thinking of Larson's career, or start thinking about your own, which is slipping seriously."

Rue's jaw clenched at the thought.

David watched the effect his words were having on the big tough-looking man he had befriended and pampered in the Larson style, under the guise of doing it for the benefit of the Larson office. Well, now it was time to cash in. David was leaving Larson. To become an agent on his own. He was taking Doug Hart, and maybe, if he could convince him, Rue McMillan.

"I could package you and Hart and that *Wild Ride* script together and go to a studio tomorrow and make a deal."

"So could Larson."

"But he hasn't."

"He thought that script was a piece of shit," Rue said.

"He was wrong."

"Then how come no one else ever made that picture all this time?"

"Because no one's right for the part but you. And Hart could play the young outlaw."

David was starting to dislike the turn the conversation was taking. He didn't want Rue to feel he was begging.

"I'm going to go," he told Rue. "You give it some thought. I'll be stopping by Larson's and then I'll be at home for the rest of the week until I find my own office. No rush."

"Does Larson know you're leaving him?" Rue asked.

"Larson has been in Europe for three weeks making some television deal for Carol Denning. He came back this morning and he doesn't know anything. He probably, for example, doesn't even know that your contract with him is up in one week. Just takes it for granted that you'll re-sign. That's it, you know, Rue. He feels like he's got you in his back pocket."

"Aw, bullshit," Rue said angrily. "He does not."

For a second David panicked. Maybe that was too strong.

"I mean—"

"I'll leave him," Rue said. "I won't re-sign the contract. I'll go with you and Hart. But you get going on that *Wild Ride* project right away. Okay?"

"Okay." David grinned. "You're making a wise decision, Rue. I'll hustle your career right back to where it should be." The two men shook hands and David tried to walk, not fly, which is what he felt like doing, down the front steps of Rue's house to his car.

Now came the hard part. Telling Larson. What would he do? David knew Larson hated to lose a client. When Barry Golden had moved in on Beau Daniels' career, David had been livid. "Listen, Barry," Larson said as he sat in the meeting with Beau and Barry and David, "the most important thing is Beau's career, and that's what we're all here to look out for. If the addition of you to the roster of people who are behind her makes her happy, it makes me happy, too."

But David knew that was bullshit. He had worked for Larson long enough to know that Larson despised anyone meddling with the careers of his clients. And Golden wasn't even taking Beau away from the Larson office. Just helping her out. David, on the other hand, was leaving with two of Larson's biggest clients.

Larson was out when David got to the office.

"Morning, Mister Kane."

"Get my wife for me, will you? And tell me when Larson gets here."

David closed the door to his office. He should probably clear out his desk. He'd already taken home the scripts he'd read that he thought would be the most valuable to his clients. His clients. Oh, boy. The David Kane Agency. And that would just be until he could get some good solid deals made. Deals for Rue and Doug, yes. But more important, deals for himself. Deals that would enable him to become a producer. A producer. He couldn't wait to tell Allyn.

The com line buzzed.

"Yes."

"Your wife's in a meeting, Mr. Kane."

"Thanks." Shit. In a meeting. Allyn was so busy lately with her fucking job. Maybe he should interrupt her meeting. He wanted to tell her about Rue. He dialed the number at Hemisphere himself. Fuck her stupid little boring meetings. Rue McMillan, superstar, was

David Kane's client. As of today. Allyn would want to know that. She'd be thrilled.

"Hemisphere Studios."

"Allyn Grant's office, please." He hated calling her Allyn Grant. Why did she have to continue to use her family name?

"It's confusing, David," she'd told him. "Everyone at Hemisphere knows me as Allyn Grant. And I love my name. It doesn't mean I'm less of a wife."

"Allyn Grant's office."

"Yeah, this is David Kane. Can I talk to her?"

"Oh, hi, Mr. Kane. I already told someone at your office. Allyn's in a meeting."

"Tell her it's me."

"She said only to interrupt for an emergency, Mr. Kane," the girl said apologetically.

David slammed the phone down.

The com line buzzed.

"Yes?"

"Mr. Larson just arrived, sir."

"Thank you."

Well, here we go, he thought. The big moment. Maybe he'd wait until later. No. Now. Before he thought about it too much. He got up, walked out of his office and into Larson's. Larson was on the phone, and he waved a little hello and made an I'll-be-right-off gesture. David watched Larson and listened to him talk. He remembered wanting to be able to be a big-time deal-maker, too. Like Larson. But ultimately, he realized that Larson was only an agent. A 10-per-cent-of-someone-else's-career agent, who only wanted to be an agent forever. Well, that wasn't enough for David. No.

"Have a nice day," Larson was saying to someone on the phone. " 'Bye." He hung up, smiling.

"Just closed the deal for Carol Denning to do a picture."

"Great."

"And you? Kane. What trouble have you gotten into while I was gone?"

"I'm leaving you, Chuck."

Larson didn't even flinch. "Sounds like an exit line from a bad B movie," he said. For a split second David was afraid to say the next part, but he didn't have to.

"Who's going with you?" Larson asked.

"Doug Hart," David said. He'd save the coup de grâce for last. "And Rue."

Larson's eyes met David's. David had imagined what this moment would be like almost from the first week he started working for Larson. Imagined it would be accompanied by a great feeling of getting even with Larson for treating him like a coffee boy, an errand boy, a gofer. He had always resented Larson and his smoothness. Yes, Larson was smooth, like Wolfson, like Greenfield. But now, instead of his feeling glad to have something over Larson, it made him strangely sad. Sad for Larson, who had probably once been as eager and aggressive as David was now, never thinking some punks like Golden or David would come along and unravel the powerful relationships he'd built with his clients. And sorry for himself, too, because for a moment he flashed on himself being the old boy someday, who would be betrayed by a young apprentice of his own. As always, he stopped the thought before it got to him. "Thanks for everything, Chuck," David said. "I know you probably don't want to shake my hand, so I'll be going."

David turned and walked out of Larson's office, through the reception area and into his own office, packed up his briefcase and, as he passed the receptionist's desk, tossed her the keys he would no longer need.

There was nothing for him to do at home. He had to find office space, but there was plenty of time for that tomorrow. Maybe he'd drive over to Hemisphere. Drop in on Allyn. Her meeting must be over by now. David headed over Coldwater Canyon toward the Valley. He couldn't wait to tell Allyn the news. She already knew about Doug Hart leaving Larson. But now. David was going to be Rue McMillan's agent.

That didn't just mean status, it also meant they'd soon have a lot of money. They'd probably move right away. Maybe buy a house in Beverly Hills. North. And eventually he'd be a producer. David Kane Productions. And Allyn would quit her job. She'd like that. And he'd like it, too, knowing she was home all day, "doing little things around the house," as Marlene used to say. Marlene. She had always wished the day would come when she didn't have to work. Well, he would give that to Allyn. The cushy job of being the producer's wife.

David could see the gold building as he drove into the Valley. He hadn't been at Hemisphere in a long time. He remembered his early days there. When he was in mourning for his mother. Maybe he was

still in mourning for his mother. He drove past the guard and toward
the casitas. Allyn's office was in one of the casitas. There it was.
David found a parking space. I'm Rue McMillan's agent. Amazing.
It felt like a dream.

"Hi. Are you Mr. Kane?"

"Yes."

"I recognized you from your picture on Miss Grant's desk," the
secretary said.

"Where is she?"

"She's on her way down from the gold building, Mr. Kane. Why
don't you go and wait in her office? I'll get you some coffee."

"Thanks."

David looked around. He had delivered mail to the casitas for
years. This office had housed several people during that time. He
wasn't sure now who they were. Allyn did have his pitcure on her
desk. A picture she took when they were in Las Vegas. Of David
standing in front of the Little Church in the West, right after the
wedding. She gave him one that she made him take of her, outside
the church, and one of them together they had asked the people to
take who were waiting to have the next wedding, but both pictures
were still in his briefcase.

He heard some voices in the outer office and Allyn walked in.

"David," she said. Putting her arms around him. How perfect. "I
couldn't wait to get down here so I could call you." She gave him a
hug. She was glowing.

"David. Guess what! I sold my show."

Her show. Her show. Yes. She told him some idea she had for a
show. A drama. About a couple trying to make ends meet during the
Depression.

"That means I'm a producer. Can you believe it?"

"Jesus," he said. "That's great."

"What happened with you?" she asked. "Did you see Rue?"

"Yeah. He's leaving with me."

"Great. Oh, honey, we really have to celebrate."

"And I said goodbye to Larson."

"Terrific. Oooh. Do you think maybe Rue would do a guest spot on
my show? A cameo? In the pilot? Wouldn't that be funny? I'd have
to negotiate for him with you."

"That would," David said, "that would really be funny."

UPWARD . . .

thirty-eight

Mickey sat alone on the floor in the large rehearsal hall at the Beverly Hills Academy. It was nine twenty in the morning. At nine thirty, he would be surrounded by twenty-five children, all under the age of ten. He was teaching them Creative Dramatics. "Exercises and games to free their imaginations and spirits and foster constructive creative thinking." That's what it said on the flyer Mickey left at all of the elementary schools and parks in the neighborhood. There was also a picture of Mickey on the flyer and under the picture it said, "Michael 'Mickey' Ashman has appeared in television commercials and television shows. He was also an employee for several years at Hemisphere Studios in Hollywood. His program is designed especially to explore your child's innate creative ability." It took him a week to write that.

The classes had begun as an act of desperation. A way for Mickey to get out of the house, to make a few dollars, to do something besides waiting for the phone to ring. After the networks passed on *I Give It Six Months,* Mickey had a few more little nibbles. A small part in an episode of *Love American Style,* a voice-over for a local Los Angeles bank. Enough to keep his unemployment going. But every day he woke up feeling empty. He remembered how the people in Jackie Levitz's comedy workshop snickered behind Levitz's back sometimes, saying things like "Those who can't do, teach." But teaching those comedy workshops gave Jackie Levitz something to live for. Kept him busy. With lessons to plan, exercises to work on, new students to talk to, individual progress reports to discuss, Levitz felt he was important to his sutdents. And now, Mickey felt that way about himself.

The door to the rehearsal hall opened slowly and Mickey looked up. It was Adam Grossman. Five. Adam had a pinchable face and a low gravelly voice that made Mickey smile.

"Hiya, Adam."

"Hello, Mickey," the little boy said. He was wearing jeans and Adidas and and a green La Coste shirt, and he sat on the floor next to Mickey. "Mickey," he said. "I got to ask you something."

"Sure, kid," Mickey said. "What is it?"

"Is your last name Mouse?"

Mickey smiled. "Yes," he said.

The little boy laughed. A gravelly laugh. And Mickey laughed, and Mickey picked him up in the air and hugged him and swung him around. He had really come to love these children. To sit in awe of their fresh and unspoiled ideas, and their confidence in expressing them. A confidence to which he felt he had contributed by praising their work. By telling the parents to either wait outside the rehearsal hall, or come back later, because he felt the children would be freer without any other adults around. "Mickey Mouse," Adam screamed as Mickey swung him in the air.

"Mickey Mouse," Mickey said laughing.

The other children were arriving now and Adam and Mickey collapsed into a dizzy heap on the floor. The air was always filled with anticipation when the children arrived, waiting for the latest exciting exercises. Mickey never disappointed them. They would be giants marching through cities, and then they would be monsters, and then goblins, and Mickey had music recorded for them to work with. And there were enormous bags of props and costumes which he made and bought and borrowed for them and they would dress up and pretend. And for those two hours be anything they wanted. There was even an exercise called "temper tantrum" where the children were encouraged to scream and yell and let out all their anger. "Like you wish you could at home," Mickey told them, and the children laughed conspiratorially with him. They knew he was on their side.

They were just about to try to be motorcycles when the door opened and one of the mothers stuck her head in and nodded for Mickey to come out. The woman was Jeffrey's mother, Mrs. Klein, and she usually sat in the lobby of the academy reading while she waited for her eight-year-old son. She looked nervous.

"Be motorcycles while I'm gone. I'll be back in a second," Mickey told the children and walked out into the hall.

"I think you ought to come downstairs, Mickey. It's that woman. The one whose little girl has the pigtails."

"Lucy," Mickey said. Lucy was a beauty. The most beautiful child he'd ever seen. Seven years old. Long blond pigtails and bangs and big blue eyes, but she was always very sad. Once the class had done an exercise called "If you could have your wish come true, what would you be?" One girl, Dawn, whirled madly around the room on her toes, to show that she wanted to be a ballerina; another girl, Debby, rocked an imaginary infant to sleep, to show that she wanted to be a mommy. But Lucy. When it was Lucy's turn, she put two chairs together and lay across them stiffly, with her arms folded on her chest. At first Mickey thought she was trying to say she wanted to be a magician's assistant because of the way she left a space between the part of the two chairs that was under her back. It looked to him as if she was going to be levitated, or sawed in half. But he was wrong.

"What's she being?" one of the kids asked.

"Yeah. What *are* you, Lucy? What's your wish?"

Lucy opened her eyes and slowly sat up. "I wish that I was dead and in my coffin," she said.

A few of the children laughed, but most of them looked at Mickey, who was trying to hide his surprise.

"Oh, Lucy," he had said. "That's silly. Try another wish. A good one. A fun one."

The seven-year-old girl looked at him through very old eyes. "I don't have another wish."

Mrs. Klein, Jeffrey's mother, ran down the stairs of the academy with Mickey. "Right out front," she told him.

Mickey pushed open the glass door and on the sidewalk outside stood Lucy's mother, a gorgeous woman who looked like a grown-up Lucy, slapping Lucy. On the face. One side. Then the other. Hard.

"You said you would. You promised me. And now you'll go to this class and do what I say. Do you hear me?"

The child was screaming and trying to pull away but the woman held her hard with her other hand.

"Please," Mickey shouted. "Stop it."

The woman turned and looked embarrassed to see Mickey. She tried to pull herself together but she still held tightly to the child's arm. Lucy's tear-filled eyes looked despairingly at Mickey.

"It's nothing," the mother said. "Just some family problems."

"No it's not," Lucy screamed. "I don't want to go to that goddamned class."

"Shut up," the mother said to Lucy, then tried to force a smile.

"She's just feeling nasty this morning," the mother said.

"I'm not. I hate acting class. I hate acting and I'm not going to be an actress no matter what you say."

There were people passing by, on their way in and out of the academy, and Mickey was worried about the twenty-four motorcycles upstairs getting out of control, but he didn't move as Lucy's mother suddenly transformed herself into a phony-voiced caricature, "Oh, my sweet girl, you know Mommy doesn't care if you're not an actress. She just wants you to be able to grow up and be successful so you can buy yourself pretty dresses and buy Mommy pretty dresses, like we always talk about. And you're so beautiful that everyone always says you could be in the movies."

Mickey felt queasy. Lucy was silent. She looked down at the ground.

"Lucy," Mickey said. "If you could do what you wanted to do on Saturday mornings, let's say, take any class you wanted to take, what would it be?"

The mother pursed her lips. Lucy was still silent.

"Lucy?" Mickey asked.

When the child finally spoke, her voice was timid and choked.

"A class with drawing and painting and crayons," she said longingly.

"Oh, bullshit," the mother said.

"Mrs.—" Mickey couldn't remember her name.

"Hill," she said.

"Mrs. Hill." Mickey was afraid. Afraid no matter what he said to this bitch she would take it out on Lucy. Little agonized Lucy. "To begin with, my classes aren't about show business. Believe me. Agents who represent child actors called me when they heard about the classes. They wanted to come here and scout. And I told them no way. Because I don't want these kids to feel pressured. That isn't going to do anything for them." He was trying to be controlled. Some people were standing around now listening.

"You see," he went on. "I've been in the business for quite a few years. And I'm real talented, and I'm devoted to the classes I take because I'm always looking to be better, and I want to be a movie star or a television star more than anyone I know, but so far the business hasn't been interested in me."

The woman looked at him blankly.

"What I'm saying is. It's hard enough to make it in show business when you're doing it because you really want to and need to. But if you're doing it because someone else wants you to do it, that's got to be impossible."

"Oh, *she* wants it—" the mother began.

"She doesn't," Mickey said. "Why don't you give her art classes? They have them right here at the academy. We'll go inside and sign her up now."

"But we already paid—"

"I'll give you every cent back right now."

"No. I don't—"

"Please, Mama," Lucy said almost inaudibly.

Mrs. Hill took a deep breath, walked inside the academy and up to the desk marked registration. Mickey had to get back upstairs.

" 'Bye, Lucy," he said, giving the little girl a hug. "Next Saturday you come over and say hi to me after art class. Okay?"

"Okay."

Mickey ran upstairs. The motorcycles had become racing cars, engines loud, brakes slamming on, crashing into walls.

"Okay," he said. "Time for the prop-bag game."

"Yayyy," the racing cars shouted and pulled to a stop around Mickey.

At the end of the two hours, Mickey was always drained. Every Saturday morning, when it was finally eleven thirty, all the kids tackled him, piled on top of him, the door opened and the parents poured in to find out what the kids had done that day. Today, as the kids ran to their parents, Mickey saw a face in the group of grownups that looked familiar to him. It was Nina's mother. That's why he'd never seen her before. Nina was signed up for the class by an Englishwoman who appeared to be a governess, and either the governess or a chauffeur always picked her up. The woman was so familiar. The other parents were looking at her shyly. She was heading toward Mickey.

"I'm Nina's mother," she said.

I know. I know. But who are you? How do I— Betty Day. Jesus. *The Betty Day Show* was the longest-running variety show on television. And Betty Day was one of the best-known and best-loved television personalities.

"Miss Day." One of the mothers handed her a pencil and paper to get her autograph. She signed it gladly, then turned back to Mickey, who was sitting on the floor. He was too surprised to get up. Betty Day sat down next to him.

"Nina talks about nothing else but your classes all week long. Last week she came home and showed me how she had acted out being an earthquake in your class. I guess that's something only a California child can do." She smiled warmly. "I appreciate your policy of not letting any adults in to watch. It's certainly made Nina feel secure with you."

"Thank you," Mickey said. "Nina's a nice girl." Betty Day. Of course. Why hadn't it ever occurred to him? The group of parents and children were gone now. Only little Nina remained, waiting for her mother, trying on the various hats from a laundry bag full of hats Mickey brought.

"I saw what you did outside this morning with that horrible woman," Betty Day said. She had sympathetic eyes. "I was passing by and stopped to listen. I thought that was really lovely of you. Actually, I was kind of a party to it myself," she said. "After you went upstairs she looked around as if she might change her mind and not sign the little girl up for art, and then she saw *me* standing there. She recognized me, and I said, 'Go on, Mrs. Hill. Sign her up.' And she did." Mickey and Betty Day laughed, and Nina came over. She was wearing a straw hat.

"Hiya, vaudeville," Betty Day said. Now Mickey noticed how much the child looked like the mother.

"I'm *not* vaudeville. I'm Nina," she said. Then she put her arms around Mickey. "I love Mickey, Mom," she said.

"Well, I understand that," Betty Day said. "Mickey's pretty lovable."

Mickey smiled.

"I'd like to help you, Mickey," Betty said. "Maybe I can. Do you know who Danny Kohler is?"

Danny Kohler. Important television producer. Three series on the air.

"Sure."

"He's my good friend. And he's casting a show."

"A pilot?"

"A sold series. And you're right for it. For the lead. Perfect. I hate to give anyone false hope. I mean you look right. And I have a hunch you're a good actor."

"I am."

"Give me your number. I'll have Kohler's office call you on Monday."

Mickey wasn't sure what to feel. He'd been this route so many times, in so many shapes and forms, that it was hard to be excited. He was afraid to be excited because he knew how crushing the disappointment was after that. He gave Betty Day his number.

"I know what you're thinking," she said. "I can see it in your eyes. And obviously I can't promise you that this time it will be different for you, because it's not my show. But I like you. Obviously my daughter likes you." Nina was hanging around Mickey's neck. "And we're in your corner."

"Thank you," Mickey said. But he wouldn't let himself fall for it this time.

thirty-nine

"Six million gross on the Minnie Kahn tour," Barry said into the phone. "And Heaven's album is three with a bullet this week. Not bad, you know?" He rocked back and forth in the leather chair behind his desk, and looked at the gold-framed photograph of Beau. That face. He loved her. He would have to locate the painter who'd done the picture of Harley and have the guy paint one of Beau that would fill the whole wall over the sofa.

"Athena will gross nearly fifty million this year," he said. Athena Records. He got the idea that night he had the fight with Jim Garland about Beau's album. In a rage Barry had tried to figure out a way to start a record company he could control. The next morning he walked unannounced into Harold Greenfield's office.

"I'll figure out a way to move all my acts to World if I can run the label," he said.

Greenfield looked long at him. Thinking. "Make the records yourself and World will distribute them," he said. Barry agreed. He wasn't sure what he was getting into, but he agreed.

He decided to call his company Athena because he remembered reading once that Athena was the goddess of war and he was certain he was in for a tough battle. The next night, after Beau was asleep, he drove into town from the beach and went to his Sunset Strip office. He went through all the files to check the dates on the contracts of all of his acts. Not their management contracts with him; there were none. His deals with the acts were always made on good faith. These were the contracts his acts had with the various record companies. He wanted to determine how soon he would be able to sign each of them to his own label. Maybe that was the night he had the first headache. He wasn't sure.

The next day he called his lawyers and business managers and Athena was on its way. By the second year, it was making a fortune and Harold Greenfield had just offered to buy it for eight million dollars and a rich contract for Barry to run it. He was thinking about it. The headaches. The fucking headaches. He would call a doctor.

"Dee Dee . . . get me . . ." Never mind. He'd dial it himself.

"Dr. Copely's office," said a voice.

"This is Barry Golden. Is Dr. Copely in?"

"No. I'm sorry. He's not. Can I help you?"

"I've been having some really bad headaches and I wanted to come in and see him," Barry said.

"He's out of town, Mr. Golden. He'll be back next Tuesday. Can it wait?"

"Uh . . . sure. Next Tuesday will be fine."

"Ten o'clock?"

"Yeah. Thanks."

He was getting one now. Maybe that's why he had finally called the doctor. Because he felt it coming on. When he wasn't having the headaches he forgot how awful it was to feel like this. The queasiness that came with it. The blurring of his vision. Migraines. That's what they must be. He remembered hearing someone who had migraines describing one to him. And the symptoms were the ones he was having now. He went to the sink and filled a cup of water. There were aspirins in the top drawer of his desk. He took the little metal box out and removed two aspirins. Fuck. The pain. He should lie down on the sofa. Yes. He'd turn out the light and lie on the sofa.

The buzzer.

"Mr. Golden, Beau is on the line."

"Hi, sweetheart."

"I love you," she said. "Where can we go for lunch?"

Right. Beau was coming in from the beach to have lunch with him. Lunch. Beau. Should he tell her he was nauseated and couldn't have lunch? No. Maybe if he could lie down for a few minutes.

"I love you, too. Anywhere you want."

"Ma Maison. I'll make the reservation. See you at your office at twelve thirty."

" 'Bye."

It was getting worse now. He closed his eyes. Lie down.

"Dee Dee . . . I'm going to lie down. Hold my calls."

"Even Minnie's?" Dee Dee asked. "She's calling from overseas at eleven."

"Oh, right. No. I'll take that." And the phone rang.

"It might be her now." Barry heard Dee Dee pick up the phone. "Yes, operator," she said. "Go ahead, please. It's Minnie," she said to him.

Barry picked up the phone and sat back down in his desk chair. Maybe if he kept his eyes closed he wouldn't see the room spinning.

"Hi, Min," he said.

Minnie sounded far away and very excited about the European

part of her tour. Barry was grateful she was rambling on because he didn't know if he could talk.

"And they loved me . . . and they mobbed the hotel . . . and the suite is gorgeous. And everyone's so polite and I got drunk with the band last night in a pub . . . and this morning Robby is so sick—but we're sold out everywhere . . . and everyone's excited about the new album . . . and how's Beau and I love you both. And I can't wait to shop in Paris. Call you from there." Click.

It was getting better. Subsiding slowly. Easing off. The aspirin must have helped.

"Can I get you anything?" Dee Dee asked.

"No. I'm fine." If he didn't move he'd be okay. Didn't think about the nausea. It was going away. Thank God. He didn't have time to be sick. There were deals to be made. He'd see Copely on Tuesday and get something he'd be able to take right away when the headache symptoms came on. He wouldn't lie down now. Beau would be here soon and they'd have a romantic lunch. He heard the phone ring.

"I'm sorry, Mr. Pearlman," he heard Dee Dee say. Irving Pearlman, Benny Daniels' lawyer. That putz. "Mr. Golden isn't available right now."

"Yes I am," he told her. "I'll take it." He was feeling better.

"Hello," Barry said into the phone. Benny Daniels' divorce lawyer was almost as slimy to Barry as Benny himself. His specialty was divorces where big money was involved. Usually he represented the wives the way Marvin Mitchelson did, but in the Daniels case it was the husband who petitioned for and was the recipient of spousal support.

"Haven't been able to reach Beau's lawyer, Golden," Pearlman said in a voice about to threaten. "But I thought Beau should be aware that if she or her lawyer fails to pay my client the support for the last two months, I will go into court and seek an order to hold her in contempt. And, buddy, I hope they send her to jail."

"Irving," Barry said. "You're a cliché. I wish I could see you right now because I know you're rubbing your ugly little hands together in glee, but Beau's been advised not to send Benny any money until he vacates the house."

"Hey, listen," Pearlman said, "I called to give you some information. Not to be insulted. Lay off."

"Pearlman, you *are* an insult," Barry said, "to the entire legal profession."

"Fuck you, you little two-bit faggot. I'll see you and that has-been girl friend of yours in court." Pearlman slammed down the phone.

Barry got up. The headache was nearly gone, but he still felt a little weak. He would lie down now. On the sofa.

Dee Dee looked in on him.

"I'm going to lunch," she said. "You feeling better?"

"A little."

"See you later."

The sofa. Barry lay down on the sofa and looked at the ceiling for a few minutes and was just dozing off when he heard the outer door open.

"Hello?" It was Beau.

"Hi, sweetheart," he said, getting to his feet. Oh, shit. He must have stood up too quickly. The pain. It was as if someone hit him with something sharp. It was . . . Jesus. He couldn't see . . .

"Beau!" he cried out.

"I wore your favorite sweater and I—" Beau walked into the office just as Barry collapsed.

"Barry? Baby? Oh, my God," she cried. "Oh, my God. Barry." She ran into the hallway.

"Help." She screamed. "Somebody help. Call an ambulance." It was lunchtime. All of the doors to the other Athena offices were closed. Beau rushed back into Barry's office. His small body was still lying in a heap where he'd fallen. He was breathing but he was unconscious. "Help me!" She picked up the phone and dialed the operator. She got the Athena switchboard. "Please," she said, "Mr. Golden is—he collapsed. Oh, my God. Call an ambulance. Oh, God. Hurry. Please."

forty

Jerri cuddled up very close to Stan. They had just made love and he was nearly asleep.

"Bob Frank is driving me crazy," she said. "You know what he does?"

"Mmmm."

"He keeps hitting on me. You know? Making passes. I'm a fucking vice-president, for Christ's sake, and he treats me like I'm some dumb bang. I don't know why he does that. I think it shows that he doesn't respect me. To think I'd go out with a married man."

Stan didn't respond. She went on.

"I also think it means he doesn't respect *you*. I mean, he *knows* we live together."

Stan hated these moments with Jerri. Moments when he knew she was lying and he was afraid to tell her he knew. Afraid to say, "I know you had an affair with Bob Frank." She usually had some motive for the lie. It wasn't just out of the blue. So each time she lied, Stan would wait to hear what was coming next.

"Maybe I should quit working for a while," she said. "Take some time off."

So that was it. Stan was relieved. Glad she wanted to leave her job. Glad she'd be away from Bob Frank. And be just his little Jerri. The girl who loved the pretty clothes he bought her, and who brought him breakfast in bed every Sunday and afterward smeared the leftover jam on her nipples and let him lick it off "for dessert."

"It's okay with me if you quit," he said.

"Oh, good," she said, cuddling closer. "Now I'll be at home all the time," she said. "Just waiting for you with my legs spread."

Jerri quit her job the next day and enjoyed her retirement for exactly two weeks. On the first day, she sat at the pool of the apartment house where she and Stan lived, and got a tan. On the second day she met her mother for lunch in Beverly Hills. On the third day she stayed in bed and talked on the phone for hours, and for the next eleven days she did some variation or combination of those same three things. By the beginning of the third week, she was getting very edgy. That's when she showed Stan the ad in *Variety:* Fabulous Benedict Canyon home. Pool. View. Lighted N.S. tennis court, master has sauna, jacuzzi, his-and-hers bath and used-brick fireplace.

Hardwood floors, beamed ceilings throughout. Poolhouse has projection room. $850,000. Ask for Elaine.

"Jesus," he said. "That sounds fabulous, Jer. But we don't need anything that big."

"The ad doesn't say it's big."

"Well, I mean that fancy."

A pout played on Jerri's lower lip.

"Honey, it's eight hundred and fifty thousand dollars," he said.

"You could offer them seven," she said.

Stan looked at her eager face. There was so much need written all over it. The daughter of a hash slinger from Culver City, she called herself.

"It would make me so happy, I'd spend every day fixing it up," she begged.

"If I'm going to pay eight hundred and fifty thousand dollars for a house," Stan said, "I hope there won't be anything about it that needs fixing up."

Jerri laughed. But she was frustrated.

"I mean decorate it," she said.

"I know what you mean," Stan told her, "but—"

"Let's just go take a peek at it. Please."

The house was empty when they got there. The people who had been living there were moved out and there was a note on the door from the real estate broker who was supposed to meet them there at two.

Dear Jerri and Stan,

Couldn't reach either of you. I won't be able to make it by two. Key is under mat. (Clever hiding place, eh?) Please feel free to look around and, if you want to wait, I'll see you at three. If not, leave the key and I'll call you later.

Elaine

Jerri opened the door with the key, and when she looked around the excitement on her beautiful face made Stan want to give her the world.

"Look at it," she said. "Just look at it."

Stan had to admit the house was better than any house he'd ever seen.

"Yes, great," he said.

When Jerri saw the bedroom fireplace, she groaned.

"Oh, please, honey. Won't you get this house for us?"

She put her arms around him and pulled him close. Stan knew what she was doing and he didn't like her little-girl approach. She always used it to get her way. But he did love this woman. "Please . . ." She kissed him and started unbuttoning his shirt.

"Jerri—"

"No one's here," she said. "No one will be here till three. Oooh, let's do it, baby. I'm so wet. And I want it. C'mon."

They fucked in the furnitureless bedroom of the vacant house with the sound of Jerri's ass banging against the hardwood floor, echoing through the emptiness. When they lay in each other's arms afterward, Stan was already figuring out in his mind what kind of down payment he would have to make on the house. It would be fine. He had plenty of money. And Jerri would be so happy.

"Maybe we should go," Jerri said, pulling her underpants on.

"No. Let's wait for the broker," Stan said. "We'll make an offer." Jerri covered his face with kisses.

He'd never been sorry about buying the house. He loved it and he loved Jerri and he loved their Sunday afternoons of tennis and swimming with friends who came over to spend the day. Besides, people were already telling him he could get "a million two" for the place. Jerri fixed the house up as she promised, but with the help of an expensive decorator. And Stan was thrilled when Albert called to say he was coming to visit and see the new house and "meet this woman I've heard so much about."

The day before Albert's arrival, Jerri cried all morning. "He'll hate me," she said. "I just know your father will hate me."

"That's crazy," Stan said, wiping away her tears. "Who could ever hate you? Go and get some pretty new outfits, and you'll knock him out."

The outfits didn't help. Albert wasn't easily knocked out. On the contrary, Stan could already see on Albert's face after the old man had been there just a few hours that he was disappointed. Not with the house. He oohed and ahhed over everything about the house. Even said he'd try to hit a few tennis balls before he went back. It was Jerri. The tension between Jerri and Albert was obvious immediately. Each of them struggled for a politeness that was so awkward they were choking on it.

"Very nice dinner," Albert said about the Chinese food Jerri had delivered from Ho Toy's one night.

"Stan and I make a great team," Jerri said another night after she'd had a few glasses of wine. "We have it down to a science. He makes a lot of money and I spend a lot of money."

Albert nodded.

"Very good caps you have," Albert said, looking at Jerri's teeth.

"Thanks," she said. "Got 'em free. The dentist was after my ass." She was flushed. Oh, shit. This was Stan's father. And a dentist.

Albert felt bad. He knew there were many women around who spent their lives being carried and taken care of by men. And that frequently the men who supported them were aware of the game. And liked the exchange. Goods for sex and affection. But Albert couldn't believe that his son, Stanley, was a man who would make that exchange. Knew he wasn't. No. Stanley sincerely loved this girl and couldn't see what she was. Stanley's mother, Lena, had died when the children were very young. Maybe Albert should have remarried. Given them a mother. Had a marriage for them to use as a model. But he didn't, and now Bonny was living with some long-haired weirdo somewhere, and worse yet, Stanley, Albert's brilliant son Stanley, was living with this trash.

"She was right," Albert said to Stan, after Jerri returned from a shopping spree one afternoon and showed them all of her purchases. "She certainly can spend money."

"It's okay, Dad," Stan said. "I make it."

Albert was pained. Stan saw it. He ached to tell his father how he felt, but they had never talked about these things before, and it seemed as if it was too late to start now. He wanted to tell his father how long he'd waited to find a woman he could talk to and relate to and who taught him sexual tricks he never dreamed existed. And how he knew Jerri was no virgin. And that she looked a little over-painted, and that though she was street-smart, he knew she had no class. But that didn't matter to him at this point. She was there for him. And hot, and loyal and his woman. End of subject.

"Maybe you and your young lady should make some kind of contract about property," Albert suggested before he got on the plane back to Florida.

Stan smiled. "You only make contracts like that if you're planning to split up, Dad. We aren't."

After Stan took Albert to the airport that day, he came home to play a few sets of tennis with Nate Shore. He was on the tennis court when Jerri called him to the phone.

"Beau Daniels," she yelled down.

"Tell her I'll call her back."

"It's okay," Shore said. "I don't mind a breather."

"She says it's an emergency," Jerri hollered.

Stan ran up the steps to the house. Barry and Beau had been happily ensconced in Barry's Malibu place for the past few years. Domestic bliss. Beau's picture had appeared on the cover of the March issue of *Ladies' Home Journal:* BEAU DANIELS: HER DIVORCE. HOW SHE SURVIVED AND FOUND NEW LOVE.

"Hello."

"Stan." Beau's voice was very faint.

"Hello?"

"Stan. It's Barry," she said. "He's in the emergency ward. U.C.L.A. They have to operate. Please . . ." She stopped talking to cry.

"I'll be right there."

Stan ran upstairs to change. Jerri was sitting on the bed putting a coat of polish on her toenails.

"Barry Golden's in the hospital," Stan said, pulling off his tennis shorts and putting on a pair of jeans from the closet.

"Hemorrhoids?" Jerri asked snidely.

Stan didn't answer. He took his wallet and his car keys and ran down the steps and out the front door.

"Stan!" Jerri shouted after him. Who gives a shit about that little drip Barry Golden anyway? she thought. Stan was already gone.

Stan could see Beau sitting on the bench in the distance as he got off the elevator. She seemed so out of place in a hospital. Who wasn't out of place in a hospital? She was staring straight ahead, deep in thought.

"Beau."

"Stan." She jumped to her feet to give him a quick hug. "I'm glad you came," she said. "We have no one."

It was true. Because Los Angeles was so spread out, visiting one's friends was a planned effort and frequently couples or families became isolated. If there was no immediate family to come for barbecues and holidays, friends could sometimes go months without seeing one another.

"What's happening?" Stan asked Beau.

"He had a brain hemorrhage," she said. Her eyes were filled with tears. "The doctor said it's something in his central nervous system."

"Where is he now?"

"They're doing angiograms," she said. "They put dye into his veins to try and see where the bleeding is. Oh, God, Stan."

Stan held her while she cried. A nurse passed and looked sweetly at Stan as if to say, "I'm sorry," and he wondered how many crying people those nurses saw a day.

The elevator down the hall opened and a few people got off and were coming toward Stan and Beau.

"It's his doctor. The surgeon who's on the case. Davidson," Beau said.

"Hello, Miss Daniels," the tall gray-haired man said gently. Stan immediately looked at Davidson's hands. They looked too big to be able to poke around inside of brains and hearts.

"This is our friend, Stan Rose," she told the doctor.

"Mr. Golden had a hemorrhage in his subarachnoid space," Davidson told Stan. "He had an arterial venous malfunction. Blood vessels that don't belong there. We're going to have to take them out, or we run the risk of it continuing to bleed."

"Brain surgery," Beau said quietly. "My God."

"He'll be coming up from the tests soon. We've given him Demerol for the pain but he is conscious. I've already discussed the surgery with him and we've agreed that we'll do it tomorrow morning. It's a long process, but it's necessary. Miss Daniels, you'll forgive me . . . but you haven't left the hospital since you came in on Friday. Have you been sleeping? Eating?"

"No," Beau said. "But I'm perfectly fine."

"Why don't you two go to the commissary and get some lunch?" he asked. "By the time you get back, Mr. Golden should have been returned to his room."

"No—I don't want to—"

"C'mon, Beau," Stan said, taking her arm. "I'll treat."

The hospital commissary was busy. Stan noticed the look of recognition that crossed people's faces when they saw Beau in the cafeteria line. Thankfully no one came over to ask her for her autograph, or to tell her they wished she'd go back with Benny. Beau put a few things on her tray: some carrot salad, a blob of red Jell-O, a cup of black coffee. Stan took a ready-made ham sandwich and a lemonade, and they found a table. Neither of them was the least bit hungry.

"It took me my whole life to find that little bastard," she said. "If he doesn't pull through this—"

"He will, Beau," Stan said. "Don't let yourself think that way."

"You know what?" she said. "I love Barry so much I could live with him in the back of a fifty-four Chevy panel truck."

Stan smiled. "As long as it had walk-in closets."

"No." Beau was very serious.

"I always had these big dreams when I was a kid about having mansions, limos and furs and jewelry, because I was a poor kid and poor kids probably all have those dreams. And then I met Benny. I was fourteen when I met Benny. I told him I was sixteen. But I was only fourteen fucking years old. And he promised me I'd have those things. Mansions and limos and furs and jewelry, and he made it come true. But always, and I know this sounds like bullshit now, you know, hindsight, but the honest-to-God truth is that what I really wanted more than any of that was to have one loving devoted man to care for me. The way Benny did at first. Or acted like he did. The way Barry has. I mean it, Stan. I've had every material thing money can buy and, as corny as it sounds, love is all there is. Everything else is bullshit."

Stan looked at her across the table. Sitting there without her makeup—in those wrinkled clothes—with her hair uncombed. She looked ordinary. She was ordinary. Wonderfully ordinary. With the same needs as everyone else.

"Let's go upstairs and see Barry," he said.

The door to Barry's room was closed and Beau tapped on it lightly. A nurse stuck her head out. "One minute," she said and went back into the room.

"Don't be scared when you see him," Beau said to Stan. "He looks awful."

The nurse opened the door. "He's awake," she told them. "But he's drugged."

Barry looked like a little boy lying on the bed in the darkened room. The way, Stan thought, that he himself must have looked when he had polio.

"Barry, honey," Beau said. "Stan Rose is here."

"Stan. Hi, pal," Barry said.

"Hiya, Golden," Stan said.

Everyone was quiet for a minute. Then Barry spoke.

"Hey, listen, Juggie," he said. His voice was breathy and almost totally without energy, and Stan smiled to himself. Demerol or not, Golden remembered the old nickname. "They're gonna operate on my fuckin' brain."

"I know," Stan said.

"I could die. You know."

"You won't die, Golden," Stan said. He looked at Beau. Her mouth was tight and her brow furrowed. She was trying hard not to cry. Barry looked so small and narrow in the bed. If it wasn't for the beard, he could have easily been mistaken for a child.

"Listen. I've got to tell you something. Harley . . . Beau . . . No. Stan." He was really spaced. He paused again for a very long time. "And you're going to hate me for saying it, but you see, if I don't, I might die and never get to tell you and you have to know."

Stan was intrigued. What could it be?

Beau looked nervous. "Barry," she said. "Go to sleep."

"No." Even under the Demerol there was an edge in the word.

Stan waited for Barry to go on.

"You have to get away from that woman. Jerri. I know you love her and I know you've been together for a while—but you have to. She's a whore."

Stan clenched his fists. He couldn't even shout at Barry to shut up.

"Barry—stop it," Beau said.

Barry was silent.

"He's drugged," Beau said to Stan. "Don't pay any attention to him."

"Does he know something?" Stan asked her. No. Please. No.

"She's a whore," Barry said. "She'll do you in. I don't want to die."

Stan walked out into the hallway. He wanted to hear more. Know it all. But he was afraid. Jerri. A whore. Golden had known her for years. What could that mean? From Golden, who had fucked boys— and then supposedly gone straight for crazy Beau Daniels. That's who was telling him that his woman was a whore. He had to know. Beau came to the door.

"I'm sorry," she said. "He's wanted to tell you that for a long time. Wanted to call you and tell you that because he cares about you."

"Who is it?"

"I think he's mostly talking about Nate Shore," she said.

Stan's heart sank. Nate Shore. He just left Nate Shore at his house with Jerri. Nate Shore's wife, Bonny Lee, was a nightclub singer when Shore met her. Shore was a William Morris agent who married her and then maneuvered her to stardom the way Benny had for Beau, and Jeff Wald had for Helen Reddy. Now Shore's career was

being Bonny Lee's manager. He had no other job than that. Without
Bonny he was nothing. Fortunately for Shore, Bonny earned millions
every year. Unfortunately for Shore, despite Bonny's big voice and
big checkbook, she was very unattractive. So he was always chasing
women. Stan told Beau he'd be back to sit with her in the morning
while Barry was in surgery—and he walked toward the elevator.

He didn't even remember the ride home. The first thing he remembered was seeing Shore's red Porsche next to Jerri's yellow Mercedes.
He was drained when he got out of the car. Golden having brain surgery tomorrow. Maybe the Demerol made him crazy. But then, why
did Beau agree?

Stan found himself turning his key in the front door lock quietly.
Oh, God. Could he stand catching her? Seeing her naked, that gorgeous naked body of hers, in the arms of another man? Was that
what he wanted? The house was quiet. He walked outside. No one
was on the tennis court, or at the pool. Shore's cock inside Jerri's
cunt. Oh, God. Maybe he should leave. Call first and make sure
Shore was gone. That was crazy. This was his house. His million-
dollar house. He wasn't leaving. Shit, no.

He heard the voices. It was Jerri and Shore. He opened the door.
Jerri looked surprised to see him. But she wasn't naked. She was
fully clothed in a tennis dress and she and Nate must have been
watching something on the television because the Betamax was re-
winding the tape.

"Hi, sweetheart," she said.

"How's Barry?" Nate Shore said.

"Not good," Stan answered. "He had a hemorrhage from the
brain. Suddenly. On Friday."

The video tape had rewound. Jerri removed it and put it into a
box of tapes near the machine.

"He's got to have brain surgery tomorrow morning."

"Oh, no," Jerri said. "How awful. Oh, honey, is Beau all right?"

She looked so concerned. So sweet and so sincerely concerned.
Maybe Golden was wrong. Maybe it was the Demerol talking. And
Beau didn't know. Shore was crazy about his wife, Bonny Lee. Shore
was a married man. So was Bob Frank. And he heard what Jerri said
to him. That night at the recording studio, outside the bathroom
door. And the next morning from the hotel in San Luis Obispo.

"Damn shame," Shore was saying. "I like Golden. Not many people in the business do, but I like him. I'll send something over to the
hospital. Bonny will want to send something from us."

Stan was in a fog. First the shock of learning about Golden's surgery, then Golden saying those things to him about Jerri. And now he was standing in this room with his lover and the man who might be *her* lover? Maybe. Maybe not.

"Well, I'd better get home to the little woman," Shore said, getting up. "Thanks for the tennis game, Jerri."

"You're welcome, Nate," she said, smiling. She was so beautiful. Stan ached . . .

"Ciao, Stan," Shore said and walked out the door.

"You must really be exhausted from all this," Jerri said to Stan. "Why don't you go upstairs and lie down. I'll straighten up in here and come and fix you some dinner."

Stan was numb.

"No," he said. "I'll stay down here and read for a while." He liked sitting in the poolhouse. There was something peaceful about it. Jerri looked concerned.

"Well, I'll stay with you," she said.

"No. I want to be alone," he told her.

He hoped she would just leave. Go up to the house and pack her things and leave because she knew that he knew. And then he'd never have to see her again. Instead of a confrontation. A showdown. Telling her he knew. Golden knew. Beau knew that Jerri was fucking Nate Shore and God knows who else.

"My poor Stan," she said, coming over to kiss him. "It must have been terrible at the hospital." More than you know. "I love you," she said.

"I love you," he said on automatic. Maybe the story wasn't true. She loved him. He loved her.

"I'll be up soon," he said.

She left reluctantly. Stan walked slowly around the lavish poolhouse. Eight hundred and fifty thousand dollars, plus everything it cost to get the place to look like this. Jesus. Projection equipment, furniture, all the equipment for the tennis court. Videotape machine. Cameras. Jerri wanted it. All of it so badly. Jerri. Maybe it wasn't true.

Stan picked up a handful of magazines. *Time. Newsweek.* Old ones. He'd read them. He flipped on the television. *Wide World of Sports* was on. It was always a good escape to stare at the television. He saw cars racing around a track and crashing into each other and crashing into walls and catching fire. He watched figure skaters gliding, lifting, turning. Downhill skiers. It was all a blur because it couldn't block out the images in his mind. He got up to turn the set off but he knew he was running out of reasons to stay down here and, if he went up to the house, it would have to be to confront Jerri.

He reached into the tape box. Later, he remembered that at that moment he was thinking he wanted to watch some old movie he had taped. This cassette didn't have a label. He slid it into place. It clicked and started.

No. My God. It was bizzare. As though the horrible pictures, my God, in his mind were somehow conveyed onto the television screen so he could see them. Oh, Jesus. Jerri and Nate Shore. Going at each other. They'd taped it. Sick. Disgusting. Taping their fucking. In his house. On his couch. Shore's ass. Jerri's cunt. Shore sucking her tits. The two of them looking at the camera and laughing. Why did she have this tape here? She didn't mean to. That was it. She wanted to take it with her. Hide it. Didn't expect Stan back before she'd taken it away. Then, when he arrived, she tried to get him out. To get him to go upstairs so she could hide that tape. The tape of her fucking Shore . . . Shore was inside Jerri now, pounding, thrusting. Stan couldn't take his eyes away. Once there was a horrible auto accident outside his office on Ventura Boulevard. A driver lost control of her car and two cars collided head on, and the ambulance came and a woman and her little girl were cut and hurt and bleeding and crying. And it was horrible and Stan hated it, hated the screaming and the blood, but he couldn't take his eyes away. Stayed at the window until everyone was gone. And now he knew he should stop watching this. Had to. No.

No. He was screaming. No. No. No. How could she? No. That whore? How? My God. No.

The tape clicked itself off and Stan, drained and hurting, looked up at Jerri, who stood white-faced and silent in the doorway of the poolhouse. Somehow he found his voice.

"Take your things and get out of my house," he said. "Be out in one hour."

"I want the tape," she said, walking toward the television.

Stan stood and got in her way. He was seething with anger. He could strangle her now. He wanted to. Wanted to hurt her. Kill her.

"Why?"

"I want it," she said. He could see she was afraid.

"No," he told her. "*I* want it."

"To torture yourself?" she asked.

"No. To show to Bonny Lee, and to the court, in case you have any insane idea about maybe asking for half of what I own."

"You bastard."

"You whore."

He slapped her hard, and again and again. He'd never hit anyone before in his whole life. When he was through, he walked away and stood facing the wall shaking. Jerri didn't even cry. She just turned and walked slowly out of the poolhouse and up toward the main house holding her head high.

Stan stayed in the poolhouse all night. At about six thirty when the sun came up, he went to his bedroom. There was a note from Jerri in an envelope on the bed. He didn't read it—just tore it to shreds and tossed the pieces into the wastebasket.

Then he took a shower and drove to U.C.L.A. Hospital. Beau was sitting outside Barry's room, just as she had been the day before. Her secretary, Connie, was with her, and she'd obviously brought Beau some fresh clothes.

"They just took him down," Beau said when she saw Stan. The three of them sat silently for a long time. Maybe an hour. At eight thirty Barry's secretary, Dee Dee, arrived, and a few minutes later Danny Kyle, the drummer from Heaven, arrived. By noon there were eight people in the corridor and a nurse came by and told them they'd have to move to the I.C.U. waiting room. David Kane arrived at two o'clock. Despite the crowd, the room remained very quiet.

At three o'clock, Dr. Davidson, still in his gown, opened the door and peeked in. His eyes scanned the room until they fell on Beau, who jumped to her feet when she saw him. Davidson spoke softly.

"He's in the intensive-care ward. We got it all, and he's going to be fine."

A cheer rose from the group. And they all hugged each other. David Kane was hugging Stan. Old Archie Andrews. He had tears in his eyes. And Beau Daniels. Sultry, hard-as-nails Beau Daniels was sitting on the floor kicking her feet happily. And she was laughing and crying at the same time. Stan, who had been so filled with agony about last night and Jerri and Nate Shore, suddenly forgot his own problems and danced for joy around the room.

forty-one

David looked carefully at the artwork. It was perfect. The sheriff's badge in the lower left-hand corner of the page. And the bold printed copy at the top. FOR YOUR CONSIDERATION . . . BEST ACTOR—RUE MCMILLAN. BEST SUPPORTING ACTOR—DOUG HART. BEST DIRECTOR—KEVIN MANN. BEST CINEMATOGRAPHER—ARTHUR HESHMAN. BEST PICTURE—WILD RIDE. A David Kane Production.

They had a chance. They had a good fucking chance. But he had to stop dwelling on it. Stop thinking about being at the Academy Awards. About what it was like that night long ago when the guys went to the Awards using Pinsky's tickets. He had been so nervous that night. But then the show started and he was fascinated. Fantasizing that it was his name that would be called next. Wondering what it would be like to run up and be handed that gold statue. And how, not so many years later, he might have a chance.

Allyn's television show was canceled after thirteen weeks. It was critically acclaimed, but the ratings were low, and now she was trying to write a screenplay, in between working with proven writers who were developing shows for Hemisphere. She was ambitious, and she liked the fact that even though most of the other movie executives' wives were "only wives and mothers," as she put it, she could sit in a room at a party with the men and relate to them because she knew what was going on in the business.

"Aren't you glad I'm your equal?" she asked David all the time. "And not some appendage who's just waiting for your command?"

"Mmmmm," he said. "Glad."

"Mr. Kane."

His secretary tapped on the office door, then poked her head in. "Can you see a Miss Collins?" she asked.

Collins. David thought for a moment. Colleen. He remembered. Doug Hart's girl. Actress. Met her on location. Stunning.

"Yes." Don't look too eager.

The door opened.

"Hi."

Should he stand? No. Christ. She was gorgeous. He remembered her twitching around the pool at the hotel where the cast of *Wild Ride* was staying for two weeks of shooting in Phoenix. And at night, after the long day. When they had all sat in Rue's suite, having a few drinks, smoking a little dope, playing cards, David had looked across the room at her. She was sitting close to Hart, rubbing his thigh, nuzzling him, and David got excited watching. Later when he went to his hotel room he called Allyn. He wanted her to be there with him, to come to the location of his first picture and sit there on the sidelines and say, "This is going to be a hit." But she wasn't, she was in production herself. "Glad it's going well," Allyn said. "Love you."

Colleen sat on the sofa. "I was just in the building so I thought I'd stop by," she said. A Playmate. Fold-out. Now he remembered. Rue had told him that. Rue met Colleen long before David did, when she first started seeing Hart. "Then one day I'm looking at a picture of this girl's snatch in *Playboy*—and it's her. I about died," Rue told David.

"Well, it's nice that you stopped by, Colleen," David told her.

"How have you been?" she asked him. Small talk.

"Fine. Just fine. You know, your boy Dougie could win himself an Oscar," he said.

"He's not my boy."

"Pardon?" He heard her. He just wanted to make sure.

"We broke up."

"Oh. Sorry."

"Don't be. He's an actor. They're all fucked up."

"And actresses?"

"Look, I'm not really serious about acting," she said. "I just do it every now and then because it falls into my lap." Her lap. David was trying to be cool. But, Jesus.

"I want to fuck you," she said.

David held on to the desk.

"I wanted to fuck you when we were in Phoenix," she added. "But I was afraid to say anything because I was with Doug."

"I'm married," David said.

"So?"

David wanted to be able to laugh and be cute about it, but this broad was serious. And he was starting to feel pretty serious, too. One time after Allyn moved in. He only cheated one time. The time that he fucked Beau Daniels. And that was business. And awful. And he felt guilty. But after he was married. Nothing. Straight as an arrow. Even though Allyn was tired a lot now when he wanted her, and sometimes they'd get into bed at night and talk about business until they both were sleepy, and it was never as hot as it had been because it was so familiar. Straight. Oh, man. He was really rationalizing like crazy. And he knew it.

"Do you want to fuck me?" Colleen asked.

"Uh . . . yes."

"How 'bout for lunch?" she said. "I live in Hollywood."

"I have a lunch meeting," he said. Asshole. This gorgeous cunt is begging for it and you have a lunch meeting? Cancel the fucking meeting. Too late. She was getting up to leave.

"Uh . . . how about seven o'clock tonight?" he asked.

"Great."

Relief. She wasn't uptight about it. She already had her address and phone number written on a piece of paper which she placed on the desk in front of him.

"See you." A smile. Allyn. He was feeling guilty already. Colleen left. David dialed the phone.

"Hemisphere Studios."

"Allyn Grant, please."

"One moment."

"Allyn Grant's office."

"This is David Kane."

"Oh, yes, Mr. Kane. She's on another line, but I'll tell her it's you."

"Thank you."

"David. Hi. I just talked to Mike Medavoy. He wants to read my script."

"Great."

"I saw your ad in *Variety*. It looked wonderful."

"Mmmm."

"I have meetings till about seven or eight tonight," she said. "How 'bout you?"

"Me, too."

"You okay?" she asked.

"I'm fine."

"Good. I've got to run. I have to be at La Serre at one."

"Right. See you later."

David's lunch meeting was with a writing team who had sent him a script about an aging Western matinee idol. They thought it would be a perfect vehicle for Rue. David read it. It was. But maybe too much on the nose. Too true. Rue was great in *Ride,* as the trade papers called the movie, but the receding hairline and the belly he was getting showed, and after the first screening Rue was nervous and drinking and finally snarling at David and saying that now he understood why Chuck Larson didn't want him to do *Wild Ride*. That Larson was smart enough to know it was wrong. And instead he'd left Larson to be with David, who was just a fucking punk. And it was the biggest mistake of his career. David had sat silently through the whole tirade. Not sure if maybe Rue wasn't right. That maybe Rue had looked foolish. That maybe the picture wasn't any good. That he, too, might be on his way out of the business once it was released. Laughed out of the business. Then the reviews came out.

"Rue McMillan's performance contained an authority never seen before in his work. McMillan was always a star. Now he is an actor."

"Rue McMillan has bridged the gap between horse operas and high art."

"A fine piece of work, beautiful to look at and profound to remember. Rue McMillan is outstanding."

Now David had Rue in the palm of his hand. And he knew he had to move fast to pick the next project for him while he was still— Colleen. Jesus, she was brazen. I want to fuck you. He had to stop thinking about it.

"Why don't you just leave the script lying around somewhere where Rue will pick it up and read it?" one of the writers was asking. "And don't tell him we want him for the old cowboy."

David smiled. "I'll think of something."

When the writers left, David began to feel uneasy. First he thought it might be his impending date, and the guilt he was feeling. But it was more than that. Bigger. These kinds of feelings were probably why everyone he knew was "in therapy," as they called it. Yes. To learn how to identify those vague unnerving feelings. Fuck it. They weren't vague. This was about Allyn and the marriage. He didn't want to be married. He never did. It had gotten away from him. Gone too far. He had hated being alone. And she seemed to want him so much. And now they were married and most of the time he was still lonely anyway. He picked up the phone and dialed.

"Hello."

"Colleen. It's David Kane."

"You've changed your mind," she said.

"Right," he told her. "Family business. But another time. Okay?"

"You bet," she said.

He was about to hang up.

"David," Colleen said. "I really want you. I watched you out there on that location every day. You ran the whole show and I thought you were fantastic. I'm really turned on to you."

"Well, thanks, Colleen," he said. "Thanks a lot."

The cleaning lady was still at the apartment when David arrived. She came to work for them three days a week.

"Afternoon, Mr. Kane."

"Polly," he nodded.

He sat in the living room and tried to read while Polly bumped around in the kitchen. He was getting more and more upset. He never could forgive Allyn for staying in her job at Hemisphere even after she knew that Greenfield considered David an enemy. Yes, she had stopped going to the Greenfields' parties, and she no longer needed or asked for advice from Julia, but she had gratefully accepted her appointment by Greenfield to the position of head of television development, and still had a great deal of contact with him. And at parties when people would ask her about Greenfield, she would say, "He's a wonderful man," and David would have to leave the room so his anger at her wouldn't show. And one night he called her on it.

"Allyn," he said. "Harold Greenfield is the one who fired me from Hemisphere because his friend, his hot-shot banker son-of-a-bitch friend asked him to—just so I wouldn't be around. And you call him a wonderful man?"

"David," she said. "Those are your problems with Greenfield. Not mine."

Disloyal. Hard. She didn't understand how overwhelming the whole thing was. About Wolfson and Marlene. Marlene would have said, "What? That man did that to you? I'll never even look in his direction again."

But not Allyn. Too ambitious for herself.

Polly left and David made himself a drink. He was hungry and nervous. Colleen. She praised him the way Allyn used to. The way Marlene used to. He sat alone in the kitchen for a while. Thinking about Marlene. When night fell he moved into the living room and sat there without turning the light on, the way he had done so often after Marlene's death.

Allyn's key was in the door.

"David?"

"Mmmm."

The darkness surprised her.

"What is it? Why are you sitting in the dark?"

He didn't answer.

"David?" Allyn said again.

Finally he spoke. "I want you to quit your job," he said.

"What?" Allyn switched the light on.

"I don't want you to work ever again." He didn't look at her. He looked straight ahead. "I want you to be at home with me. For me. I want all your time. And all your attention and I don't want to share you with your work."

"That's impossible, David," she said quietly. "And it's wrong of you to ask it."

"It's not wrong," he said. "It's what I have to have."

"Then I'd better pack my things and go," she said, and walked to the bedroom.

David turned the television on. *All in the Family.* Edith Bunker was telling Gloria the facts of life and she was worried and trying very hard to tell it right. The audience was laughing. By the time *All in the Family* was over, Allyn was standing by the front door with a large suitcase in one hand and her briefcase in the other. She put the suitcase down for a moment.

"Lawyers and all that, I guess," she said.

"I guess."

Allyn opened the door, then turned to look at him.

"David," she said. "I guess this doesn't matter much now, but I'm pregnant."

It was a lie. She was lying to make him change his mind.

"Are you sure?"

"Yes."

"Then why did you say no it was impossible when I said you had to quit your job? You *can't* work if you're pregnant."

"Of course I can. Plenty of women do. Marcie Carsey at ABC did it beautifully, and—"

"Not *my* wife."

"David, you've got some strange archaic idea about what marriage is, and I can't live up to it. I'm leaving. I'll get an abortion." She turned to go.

"No."

"David."

David jumped to his feet.

"You're not getting any goddamned abortion."

"David, I'll go to a nice safe hospital where they do them fast and easily. I don't want to have a baby now. Not with you feeling this way. I'm not going to abort myself the way your mother did, so I won't die."

He hated the scorn he heard in her voice for Marlene. Marlene. For a moment he'd forgotten.

"No!" he shouted. "No abortions! No!"

He grabbed her shoulders and shook her hard. "No goddamned abortions." Harder.

"David, stop it."

"I love you," he said, "and I won't let you die." Allyn was afraid.

"David, no—"

Again. Shaking her harder.

She dropped to the ground to get away from him, and when he looked down at her, sitting in a terrified heap on the floor, he realized what he had done.

"Allyn," David said, barely able to speak. Her mouth was open, and her hands were holding her face. She looked at him with fear and pain in her eyes.

"Oh, my God. Oh, Christ. I'm sorry. I'm sorry. Please, please forgive me. I'm sorry," he said.

Allyn didn't speak.

"Stay with me, Allyn, and have our baby," he begged. "Please. I swear to God I'll treat you good from now on. Better. I promise. I'll never hurt you. Please. I want you and our baby. Please."

Allyn didn't answer him with words. Instead, she stood and walked into the bathroom, and washed her face. Then she went into the kitchen and cooked dinner.

forty-two

The minute the screening of the pilot was over and the lights came up, everyone in the room crowded around Mickey.

"Great!"

"Loved it!"

"Big hit!"

"You were so funny!"

"Mickey, you're fabulous."

Network executives. Friends of the producer. The rest of the cast. It felt so good.

And now Mickey was having lunch in the commissary with Danny Kohler. He wanted to pinch Danny Kohler just to be sure the gorgeous glorious son of a bitch was real. Kohler was famous for discovering and making giant careers for some of the biggest names in television. He had three shows on the air now. Three. More than anyone else. "A major supplier," the trades called him. And there he was. Across the table. Talking about the network's reaction to Mickey Ashman.

"If the first show drove them crazy, wait till they see the next two," Kohler said. He was a cute man with lots of gray hair and a bushy gray mustache, and he was wearing a yellow jogging suit. Yellow was his favorite color. His lucky color. So everything in his life was yellow. The walls of his office, the Kohler Company T-shirts, the script binders for his shows, his cars.

"They loved you so much," Kohler said, "and they laughed so hard they couldn't see straight."

More, Mickey thought. Say it some more. Oh, yeah.

"We're gonna take the night," Kohler said grinning. "We've got the best time slot, and I guarantee you we'll run away with the night. You're gonna be a star. Are you gonna give Betty Day ten percent?" he joked.

Mickey laughed. "I guess I'll have to."

"Your agent's adorable," Kohler went on. "I've known Miltie since I was a kid. I was a singer, you know." Mickey didn't know. Mickey didn't care. He just listened and smiled. This was the best moment of his life so far.

"Miltie made sure I put a fancy dressing room for you in the deal and top billing. You know, lots of people laugh at him just because he's old, they think he's senile. Bullshit. He knows everything. He knew enough to sign you, and he made you a good fucking deal, too. You happy with it?"

"Yeah," Mickey said. "Sure, I'm happy."

Happy was hardly the word. Five thousand a show. Thirteen shows. On the air. If the show was picked up he'd get an increase the second season to seven thousand a show, with "appropriate raises annually," as Miltie explained it to him. And Mickey was the star. He couldn't quite believe it, but this time there was no mistaking it. The show was called *Hey, Richey!* It was about a guy who owned a drugstore where a bunch of neighborhood kids hung out. The guy gave the kids advice and became the good parent to them that they weren't getting in their ghetto homes. Richey. That was Mickey. He had all the jokes and all the wisdom in the script. And the five young guys were foils for him.

The word was already out, around the industry, that the first three shows had been taped and were dynamite. Good stories. Good writing. Good jokes. Good casting. And that Ashman guy is so incredibly funny. He does a bit where he's making a banana split and talking to a gorgeous doll who's sitting at the counter. And it's like Chaplin. The timing is exquisite. That's what they were saying. Like Chaplin or Woody Allen. And the comments were getting back to Mickey. Through his agent. And through Jackie Levitz, and people in his workshop, too. In the trades there was a blurb—"Danny Kohler, famous for never making a mistake in the discovering new talent department, has picked another winner. Mickey Ashman as Richey on Kohler's new sitcom *Hey, Richey!*"

TV Guide called Mickey at home. They wanted to do an article on the making of a hit show. And since Kohler was involved, they were reasonably sure *Hey, Richey!* would be a hit. Mickey was working with Kohler's publicist. They were mapping out a plan for the fall season. Milt Stiener was trying to get commitments for Mickey to do guest shots on some fall variety shows. It was a bit-time career push. Mickey couldn't believe it.

Every morning he would get into his new MG, leave his house in the Valley, and drive to work. Most of the time he'd get there before the others, and he would study his lines, either sitting at the counter of the soda fountain on the set or sitting on the sofa opposite the dressing table in his dressing room. His dressing room. Mickey still couldn't get used to it. He'd walk around the room and run his hand across the formica dressing table that was his, and look into the mirror that was his, and walk into the little bathroom that was his, shaking his head. It was true. It had happened. It was worth everything. The classes he had taken, the classes he had taught, the years of terrible auditions, even the job at the waterbed store. Once, this week, just for the hell of it, Mickey decided to try to make a list of his biggest problems and the worst thing he could think of was that the shower head at his house was broken. Boy, oh boy, life was good.

Tonight at the taping of the fourth show, thanks to special permission from the network, because children under twelve were usually prohibited from attendance at the tapings, some of Mickey's students were coming to watch. Betty Day and her little daughter Nina were meeting the others at the Beverly Hills Academy at five, and they were all coming to the studio together. Mickey smiled to himself thinking about how they would look. Adam and Dawn and Jeff, and Betty said she'd try to reach little Lucy Hill.

Mickey sailed through the rehearsal. There was a still photographer from *People* magazine. The first episode of *Hey, Richey!* would be airing in six weeks, and the magazine wanted to be ready with a story when it did. When Mickey was in his dressing room getting made up, the door opened and Jackie Levitz came in. Levitz had been at every taping. Supportive. Encouraging. "That was a great moment, Ash," he'd say about some scene or other.

"How do you feel, kid?" he asked. Mickey knew the old comic was proud of him, but envious, too.

The makeup man powdered Mickey. "There you go," he said and left. Today Mickey had some news for Levitz.

"Jackie," Mickey said. "I talked to Danny Kohler about you today."

"Yeah?" Jackie said, lighting up. "I met Danny Kohler. He's a nice guy."

"I told him I think my character of Richey ought to have an uncle. They should write one in. A guy who comes to work at the soda fountain with him. You know. There could be lots of stories about how Richey and the uncle have different ideas about how to treat the street kids and stuff, and I told him that I wanted the part of the uncle to be played by you."

Jackie Levitz didn't know how to react. It was a feeling Mickey had had many times himself.

"So . . . uh, what did Kohler say?" Levitz asked guardedly.

"He said yes. He's seen your work. He loves the idea and he loves you. He's calling your agent on Monday."

"No kiddin'?"

"No kiddin'."

The sweet little guy Jackie Levitz threw his arms around Mickey's neck.

"No kiddin'?" he asked again. When he looked at Mickey, Mickey saw Jackie was trying to control his tears.

"I'll go find Kohler right now if you want," Mickey said. "And let *him* tell you."

"No. Oh, no. That's not necessary. I'm just—I'm so glad. A good part. Richey's uncle. Oh, wait till I tell the class. But I won't tell 'em till after the deal's made. Hey, thanks a million."

There was a knock.

"They're ready for you, Mickey," the stage manager said.

"Knock 'em dead, kid," Jackie Levitz said. "You're the best. I'll see you later."

The show went well. Mickey could pick out the giggles of his creative dramatic students, and when he came out to take his bow at the end of the show, the children let out with a cheer that was so filled with adoration the rest of the audience turned to see where the voices came from.

The dressing room was filled with friends and fans. This was always Mickey's favorite part of the evening. Everyone coming in to tell him how great he'd been. The feeling was so terrific; it lasted nearly until the next week when they came in again. Ruth Levitz, Jackie's wife, gave Mickey a special hug.

"Jackie told me what you did. You're an angel."

Then the children came in. With Betty Day. Mickey made a face of mock surprise. They all giggled. Mickey ran over and hugged them all in one big hug. Lucy Hill wasn't there. But the others jumped all over him.

"Mickey, we saw you on television and real at the same time," Dawn said.

"She means on the monitors."

"Yeah."

"Can I sit in your chair?"

"If I be an actor when I get big, how do I get a job here?" little Adam asked.

Mickey grinned. All the grown-ups waited for his answer. "With great difficulty," he said.

Lots of laughter.

After the children had explored every corner of the dressing room,

Betty Day ushered them out and the others left one by one, and Mickey took his makeup off and he looked at himself in the dressing-room mirror. There was a knock at the door.

"Yeah?"

"Costumes, Mr. Ashman," a girl's voice said.

"I'm decent," he answered, still looking at himself in the mirror.

The young costume girl, Mary, had long straight California blond hair and a turned-up nose and braless bouncing breasts. She was shy with Mickey, even though he'd seen her flirting and laughing with the grips and propmen.

"Just want your dirty clothes," she said, not looking at him.

"You pervert," he joked. "I'll bet you want to take them home and sniff them till you get high."

She giggled.

"Mary," he said. "You're pretty."

"Thanks, Mr. Ashman." She was blushing.

"Want to come home with me?" he asked, looking at her hopefully. "I may be a big star, but I'm humble in bed." He smiled boyishly. She was really pretty. It would be good with her. His life had been so busy there hadn't been time for women in ages. But this cute little blonde would change all that and—

"I can't," she said. "My boy friend's waiting for me."

She shrugged apologetically and walked out the door carrying the dirty laundry. Mickey sat silently in his makeup chair. After a while he got up and picked up his plastic duffel bag. It still had the piece of masking tape on it that he'd removed from his trailer dressing room on *I Give It Six Months*. He looked in the mirror one more time.

"Well, kid," he said to himself, "it's pretty lonely at the top. Ain't it?"

Then he smiled. He *was* lonely. But he wouldn't trade what he had. Not for anything.

TO THE TOP

forty-three

Barry recovered slowly. When the doctors finally agreed he was ready to leave the hospital, Beau, who had been there every day, with toys and flowers and food from his favorite restaurants, arrived excitedly to pick him up. She was very early and she came in a limousine she'd hired for the occasion. She'd been up since six that day, singing in the shower, dressing, putting on makeup. Looking like the perfect Beau Daniels. The television Beau Daniels. She almost never looked like that anymore. But Barry was coming home. Her delicious Barry. Her love.

One of the nurses helped Barry into a wheelchair. He was so frail now that Beau could have lifted him herself. But she didn't. She watched instead. The bandaged head, the tiny face with the scraggly beard. He looked like a— She stopped herself from thinking it. But the thought kept coming back. He was so small and loose. He looked like a ventriloquist's dummy.

And then Beau and the nurse were in the elevator standing behind the wheelchair and the silent Barry. And there was no sound but the elevator's hissing. And then the door opened and they were on some strange cement level of the hospital. It was a back exit. A way to get out of the building and avoid the paparazzi who were hovering around the front of the hospital, waiting. For Barry and Beau. Beau Daniels who only made one TV special a year now because she didn't want to do anything that would take her away from Barry for even a few hours. Now she and the nurse pushed the wheelchair down the cement corridor. It was endless. Later Beau would have nightmares about that corridor. Her footsteps, the nurse's footsteps, the creaking of the chair. And Barry's silence. His very obvious silence.

At home Beau tucked Barry into bed. The room was filled with flowers and balloons from friends and well-wishers. People Beau had told happily, earlier that week, "My man's coming home." Barry didn't notice the balloons or the flowers. For days he hardly spoke. And when he did it was always about death. Harley's death, Eugene's death, his own death. Still deep in the shock of what might have been. Small caskets. For Eugene and Harley. They only needed small caskets. And for him. Only need two pallbearers. He'd overheard someone make that joke at Harley's funeral. A joke? A fucking joke? At Harley's funeral. It's a good thing he didn't see who it was who made it. Fuckers. Death. Meningitis. He hardly ever even looked at Beau, who told him funny stories, and who lay next to him, singing to him softly, with the ocean beating against the beach as her accompaniment. Mostly she sang love songs. And when Barry fell asleep, she would tiptoe down the stairs and curl up on the living-room sofa and read until she fell asleep there, so she wouldn't disturb him.

Weeks went by when the only voice Beau heard was her own, or the delivery boys from Jurgenson's who brought the groceries, or the doctor she called to report Barry's progress.

"He can't stay in bed, Beau," the doctor told her. "He has to be up and active."

"Fuck that," Barry said when Beau told him what the doctor said.

"So that's what your voice sounds like. I recognize it," she said. "Now get your candy ass out of bed."

Barry continued to look at the ceiling.

"I could have died," he said.

"But you didn't."

"But I could have."

"Yes. You could have. Is that why you're acting like you already did?"

"Easy for you to be glib," he said angrily.

"I'm not glib, you motherfucker. I was there for all of it."

"Not where *I* was."

"If I *could* have been I would have traded."

"Bullshit."

"I swear to God, you ungrateful bastard. I would have." Barry looked at her.

"Beau . . ." He reached out his arm. He looked so helpless. She went to him and held him. She was very careful now when she touched him. Gentle.

"Please. Barry. Walk with me on the beach."

"No."

"Please. Just today. Then if you don't like it, tomorrow we can play Esther Blodgett and Norman Maine."

"What does that mean?"

"Judy Garland and James Mason. In the second version of *A Star is Born*. You see, I'm her, so I stay up at the house and sing and make breakfast, thinking you're going for a starting-a-new-life morning swim—because you're him. Then you walk out into the ocean. And you keep walking to Japan. Get it?"

Barry was laughing. He remembered the movie now.

"Oh, but you have to leave your robe on the beach as a memento," she said. "Do you have a white robe?" He was laughing. She ran to the closet.

"Let's see. Red robe. Black robe. Green robe. No white. You creep. What are you trying to do? Ruin the picture?"

Barry was laughing hard now.

"Don't try and make up," Beau said with a mock pout. "You've ruined my whole fantasy."

Barry turned slowly, put his feet on the floor and stood. He was pale and the size-small blue cotton pajamas hung around his slight body.

"I'll go put on a sweater and we'll be Streisand and Redford in *The Way We Were* instead," she said.

They walked on the beach every day, and most of the time, for the first two weeks, it felt to Beau as if she was holding him up. But soon he was a little stronger. Beau was making him eat, and he had a doctor's appointment and was told he was progressing nicely, and one day he called in to Beau, who was taking a shower, and said he wanted to take a walk alone.

"You're not wearing a white robe, are you?" she shouted back to him.

He laughed. He loved her. They hadn't made love in six months.

Dr. Lutz sat cross-legged in the chair. Barry remembered now how Beau had described Lutz as looking like Humpty Dumpty. Perfect description. Barry and Beau sat across from Lutz on a leather sofa. They were holding hands.

"He doesn't fuck me enough," Beau said to Lutz.

There was a long pause. Lutz looked at Barry.

"Barry," he said. "Fuck her more." Then back to Beau. "What else?"

Beau laughed. "That's all."

Everyone was quiet again. Lutz looked as if he might fall asleep.

"I can't," Barry said, breaking the silence.

Both Beau and Lutz looked at him.

"I love her, but I can't."

"Is it *because* you love her that you can't?"

"What?"

"Many people are unwilling to connect sexuality with feeling, Barry," Lutz said.

"That's not it," Barry said.

"Then what *is* it?" Lutz asked.

Barry was getting tense.

"I don't know."

Beau was no longer holding Barry's hand. She was picking at a place in the arm of the leather sofa where the leather was ripped. She was making the tiny tear a little bigger, and bigger still.

"Maybe it's just that I'm a fag," Barry said.

No one knew how to respond. Fat Lutz pursed his lips. Beau kept picking at the leather. Then Lutz spoke.

"Maybe," he said.

"That's crazy," Beau said, but her voice was choked with emotion. "We had great fucking until you got sick. Great. Why are you doing this to yourself? And to me?"

Barry didn't have an answer.

"Do you love me?" she asked.

"Yes."

"Do you want to be with me? Live with me?"

Silence.

"Barry?"

"Beau, I'm a homosexual. I love you but I don't think I can—I don't know."

Beau was crying. "But we talked about it. In the beginning. And it's been so good for so long. Why now? Why are you telling me this now?"

"Maybe it has something to do with my having been so close to death," he said. "But I started feeling as if my lying to you was like lying to my mother, pretending to be straight when I wasn't."

"I knew you weren't straight. I always knew the truth about you."

"But what you didn't know was that sometimes when I was fucking you, I was picturing Harley or Andy May, or some twelve-year-old little groupie boy who—"

"So what?" Beau said. "I thought about Benny plenty of times when I was with you, because Benny got me hot. Even though I hated his guts. Does that matter?" She turned to Lutz.

"Not to me," Lutz said.

Beau was getting angry. "Lutz, you asshole. You know what I mean. Isn't it just important that everybody comes? And not why, or how?"

Lutz laughed. "Well, I wouldn't have quite put it that way," he said.

"Don't leave me," Beau said to Barry.

"I won't."

But still there was no sex, and Beau tried. She wore her most provocative clothes, she wore no clothes, she bought books of erotic art and kept them by the bed. And the more she tried, the more difficult it became. And the more tension there was between them. And the less Barry spoke. And the more she loved him. So when she woke up that morning and he was gone, she ran right to the garage, because she already knew that he hadn't just gone for a walk on the beach, and when the Corniche wasn't there she came inside and pulled the telephone out on the deck with her, and kept her hand on the receiver, praying that Barry would call from wherever he had gone, to tell her he was all right. She didn't hear from him for three weeks.

"Beau."

"Please tell me you were kidnapped by the Symbionese Liberation Army. Please," she said. She hadn't left the house.

"Beau," he said gently. "I can't come back."

"Where are you?"

"I'm in New York."

"I'll come there. I'll leave in one hour. I'll be there by tonight."

"No."

"Don't tell me no, you bastard."

"Beau, I miss you and I love you, but no."

The limousine driver thought the little guy with the beard was crazy. Every day for the last ten days, the same thing. Pick him up at the Sherry Netherland and drive him to Brooklyn, park the car on the same street, and then sit there. All day. While the little guy looked out the window of the car at this one particular building. It was so frigging dull. And sometimes if the driver had to take a piss, he'd say to the little guy, "See ya in a little while," and he'd go take a piss and get a newspaper too, so he wouldn't die of boredom. Today, just when the driver was getting back to the car from a walk around the block he took to stretch his legs, he saw the little guy get out of the car and walk across the street toward the front of that place he'd been watching, where a woman was getting out of a taxi.

This was like some kind of detective movie, for Christ's sake.

"Aunt Eleanor."

The woman was startled. She turned her head nervously and looked at the bearded young man. Then she looked more closely.

"Barry?"

"Yes."

There was a moment when it looked as if she might turn and run, but instead she moved toward him and embraced him, and the smell of her perfume was first familiar and then overwhelming because it brought back all of his past, and he fought back tears.

"Make my mother see me," he said.

"What do you mean?" Eleanor asked.

"I called her once, a few years ago, and I begged her to let me come over and be with her, and talk to her. I asked her if I could take her to dinner or the theater and she said no. She was busy. I've never spoken to her since."

"She never told me that," Eleanor said. "In fact, when Mashe died, she said at the funeral, 'It's too bad Barelah isn't here, but I don't know how to reach him.'"

She said that. Mashe died. She said that.

"I didn't know about Uncle Mashe."

"Two years already. A massive coronary. I'm dating."

"Of course you are," Barry said. "You're a very attractive woman, Aunt Eleanor."

"That's your limousine?" the aunt asked.

"I rented it."

"Why?"

"So I could sit outside here and wait for her to come out."

"She won't be coming out," Eleanor said. "She had a cerebral hemorrhage a few months ago. She's totally paralyzed. Your father sits and reads to her all day. No one knows if she understands or not. She could stay like this forever, or die. I come over a few days a week. I pay my respects. I'm dating."

"You told me."

"You want to come in there with me?" she asked, nodding toward the door.

Barry didn't know what to say.

"At least you know she won't call you names," Eleanor laughed. A kind of hysterical laugh. Black humor. Like the joke about two pallbearers.

"No," Barry said, and turned and walked across the street toward the limousine.

"Barry," Eleanor shouted after him, "I was kidding what I said about her not being able to call you names."

He turned and stood in the middle of the street looking back at his aunt.

"Maybe she wouldn't have," Eleanor said.

Maybe she wouldn't have.

"Please, Barelah, go inside with me," Eleanor said, reaching out her hand for him to come and take.

The limousine driver had been watching the little guy in the mirror. Starting across the street, then stopping right in the middle of the goddamned street and starting to talk again, and then going back across the street and disappearing with that woman, inside the place he'd been staring at for days.

All the way up the three flights behind Eleanor, Barry was nervous. Now they were at the front door. Barry was sweating as he looked at it. Remembering.

"Aunt Eleanor—I—"

Eleanor produced a key from her purse and turned it in the door. Nothing had changed. The same grandfather clock and umbrella stand in the tiny foyer. The same musty smell. Barry was shocked at himself for feeling so nervous. He was Barry Golden, he told himself. A self-made multimillionaire, a major force in the music business, the lover of exotic Beau Daniels. Beau. He missed her. But it couldn't work with her. And the agony of trying to make it work every day had been worse than the pain of feeling her absence. Maybe. The living room looked the way Barry remembered it before the days when the racks of Eldor seconds lined the room.

"Hiya, Jeanie," Eleanor shouted.

"Good mornin'," came a voice from the kitchen.

A fat black woman in a white nurse's uniform.

"How's she doing?" Eleanor asked the woman.

"Same."

"Jeanie's a good nurse," Eleanor said. "The day nurse."

Nurses. Day nurses? That must mean there were night nurses too. Who was paying for it all?

Aunt Eleanor tapped lightly on the door to Barry's parents' room.

"Yes?" His father's voice.

"I have a surprise for you," Aunt Eleanor said, opening the door.

Barry saw his mother now. Her eyes were closed but the lids were not shut tight. And they fluttered.

And there were tubes moving liquids in and out.

Intravenous. Catheter.

A wave of nausea swept over him. But before he could run away, he caught a glimpse of his father. So small and old. Wrinkled. And bent. It was frightening.

"Is it Barelah?" His father was squinting. "I'll get my glasses."

"It's Barelah," Eleanor said.

"No."

"Yeah, Dad," Barry managed to say.

The two of them. His mother with the intravenous and his father looking like an old troll. No. It was a nightmare. He had never imagined a homecoming like this. And he had imagined a homecoming many times.

"With a beard, yet," his father said, coming toward him. Toward him.

Barry extended his hand. His father took it. The old man's hand was bony and small and weak.

"Nu?" his father said nodding. "Nu, Barelah. It's been a long time. Yes?"

"Yeah, Dad. A long time."

He looked into his father's eyes. Maybe if he kept looking into his father's eyes he wouldn't have to look at his mother. Tubes. Intravenous. Catheter.

"You're a handsome guy," his father said with a smile. Was that pride in his eyes? "Rich, too, no?" he asked smiling and nodding. How do you answer that question?

"I'm doing okay, Dad," Barry said, realizing that he was nodding too. "I can't complain."

What was going on here? Small talk with his father whom he hadn't seen in twelve years, in a room where his mother was lying in a coma. The same room where she'd thrown herself across her bed all those years ago and informed Barry that his father was too ashamed to even be in the same house with him. The impulse to turn and run out the door and down the steps to the waiting car was overwhelming.

"Talk to your mother," his father said.

Oh no. Now he would leave. This was too much.

"Don't be afraid," his father said, giving him a shove in the direction of the bed. "She understands everything."

Barry glanced quickly at Aunt Eleanor, who gave him a shrug that said, No she doesn't understand at all, but as long as your father thinks she does, we humor him.

"Go ahead," his father said, nudging again.

Barry took a few steps toward the bed. He didn't want to get any closer.

"Sweetheart," his father said loudly to his mother's inert body, as if to a deaf person. "It's our Barelah. He looks very handsome. And he came home just to see you."

His father gave him another little nudge. Barry stood looking at his mother for a long time. He remembered how vain she was. If she could speak now, she'd probably say, God, I look like hell, don't I? After a while he realized his father and Eleanor had left the room and he was alone there with her. And those tubes. Maybe she understood.

"Mah," his voice cracked. He swallowed and tried again. "Mah," it was almost a whisper this time. She would never hear that, if she was hearing at all. Louder. "Mah, Dad says you can hear me . . . and understand me, too. Aunt Eleanor says no. So, I figure I'll tell you what I have to tell you, and if you can hear me and understand, that'll be good. And if you can't, it couldn't hurt. Remember that joke, Mah? About giving the guy the enema? And the punchline was 'It couldn't hurt?' Remember? Mah? It was one of your favorite jokes."

He took a step closer to the bed.

"Mah." He couldn't believe that was her—so lifeless. So silent.

"Mah, I'm gonna pretend that you can hear me, because I need you to hear me. I need you to hear what I have to tell you and maybe telling you will make me feel better about myself, and I need to feel better about myself, because every day I still look in the mirror and you know who I see? I see Barry Golden, the boy whose mother threw him out of her house and wouldn't take him back. And that's all I'm ever going to be, Mah, unless you let me know that you wish you hadn't done it. That you're sorry. That sometimes late at night you sat and looked at the articles about me in *Newsweek* and you kvelled, and thought to yourself proudly, that's my son, that's my joy, that's my little jewel.

"Remember why you started calling me your little jewel? Right after you told me the story about the little jewel in the turban of the sultan that made the sultan smile every day, you called me your little jewel because you said I made you smile every day. And remember, Barelah Schmarelah pudding and pie, Mah? You called me that too. Like Georgie Pordgie. Barelah Schmarelah pudding and pie, kissed the girls and made them cry. It ran through my head, that poem. All my life. Because I didn't want to kiss the girls, Mah. And that made *you* cry. But you didn't know why you were crying, and *why* was because you were afraid if I was a homosexual I was doomed to live some sleazy, back-door existence for the rest of my life. Right, Mah? And you didn't want that for me because I was your only child. Your little jewel. Right?

"So, Mah, because I know how you felt, that's why it's important to me that you know that my life has never ever been sleazy or back-door. Not since I left New York.

"I've had two really good relationships. Which is more than most people can say about their whole lives. And one of them with a woman, Mah. Honest to God. Not just a woman, but a star, too. Beau Daniels. From television. Did you see us together in *People* magazine? We were at a concert when those pictures were taken. Beau Daniels is in love with me, Mah. She was married once, but she got a divorce, and she— You would like her, actually. I mean, she's not Jewish, but she's a very good person and she— Mah, I—"

The tubes, the intravenous and the catheter, made strange slurping sounds which punctuated Barry's speech.

"Mah, you were kidding that day I left when you told me you'd say kaddish for me. Right? You *were* kidding, weren't you? I thought about that for a long time after I left. I wondered if someone saying kaddish for you made God think you were dead and then he didn't help you anymore. So I was scared. Isn't that funny?"

Barry moved closer to the bed.

"Maybe I was scared because I was very sick too for a while, Mah, and I had to have surgery, and I was in the hospital, and Beau was with me, and I thought about asking her to call you to tell you I needed you. But I was scared to do that. Isn't that stupid? You would have been there in a minute if you knew how bad it was. Wouldn't you?

"Do you still have those little blue boxes where you put away money for charity? The pushkes? When I was a little boy you gave me a spanking one time, and you felt so guilty you said to me, 'Barelah, I put a dollar in the pushke because I felt so bad that I made you cry.' Well I got news for you, Mah. You owe the pushke ten thousand dollars."

Barry laughed a nervous laugh.

"I cried so many times over the last twelve years. You wouldn't believe it. But I know you cried too. Right? Cried because you were" —Barry took a big breath—"because you were sorry, Mah. Very, very sorry that you threw me out. Right?" He was leaning over the bed.

"Mah, I forgive you. I forgive you and you forgive me. Isn't that right?"

"It's right, Barelah." His father had returned and was standing in the doorway. "She forgives you."

Barry looked at the old man who was like a stranger to him, and then back at his mother on the bed, and he walked to his father's side. The two men embraced. The old man felt like a skeleton to Barry and it was strange when he realized that this was the first time he could remember his father holding him in his arms.

Eleanor stood in the doorway looking on. Barry let go of his father and walked toward the bed slowly. Then he reached out and lightly touched his mother's hand. The one with the intravenous.

"I'm leaving, Mah. I have to go now. But I'm glad I came and maybe I'll come back tomorrow," he said. "Okay?" he asked a little louder, as though he hoped she would suddenly turn to him and beg him to stay.

By the time Barry walked out of the room and closed the door behind him, Eleanor and his father and the black nurse were in the kitchen having tea. Barry felt weak. Like sitting down in the kitchen, the old family kitchen and never moving again. Barry walked to the kitchen and looked at his father.

"Who's paying for Mother's care?" he asked the old man.

His father didn't answer.

"I am," Eleanor said.

"From now on, I am," Barry said.

"It's only the nurses, and an occasional visit from the doctor," Eleanor said. "They can't operate. It's just a matter of time."

"From now on I'll send you money every month, Dad." His father began nodding again.

"How 'bout dropping me with your fancy limousine at Eldor?" Eleanor asked.

Eldor. "Sure," Barry said. Another spindly embrace from his father.

The ride to the garment district was long. Aunt Eleanor told Barry about the two men she was dating. One was a widower who was "fabulously wealthy," and another was a man who lived in her building who had never married, a very fine gentleman, retired from the banking business. Probably gay, Barry thought to himself.

"Want to come up?" Eleanor asked him as the driver pulled up at the curb in front of the building.

"No."

"I use Mashe's office," she said. "I redecorated it. But I'm just a figurehead. You know. I'm the president. But the vice-president runs the whole thing. Andy May is still with us." Barry could tell Eleanor was looking at his face carefully to see how he would react to that. In fact, he was curious about Andy May. But no.

"Come up," she coaxed.

"All right."

The reception area of Eldor looked the same. Except now the girls who answered the phones had frizzy perms and long red fingernails. They waved to Eleanor as she passed, and eyed Barry. Barry and Eleanor walked down the hall and into Eleanor's office, formerly Mashe's office, where Barry had stood all those years ago, telling Mashe he was going to California. Wondering often after that, what made him say it. Eleanor, or the decorator, had totally changed the office. There was an orange paisley sofa and orange velvet chairs. A burlwood table instead of a desk. It looked like Eleanor's living room. Only the portrait of Eugene in his tallis and yarmulke was left from the days of Mashe.

"Andy May is still here," she said to Barry again as she sat on the orange paisley sofa.

"That's the second time you've told me that, Aunt Eleanor," Barry said.

"I just thought you'd want to say hello to him."

Andy May. Andy May would be in his forties now. Forties. Yes, Barry was curious.

"No," he said. "I don't."

"You want some coffee?" Eleanor asked.

"Nothing, thanks. Eleanor. I'd like to reimburse you for the money you've spent on my mother since her illness," he said.

"Oh, no," Eleanor said.

"Yes, Aunt Eleanor."

"Barry. Please."

"I insist."

It was as if they were arguing over a check at Ma Maison.

"How much would it be?" he asked.

"Twelve thousand three hundred and fifty dollars."

She knew exactly.

"I'll have my business people send you a check as soon as I get back to California," he said. "And I'd be grateful if you'd see that my father is comfortable."

"Of course," she said.

He stood.

"I'd better go and leave you to whatever it is you have to do here," he said.

"Barry, Mashe was very fond of you, you know," Eleanor said. "After you moved away, he was sorry. He even cried a few times about what he'd realized he'd done to you. And to your parents."

Barry was tired. He wanted to be home. At the beach. Instead of here in this strange place. Eldor.

"I cried about it, too, Aunt Eleanor," he said. "I'll be in touch."

Eleanor didn't get up from where she was sitting, next to the burl-wood table. Barry walked out of her office and closed the door. He stood for a moment trying to decide. If he turned right he would be heading for the receptionists' area and the elevator. If he turned left he could walk down to where the designers' offices were. Andy May. Forty. Barry headed for the elevator.

"I want you to wait for me," he told the driver as he got into the car. "I'm going to check out of the hotel as soon as I get back there and then you can take me to the airport."

"Yes, sir," the limousine driver said. He was glad the little guy was leaving New York. It meant he wouldn't have to spend any more dull days sitting parked on the same street in Brooklyn.

It cost Barry sixty dollars to get the Corniche out of the airport parking lot at the Los Angeles Airport. Even to him that seemed expensive. As he drove down the freeway toward the Coast Highway, he wondered again about what he would say to Beau. There wasn't a cliché for this in old movies. I love you, baby, but a man like me can't be tied down. Or, I'm no good for you, sweetheart, I have to be free. That was all bullshit. The truth was he *did* love her, and he did want to be tied down, but eventually, if they stayed together, she would hate him.

It had been raining in New York when Barry walked out of the Sherry Netherland with his bags to get into the car. And he looked at the chic New Yorkers scurrying past in their London Fog raincoats trying to hail taxis. And he thought to himself, at that moment, how much he liked it there, and how maybe he would move there, and start a new life. He could run Athena from New York. Why not? But now, on the Coast Highway again, seeing the Pacific Ocean, which was his back yard in the Malibu Colony, he knew he couldn't leave.

The guard waved him past and he turned the corner and pulled into the open garage of his house. He'd leave the bags until later.

The front door was unlocked. Beau must be at home. "Beau?" Nothing.

He looked out at the beach. There. She was sitting alone, in a lotus position on a towel, facing the ocean. After about a minute, as though she felt his look on her back, she turned. When she saw him she jumped to her feet and ran. God, she was beautiful. In a tank top and bikini bottoms, running toward him with her arms outstretched, grinning.

Beau threw her arms around him and they held each other very tightly.

"Barry, honey."

"Beau."

"I love you."

"I love you."

She kissed him and then moved away to look at him happily, and then grabbed him and kissed him again, and then stepped back again to look, as if to make sure it was really him.

"Well," she asked finally. "What did you do?"

"I missed you," he answered.

"Besides that."

"Isn't that enough?"

"Yes."

She embraced him again. "Barry," she said. "I made an offer on a house. In Beverly Hills. Escrow closes next week. I'm going to move in there, and Connie will move in with me until I feel comfortable about being alone. Maybe she'll even stay there through the summer. It's got a pool and a jacuzzi and it's cute. You'll visit us." He couldn't see her face. He was afraid to see it.

"I don't want to visit you," he said.

He felt her stiffen.

"Beau." He held her arms and moved her away from him, still holding on so he could look at her. Beau Daniels. The Beau Daniels nobody ever saw. Afraid. Trying to be tough, but afraid.

"Why not?" she asked sadly.

"Because I want to marry you."

Her face relaxed and then she smiled.

"Yeah?" she asked.

"I don't know what will happen, and if it makes either one of us unhappy or crazy, we'll end it. But I love you. So call the real estate broker and call Connie and tell them you've had buyer's remorse, and you don't want any house in Beverly Hills. Okay?"

"I'll do it now," she said, starting for the phone.

"Wait, Beau," Barry said, looking after her. "Not yet. There's one more thing I really want to do now."

"What is it?" Beau asked. But she was already grinning because she saw a familiar look in Barry's eyes.

"I want to fuck your brains out."

Slowly and seductively Beau pulled the tank top over her head, and Barry unbuttoned his shirt and took it off as he followed her upstairs. He was hard. He wanted her. Wanted that lean perfect body. When they got to the bedroom Barry looked out at the ocean as Beau undid his belt and unzipped his trousers and then he hugged her gently with one hand and tugged at her bikini bottoms with the other. And soon they were naked and rocking and floating in one another's arms, kissing and touching and speechless with the ecstasy of making love to the person each of them loved most of all.

forty-four

STAN ROSE PRESENTS. Even now, when Stan looked at his own ads in the paper, it felt strange to see his name above the name of the rock stars. He and Barton had discussed the idea years ago, before they had the sign painted on the door that said ROSE AND BARTON CONCERTS. Stan suggested they call the company by a company name.

"Like West Coast Concerts, or Far West Concerts," he said. "Or how about a drug reference? Far Out Concerts."

Barton didn't laugh.

"If you don't put your name on the company, Stanley, you're nowhere. Look at Bill Graham and Wolf and Rismiller. Those guys are known. You wanta be known, Stanley?"

Stan wasn't sure. He knew he wanted success. But he wondered if he wouldn't feel more comfortable as a quiet and anonymous success, rather than a public one. Maybe those things were synonymous. Success and public. So many times he still felt like the shy boy whose favorite pastime was watching television, or sitting alone reading the collection of weekly news magazines that come in the mail.

He sold the Benedict Canyon house one week after Jerri moved out, and moved into a subleased furnished apartment in the Sierra Towers on Sunset. He had loved that house, but the feeling of Jerri was all over it, and after she left, and he found out that Barry Golden was going to recover, Stan did nothing but walk from room to room, thinking about life and relationships, and trying to figure out how he could have been so foolish about Jerri.

This room will be for our baby, she'd said about the sunny front bedroom the day they moved in. It's so bright and pretty. And he remembered wondering, when she said that, if she had ever talked about wanting babies when she was with Nick Jonas, or when she was with Bob Frank. Or was it that she realized that wanting a family was Stan's particular weakness? What he sometimes jokingly told her was his "barbecue fantasy." To have a Kennedyesque family where everyone related well to each other. And adored each other. No. It was just an act. Yes, the house was much too much Jerri.

The real estate broker was thrilled to get Stan's call offering her the listing. She wouldn't even have to advertise, she said. She already had a client she was sure would want the place.

Stan sat in the poolhouse and read while the broker showed her
clients around his house. Ironically, the broker's clients were a perfect family. Dr. and Mrs. Lawrence Burns. Tan, smiling, slim and
affluent. And they had two children. A girl and a boy. While the
grown-ups looked at the house, the children chased one another
around the tennis court.

Lawrence please-call-me-Larry Burns made an offer on the place
immediately, because if he didn't, the broker assured him, by next
weekend it would just be gobbled up. Stan was asking a million two
for the place. Burns offered him a million. Stan accepted the offer.
What was two hundred thousand dollars? Particularly in the face of
having to stay longer in this memory-filled place.

The apartment seemed small and depressing after the sprawling
Benedict Canyon house. But Stan promised himself it was temporary.
Until what? Until he found another woman who turned him on the
way Jerri had?

The concert company was grossing millions of dollars. Stan had
moved the offices into town from the Valley building, which he now
owned, into another building he owned in Hollywood. And he hired
several bright young music-conscious boys to be his associates. The
whole setup ran like a top. There was a head of advertising, a head
of publicity, a head of merchandising, and a year ago Stan had devel-
oped a partnership arrangement with some smaller concert companies in other parts of the country, so one of the new employees
served as liaison between Stan Rose Presents and those smaller promoters.

Stan tried hard to block Jerri out of his mind and the way he
missed her. But it was painful. Glad you're not with that cheap cunt
anymore, someone said to him at a party. It was a woman who said
it, and Stan didn't know how to react. Did you hear Nate Shore left
Bonny Lee for a few months, he overheard at a party. Living with
that whore, what's-her-name. And then he went back to Bonny.
Cheap cunt. Whore.

Women phoned Stan daily. Attractive women. And young girls,
too. They called him at the office. Groupies, some of them. But
others who were simply pretty young girls who honestly seemed to
find him attractive. It was boring. He was and always had been in the
music business because of the business, not the music. He was a good
promoter. He had no love for rock 'n' roll. So when the girls asked
him the question, don't you really get off on the mindbender's lead
guitar, he made an educated guess that the answer should be yes,

offered that answer with a smile, got laid, and then stayed up all night watching the pretty young girl sleep, feeling very lonely.

He remembered when he was in the mail room delivering mail to the office of Tom Rich the casting director. Enid, Rich's secretary, ripped all the letters open and shouted in to Rich, "You got anothah bunch of love lettahs from actresses, Tommy." Rich laughed out loud. "They're crazy about me," he said back.

Enid winked at Stan, then shouted back at Rich. "Yeah, but would they still be crazy about you if you were a Volvo dealer in Van Nuys?"

Now Stan found himself asking that question about the young women who were so hot to go out with him. The answer was always no. But maybe it didn't matter. After all, business was great. He was leaving tomorrow for New York to meet with Joe Rio about what Rio said were some business ventures outside the concert world. Fucking Rio. Always mysterious.

The office door opened. Patty, Stan's personal secretary, stood there. She was his longtime through-thick-and-thin pal. He'd urged her to play a more powerful role in the company but she'd refused.

How 'bout the same job and more money? she'd asked.

You got it.

Now she made more money than anyone at S.R.P., except for S.R. himself.

It was something unusual. Stan could tell because Patty's eyes were big with excitement.

"Harold Greenfield," she said.

"What about him?"

"He's on the phone and he wants to talk to you."

Only once before had Stan seen Patty so impressed with the name of one of his callers. That time it was Bob Dylan. Mostly she was used to the stars who called requesting special tickets, or better seats, or backstage passes. Frequently those people didn't get past her to talk to Stan now that the company was so busy. But Patty knew Greenfield had been a big honcho when Stan was a mail room underling and she loved it that he was on the phone waiting for Stan now.

"Without a secretary," she said. "It's just the man himself."

"Why didn't you just buzz and tell me that, Patty?" Stan asked, knowing the answer.

" 'Cause I wanted to see your face."

Stan grinned and pushed the button on the telephone line with the blinking light.

"Harold!" he said playfully into the phone.

Patty giggled and closed the door behind her.

"Got any of my stationery left?" Greenfield asked.

Stan shook his head. Jesus. Greenfield had a mind like a steel trap.

"Could be," he answered. "I'll look around."

"Well, if you find some, write yourself a note that says I'd like to have a meeting with you as soon as I can. Then sign my name, you no-good forger. Okay?"

"I'm leaving for New York tomorrow, Harold," Stan said. What could Greenfield possibly want? "It'll have to wait until I get back."

"How about today?" Greenfield asked. "It's important."

"I'll be right over."

Stan paused in the lobby of the gold building to look around. It seemed exactly the same. Willie the guard sat with the back of his chair leaning against the wall near the elevator. His feet, wearing black tie shoes and white socks, were dangling and his heels were tapping on the legs of the chair. He looked half asleep as the Hemisphere employees hurried past him to get on and off the elevators.

"Hiya, Willie," Stan said.

"Hiya," Willie said, automatically. Then he looked up. "Well, I'll be darned if it ain't Rosie the mailboy," he said. "Long time no see, kiddo. Long time no see."

The old man got up and shook Stan's hand.

"See your name in the paper all the time, Rosie," he said to Stan. "Always show your ads to the wife and tell her, 'That was one of my boys.' Big-time now. You and that there guy that plays Richey on TV. That funny son-of-a-gun. Ahhh, what the heck's his name?"

"Ashman," Stan said. "Mickey Ashman."

"Yeah, Mickey. He's good on there, too. Big television star now, ain't he?"

"He sure is," Stan said.

"So what are you doing here?" Willie asked, smiling broadly. "Come to try and get your old mail route back?"

"Not yet, Willie," Stan said. Then he leaned toward Willie in mock confidentiality. "But in this business, you never know. It could happen."

"Who you here to see?" Willie asked.

"The big boss."

"You mean H.G.?"

Stan nodded.

"Well, well." The old man looked impressed, and Stan thought for a second it looked as if Willie was about to ask what Stan and Greenfield were going to talk about. After all, just as the mailboys were privy to all the studio off-the-record information, old Willie, who locked the doors of the elaborate offices in the gold building every night, had probably seen it all and known it all.

"Well, good luck to you, Rosie," Willie said. "Hope you get what you want out of the old boy. And don't be a stranger around here no more."

Stan shook Willie's hand. The elevator door opened.

"See you, Willie," Stan said, getting on the elevator and pushing the button for twenty. "And keep up the good work."

The elevator door closed. Stan looked up and watched the floor numbers go by, remembering when this was his mail route and wondering what Greenfield wanted. Twenty. He knew the route as if it were his way home. Vi, Greenfield's secretary, was still there. Old.

"Hello, Vi."

"Hello." She had no idea who he was.

"Stan Rose," he said to remind her.

"Oh, yes, Mr. Rose," she said. "He's expecting you. You can go in." She still didn't remember him.

Greenfield stood as Stan walked in. The man had always looked distinguished, but age made him look even better.

"Don't get up, Harold," Stan said. "I'm just delivering your trade papers."

Greenfield laughed. "Rose," he said. "I'm amazed. How did a guy who spent his childhood being crazy about TV become the king of rock 'n' roll instead of a network boss?"

"I'm flattered, Harold," Stan said, "but I like to think that Elvis Presley was the king of rock 'n' roll, and that after he died the title went to Wolfman Jack."

Greenfield smiled. He didn't get it. He came from behind the desk, put an arm around Stan and walked him to the window. The bustling Hemisphere lot was something to see from the twentieth floor of the gold building. Both men stood looking down at it without speaking. There were actors in all sorts of costumes, limousines, tour trams. Stan wondered if Greenfield still thrilled at the sight of it.

"Christ, it's exciting down there," Greenfield said.

Stan smiled. "It's your empire."

"Yes, that's what it is," Harold said, without a trace of pretense.

"Do you see that huge grassy area out there past the last sound stage?" he asked Stan.

"Uh-huh."

"That's what I called you about," Greenfield said, looking at Stan.

"Why me?" Stan asked. "I don't even own a lawn mower."

"Let's sit down, Rose. I've got a proposition for you. Want some coffee?"

"Never touch the stuff."

"I want to do a rock festival on this lot. In that field. With a stage, and terrific lights and sound, and all the top groups. Every month. Maybe every week. And sell it to the networks as a big new TV show. Pay big money to the best acts, get a hotshot TV director, have rock stars host it, and get youth-oriented sponsors to pay the bill. What do you think?"

"Sounds great. Probably impossible to put together, but a great idea."

"Why impossible?"

"Okay, I take it back. Next to impossible. Harold, most of those groups are difficult to handle, frequently only interesting to see in person, and many times, too sexual for prime-time television."

"What about if it was aired as a late-night show?"

"Late-night, maybe," Stan said.

"What about calling the show Stan Rose Presents?" Greenfield asked.

Stan thought Greenfield was kidding, so he kidded back.

"What about calling it Bill Graham Presents?" he asked.

"I mean it. Because people know about you, Rose," Greenfield said. "The kids do. Even in cities where you don't promote shows they've heard of you. And the acts know you, and the agents trust you. So you'd be the executive producer, or the producer, or whatever the hell. But you have to do it. Because if you don't, the network will think I'm a liar since I already told them you would."

Jesus. Harold Greenfield. Stan Rose Presents. Producing a television show. It would be an adventure.

"We'll use acts from World Records," Greenfield said. "And Barry Golden, he can send some talent our way. Maybe his girl friend would host the thing one week—Beau?"

"Let me think about it," Stan said. "I'll try to put it together while I'm in New York."

Greenfield shook his hand.

"Good," Greenfield said. "Very good."

On Stan's way out, when he reached the lobby, he noticed that Willie the guard was still in his chair, tipped against the wall, feet dangling as before. Only now he was fast asleep. With his mouth open. Great guard, Stan thought. The old guy must know where some pretty important skeletons were buried.

Stan loved New York. Sometimes he would stand by the window of his suite at the Warwick looking down at the corner of Fifty-fourth and Sixth and count the yellow taxis as they went speeding by, knowing there was no end to the parade, but trying to keep up with them as they careened around corners, most of the time barely missing one another and the pedestrians. This was his best trip to New York yet. He'd had meetings at William Morris about some new acts, meetings with Joe Rio about some investments, and a slew of telephone calls back and forth with the Stan Rose Presents lawyers in Los Angeles about the deal Harold Greenfield wanted to make for the rock 'n' roll television show.

And tonight his father, Albert, was flying in from Florida. Albert was finally involved in a relationship with a woman. Stan was glad for him. Albert described the woman as a "hell of a nice gal."

"Great," Stan said. "Why don't you bring her along?"

"Oh, no," Albert said, laughing. "She ain't *that* nice."

The two men would go to the theater. Stan had tickets for *A Chorus Line*. Great seats. It was only one o'clock. Albert wouldn't arrive until six. Maybe Stan would go shopping. Surprise Albert with some new ties.

The elevators at the Warwick were slow, and Stan stood in the hallway, tapping his foot as he waited. Bloomingdale's. It would be a nice walk to Bloomingdale's. Then later he'd wander along Fifth Avenue and look in the windows. The elevator doors opened. A blond woman. By herself. Pretty and—

"Jerri?" Stan didn't know whether to get on the elevator or not, and the door began to close. Jerri must have pushed the button marked "door open," because it opened again, and as he started to get on the elevator, she started to get off the elevator, and they collided and they both laughed.

My God, she was beautiful. So beautiful he could feel an ache in his chest just looking at her. She was wearing a black wool suit and a red silk blouse, and black boots. She looked very chic and better than he remembered her. Maybe because in some of his memories she was very ugly.

"Hi, Stan," she said softly. "Here on business?"

"Yes."

A few days after he'd found the cassette of Jerri with Nate Shore, he came back to the poolhouse and threw the cassette in the pool, and left it there for days, until he was sure the chlorine and chemicals had destroyed it. Then he fished it out and threw it in the trash, imagining that if in some way the picture was still intact, the trash man would take it home and watch Jerri fucking Nate Shore. Then Stan laughed at himself for thinking the trash man had a videotape machine. Jesus, he was jaded. Everyone in his world had videotape machines. So why not the trash man?

"I am, too," Jerri said.

They looked into one another's eyes. It was amazing he hadn't bumped into her before. At concerts. At parties. Not so amazing. She'd probably avoided him carefully. Stan searched his mind for something to say. All he could think of was I love you, I want to be with you. Come to my room with me. Now. Let me hold you. Make love to you. Jerri.

"Where are you headed now?" he asked her.

"Shopping," she said.

"Me, too," he said, forcing half a smile.

"Bloomie's?" she asked.

"Uh-huh."

Jerri pushed the button for the elevator, and when the doors opened they got on silently. In the elevator he could smell her perfume. Joy. He'd bought gallons of it for her. They walked through the lobby and out the side door and headed east toward Lexington Avenue. Jerri. He was with Jerri. He had this strangely guilty feeling about being with her, as if he should try to avoid being seen. As if being with her was illicit. Maybe it was. Maybe that was her charm.

She put her hand through his arm when they crossed the streets, and he loved feeling her touch him. And as he caught another whiff of her perfume, he was filled with memories of her in bed. And how she looked in the mornings. So beautiful. So incredibly beautiful.

In Bloomingdale's, the crowds moved quickly. Consuming. Taking.

"Look," Jerri said, gesturing with a nod of her head as they walked on the first floor. A fat older woman being made up by a clownishly over-made-up salesgirl. "Glamour," Jerri said. Stan laughed.

And they continued to walk from floor to floor of the big store.

Neither of them saying much. Neither of them shopping. Just looking. At one another, and the clothes, and the people.

On the floor where the furniture was displayed, there was a bed
for a child's room shaped like a huge tennis shoe. Other people were
gathered around the bed, looking and pointing.

"Lovely bed for a little boy's room," a middle-aged woman said.

"Or just for somebody very kinky," Jerri said loudly, and laughed.
The woman gave her a disapproving look and turned away. Jerri
laughed again. Louder. As they walked on, Stan remembered all the
times in the last few years he swore to himself that if he ever ran into
Jerri again, he would ignore her. Turn away. Resist even looking at
her, knowing that the longing he had for her was so powerful. And
here he was now, walking through Bloomingdale's, as if they were a
couple of old college chums just hanging out together. And he didn't
want it to end. Prayed that it wouldn't. Albert. Maybe he could stop
Albert from coming in. Ask Jerri to go to the theater with him. Then
later, they would sit in some dimly lit restaurant having supper, and
he would tell her how he missed her, and she would have some
reason, some perfectly logical reason for what happened with Nate
Shore. And she would say that all the stories Stan heard about her
past were lies and she could prove it, and Stan would believe her and
say, Of course, that makes sense, now let's get married, and—

"I have to get back," she said.

No. No. You don't, Stan thought. You can't, Jerri.

"Me, too," he said.

They were silent all the way back to the Warwick. Onto the elevator. He pushed eight. She pushed eleven. The door opened at eight.
Now. He had to say it. Please. Be with me, Jerri. We've been apart
for too long, and no one does it for me the way you do. I know about
you and still I have to have you. Come to my room with me.

"Nice to see you," Jerri said to him.

"You, too," he answered.

The elevator doors closed. Stan walked to his room, took the key
out of his pocket and opened the door. Albert Rose sat in the living
room of the suite reading the newspaper.

"Dad," Stan said.

"Hi, baby," Albert said, getting up. "I got an earlier flight. Where
you been?"

"Shopping," Stan said. He could have had Jerri with him now.
What would Albert have thought?

"You didn't buy anything?"

"Just window shopping."

"Hell," Albert said, grinning. "Don't do that. I can get you a discount on windows."

Stan smiled.

"Let's go get something to eat," Albert said.

"Great."

When Stan and Albert got on the elevator to go down to the lobby, the smell of Joy still hung in the air.

The outdoor stage was so well put together it was hard to believe it had been built as a temporary structure in a matter of a few days. The dressing-room facilities were well planned and comfortable. With showers and heaters and excellent lighting. The power trucks were lined up and a few of the groups had begun to straggle in to do sound checks. Stan Rose and Harold Greenfield stood together at the end of the field watching the scene.

"I'm impressed, Harold," Stan said. "Once I agreed to do the show and signed the groups, you had that damned thing put up in three days."

"Don't be so impressed," Greenfield said. "When I did *Atlanta's Burning,* I made the whole South in *two.*"

"Call for you, Mr. Rose," came a voice over the P.A.

Stan was worried as he headed for the phone. He'd tried to get Beau to host the show. This was a pilot, important, could decide what the show's future would be, and Beau was still a big draw to the kids. Great to look at, slinky, sultry, perfect. But Barry and Beau were in Europe. Rumors said, maybe even getting married. So Stan had called around trying to find someone equally impressive as Beau.

Agent after agent called him. "How 'bout Neil Slocum?" one agent asked.

"No," Stan said.

The Slocum Brothers Band. They were trouble. Drugs. Fast cars. A history of near-miss accidents in the Ferraris they bought with the money they got from their first hit albums. Neil Slocum, the eldest brother, was the current bad boy of rock 'n' roll. In and out of jail, doped out and then into rest homes for a few months and swearing in an interview in *Rolling Stone* that he was clean. No. Not Neil Slocum.

But during the time that passed, as Stan tried to reach this unreliable star or that, Neil Slocum's first album alone, without the Brothers, shipped platinum, and the agent called again.

"He's clean," the agent said. "I swear to God it's cool. I'll bring him there myself."

Stan picked up the backstage phone.

"Hello."

"Uh, Stan. It's Freddy Britz." The agent who had sworn to God. "Uh, listen," Britz said. "Neil is—uh—he's running a little late today and—he won't be able to make the rehearsal."

Stan bit his lip. "Freddy," he said. "You swore to me that—"

"I know. I know. He'll be there. He'll be fine. He'll be there in plenty of time to do the show. I swear to God. But he just can't make the rehearsal. See you soon. I will. I'll be there real soon. With Neil. Honest to God."

Stan put the phone down. Matty Greer, the director, stood a few feet away.

"Problems?" Greer asked.

"You said you wanted to run the show down just for the order," Stan said. "Well, Neil Slocum's going to be late."

"Shit," Greer said. Greer was a television director. Very tan with gray curly hair. He'd been directing TV variety shows for years. The word on him was he wasn't a genius, but he took pretty pictures. And after years of working with temperamental television stars, and being pushed around by television producers and network brass, he rolled with the punches.

"Why don't *you* just walk it through for me then, Rose?" he asked.

"Me?"

"You know. Just kind of block it out for me so I can make sure my boys have it all down, and the groups know when to get on and off so we don't have to keep stopping later. Okay?"

"Yeah. Sure."

Some more people had arrived from the groups. Their "old ladies," friends, and also the concessionaires. They were all milling around and Greer rolled the tape with the theme music on it and Stan walked out onto the stage. Most of them knew him so they began to whistle and applaud. And Greer was on the truck watching and the crew was laughing. And Greer said to Stan over the P.A., "Okay, Stan, bring out the first act."

Stan grinned because he caught sight of himself in a monitor.

"Hi," he said, "I'm sure you know I'm not Neil Slocum because my eyes are focused."

Everyone out on the vast grassy area laughed.

"I'm Stan Rose," he said, "and this is Stan Rose Presents."

More people had come in. Everyone was applauding.

"Tonight my guests are the beautiful Bishop Brothers Band, featuring Jay Tarmack." Wolf whistles from the crowd. "An old favorite, Magic Hat, and my special friends, Twilight. So get ready to rock, right after this word."

Greer's voice came over the box. "You're great, Stan, just great. But I'm putting *my* money on the freak with the guitar."

Stan walked through the rest of the rehearsal easily, making jokes, teasing the acts, poking fun at the director in the booth. Even telling a brief story now and then about the first time he'd seen this group or that one, and what guy had a new old lady, and giving away well-known secrets that made everyone laugh. It was late morning when the rehearsal was over. The show was scheduled to start taping at noon.

"Any sign of Slocum?" Stan asked a group of his employees who were backstage.

"Yeah," one of the Stan Rose Presents henchmen said. Stan didn't like the look on the kid's face that went with the yeah. He headed for Slocum's dressing room and knocked on the door.

"Whosit?"

"Stan Rose."

"C'mon in."

Freddy Britz, the agent, looked nervous.

"Uh, hi. He's here. He's in the john."

"Britz," Stan said. "If anything is wrong, you better tell me now, because—"

"Hey, man, nothing is wrong," Neil Slocum said. Stan had left the door open and Slocum was standing in the doorway. His long black hair flowed down his back. He was very pale, and he wore a flowered caftan. He looked like a refugee from the sixties.

"My man," he said to Stan. Stan had used the Slocum Brothers as an opening act on one of the earliest Rose and Barton Concerts, and many times since then. When Stan took Slocum's hand to shake it, he could feel the rock star trembling.

"You okay, Neil?" he said.

"Oh, shit, yes," Slocum assured him.

Stan remembered that at one of the early Slocum Brothers Concerts Neil had come by the hall early to do a sound check alone. It was at Santa Monica, and after the sound equipment was in order he asked Stan to have dinner with him, and the two of them went to a restaurant on the pier. They had a few beers and talked about growing up, and Slocum told Stan that he was from Florida too. Jacksonville. Stan knew some guys from the University of Miami who were from Jacksonville. When he mentioned their names and Slocum knew them well, it seemed weird to Stan that someone as freaky as Slocum had a childhood that sounded a lot like his own.

"We start in about an hour, so relax," Stan said. "There's cue cards so you can read off those, and I'll be around in case you need any help with anything else."

"Thanks, man," Slocum said.

Freddy, the agent, gave Stan a smug smile, and Stan walked out to visit the other dressing rooms before the show. As he passed the stage area again he could see the hordes of kids beginning to crowd through the newly constructed gate that surrounded the field.

"A beautiful sight," he heard a voice say. Harold Greenfield was watching the kids come in. "Say, Rose," he said, "you were a great host. I was out there watching your rehearsal."

"Thanks, Harold," Stan said. "It was fun."

"You ought to be the one who hosts the show. You were funny. Charming, I might add."

Stan smiled.

"Gee, Harold. Next thing I know you'll want to star me in one of your pictures."

"I mean it," Greenfield said. "All those stories you told. The kids would love those."

"But I'm too shy, Harold," Stan said, and opened the door to go into Magic Hat's dressing room.

"We want Neil! We want Neil!" the kids in the audience were screaming, and Slocum stood in the wings with Freddy Britz and Stan Rose and Magic Hat, who were waiting to make their entrance, and Harold Greenfield. It seemed funny to Stan to see Greenfield in his three-piece suit with that group of rock people.

"We want Neil! We want Neil!" The screams were loud now, as Stan put an arm around Slocum to wish him well. The man was trembling a lot now, but before Stan could ask him if maybe he wanted to sit down and relax for a while, to let Greer go out and do an audience warm-up, Slocum pulled away from him and walked onto the stage.

The thousands of kids who were sitting on blankets spread on the grass jumped to their feet when they saw him. Cheering. Screaming with adoration, "Neil! We love you, Neil!" And Neil Slocum smiled at them weakly. He raised a hand to wave, and then, as if in slow motion, sank to the ground. There was a horrified reaction from the crowd and people running toward the stage, until one of the Magic Hat group and a member of their road crew ran out, lifted Slocum's limp body and carried him off. Greer's voice came over the P.A. to ask that everyone please sit down.

As Slocum was carried offstage and past him, Stan held his breath. Bizarre. Was it the music business that was bizarre or just the whole world in general? At least once a day someone asked Stan the question, Why is a straight guy like you involved in this world of freaks? And he would laugh. Now he was wondering what the answer was. He looked at Harold Greenfield. Greenfield must be wondering the same thing about himself. The old man really looked at a loss.

"Say something," Greenfield said to Stan and turned him toward the stage and marched him forward. Shoving him. And Stan found himself on the stage holding the microphone. The kids were very loud.

"Neil is okay," Stan said very loud into the microphone, hoping he was telling the truth. "Just exhausted," he added. The crowd was getting a little quieter. "So if you're very cool, in about five minutes, we'll start shooting the show again. I'm Stan Rose and we've got really terrific acts coming down today, so hang in. Thanks."

Stan walked off. He could hear the ambulance making its way through the Valley traffic toward the studio to get Slocum. Greenfield and Greer were waiting for him in the wings.

"Slocum's dead," Greenfield said. "But we won't tell the kids. Let them find out on the news when they get home tonight."

Stan was numb. Neil Slocum. Another casualty in the world of the music business. In the last ten years he'd seen so many it didn't even startle him. Neil Slocum. Stan's reaction to the news came out as a joke.

"I guess that means he won't be going on," he said.

"That's right," Greenfield said. "*You* are."

"You're crazy, Harold."

"Rose, you were great out there in rehearsal. If you stink we'll forget we ever tried it, and if you're even half decent, you'll be a star."

Stan was laughing nervously.

"What'll I wear?" he said. "I can't go on a television show. Look what I look like." He was wearing a plaid shirt and khaki pants.

"Rose, this is Hemisphere Studios," Greenfield said. "I can make you look like Errol Flynn or King Kong within ten minutes. I've already sent for makeup and wardrobe."

The network wasn't sure about the show. Neither were the sponsors. That guy. The emcee. No one ever heard of him. They decided to test it at a preview center where they brought in audiences who were hooked up to computers, which recorded their responses. They ran the test for only seven days, because on the eighth day, the head of the preview center called Harold Greenfield to tell him that they would be unable to test "Stan Rose Presents" tonight, because last night the audience was so excited by it they had overexerted the computer. When they heard that, the network and the sponsors reconsidered, and the show was scheduled to go on the air.

forty-five

Allyn looked at the gold face of her Rolex watch. She loved that watch. David had given it to her the day after Mandy was born. To make up for the fight they had had in the hospital about the name. "It's too soon, David," Allyn said to him. "Too soon to name the baby after your mother. I know you loved her, but we mustn't treat our daughter as if she's a reincarnation of Marlene. She's not. And calling her Marlene seems unhealthy to me." David was furious. He stormed out, and Allyn was relieved. Maybe now she could get some sleep.

And in the morning he was back. Sheepish, loving, apologetic, with the box from Tiffany's. He'd somehow managed in that short amount of time to have the watch engraved, too. On the back it had the date and then the words "Thank you for Amanda." Capitulation. Amanda. The name Allyn wanted to use for the tiny orange-haired baby girl. The name her mother and grandmother wanted for the baby. After Abraham Cutler, Allyn's grandfather.

The Rolex cost David more than two thousand dollars, and it ran fast. Now it said ten. Close. Maybe it was a few minutes before, and David was on the phone with his lawyer Ben. Allyn could tell because the light on the phone was still lit under the seven eight three number and Ben had called David on that line two hours ago. It must have been important because David closed the door to the den and gave Allyn the look which meant she shouldn't disturb him with anything mundane like good-nights from Amanda. Allyn decided to go and look in on Amanda, but as she got to her feet, she saw the phone light go out, and heard the door to David's den open.

"Allyn?"

David was hurrying up the stairs. Unusual. He opened the door to her office. He was smiling.

"That was Ben," he said.

"I know. What did he want?"

"Remember that conversation I told you I had with Mel Eastman last week?"

"Yes."

Mel Eastman was the chairman of the board of Premier Films. He was an idol of David's. A studio bigwig who was vital, tough and smart. A man David had observed from afar and admired enormously. After they'd met, and Eastman praised David's work, even *Wild Ride,* which David felt now, two pictures later, was only a primitive effort, David rushed home to tell Allyn. I met him. I met Eastman, David said, and he had the same look on his face Amanda had on hers when she walked into the toy department at Bullock's and saw Santa Claus for the first time.

"Eastman called Ben. He's offering me a job. I mean Premier is. They want me to be president."

"What about Neiman?"

Wayne Neiman was the current president of Premier Films.

David shrugged. "Moving on, I guess. Ben says Eastman wants me so much he thinks we can ask for the moon."

Allyn smiled. "That's wonderful, David, I'm really proud of you." She was. Her husband. He was just thirty years old and he'd already produced three major motion pictures. One which was nominated for an Oscar, and the other two which were critically acclaimed for their excellence.

Yes, excellence. David was committed to that. He would become riveted to a project, consumed by his need to make it perfect. So that even after hiring the best director and film editor and cinematographer, and finding the perfect cast, and handpicking the crew, still he would be watching, checking, examining every frame, considering every beat. To prove that he wasn't just a businessman, but a skilled overseer with a discerning and critical eye. And mediocrity would never slip past him. Well, now it was paying off. He was hot. Becoming. Emerging. Verging on enormity. Fight back the rest, Allyn thought. Fight back the part that begins with the words Yes but at the expense of . . . She loved him. She knew what he was, but she loved him. She would tell him and maybe they would celebrate his potential new job by getting into bed now and making love. It had been weeks.

David paced back and forth across Allyn's tiny office.

"I love you," Allyn said.

"Ben told me he's going to write a contract that'll blind those bastards, it'll be so dazzling. But he thinks they'll buy it. They want me." His eyes were dancing. He hadn't heard her.

"And I want you, too," she said.

This time he did.

"Ahhh, honey," he said, taking her in his arms. "I wouldn't be anywhere without my sweet wife and my little daughter Mandy."

"Thank you, darling," she said. She recognized those words. She'd heard them before. They were part of his never-used-but-often-rehearsed Oscar acceptance speech.

"Let's go to bed, David," she said. Why, she wondered, was she trying to seduce him when he was so uninterested? So obviously into his own moment. Maybe so she'd feel more as if she were a part of the high he was on.

"Naah," he said distractedly. "You go ahead. I want to do some reading."

He gave her a pat on the arm and ran back downstairs.

For the next few days it seemed as if David was either out some-where at a meeting or, when he finally arrived home at night, ex-hausted. He would stand in front of the refrigerator, forage for left-overs, then close himself into his den and get on the phone. Sometimes Allyn would walk past the den and stand at the door, hoping David couldn't tell that she was there, and that maybe she'd overhear a part of his conversations. "Stock options" was a phrase she heard repeatedly. "Control." He said that one a lot. Sometimes with the word "creative" in front of it. Must have full Creative Con-trol.

Eventually she would tiptoe away and go upstairs and try to fall asleep without staring at the light on the phone under the seven eight three number. By the time she woke up in the morning, David would be gone for the day. And the only clue that he'd actually slept in the bed with her was the rumpled sheet on the other side.

Allyn would get up, feed Mandy breakfast, give instructions in broken Spanish to Berta, the housekeeper, and sit down and try to work.

Work. Was she kidding herself about the goddamned work? Ever since the day she left Hemisphere and stopped getting a steady pay-check, it didn't feel right to call the writing she was doing at home her work. She tried to make it seem more like real work by setting up an office for herself in the new house. A desk. A lamp. A filing cabi-net. A perma-plaqued picture of the cast of her TV show on *TV Guide,* which had been signed to her by each of them, and a perma-plaqued eight-by-ten picture of herself with Jay Masters, the star of the show. But perma plaques couldn't cure the crippling feeling she had about writing a script. The way when she finally got herself to sit down, to ignore the chores in the house that suddenly seemed very important, she couldn't get herself to write. She started countless times, and filled her wastebasket with crumpled pages that always sounded pitifully sophomoric and made her furious at herself. Why couldn't she just be happy being Amanda's mommy? Happy as the lady of this beautiful Brentwood house? Mrs. Kane. Wife of producer David Kane, and now maybe studio head David Kane. My God. There was a time not so long ago when that would have been the answer to her every prayer. A time when having a husband and a child was all she wanted. Phil Gruber. Allyn smiled. She hadn't thought of him in a very long time. About two years ago, Allyn's mother had told her on the phone that she was going to have her eyes checked. She went to Phil Gruber.

"Divorced," she told Allyn.

It was amazing to Allyn that simply by the way she had spoken that one word, her mother had managed to convey, not only the information that Phil Gruber was divorced, but also the message you-should-be-glad-you-didn't-end-up-with-him-because-he-couldn't-even-stay-married, as well as her opinion of people who got divorces, which was that they were failures.

"Too bad," Allyn had said about Phil Gruber's divorce. And then she had a flash of fantasy that maybe she and Amanda would rush off to Pittsburgh to visit Grandma, and one night in Weinstein's Delicatessen there would be Phil Gruber and he'd beg her to leave David and be his wife, now that he finally had Janet Blumenthal out of his system.

The electric typewriter was humming, and Allyn was sorry that she bought it. There was something about the way it hummed that got on her nerves. Okay. Let's go. Okay. C'mon. Ready, it said. And she knew she had two choices. She could turn it off and fall asleep, which is what she'd done for the last several days after she tried to work, or she could leave it on and insert a piece of paper, and start typing anything. Anything. She looked out the window. Amanda was playing on the front lawn with Berta. Allyn knew she should type and not look out the window and watch them, but— The phone was ringing. Thank God.

"Hello, Mrs. Kane?" It was David.

"Who's calling?" she asked, smiling.

"The president of Premier Films."

"David! They agreed to everything?"

"Every single thing."

"Fabulous. Terrific. Oh, David . . . I'll chill champagne."

"I won't be home till late. I'm going over to Eastman's office now to talk."

"Okay," she said, "I'll wait up and we'll celebrate later. And maybe I'll make some kind of a light supper and . . ."

Allyn rambled for quite a while before she realized that David had hung up.

By the end of his fourth week, David knew everything about Premier Films. Every night he read. Company financial reports. Projects the studio was considering acquiring. Projects the studio had already acquired, some of which had been given "go" status, others which were fraught with problems and needed to be bailed out of trouble. And he screened and watched films. Every one Premier had made in the last ten years.

And during the day he took meetings with every executive in the company. Called them to his office. Individually. And asked them to lunch with him, talk with him, explain to him how the studio worked best in their opinion. First the lawyers. David made them bring copies of all the contracts the studio had with creative people, so he could see who was worth how much. Then he met with Larry Deebs, the vice-president in charge of finance. David sat with Deebs for hours on end. Asking him questions, reviewing expenses, learning, remembering.

"Jesus," Mel Eastman said to David one morning, during what had become their regular breakfast at the Polo Lounge. "You know as much about Premier as I do, and I've been there fifteen years."

"That's not true, Mel," David said. "I know *more* than you do. For example, I know you've only been at Premier for fourteen years and three months."

Both men laughed. Later that day, Eastman called David on the phone that was the private line between their offices.

"I just got a call from Isaac Wolfson," he said.

David closed his eyes and held the phone very tightly.

"You know?" Eastman went on. "Over at the First Bank of Beverly Hills."

"Yes," David said.

"Seems he got a notice saying we wanted to move our business elsewhere. He's upset."

"Oh?"

"We've done business with the Wolfson brothers for years," Eastman said.

David listened carefully. There was nothing in Eastman's voice to indicate that he had any feelings other than curiosity about this issue.

"Deebs told me about the studio's relationship to the Wolfson brothers," David said. "But I've looked at the numbers very closely, Mel, and I know we can get much better terms at Greater Los Angeles. I'll send you the specifics."

"No need to," Eastman said. "I'll put the resolution to the board and it's done. Makes no difference to me."

He hung up. David placed the telephone receiver carefully back in its cradle, still holding it tightly. The Wolfson brothers. Isaac, Charles and Jack. Would Charles Wolfson tell his brothers why Premier Studios, a multimillion dollar account, was pulling their money away from the First Bank of Beverly Hills? Not likely.

A large color photograph of Amanda Melanie Kane sat in a frame bought by her mommy on the left-hand side of her daddy's desk. David looked at the picture and smiled.

"Hi, Mand," he said. "Everything's going great."

Everyone who met Amanda commented on what a beautiful child she was. Today, while her daddy was lying on his stomach in the park reading a script, she sat on his back playing horsey-horsey. But Amanda was only two and a half years old, and the fascination of horsey-horsey was brief. That's why when the yellow-and-black soccer ball went rolling by and caught her eye, she decided to get up and play with it.

The bigger children kicked the ball and ran happily, then kicked it again and ran some more. Maybe they would give her a turn. She followed them. Her green eyes huge with excitement and her little hands clapping. Doggie. The fluffy little white doggie that had been sitting on a blanket next to the man and lady who were kissing now ran at Amanda's heels. Amanda laughed out loud.

David was nodding now. That was a bad sign. The script was boring him to sleep. He wouldn't even finish it. He'd try reading one of the others he'd brought with him. The property he chose for his first project as the president of Premier Films would have to contain irresistible roles, so that he could attract someone like Jane Fonda or Jon Voight or Jack Nicholson by showing them the script. That was crucial. But this script wouldn't do. He was sleepy. Up and dressed every morning by six to spend a few hours getting his calls to New York out of the way. But today was Sunday. As soon as Allyn got here to relieve him of Mandy, he'd go home and sit by the pool and nap on a chaise lounge in the sun. The maid's day off. Allyn said she wanted to get some work done.

Allyn's work. At least she was home all day now. She'd set up her little self-important office in the new house, with the perma-plaqued notices from her television show hanging on the wall. And every day she sat in there and did something. Typed and talked on the phone and teased David that she would emerge from that room eventually with a script he would beg her to let him produce.

"Hi."

David looked up. He had to admit she was beautiful. Still beautiful.

"Sorry I'm late, but I got caught up in what I was doing and I didn't want to quit. Where's Mandy?"

David looked around. "I don't know."

"David, stop it," Allyn said, smiling nervously.

Mandy. She was just playing horsey a minute ago. No. Ten minutes ago.

"Mandy!" David called out.

"David." Allyn couldn't believe it. "Are you crazy? What were you doing here?"

"Shut up," David said. "Mandy," he shouted. He didn't know which way to go. Where to walk. The park was enormous. And filled with people.

Allyn looked around. It couldn't be. A little girl like that. Someone would know.

"Excuse me," Allyn said. The couple on the blanket had a fuzzy white dog. "My husband was sitting with my little girl over there." The white dog sniffed Allyn's shoe. "She's two and a half, very little, has red hair, did you—" Blank faces. "Thank you."

The white dog yapped at her feet.

"Mandy," Allyn shouted, walking back to where David was.

"I'll call the police," he said.

Allyn felt weak. Again her eyes scanned the park. That bastard, David. That self-absorbed son of a bitch.

"Don't leave," she said, grabbing his arm. "She's probably around here someplace looking for us. For you . . . She knows she came here with you. If she doesn't see you she's liable to—" Nowhere in sight. No Mandy anywhere. Allyn began to cry.

"How could you, David? My God."

"Stop it! We'll find her. She's a tiny little girl. She can't have gone far."

"You stay here. I'll look," she said.

The laughing picnicking crowds in Roxbury Park were a blur to

Allyn as she walked, stopping people who only shook their heads when she asked them if they had seen her baby. Or they looked at her sympathetically for an instant, then back to their game, or their sandwich or their book. That son of a bitch David.

"Mandy," she shouted.

The tennis courts were filled. Tans. White shorts. Bounce. Hit. Bounce. Hit. Nice shot. Deuce. Bounce. Hit. Mandy. My baby. Where is she?

"Mandy!" Allyn's voice rang in her own ears. A German shepherd and a golden retriever romped on the grass barking noisily at one another. The little white dog ran off to join them.

Kidnapped. No, she wouldn't think of it. A kidnapper wouldn't just pick a child up from the park. Too many people around. Besides, here in the park, it could be anybody's child. No one could tell by looking at Amanda that she was the daughter of a rich powerful man.

Allyn stopped walking. She was probably going about this all wrong. She remembered when she was a little girl, she took an I.Q. test. Stanford-Binet was it? Where they showed her a square. A box drawn on the page. And the box had an opening on one end. This is a field, the psychologist said, or did it say that in the directions? And you have lost your wallet in the field. How would you go about finding your wallet? With your pencil, draw the path that you would take. Allyn remembered her answer. She drew a straight line into the middle of the square and said, I would walk into the middle of the field, turn around in a circle, and if I didn't see my wallet, I would start to cry. The psychologist told her her answer was unacceptable and went on to another section of the test. But that's what she wanted to do. Stand and cry.

Maybe she should go back and tell David to call the police after all.

"Mandy!" No answer. People were looking at her now and she realized she was crying.

"Mandy!" Her voice was getting tired.

She was almost near the parking lot on the far side of the park. The screeching of brakes was loud. And then the thud, and the voice, screaming.

"Ohhh. Nooo!"

People were running. Gathering. A crowd in the parking lot. The driver of the car had gotten out and was moving toward the center of the crowd.

"Oh, dear God. I'm so sorry."

More people were running to see.

Mandy. I have to get there. A nightmare. I'll wake up. It felt to Allyn as if she were walking under water. Against some strong force, as though no matter how she tried to get to the accident she couldn't advance. Have to get there. Mandy.

"Please," she said. "Please, someone, please. My daughter. Please." She was grabbing people in the crowd by their shirts, their hair, anything she could do to push them, force them, move them out of her way so she could get to the front.

"Please, my baby. Please. You have to move."

"Jesus, lady," a man in a gray sweat suit said. Allyn, ridden with terror, looked at the ground in front of the car, where the little white dog lay dying.

"Your dog?" the man in the gray sweat suit asked.

"I'll take it to a vet," the driver of the car announced to the crowd. "Maybe it can be saved." As the man knelt next to the dog, the crowd began to disperse. Allyn took a deep breath. Mandy.

"Doggie."

Allyn looked around. About ten yards away, next to the water fountain, playing in the mud that had been made by the spilled fountain water, was Mandy.

"Mandy. Oh, Mandy. Oh, my God," Allyn said, rushing toward her baby girl, reaching for her, touching her, grabbing her, holding the child against her tightly. Thank you, God.

"Mandy," Allyn said, her eyes blinking to hold back the tears that spilled out in spite of her.

"Mandy, oh, my baby, Mandy."

As Allyn cried, her tears fell into her daughter's bright-red hair. The beautiful red hair that Allyn combed and braided, and sometimes even envied. There were leaves in Mandy's hair, and dirt, and Allyn's tears turned to a smile when she saw there was a ladybug too. Gently she took it and let it walk along her hand.

"Look," she said to the little girl.

"Lucky!" Amanda said, grinning. Allyn had told her that once as they sat by their pool and she remembered. Mother's brilliant girl.

"Very lucky," Allyn said, kissing her baby's sweet pink face on each pudgy cheek. "Very lucky."

"Manda," Allyn said, pulling the leaves one by one out of the child's hair. "When you come to the park with Daddy, he sometimes gets very busy. Do you know what I mean?"

"Daddy's reading strips," Amanda said, repeating what she thought she'd heard Allyn tell her, when David didn't want to be interrupted in his den.

"Yes, he's reading scripts," Allyn said. "But you mustn't wander away from Daddy when he's reading. Because then he won't know where you are."

"Okay," Amanda said. "I'm hungry."

"Me, too," Allyn said. She brushed the sand from the seat of the child's overalls.

"Dirty tushie?" Amanda asked.

"Yes. Dirty tushie, and dirty everything else, too."

Allyn took Amanda's hand. "Let's find Daddy," she said, and they walked slowly back toward the grassy area where she knew David would be waiting anxiously.

"Oh, good. You found her," an older woman Allyn had approached earlier said.

"Yes."

David. She could see him now in the distance under the same tree where she'd found him earlier. She couldn't believe it. He was lying down again. Reading.

"Daddy!" Amanda shouted. "Daddy!" David turned, gave a casual little wave, and went back to his scripts.

That night, after Amanda was asleep, Allyn sat in the bedroom and watched the light over the seven eight three number. The minute it went off she got up slowly and walked downstairs, through the darkened hallway to the door of David's den, and tapped on it.

"Yeah?" he said.

Allyn opened the door slowly.

"David. I want you to find another place to live immediately. I'm divorcing you. You're a self-involved unfeeling man, and I've lived with you as long as I can."

David looked at her, saying nothing. She went on.

"I loved you so much for so long, and I always thought, or at least hoped, the situation could change. That you would change. That being a husband and a family man would make you try to be responsible to someone besides yourself. But it didn't. And it's painful for me to live like this, and it's wrong for Mandy to live like this, too."

Allyn was surprised at how calm her voice sounded, because her fists were clenched so tightly her nails were digging into her hands.

"Allyn—"

"There won't be a discussion, David," she said. "I've been holding this inside since this afternoon. If the baby hadn't been there to see, I would have strangled you. Killed you. Torn you apart for your indifference and your negligence. Toward Mandy and toward me, too." She hated her voice for sounding so shrill. She wanted to be calm.

"You can let me know where you'll be and I'll have Berta pack your things and send them to you."

David stood. "Allyn, please sweetheart. I think you're over-reacting."

That bastard. "David," she said, "I can hear you using your sweet killer voice. The one that makes everyone in this town tremble when you call them. Well, it won't work on me anymore. Or on my daughter."

"Our daughter," he said. This was getting out of hand.

"Our daughter now," Allyn said angrily. She was losing control. "But not in the morning when it's time for breakfast and you're gone. Or not when it's time to go to bed and you aren't home yet, or you're locked in this goddamned den. And not when it's time to decide which nursery school, and not even in the park when you're sup-posed to look up every now and then from your reading to make sure she doesn't get kidnapped or run over by a car, which she almost did. David, she could have. Do you realize she could have?" Allyn was screaming. "But you couldn't watch her. You had to pick the right script for your studio so you could be David Kane, the young Harry Cohn, or Jack Warner or Harold Greenfield. Well, fuck your scripts and your studio and your artistic control, you egomaniac. And get out of this house tonight. Because I can't stand you. And I can't stand what I've become from living with you. And I won't have Mandy become that either."

For a moment it looked to Allyn as if David was stung. Hard. And she was glad. She had shown him. Now she had shown him. But then she saw his jaw set and his eyes narrow, and he was saying something which she almost didn't hear at first because she was caught up in lis-tening to the sound of his voice again. That sweet killer voice.

". . . wish I could contradict you, but I can't," he was saying. "Wish I could tell you how wrong you are, prove to you everything, all of it is some kind of paranoid bullshit, some middle-class house-wife's complaint that she gets because she's watching her tits start to sag, and just write it all off to that, but too bad for me 'cause I can't.

I've never wanted any of this, Allyn. This marriage, that child, or a life like this. Never."

He didn't. Ever. She knew it. She'd always known it, but she thought it could change.

"But I tried," he went on.

Allyn wanted to interrupt him and scream, "No you didn't, you did not try." But she didn't.

"Tried because I kept thinking I'm supposed to care about having a family. I'm supposed to love a child who looks like me. I'm supposed to be grateful and delighted that a woman who's as beautiful and as bright and as devoted as you are is in love with me and giving all of her energy to the David Kane family. Supposed to be glad. But it doesn't mean shit to me. You nailed me, Allyn. It doesn't mean shit."

She was crying, crying hard. Her eyes were still sore and swollen from crying in the park earlier and the new tears burned. She put her hand on the desk and leaned on it for support. David put his hand on hers. That familiar freckled hand she had kissed and touched and held for so long. She couldn't understand. How could she hate him so much and love him so much all at once?

"Don't cry, Allyn," he said. "You have you and Mandy and I only have me."

"David, can't we—" She had never heard him like this, never heard him open up this way. Talk about his feelings, his inability to connect with her, with Mandy. Maybe it meant there was a chance they could work on it. Work it out.

"No," he said. "We can't. I've been waiting for you to throw me out for a long time. If you hadn't, eventually I would have left on my own."

He started toward the den door. Allyn ached looking at him.

"I love you," she said.

He didn't turn around.

Allyn sat down in the chair by the desk where David had been sitting while he was on the phone. She was numb. Unthinkingly she pushed the buttons on the phone. Hold. Seven eight three. Seven eight four. Seven eight five. Hold. Even after she heard him walking out the front door she continued to sit there, pushing the buttons. Pushing the buttons, until finally she leaned back in the chair and fell asleep.

It was Mandy's voice that woke her.

"Mommy? Where are you? Berta, were's my mommy?"

"I'm in the den, Mandy honey," Allyn said.

Amanda was carrying Winnie the Pooh and still wearing her yellow shortie baby doll pajamas, and she climbed up onto Allyn's lap and nestled against her mother.

"Daddy's gone, Mandy," Allyn said.

Amanda looked at her mommy's face.

"I'm hungry," she said.

Allyn set Mandy's feet on the floor, gave her a little pat, then got up and headed for the kitchen. It was eight o'clock. At ten, she would call Harold Greenfield and ask if she could have her job back.

forty-six

The Grammy Awards Show was usually in March. This year it was on the third. It was Mickey Ashman's birthday, and Mickey was going to be a presenter. Even though he wasn't in the music business, the producers of the Grammys chose him because his show had been on the air for four seasons, and he was a big star. Everywhere he went, people yelled out the greeting to him that was the title of his show. *Hey, Richey!*

At the taping of *Hey, Richey!* the night before Mickey's birthday, the cast had a huge cake for him. The baker had done a caricature of his face, and on the cake it said, HEY, MICKEY, HAVE A HAPPY. Jackie Levitz, who played Richey's uncle, had designed the cake. The cast and crew pitched in for it.

And the new girl was there. Sally Strock. She was tiny and pretty with a cute short hairdo, expressive eyes and an adorable laugh. The writers had written her in to play a new character, Pam, Richey's girl friend. Mickey had been thinking at rehearsal all week that he wished she were his real girl friend. And after they had the cake, he said to her, I know this is very short notice, but I was wondering if you'd be my date at the Grammy Awards tomorrow night, and she said she would love to if she could get a dress in time, and he said he'd use his influence so somebody on the show's wardrobe staff could help her find a dress. She laughed and told him that would be great, and Mickey took her phone number and headed for his dressing room. But he turned around as she was walking away and called to her.

"Pam . . ." She kept walking. That was the name of her character, not her.

"Uh, Sally." Now she turned.

"You didn't say yes just because it's my birthday, did you?"

She laughed her adorable laugh.

"Nope," she said, and waved and kept walking through the door and outside to the small trailer that was her dressing room.

She looked beautiful when he picked her up for the Awards. She borrowed a dress from her sister Jan, who told Mickey she was looking forward to the taping next week, which would be Sally's first show, and then looked out the window and saw the waiting limousine, and when she thought Mickey wasn't looking, Jan mouthed the word "Wow" to Sally.

* * *

Mickey's limousine pulled into the line of limousines outside the
Palladium. Through the windows he saw the fan-magazine photographers and the fans waiting for their favorite stars to emerge. They
were like children at a party watching the opening of birthday gifts.
Oohing and aahing and yayying.

It was Mickey's turn. They screamed when they saw him. Mickey.
Richey. Heyyy, Richey. He loved it. It made him shake. He smiled
and waved and blew kisses, and then remembered Sally, who was
standing behind him, and he turned and took her arm and led her toward the lobby of the Palladium.

People. The lobby was filled with people. Mostly music-business
people. If this was the Emmy Awards, Mickey told himself, he would
know more people. He would show Sally to her seat in the auditorium
and then get backstage.

"Reggie," a voice called. Maybe the voice said Richey. No, Reggie
for sure. Mickey turned. What a sight. Stan Rose, old Juggie. And
Golden. With Beau Daniels. Mickey felt Sally's hand tighten on his,
and he realized that these famous faces must be intimidating to her.

"Old friends," he said, guiding her toward them.

Golden and Stan embraced Mickey, and Beau and Sally were introduced, and Mickey made a joke about the fact that he and Beau
and Stan were all big TV stars, and Golden would just have to go
home because he wasn't one, and then he felt badly because Sally
wasn't one either, and he had acted as though she weren't there. But
Sally didn't seem to notice.

"Arch is supposed to be here tonight, too," Stan said.

"The old gang," Mickey said. God, he felt good.

"Where are you sitting?" Barry asked Mickey.

"I'm not," Mickey said. "I'm a presenter."

Barry and Stan exchanged mock impressed looks.

"Well, big fucking deal," Barry said. "A presenter."

"*I'm* not even a presenter," Stan said, "and I'm in the music business, and on television, too. And Beau's not even a presenter and
she's a superstar. How do you account for this, Ashman?"

Mickey grinned. "Well," he said. "Beau's show is off the air. And
yours is on so late only insomniacs know who *you* are." The others
laughed.

"Well, if this isn't a motley-looking group." It was David Kane
and a date.

"Arch!" "Hey, Archie."

"David Kane, this is Sally Strock."

"Hi."

"Colleen Collins, meet Mickey Ashman, Stan Rose, Barry Golden."

"I love your show," Colleen said to Mickey.

Mickey recognized her. She was a Playmate fold-out. And he thought he remembered she once went with Doug Hart, the movie star.

"Thank you," Stan answered, as if she were talking to him.

Everyone laughed. Colleen didn't know why.

"Thanks," Mickey said.

"Yeah, Ashman, it's a good show," David said. "And you're good on it, too. I think I might have a part in a picture for you."

"Terrific," Mickey said.

"We'll have lunch," David said.

"Yeah," Mickey said.

The crowd was moving into the auditorium.

"Can we all sit together?" Barry asked.

"Probably," Stan said. "Only the nominees get good seats anyway."

"Come with us, Sally," Beau said.

Sally smiled, glad to be included.

"Okay, then," Mickey said. "I'll see you guys later."

On top of the world. On top of the fucking world. No coke and the highest he'd ever been. Maybe Sally Strock was good luck. Maybe he'd marry her someday. Only this morning Harvey and Libby called from Chicago to say hello, and Mickey's mother was at their house, and she got on the phone to talk to him.

"Hi, darling," she said to him. "How's my famous son? I tell all my friends. I have one son who's smart and one son who's famous." Jesus. She never quit. "Now, when are you going to invite Mother to a wedding?" she asked.

"Don't know, Mah," he'd said.

Sally Strock Ashman. She was very cute, and a nice person, and she was very gracious about sitting out there with people she'd never met while Mickey went backstage.

Backstage. There were a lot of stars milling around. Many of them greeted Mickey warmly. A few other television people. They were like a club, he thought. All of them in this club of successful people who asked each other questions like, When do you hear if your show was picked up? And how are your ratings? And, I noticed your show was number four last week. Congratulations.

Mickey was presenting the award for the best female vocalist, and he stood backstage for a long time, listening for his introduction. "A man who not only makes a mean banana split, but makes your sides split as well . . . Hey, Richey himself . . . Mickey Ashman!!!!"

There was a huge ovation. A lot of Hey, Richeys, and whistling and stomping from the crowd. Mickey was turned on, and as he walked out onto the stage and looked out at the crowd, they were a mass of faces, until he focused for a moment and caught sight of David Kane's bright red hair. Jokes. He did jokes about the characters on his show and the audience laughed a lot. They loved him.

"Nominations for the best female vocalist are . . ."

Kane, that fucker. Waited to offer his help until now. Now when he didn't need him.

". . . Lita Collins . . . Minnie Kahn . . ."

Rose. Alone. A good man, Stan Rose. A real good man. And he deserved every drop of his success. Golden with Beau Daniels. A weird duo.

"The envelope, please. I'm good at envelopes," Mickey said. "I used to work in a studio mail room."

The audience only tittered. Golden, Rose and Kane broke up.

"And the winner is—Minnie Kahn." Rush of applause and Mickey was off.

"Great," a few people said.

"You were terrific. Thanks, Mickey."

When the show ended, Mickey was more swamped by autograph seekers than any of the other stars.

"Richey. We love you."

Sally waited patiently, and when Mickey had signed the last autograph, the two of them walked hand in hand toward their waiting car.

"Is your sister going to be at your place when we get there?" Mickey asked Sally as the limousine driver headed toward Hollywood.

"No," Sally said, and Mickey pulled her toward him and they kissed. And then kissed again, and again. And he was so high about everything in his life. He would make love to Sally when they got to her apartment. Make love to her and hold her all night.

"How 'bout if I tell the driver to go and I spend the night?" he asked at her door.

"No, Mickey," she said softly. "I really want to go to bed with you, but we'll be working together all year, and we'll have lots of time for that. You know?"

Mickey was disappointed, but still very high.

"I know," he said, nodding. "And you're right. I guess we do have lots of time. Another kiss and he ran happily back to the car to go home. He had everything. Soon he would have her, too. She'd be his. He knew it.

"Home, driver," he said.

He couldn't possibly sleep now. He had a glass of milk and tried the television on every channel until he was sure there was nothing on he wanted to watch. He took off his tux and read some old issues of the trades. He loved to look at Thursday's papers because they had production schedules in them. HEY, RICHEY! A DANNY KOHLER PRODUCTION. CAST: MICKEY ASHMAN. He would never get tired of it. He couldn't get tonight out of his mind. His triumph. At last. Ashman the schmuck. He laughed to himself. Ashman, the putz, who looked like he was going to be in the mail room for life, was the one on the stage. The one who got the laughs. He probably gave out more autographs tonight than Beau Daniels.

He read next week's script. It was about Richey and Pam falling in love. There was no rehearsal tomorrow. Maybe he'd take Sally to the beach. Maybe he'd even get a place at the beach. It was expensive, but he had money now. A lot of money. Mickey yawned. It was 4 A.M. Maybe he'd fall asleep if he just closed his eyes for a few minutes. Yes. Close his eyes.

The loud crash woke him, and he opened his eyes and lay there frozen. Maybe it was in his dream. Please. Maybe it was outside. Yes. Not a sound. But then he saw the beam of the flashlight. No. A nightmare. It had to be. Footsteps.

"Who's there?" Mickey asked.

"Stay where you are, motherfucker," a young man's voice said. "I'm just here to rip you off, but you move and I'll blow your fuckin' brains out."

Stan was having a dream he'd had before. Several times. The dream was about Jerri. She was lying in bed, in the house where they'd lived on Benedict Canyon, and she looked very frail, and Stan sat next to her holding her hand. She smiled at him weakly and thanked him for loving her even though she was the way she was. Then Stan asked her to tell him what she meant by that, the way she was. The other times he'd had the dream she said I mean sick. I'm sick. I don't mean to be, but I'm sick. This time she started to tell him something, but he couldn't hear what she was saying because the phone was ringing loud. He wanted to hear her, strained to hear her, but the phone kept ringing. Shit.

He opened his eyes. He was in bed in his apartment. It was his phone that was ringing and he reached for it reluctantly.

"Hello."

"Jug? It's Arch," the voice on the phone said.

"Huh?"

"It's David Kane, Stan. I didn't know if you'd heard or not, about Mickey Ashman."

Stan sat up. David Kane. Calling about Ashman?

"Heard what?"

"He was shot," David said. "Shot. By a robber. Late last night, or this morning after he got home from the Grammys. I just saw it on the news."

"Oh, Christ," Stan said. "Oh, no. Ashman. My God."

"I know," David said. "It's the fucking worst."

"Who did it?"

"They don't know."

"Why? What motive? Was it a fan?"

"No one knows."

"What about that girl? From last night?"

"She wasn't there. He took her home right after the show. Danny Kohler was on the news early this morning. They had film of him coming out of the morgue. They must have called him to identify the body."

"Oh, God," Stan said. "What can we do? Is anyone arranging the—" Stan couldn't go on. He couldn't make himself say the word funeral.

"I'll have my secretary call Kohler," David said, "and I'll call you with the details."

"Yeah," Stan said. "All right." He was about to put the phone in the cradle when he heard David Kane say something else so he moved the phone back to his ear.

"Wait—Rose—" David was saying.

"Yeah?"

"Do me a favor and call Allyn and tell her about Ashman, will you?"

"Sure," Stan said.

He hung up the phone and shook his head. Poor Mickey Ashman dead. And Kane couldn't even call Allyn to tell her.

forty-seven

Beau liked waking up early at the beach. If it was very early so no one was out yet, and the tide was high, she could imagine that the house was a big boat at sea. She would go outside to the upstairs deck, opening the door carefully so she wouldn't wake Barry, and then she'd sit on a lounge chair, and listen to the screeches of the sea gulls and Barry's snores, feeling that she was the luckiest person in the whole world. Yes, she was. Eggs Benedict. That's what she'd do for him today. Her man. Make him Eggs Benedict. He'd love that. She'd bring it to him in bed.

She opened the door and tiptoed through the bedroom, grabbing a pair of jeans and a T-shirt from a chair where she'd tossed them and heading downstairs toward the kitchen to see if she had all the ingredients. Butter. No butter for the hollandaise. And no Canadian bacon. Shit. What time did the market open? The Market Basket in the shopping center. It must be open early. The car keys were on the living room table. She'd be back and Barry wouldn't even know she'd been gone. Maybe a note. Gone for bacon. Nah. She'd be back in five minutes.

She got into the Corniche and started the engine. Barry must have forgotten to turn off the car radio last night when they got home from the Grammys and the loud burst of music startled Beau. She reached for the dial quickly and turned down the sound. When she got to the highway she fiddled with the radio dial again, the way she always did when Barry was driving. No music she wanted to hear. She tuned in to station KISS. That was good. Cher was singing "Take Me Home." Beau pulled into the parking lot. Hooray. The Market Basket was open. There was definitely something special about being up early at the beach.

"Police are combing the San Fernando Valley looking for the robber who shot and killed well-loved television star Mickey Ashman in his North Hollywood home this morning. Ashman, who was a presenter only last night on the Grammy Awards, was the star of the television series *Hey, Richey!*"

Mickey. Now. After he had finally made it. Barry had told her all the stories about Mickey and how he'd been in the mail room longer than all of them, and nothing good seemed to happen for him until

Hey, Richey!, and now. Fuck the Eggs Benedict. She'd go and wake Barry.

When Beau got back to the house Barry was awake.

"Stan Rose just called me," he said. He was sitting on the edge of the bed. "The funeral's going to be tomorrow at Forest Lawn," he said. He was pale. "Kohler asked if Stan and Kane and I would be pallbearers."

He looked at her with eyes that didn't see her, then added absently, "It wasn't so long ago I thought those guys would be carrying me."

Beau sat on the bed next to Barry and they held hands quietly for a long time.

"I'll call a car and a driver to take all of us tomorrow," Beau said. "It will be better if we're all together."

Jackie Levitz stood at the podium. His was the last eulogy.

"Mickey Ashman was what my ancestors from the old country would have called a mensch. I guess loosely that means a solid citizen, a man, a person of substance. He got me my job, but that's not why I loved him. I loved him because he cared about people. The children and grown-ups alike. I loved him because he was the star of *Hey, Richie!*, a show that was in the top ten from the first week it was on, and never, not once, did he ever act like a star to anyone on the set. Or to any of his friends. I loved him because—" Levitz's voice broke and he waited until the rush of emotion subsided before he went on.

"Because he always had time to tell a joke, or kid around and be a pal, and I'm gonna miss him like hell."

A loud sob from Mickey's mother.

When the service was over, the people started moving toward their cars. Everyone was there.

Mickey's parents and Mickey's brother Harvey and his sister-in-law Libby. Danny Kohler put an arm around Harvey. For a second, Harvey's resemblance to Mickey was eerie to him.

"Your brother was a prince," Kohler said to Harvey. "A fuckin' prince."

Harvey nodded and began to cry and Kohler hugged him.

Jackie Levitz and his wife Ruth were with Sally Strock. The news media were there. A TV newswoman asked Danny Kohler if he would make a statement, and he said no.

Jimmy Komack was there, and Garry Marshall and Norman Lear.

Also an actress named Ginny McConnel and Tom Rich from the casting department at Hemisphere Studios, and Don Morgan from personnel at Hemisphere, and Harold and Julia Greenfield were there with Allyn Grant, and Arlen White and a director named Jeff Bain and a man named Dick Snyder who used to own a waterbed store in the Valley, and Willie the guard from Hemisphere and Barney Lautner who had a column in one of the trades, and his wife Nadine who went everywhere with him because she knew who all of the stars were, and she would point them out to him so he could write in his column that they were there.

After they lowered the coffin into the ground, Barry and Beau and Stan and David walked together slowly. Stan noticed the Greenfields and Allyn Grant getting into a limousine ahead, and he knew that David noticed too but turned away. Stan looked back at the crowd.

"I heard my father say once that when you get into your fifties you should start getting used to the idea of losing your friends to death one by one. But this is too soon for us," he said. "Too goddamned soon."

"Especially for Mickey," Beau said. "He was just starting to make a life for himself."

"I have to get going," David said. "Is that our driver?"

"I'll go check," Beau said and walked away in the direction of the cars.

"Listen, you guys," Barry said. "Why don't you come out to the beach on Sunday to my place and we'll all have dinner?"

"Sure," Stan said.

"Yeah," David said. "Okay."

Beau was waiting to tell them that she'd found their driver. The three of them walked together to join her.

Nadine Lautner elbowed her husband, Barney, the columnist, when she saw Beau Daniels getting into the limousine.

"Barney," she hissed to her husband. "That's some fancy group. That's Beau Daniels. Write it down. And Barry Golden. And Stan Rose from Stan Rose Presents . . . and that other guy with the red hair. Goddamn it. He's someone big, too."

One of the secretaries from Hemisphere heard Barney Lautner's wife, and nudged her friend.

"Those men," she said to her friend. "I think that they're big in the business."

The friend looked at the three men who were getting into the limousine behind Beau Daniels. It must be true, they all looked so hand-some and successful.

"Listen," the second woman said wistfully, "when you're big in the business, what else is there?"

The line of limousines pulled away from the curb and headed out of Forest Lawn and west toward Hollywood, Beverly Hills, Brent-wood and Malibu.